Pictures
of
Perfection

Pictures of Perfection

A Dalziel/Pascoe Mystery in five volumes

by

Reginald Hill

Pictures of perfection, as you know,
make me sick and wicked

Delacorte Press

Published by
Delacorte Press
Bantam Doubleday Dell Publishing Group, Inc.
1540 Broadway
New York, New York 10036

ISBN 0-385-31270-9

Manufactured in the United States of America

TO

THE QUEEN OF CRIME EDITORS,

ELIZABETH WALTER,

THIS WORK IS,

WITH HER GRACIOUS PERMISSION,

MOST AFFECTIONATELY

DEDICATED,

BY HER ADMIRING

AND GRATEFUL

FRIEND,

THE AUTHOR.

Nullum quod tetegit non ornavit

AUTHOR'S NOTE: The epigraph and all the chapter
headings are taken from Jane Austen's letters.

Volume the First

PROLOGUE, being an extract from the draft of an
uncompleted
HISTORY OF ENSCOMBE PARISH
by the
Reverend Charles Fabian Cage, D.D. (deceased).

It is a truth fairly universally acknowledged that all men are born equal, but the family Guillemard, pointing to the contra-evidence of their own absence from the Baronetage, have long been settled in Yorkshire without allowing such philosophical quibbles to distress or vex them.

The first stirrings of populism in the last century had been shrugged off as a mere Gallic infection, susceptible to applications of cold iron and a diet of bread and water. But the virus proved a virulent strain, eventually getting a firm grip on a country weak and convalescent after the Great War, and by the nineteen thirties even the Guillemards had begun to suspect its presence in their own Norman blood.

And by 1952, when Selwyn Guillemard, the present Squire, inherited the estate, he was ready to accept, without prejudice, that there might after all be something in this newfangled notion of the Rights of Man.

The Rights of Woman, however, remain very much a theme of science fiction.

About thirty years ago Squire Selwyn had the ill luck to lose his only son and daughter-in-law in a motoring accident, a grievous loss and one which, despite all my urgings, he seemed more inclined to bear with pagan stoicism than Christian fortitude. Nor did he at this stage *derive much consolation from the survival of his infant granddaughter, who henceforth was brought up at Old Hall.*

A child reared in an aging household is likely to be either precocious or withdrawn, and little Gertrude Guillemard showed few signs of precocity. Indeed so quiet and self-effacing was she that even her antique name seemed too great a burden for her, and it was soon alleviated to Girlie.

The Enscombe Old Hall estate is naturally entailed upon the male line. Modern law has rendered such archaic restrictions easily removed, but whichever way he looked, Squire Selwyn could see little incentive to change. Behind, he saw the sternly admonitory face of tradition; ahead, he foresaw that the diminished and diminishing estate was going to need a more vigorously heroic hand than his own to keep it from total collapse, and no one who had ever seen Girlie Guillemard in her infancy could have supposed her to be a heroine. So the Squire had few qualms about admitting his great-nephew, Guy, as heir apparent.

His wife, Edna, nursed hopes that the main and collateral lines might be joined by a marriage of cousins. These pious hopes survived their adolescence, which saw Girlie mature into a self-contained and biddable young woman and Guy sprout into a bumptious, self-confident public schoolboy, though a more perceptive woman than Edna Guillemard might have been rendered uneasy by the infrequency of Guy's visits to Yorkshire (which he designated megaboring) and the stoicism with which Girlie bore his absence. Then, shortly after the young folk reached their majorities and could decently be given some firm prothalamic nudges, tragedy struck the Guillemards again, and Edna died of a too tardily diagnosed adder bite. Once more I officiated at a Guillemard funeral.

Afterward the Squire invited me to join himself and the youngsters in his study for a glass of sherry. We talked for a while, as one does, of the virtues of the dear departed, then the Squire took a huge meerschaum from his crowded pipe rack, slowly filled and lit it, and seemed to go into a reverie with his eyes fixed on the furthermost left-hand corner of the room. Finally he nodded, turned his attention to me, and said, "Edna had a fancy to see these yonkers in church again pretty soon, getting married. What do you think?"

"More to the point, what do they think?" I replied.

Now Guy, too, produced a pipe, all gleaming with stainless steel, pulled the tobacco jar toward him, and went through a similarly

lengthy filling and lighting process before saying, "I think I'm a bit young yet to be thinking of marriage, Squire. But a few years on, who knows? In the meantime I'm happy to admit some kind of gentleman's understanding."

Then he sat back in his chair, smiling complacently, I presume at what he took to be his diplomatic dexterity.

The Squire looked at Girlie. Slowly she reached forward and took a smaller meerschaum from the rack. Slowly she filled it from the jar, slowly she lit it. Satisfied at last she sat back in her chair and took two or three appreciative puffs. Finally she spoke.

"As for me," she said, "I'd rather screw a rabid porcupine. Now if you'll excuse me, I have to see about lunch."

When she left she took the pipe with her. What had been a gesture became first a symbol, then, alas, an addiction. There were other changes too. All the Laura Ashley dresses her grandmother thought so became her were discarded (though not destroyed, many of them reappearing a short while later when little Frances Harding came to live at the Hall), and Girlie took to wearing jeans and Wellies during the working day, and stark black and white for formal occasions. Her Alice-length hair was reduced to a helmet of turbulent curls, and very soon the great local debate about who would now run the household was rendered superfluous as it became apparent that Old Hall had a new and formidable chatelaine.

The estate was managed by a factor under the notional supervision of the Squire, but the latter, never the same since the loss of his son, now retreated even farther into a protective eccentricity. The task of checking the books soon devolved upon Girlie. These were the insane eighties when the psycho patients took over the surgery and started remodeling society in their own image of perfection, without benefit of anesthetic. Trevor Hookey, the factor, soon revealed himself as a dedicated Thatcherite, wielding his knife with a zealot's glee, crying, "If it doesn't hurt, it's not working!" and assuring Girlie proudly that the new sleek and slimline Old Hall estate was the superefficient model of the future.

Girlie listened politely to this liturgical formulary for a couple of years. Then as her calculator squeaked up the dismal "grand" total at the annual Reckoning of 1986, she interrupted the zealot, saying, "Enough. I have seen the future and it sucks. We aren't sleek and superefficient, we're emaciated and moribund. There's only one large economy left for us to make."

4 REGINALD HILL

"And what's that, my dear?" asked Hookey with a patronizing air.
"Your salary," said Girlie Guillemard.

These Reckonings, by the way, take place on Lady Day, that is the
Feast of the Annunciation, March 25, which is in England a Quarter
Day, and has in Enscombe since time immemorial, or at least since
1716, been the day for the settling of accounts. That it survives as an
occasion is a tribute to Yorkshire doggedness. Naturally the largest
and most general payments to be made in the area are the Squire's
rents, and while the Guillemard estate was still extensive and ways
were rough, it was common courtesy to offer the tenants some refresh-
ment before they set off home.

But over the years, even before the awful eighties, the estate was
contracting and roads were improving, and gold coin under the floor-
boards was giving way to paper money in the bank, and eventually
checks and giros and standing orders made it hardly necessary for the
physical collection of rents at all. In any other county the Reckoning
would have ceased to exist save in the memory of graybeards and the
annals of antiquarians. But the difficulty of prizing a Yorkshire ter-
rier's teeth from the neck of a rat is as nothing to that of persuading a
Yorkshire tyke to give up a long-established freebie. So the Reckoning
has evolved into an annual tea party at which the collection of rents
occupies only a couple of minutes, and the refreshment and gossip a
couple of hours.

From '86 on it was Girlie who sat in the seat of custom and Girlie
who ran the estate. With the factor's departure the village had antici-
pated that perhaps Guy the Heir would appear to nurture and protect
what would one day be his own. But the eighties, which had turned
England into a valley of dry bones for so many, had rendered it a
loads-a-money theme park for others, and Guy the Heir was far too
busy plunging his snout in the golden trough to be concerned with a
run-down, debt-ridden estate in megaboring Yorkshire.

But they were not long, the days of swine and Porsches. And by the
early nineties the smartest pigs, those who could still remember how to
walk on two legs, were putting as much distance as they could between
themselves and the wrack of the Thatcherite economics they had
worshiped in vain. It would be comforting to see this as conversion.
Alas, I fear that they are merely searching for new horizons to pollute,
new territories to exploit. I fear nowhere is safe, not even the green
grass, clear air, translucent waters, and simple country folk of a
distant, megaboring Yorkshire dale.

One

*How horrible it is to have so many
people killed!—And what a blessing
one cares for none of them!*

It is the Day of Reckoning.

The sun is shining. The inhabitants of Enscombe will tell you the sun always shines on Reckoning Day, meaning it hasn't rained much above a dozen times in the last twenty years. But this year they are right. After a week in which March seemed always looking back to January, suddenly it has leapt forward into May, and even in the shade, the air hangs warm and scented with blossom.

The village lies still as a painting, an English watercolor over which the artist has labored with furious concentration to fix forever one perfect moment. What problems it must have posed! How to capture the almost black shadows which the sun, just past its zenith, gives to the left-hand side of the High Street without giving a false Mediterranean brightness to the buildings opposite? And then the problem of perspective, with the road rising gently from the Morris Men's Rest at the southern end of the village, widening a little beyond the post office to admit the cobbled forecourts of the sun-bright bookshop and café opposite the shadow-dark gallery, then steepening suddenly into a breathless hill as it climbs alongside the high churchyard wall over which headstones peep as though eager to see how the living are doing in these hard times. Nor is the curiously slouching tower of the church easy to capture accurately without making the artist look merely incompetent! And that distant pennant of kingfisher-blue which is all that is visible of Old Hall above the trees beyond the church, were it not better with an artist's license to ignore it as a distraction from the horizon of brooding moorland which is the picture's natural frame?

But it is that blue pennant which explains the village's stillness, for it betokens that the Squire is hosting his Reckoning Feast. And, more important still—for any daubster can paint a house, but only the true artist can hint the life within—the pennant signals that behind this picture of still beauty there is warm, pulsating humanity always threatening to burst through.

Now there is movement and the picture starts to dissolve. A woman comes hurrying down the shady side of the street. Her name is Elsie Toke. She is a slight, rather fey-looking woman in her forties, though her face is curiously unmarked by age. But it is marked now by anxiety as she looks to the left and right as though searching for someone. She catches a movement ahead of her on the sunny side of the street. A figure has emerged into the light, not very sensibly dressed for this place and this weather, in combat fatigues with a black woolen balaclava pulled over his head so that only the eyes are visible. And crooked in his right arm he has a heavy, short-barreled gun.

He has not seen the woman yet. His mind seems boiling like the sun with more impressions and ideas than it can safely hold, a maelstrom of energy close to critical mass. He recalls reading somewhere of those old Nordic warriors who at times of great crisis ran amuck. Berserkers, they called them, responding to some imperative of violence which put them in touch with the violence which lies behind all of nature. He had found the idea appealing. When all else fails, when the subtlest of defense strategies prove futile, then throw caution to the winds, go out, attack, destroy, die!

The woman calls, "Jason!"

He becomes aware of her for the first time. She is hurrying toward him, relief smudging the worry from her face. He registers who she is but it means nothing. To a berserker all flesh is grass, waiting to be mown down. If any thought does cross his mind it is that he has to start somewhere. He shifts the gun from the crook of his arm to rest the stock on his hip. The expression on her face is changing now. She opens her mouth to speak again, but before the words can emerge, he fires. She takes the shot full in the chest. She doesn't scream but looks down in disbelief as the red stain blossoms and the sour wine smell of blood rises to her nostrils.

The berserker is already moving on. There are other figures in the long High Street now and his mind is reeling with delight at the prospect of conjuring fear into familiar faces as they admit the unbelievable.

Here comes Thomas Wapshare, eyes bright with curiosity, chubby cheeks aglow, mouth already curving into his jovial landlord's smile, and curiously the smile still remaining even as the eyes at last grasp what is happening, even as the muzzle comes up and at short range blasts him in that oh-so-comfortable gut.

And there across the street unlocking the post office door is Dudley Wylmot, a thin, gangling man with a weak chin and a spiky moustache under a rather large nose which gives him the air of a self-important rabbit. There is certainly something of the rabbit in him now as he turns with his key in the door and becomes aware of the gun barrel pointing straight at him. The berserker waits just long enough for Wylmot to register fully what is happening, then he fires. The shot takes him in the neck, and he spins around, slamming against the blood-spattered door.

Now the berserker moves faster. Up ahead he has seen Caddy Scudamore opening the door of the Eendale Gallery. Luscious, gorgeous, infinitely desirable Caddy, who looks at you as if you aren't there unless she takes a fancy to paint you. Shared, her indifference is bearable. But what right has she to select one out of the mass? She has the door open. She steps inside. He blasts her right between the shoulder blades, smiling beneath his balaclava to see the fresh red blood blot out all the other colors on her paint-stained smock.

"Hey!"

The voice comes from behind him. He turns. In the doorway of the Tell-Tale Bookshop stands the distinguished gray-haired patrician figure of Edwin Digweed. He must have seen the attack on Caddy through his window. A wise man would have dived behind his bookshelves! He snaps off a shot without conscious aim and feels a surge of superhuman power as the bookseller grabs for his stomach and feels the sticky blood oozing through his fingers.

Out of sheer exuberance the berserker lets one off at the window of the empty Wayside Café, then, holding his weapon at the high port, begins to jog up the hill past the churchyard.

He is slowing down by the time he reaches the war memorial set in a nook of the wall, so he takes a breather and gives the bronze soldier, who has been gazing nobly into space for more than seventy years, a reminder of what it was all about.

The driver of an open-topped cabriolet in a striking shade of metallic aubergine slows almost to a halt as he observes the berserker's assault on the memorial. His name is Justin Halavant and he has a slightly off-key sense of humor which inspires him to call, "I say: has war been declared on all statuary or just the military genre?"

He realizes his mistake at once. Startled, the berserker swings around and pumps off two rapid shots. The first hits the car door, but the second hits Halavant high on the side of his head, his muscles spasm, his foot rams down on the accelerator, and the car goes screaming down the hill into the village.

Not waiting to see what becomes of it, the berserker jogs up the hill and turns into the churchyard.

Here he pauses, leaning against a headstone, to check his ammunition. He is tempted to do a bit of damage to the church, but ammo is running low and instinct urges him on to surprise the great bulk of villagers still at the Reckoning Feast before rumor of his activities reaches them from the village. But he does waste a shot at the Guillemard coat of arms above the arched gateway which leads from the churchyard into Green Alley and the Old Hall estate.

Now the climax is close—which is just as well, as the energy which not long before had seemed set to last him forever is now fading fast and the weapon which had seemed like a willow wand in his hands pulls at his muscles like a pig of iron.

Out of the corner of his eye he glimpses a figure, and instinctively he pumps a shot at it before he realizes it is only a marble faun leering over a low stone bench. His snap shot hits home and as he watches, the leering head slowly topples off.

Now he is close enough to the Reckoning to hear its noise. Not the usual hubbub of vacuous gossip and the chomping of greedy teeth. No, now it is the throb of a passionate cello and an old but still piercing voice raised in rhythmic incantation.

> Who has not seen in windy March
> Flocks fleeing through the fields,
> 'Neath arching ash and leaning larch,
> With winter on their heels,
> His breath with strength to drench or parch,
> More fierce because it fails?

It is the Squire inflicting his ballad on the captive audience. It occurs to the berserker, across whose dark and stormy mind an occasional shaft of rationality shoots, that some of the listeners might, to start with, regard his interruption as a blessed relief.

But not for long.

He comes into the seated villagers from behind. He reckons he can only spare half a dozen shots for this lot. There's old Ma Pottinger, always droning on about that precious school of hers. She glances his way, opens her mouth to utter the sonorous admonition which is her trademark, but it turns into a piercing shriek as he drills one into her ample bosom.

People turn to look. The Squire carries on chanting.

> So fled the Gaels from Guillemard
> As he came galloping on,
> More fearsome than the pouncing pard
> In leafy Lebanon,
> And yet his lifeblood spouted hard
> Beneath his habergeon.

But the cellist sighs to a halt as the berserker advances like Moses through the Red Sea, an apt image as he paints with blood to left and right, catching Daphne Wylmot high on her golden head and knocking old Mr. Hogbin clean out of his walker.

In the front row they rise as if to greet him, and he gives each in turn the greeting they deserve.

There's Larry Lillingstone, the young vicar—here's something for your sermon! Whoops. Kee Scudamore, either deliberately or trying to escape, has got in the way. Not to worry, here's one in the cassock for you, Vicar, anyway. And who have we here? Farmer George Creed and his so holy sister whose pies are a lot tastier than her piety—there's for you! And bossy Girlie Guillemard comes next, her teeth biting clean through the stem of her pipe as her belly blossoms redly. And now the smell of blood is hot in the evening air, and hotter still in the berserker's mind as he leaps onto the table in full and ineffable fury. At point-blank range he pumps a shot into little Fran Harding's cello, which she is vainly trying to shelter behind. Then he turns to the Squire. Their eyes meet. "Here's one for your ballad, Squire," says the berserker. And laughs as the force of the shot drives the old man's script back into his chest, where it hangs redly, like a proclamation on a blasted tree.

Now the berserker turns to face the crowd. Or rabble, rather, for they are all in retreat. Except for three. The Holy Trinity! The Three Stooges! The Good, the Bad, and the Ugly!

He can't remember their names. Doesn't matter. You don't give pigs names, not when you're planning to kill them.

They are moving slowly toward him. He glances down and regrets the shots wasted at nonhuman targets, for he sees he has only one shot left.

Not to worry. One's enough to make a point.

But which one?

The Good? The Bad? Or the Ugly?

He makes his decision.

He raises his gun.

And he fires.

Two

*I do not want people to be very
agreeable, as it saves me the trouble
of liking them a great deal.*

Two days before the events just described, late on a cold
March afternoon buffed bright by a skittish east wind,
Enscombe's peace had been less dramatically shattered by
the arrival of three motorcycles and a long-base Land
Rover.

The Land Rover had the words GUNG HO! stenciled on its
sides in scarlet with, above them, the image of a swooping
bird of prey. The same logos appeared on the white helmets
and pale blue leathers of the riders and passengers of the
first two motorcycles. These were Harley-Davidson Fatboys,
and they and the Land Rover bumped up the cobbles of the
narrow forecourt of the Wayside Café and came to a halt
with a deal of exuberant revving.

The third solitary rider brought his old Triumph Thunder-
bird to a more decorous halt in front of the neighboring Tell-
Tale Bookshop (Rare & Antiquarian: Prop. E. Digweed,
D.Litt.). His helmet and leathers were a dull black, unre-
lieved except by a star of silver studs at the breast.

The first Harley-Davidson team had removed their helmets to reveal a shag of black hair, male, and a shoal of
herring-bright ringlets, female, which its owner shook down
over her shoulders as she stretched her arms and said, "Un-
zip me, darling. I'm dying for a pee."

At this point the door of the café opened to reveal a
statuesquely handsome woman in a blue checkered apron.

She looked the new arrivals up and down and said, "No hippies. No bikers. In the Name of the Lord."

The ringleted rider shrieked an incredulous laugh, and her companion said, "What's the Lord got against bikers, then?"

" 'God hath made man upright, but they have sought out many inventions,' " replied the woman in a perfectly matter-of-fact voice.

The second passenger had removed her helmet to reveal a Nefertiti skull whose close-napped hair was, aptly, a billiard-table green. She lit a cigarette and said, "Jesus Christ!" The café owner gave an outraged snort and took a step forward to put baize-head within reach of either the Third Commandment or a left hook, but before this could be made clear, the fourth biker, who'd been conferring with three young men climbing out of the Land Rover, whipped off his helmet with a flourish and said, "Dora, my sweet, it is I, Guy. And I have brought these good people to a halt within sight almost of our destination with the promise that here they would get the best apple pie this side of Paradise."

He was in his late twenties, with curly brown hair, eyes that twinkled at will, and a charming smile that couldn't quite conceal its complacent certainty of success. His voice was vibrant with sincerity and those reverse-*Pygmalion* vowels which old Etonians imagine improve their street cred. He advanced as though to embrace the café owner, but she folded her arms in a counterscarp which repulsed familiarity and said, "I'm sorry, Master Guy. It's got to be the same rule for all, else the law is mocked."

For a second the biker's charm looked ready to dissolve into petulance, but reason prevailed and he said, "All right, Dora, our loss is your loss. Come on, boys and girls. The good news is the Hall's only a minute away. The bad news is, you're going to have to make do with cousin Girlie's marble cake, which does not belie its name. Ciao, Dorissima! Avanti!"

The male trio got back into the Land Rover, the mixed quartet replaced their neuterizing helmets, while the solitary rider who had been observing the incident with quiet interest removed his. Behind him and to his left a nasally upper-class kind of voice said, "I say. You. Fellow."

Slowly he turned his head, which had all the unlikely rugosities of a purpose-built Gothic ruin.

In the doorway of the bookshop stood a tall, slim man with an aristocratically aquiline face under a thatch of silver hair with matching eyebrows that shot up in surprise as he got the full frontal view, then lowered to echo the sardonic twist of his lips as he said, "You are, I hazard, not a customer?"

"Not for books, if that's what you mean," said the biker politely. "It were more a cup of tea—"

"I thought not," interrupted the bookseller. "Lacking as you clearly do those basic skills of literacy which would have enabled you to read the sign."

The sign he was pointing at was fixed to the wall beneath the window. In a diminutive version of the elegant cursive script used for the shop name above, it read CUSTOMER PARKING ONLY.

It would have been possible to argue that where the message is monitory, the medium should place clarity above aesthetics. But all the biker said was "Yes, well, I would have parked in front of the café, only there wasn't room. . . ."

"Indeed? I suppose by the same token, if the café were closed, you would expect high tea to be served in my flat? Besides, there seems to be a plenitude of room now. . . ."

It was true. The rejected convoy was moving off in an accelerando of engines and a brume of fume.

"Sorry," said the biker, wheeling his bike the few feet necessary to take him from one forecourt to the next.

The aproned chatelaine remained in place.

"Your friends have gone to the Hall, God preserve them," she said.

"Amen, but I'm not with them," said the solitary.

" 'He that toucheth pitch shall be defiled therewith,' " said the woman. "No bikers. No hippies. Not even if they're old enough to know better."

The biker looked slowly around as though in search of help. The convoy had already vanished up the hill beyond the church. A cyclist appeared from the bottom end of the High Street and passed rapidly and silently by. The rider was a pale-faced young man wearing a forage cap and fatigues. The bike had panniers and along the crossbar was strapped a shotgun. He could have been a youngster who'd lied about his age in 1914 to join a bicycle battalion. But slight though his build was he drove the machine up the hill past the church with no diminution of speed.

In the doorway of the Eendale Gallery directly opposite the book-shop, a youngish woman watched his progress, her face as coldly beautiful as a classical statue's.

The biker, finding no hope of relief, returned his attention to Dora Creed and said, "This Hall that lad mentioned. Have they got a tearoom there?"

He saw at once he'd touched a nerve. She drew herself up and said, " 'They have made it desolate, and being desolate, it mourneth unto me; the whole land is desolate, because no man layeth it to heart.' "

"I'd not argue with you there," said the biker. "But there'll be another election sometime. Meanwhile, this Hall . . . ? I'm parched."

Suddenly she smiled with a charm reminiscent of Master Guy's but lacking his contrivance, and for a moment the biker thought he'd got inside her principles. Then she said, "Carry on up the hill past the church. You'll see the estate wall on your right. There's a big set of gates and a lodge after about two furlongs. That's Old Hall."

"Thank you kindly," said the biker.

He replaced his helmet, restarted his engine, and set off at a sedate pace up the High Street.

The church, which dominated the village from the first plateau of the rising ground to the north, had a curious feature which might have tempted some men to pause. The tower looked as if it had fallen out with the nave and was leaning away from it at an angle disconcerting to the sober eye and probably devastating to the drunk. But the biker was not in a mood for archaeological diversion. A cup of tea was what he craved and he doubted if old traditions of ecclesiastic hospitality still obtained in rural Yorkshire.

Beyond the church, as promised by Miss Creed, a high boundary wall reared up to inhibit the vulgar gaze. But after a quarter mile a large sign advertising the imminence of Enscombe Old Hall suggested the vulgar gaze might no longer be considered so unbearable.

A little farther on, the wall was broken by a massive granite arch fit to harbinger a palace. In the headstone of the arch was carved a bird with a long, thin neck, perched on a heraldic shield whose quarters variously showed a rose, a sinking ship, a greyhound couchant, and what to the biker's inexpert eye appeared to be a dromedary pissing against a Christmas tree. Beneath this dark escutcheon ran the equally obscure words *Fuctata non Perfecta*.

On the gate columns, however, had been hung signs of compensatory clarity which in a style and coloring designed to catch the motoring eye advertised the delights on offer at Old Hall.

For a mere £5.50 you were invited to tour this fortified Tudor manor house, the home of the Guillemard family since the sixteenth century.

Or for £2 only, you could explore the extensive grounds (except when the red flag was flying, which meant they were being used for "skirmishing"—details on application). In addition the visitor too frail to skirmish, tour, or explore could seek care and perhaps cure in the new Holistic Health Park centered on the refurbished stable block, where it was proposed to offer acupuncture, reflexology, aroma therapy, metaplastic massage, and Third Thought counseling.

Only one word in this multifarious menu really registered on the biker's brain. It was *Refreshments*.

Strictly observing the five-mph speed limit imposed by yet another sign, the biker passed beneath the arch into a greening graveled drive curving out of sight between high banks of rhododendrons in need of pruning.

To the left just inside the gateway stood a square single-story building, presumably the lodge, its rather forbidding front made gay by window boxes full of daffodils. The biker glimpsed the figure of a man standing in one of the windows and he gave a friendly nod. In that brief moment of distraction a girl of five or six came hurtling out of the shrubbery to his right, hit the front wheel of the bike, bounced off, and sat down on the gravel.

"Bloody hell," said the biker. "You all right, luv?"

She put her hand to her mouth and let out a strange noise which it took his tear-anticipating ear a little while to identify as giggling.

Then she rose, dusted herself off, and ran past him into the porch of the lodge, where she turned to look back and wave.

He watched her easy movement with relief till a strangely situated knocking sound made him turn his head, when he found himself looking into the face of a uniformed policeman who was rapping his knuckles against his crash helmet.

Correction. Almost uniformed. He was wearing tunic and trousers but was hatless, his vigorous red hair tousled by the gusting wind. Even the serious expression he was wearing and a fading bruise high on his right cheekbone couldn't disguise how young he was.

He brought his face close enough for his breath to mist the biker's plastic visor and demanded, "Can't you read?"

The biker sighed at this further aspersion on his literacy.

"Yes," he said. "I can read."

"Then you'll know the sign back there says five miles an hour."

"Aye, I noticed, and that was what I were doing."

"Oh, yes?" sneered the young policeman.

Slowly he began a circumambulation of the motorcycle. He moved with an easy grace, like a man who was proud of his body, which to the biker's keen eye, with its breadth of shoulder and narrowness of waist, looked a body to be proud of.

His circle complete, he halted, and with his eyes still focused on the machine as though by sheer force of will he could create a fault, he thrust his left hand under the biker's nose, snapped his fingers, and said, "Documentation."

The biker examined the outstretched hand, which had half a dozen stitches, perhaps more, in a cut which ran from the thumb ball along the wrist under the shirt cuff. Then, with a sigh, he unzipped his jerkin, reached inside, and came out with a wallet.

"Any particular reason I should show you this?" he asked mildly.

The constable's handsome young face slowly turned.

"Because I'm *asking* you, that's one particular reason. Because I'm *telling* you, that's another particular reason. Two enough?"

"Plenty. As long as you'll be putting 'em in your report."

"What I put in my report's got nothing to do with you," said the constable.

"You think not? Here," said the biker. He handed over the documents he'd removed from his wallet, then slowly removed his helmet.

The youngster looked from the documents to the face then back to the documents, like a soldier trying not to believe a dear-John.

"Oh, hell," he said unhappily. "You might have let on."

And Detective Sergeant Wield said, "You need documentation to get treated politely around here, do you?"

"Yes, I mean, no, of course not, only you've got to keep a sharp eye open for strangers out here. . . ."

He was nobbut a lad, thought Wield, noting how the embarrassed flush blended in with the rich red of his windblown hair.

He said abruptly, "Worried about strangers, are you? Seems to me that come Easter, you're going to have a lot more to worry about, and from that sign on the gate, some of 'em will be very strange indeed. You got a hat, lad?"

"Yeah, I'm sorry, Sarge, it's back there . . . in the car. . . ."

"Wear it." Wield's brain, which his CID chief, Andy Dalziel, opined should be pickled in strong ale and sold to IBM after the sergeant's death, had been punching up references to Enscombe.

He said, "Post office here got done, twice, wasn't it? Once before

Christmas, once just after. We never got anyone, as far as I recall. That'd be strangers, too, I supppose?"

"I expect so, Sarge."

"And wasn't there some bother about the war memorial last Remembrance Day?"

"Yes, Sarge. It got desecrated. I'd just started here then."

"Did you get it sorted?"

"I think so, Sarge."

"Anything else important happen here since you came?"

"No, Sarge. I don't think so."

"What about those stitches in your arm? And that bruise on your face? You been in a ruck?"

"Oh, no, Sarge." He laughed, not wholly convincingly. "Walked into the branch of a tree, fell, and cut myself on a rock."

"Oh, aye? So. Two break-ins and an attack by nature. Real crime wave! No wonder you're neurotic about strangers. But the rule is, nice first, nasty when you see a need. You got that, Bendish?"

The name had popped into his head. He must have seen it on a report. He'd had nothing to do personally with either of the PO jobs here.

The young constable was clearly impressed and disconcerted at this degree of knowledge. His mind was trying to fit it in with the appearance of a detective sergeant, some way past the first flush of youth, wearing black leather and riding a high-powered motorcycle.

He said, "You're not here officially are you, Sarge? I mean under cover . . . ?"

Wield barked the sound which friends recognized as his way of expressing amusement—though others often took it as a sign that the interrupted lycanthropic process suggested by his face was about to be resumed.

"No, son. Just out enjoying the countryside. And dying for a cup of tea. It said something back there about refreshments."

"You're out of luck. Sorry," said Bendish, as though he felt personally responsible. "Place isn't open to the public till Easter; it does say so on the sign. You must have missed it. But there's a café in the village. Dora Creed's place. She's a smashing baker. Very welcoming."

"Oh, aye?" said Wield. "I saw it. Next to a bookshop. Make me welcome there, too, would they?"

"Oh, yes. Old Digweed'll talk to you for hours about books if you let him."

"So," said Wield. "If we add you, that must make Enscombe about the most welcoming place in Yorkshire. It fair wears a man out. I reckon I'll head on home and make my own tea."

To give unalloyed joy is a rare privilege. Observing the undisguisable relief and pleasure which broke out in the young man's face, Wield thought, Mebbe I should say good-bye to folk more often.

"Sorry about the misunderstanding, Sarge," said Bendish.

"You'll be sorrier if I catch you wandering around again baht 'at," said Wield heavily. "This isn't Ilkley Moor. Take heed!"

He revved up and set off slowly through the gateway. The watcher at the window had vanished but the little girl was still standing in the porch. He waved at her as he passed and she waved back, then ran into the house.

The young constable watched him out of sight. Then he flung up his right arm in a gesture as much of exultation as derision and yelled, "And good-bye to you, too, you ugly old sod!"

Then, laughing, he turned and ran back into the rhododendrons.

Three

*... so young, so blooming, and so
innocent, as if she never had a
wicked thought in her life—which
yet one has some reason to suppose
she must have had ...*

Kee Scudamore watched the last motorcyclist move away, then crossed the street. She walked with an easy and unconscious grace untroubled by the gusting wind which unfurled her long flaxen hair and pressed her cotton skirt to the contours of her slender thighs. Under her left arm she carried a box file.

"Dora, Edwin, good day to you," she said in a soft voice with just enough music in it to take the edge off a certain almost pedantic note. "And what did Guy the Heir want with you?"

"Pie for his cronies," said Dora Creed. "I sent them packing. Rules's no good if you make exceptions. No hippies, no bikers."

"Take care, Dora. Once he comes into his own, it will be his decision who caters for the Reckoning, not to mention the new café."

Dora shrugged indifferently and said, "Hall may stand higher than the church, but it's the church I look up to."

"Well said," replied Kee. "I wish everyone had your principles, especially up at the Hall."

"Oh, Jesus," said Digweed. "Not more revelations?"

Dora Creed shot him an indignant glance and said, " 'The Lord will not hold him guiltless that taketh His name in vain.' "

Digweed replied with some irritation, "If the Lord can

tolerate the enthusiasm of a vessel as holy as yourself for the works of Harold Robbins I am sure he will permit me the occasional profanity. Kee, what now?"

"It's this gift shop Girlie's planning. First there was your brother's carved crooks, Dora. Not that I can really complain about that. George is a free agent and goes his own way."

" 'As an ox goeth to the slaughter, or as a fool to the correction of the stocks,' " said Dora Creed fiercely.

Kee raised her eyebrows questioningly at Digweed, who shook his head as if to say he didn't understand either.

"However," resumed the blond woman, "Beryl Pottinger's a horse of a different color. I've put in a great deal of time and effort there, and she's learned a lot from Caddy. Her watercolors have become our best-selling line. Now she tells me Girlie's offering her a better deal. This is blatant poaching."

"I cannot believe Beryl would let herself be bought."

"With her job at the school on the line, money may seem a little more important."

" 'He that hasteth to be rich shall not be innocent,' " said Dora.

"Let's hope we can save her job," said Digweed.

"By selling the Green, you mean? Even if that's what the village opts for, would it raise enough?"

"With planning permission, possibly. The Parish Council put out some unofficial feelers and got a working estimate. But let's leave all that till the meeting tomorrow night, shall we? Meanwhile I hope you get your differences with Girlie sorted out. She's a reasonable woman."

"She's also a Guillemard, and *Fuctata non perfecta*'s a hard virus to get out of your blood. Holistic healing and executive cowboys and Indians may save the Hall, but what kind of people do you think they'll be bringing into the village?"

"Hippies. Bikers," said Dora promptly. "They go to and fro in the evening: they grin like a dog, and run about through the city."

Digweed and Kee laughed out loud and the bookseller said, "Certainly that last creature that was here, the one by himself, he was straight out of Mad Max! But there can't be many around like him, thank heaven. Kee, that deed of gift you want me to look at . . ."

"I've got it here," said the woman, opening the box file, which was full of what looked like old legal papers. "Here you are."

"My law is very rusty," he said warningly as he took the document she handed to him.

"Mine's nonexistent," she replied, closing the file. "I've probably got the wrong end of the stick. Nevertheless, it could be worth a look. Meanwhile I'll drop the rest of this stuff off at the vicarage and I might just carry on to the Hall and have a talk with Girlie about Beryl. Edwin, if you see anyone going into the gallery, you might pop across. Caddie's supposedly in charge, but once she gets stuck into something in her studio, you could blow up the till and she would hardly notice."

She set off up the street with the wind dancing attendance.

Digweed, watching her go, said, "Interesting how well Kee managed to suppress her fascination with parish history while old Charley Cage was up at the vicarage."

Dora said, "A vicar needs a wife. It's not natural else."

"Indeed? Perhaps you should drop a line to the pope. I think I'll just pop over and check that Caddy's okay."

He patted his silvery hair as he spoke, though unlike Kee's silken mane, it was too coarsely vigorous to be much disturbed by the wind.

Dora Creed said, " 'The hoary head is a crown of glory if it is found in the way of righteousness.' "

"True beyond need of exegesis," said Digweed.

He crossed the street and entered the gallery. Converted from the old village smithy, it was a spacious, well-lit room, the upper walls of which were crowded with paintings and the lower shelved with tourist fodder. Behind the unattended till a door opened onto a narrow, gloomy passage. Digweed went through it and called, "Caddy?"

"Here," a voice floated down a steep staircase.

Digweed ran lightly up the stairs and along a creaking landing into the studio. This consisted of two rooms knocked together and opened into the attic, whose sloping roof was broken by a pair of huge skylights. These spilled brightness onto a triptych of canvases occupying almost an entire wall. On them was painted a crucifixion, conventionally structured with the cross raised high in the central panel and a long panorama of landscape and buildings falling away behind in the other two.

Here conventionality ended. Though much was only sketched in, the background was clearly not first-century Palestine but twentieth-century Enscombe. And the as yet faceless figure on the cross was a naked woman.

At one end of the chaotically cluttered room Caddy Scudamore, as dark as her sister was fair, and as luscious as she was lean, stood in front of a cheval glass with her paint-stained smock rolled up, critically examining her heavy breasts.

"Hello, Edwin," she said. "Nipples are hard."

"Indeed," said Digweed, his gaze drifting from reflection to representation. "And perhaps one should ask oneself whether in the circumstances they would be. Caddy, I think the time has come for you and me to have congress."

And he carefully closed the door behind him.

Four

*... he gave us an excellent
Sermon—a little too eager sometimes in his delivery, but that is to
me a better extreme than the want
of animation especially when it
comes from the heart.*

"The church of St. Hilda and St. Margaret, in Enscombe,
dominating the village from the high ground to the north
where the valley of the Een begins to climb up to the moors
which give it birth, has two immediately striking unusual
features. One is the double patriotic dedication and the other
is the famous leaning tower which, though no challenge to
Pisa, is certainly more inclined to Rome than a good Prot-
estant church ought to be."

(Pause for laughter.)

The Reverend Laurence Lillingstone paused for laughter.

His audience, which was himself in the pier glass set in
his study wall, laughed appreciatively. So, too, he hoped,
would the ladies of the Byreford and District Luncheon
Club. "Not too heavy," Mrs. Finch-Hatton had said. "Save
your fine detail for the Historical Association."

He had nodded his understanding, concealing his chagrin
that the Mid-Yorkshire Historical Association had just rejected his offer of a talk based on his researches into the
Enscombe archives. "Sorry," the secretary had said, "but
we've got old Squire Selwyn doing his ballad history. Don't
want to overdose on Enscombe, do we?"

Dear God! What sort of world was it where serious scholarship could be pushed out by a music-hall turn?

The handsome face in the glass was glowering uncharitably but as he met its gaze, the indignant scowl dissolved in a flush of shame.

What right had he to mock old Selwyn's verses when God who knows everything knew it wasn't serious scholarship that drove him to his own historical researches, it was serious sex!

He'd thought he'd put all that behind him when, after a highly charged episode during his curacy, he had taken a solemn vow of celibacy.

This was, of course, purely a private matter, as the Church of England imposes no such restraint upon its ministers. But when he was offered the living of Enscombe, he felt duty bound to apprise the bishop of his condition—"in case such a rural community might expect eventually to have a vicar's wife to run the Mothers' Union, help with the Women's Institute, that sort of thing."

The bishop, of the Church's worldly rather than otherworldly wing, replied, "You're not trying to tell me you're gay, Larry?"

"Certainly not!"

"I'm relieved. Not that I've anything against gayness. Some of my best friends ought to be gay."

"But you don't think Enscombe is ready for such an imaginative appointment?" smiled Lillingstone. "Not even after putting up with the Voice of the People for so many years?"

"Charley Cage, your predecessor, was my predecessor's predecessor's revenge on the Guillemards. Shortly after his elevation to the episcopate back in the thirties, he gave way to pressure from the then Squire to move the then incumbent, Stanley Harding, on. Later, as he grew into the job, he much regretted this weakness, so when, just before his own retirement in the fifties, the living became vacant again, he looked around for someone whose views were likely to cause the Guillemards maximum pain, and lit upon young Charley."

"What was Stanley Harding's crime?"

"Oh, social awareness, Christian charity, the usual things. But worst of all he had the temerity to marry the Squire's daughter!"

"Good Lord. And the bishop got his own back with Cage."

"This is only my own theory, you understand," laughed the older man. "In fact, it rather backfired. The old Squire died and his son, the present Squire, got on rather well with Charley. At least they never fell out in public. But to get back to your nongayness, I'm relieved because old Charley was in every sense a confirmed bachelor, and I feel that after forty years, the blushful maidens of Enscombe deserve at least a level playing field."

"I haven't made my vow lightly," said Lillingstone, slightly piqued.

"Of course you haven't, but the strongest oaths are straw to the fire i' the blood, eh?"

"Saint Augustine?" guessed Lillingstone.

"Saint Bill, I think. No, you'll do nicely for Enscombe, Larry. But be warned, it's a place that can do odd things to a man."

"Such as?" enquired Lillingstone.

The bishop sipped his screwdriver and said, "Old Charley used to claim, when the port had been around a few times, that after the Fall, God decided to have a second shot, learning from the failure of the first. This time He created a man who was hard of head, blunt of speech, knew which side his bread was buttered on, and above all took no notice of women. Then God sent him forth to multiply in Yorkshire. But after a while he got to worrying he'd left something out, imagination, invention, fancy, call it what you will. So he grabbed a nice handful of this, intending to scatter it thinly over the county. Only, it was a batch He'd just made and it was still damp, so instead of scattering, it all landed in a single lump, and that was where they built Enscombe!"

Lillingstone laughed appreciatively and said, "I wish I'd known Cage."

"He was worth knowing. He died in the pulpit, you know. No one noticed for ten minutes. His dramatic pauses had been getting longer and longer. He was extremely outspoken both on his feet and in print. For recreation, or as he put it, to keep himself out of temptation (though he never specified the nature of the temptation), he was writing a history of the parish. You're a historian yourself, aren't you? If you feel the flesh tugging too strongly, you could do worse than follow Charley's example. All the archival stuff's at the vicarage. It'll need sorting out before our masters sell the place from under you."

"Sounds interesting," said Lillingstone. "But if Cage's work was well advanced . . ."

"Oh, yes. He showed me various drafts. Fascinating, but much of it utterly unpublishable! No, you take my advice, Larry. There's nothing like the dust of the past for clogging an overactive internal combustion engine!"

The young vicar had taken this as a joke till a few days after his induction, when his desire to meet those of his flock who hadn't been at the church (i.e., the majority) took him through the door of the Eendale Gallery.

He had been instantly aware that there were paintings here of a quality far above that of the usual insipid watercolors of local views which filled much of the wall space. One in particular caught his eye, a small acrylic of his own church, stark against a sulphurously wuthering sky, with the angle of the tower so exaggerated that it looked as if the building had been caught in the very act of being blown apart.

The gallery had been empty when he entered and so rapt was he in studying the picture that he did not hear the inner door open.

Then someone coughed gently and a voice said, "Need any help?"

He turned and saw the Scudamore sisters, or rather he saw Caddy, and he knew instantly he needed more help than anyone here below could give him.

It was a coup de foudre, a surge of longing so intense, he felt as if every ounce of his flesh was on fire.

He stammered thickly, "The church . . . I'd like to look at the church. . . ."

Kee Scudamore, whom he'd registered merely as a pale presence, bland and bloodless alongside the vibrant carnality of Caddy, said, "The church? Perhaps you should ask the vicar."

He heard himself say idiotically, "I *am* the vicar," and the smaller, darker, infinitely more luscious girl put a paint-stained hand to a mouth made to suck a man's soul out of his body, and tried to stifle her giggles.

"You mean the painting? Of course," said the cool blonde.

She moved past him, unfolded a set of steps, mounted, and unhooked the picture.

He had left with the painting wrapped in brown paper under his arm. It had cost him more than he could afford, but what was money when he was already aware of the incredibly high price he was likely to pay for his visit?

He was in love, a man who had nothing to offer, a man bound by a vow no one could release him from. He didn't doubt that if he consulted his friend, the bishop, he would be offered all the reassurance which that pragmatic prelate could muster. *It is better to marry than to burn* would be trotted out. But it all depended where you were going to burn! He wasn't sure just how much credence he gave to a physical hell, but he knew he had a belief to match Thomas More's in the nature of a vow.

So he had thrown himself into his parish work with a fervor which soon won golden opinions, and he put himself out of temptation in his "spare" time by following the bishop's suggestion and Charley Cage's example by plunging into the past. Sorting out Charley Cage's chaos of archival material was a necessary as well as a therapeutic act. As forecast by the bishop the diocese's business managers had decided to do what Cage's obduracy had inhibited them from doing much earlier, which was to build a modern bungalow and sell the rambling old vicarage into private occupancy. So Lillingstone had a great deal to occupy himself with. Yet in a small place like Enscombe not all the business in the world could prevent occasional encounters with Caddy, and the merest glimpse of her was like a tot of whisky to an alcoholic, producing instant relapse. Fearful that the physical effect of her presence would be too visible to sharp country eyes, he had abandoned the telltale tight jeans which were his preferred off-duty garb and reverted to the protective folds of the traditional cassock, a move which mollified his older parishioners, who liked a parson to look like a parson.

His efforts to avoid Caddy did not extend to her sister. On the contrary he found much solace in Kee's grace and composure. Here was the still center of the Scudamore household, its domestic and commercial strength and its tutelary spirit. And while Lillingstone would not have dared to be alone with Caddy, the company of Kee permitted a pale but safe shadow of contact.

"Larry? Are you all right?"

He turned from his mirror to find Kee Scudamore, like a conjuration of his thought, standing in the open French window. A quick glance reassured him she was alone and he went toward her smiling.

"I'm fine," he said. "Just rehearsing my Luncheon Club talk."

"Indeed? Well, if that was a dramatic pause, I'd be careful. There are ladies there who will not hesitate to rush forward with offers of mouth-to-mouth resuscitation."

"I think you overestimate my charms," he said glumly.

"Perhaps," she said. "I'm on my way to Old Hall and I thought I'd return these documents. Fascinating."

She placed the box file on his desk.

"I've hung on to the deed of gift," she said. "By the way, what exactly is a tithe?"

"Old English *teopa*, Middle English *tipe*, a tenth," he said promptly. "Specifically that tax of one tenth of produce or labor paid for the upkeep of clergy. Last century as the produce-and-labor thing became uncollectable, or just undesirable, a rent charge was substituted. And in 1936 the Tithe Act abolished tithes completely, except as purely voluntary payments. Why do you ask?"

"It was just something in the deed," she said vaguely.

He glanced at her sharply and said, "You've not been nobbled by the antediluvians, have you? The ones who think the vicarage shouldn't be sold because it was a gift from the parish?"

"It does seem a mite ungracious."

"Kee, it was two hundred years ago!" he said in exasperation. "And even if it were yesterday, a gift's a gift. You don't retain rights."

"So you'll be happy to move into some little breeze-block bungalow?"

"Of course not. I love it here. But you must admit it's absurd for one single man to be rattling around in a place this size. Anyway, it's not my decision. I have got masters."

"I thought you worked for God. Sorry. Let's not fall out. I noticed your For Sale sign says UNDER OFFER. Anyone I know?"

"Indirectly," he said, not too happily. "Phil Wallop."

"What? As in Philip Wallop, Contractor, who's doing Girlie's improvements at the Hall? What's he going to do with the place? Turn it into a massage parlor?"

"No," he said. "There are of course restrictive covenants. Domestic use only. The positive way to look at it is a man doesn't make a mess in his own backyard."

"You're losing me, Larry," she said. Then her sharp mind made the leap. "This wouldn't have anything to do with this working estimate for the Green Edwin was just telling me about? It would, wouldn't it! My God, Wallop's going to turn us into a suburb!"

Her face flushed with anger, she strode through the French window and across the lawn. Lillingstone hurried after her, catching up as she passed through the arched gateway leading into the churchyard.

"Look," he said, "if the Green's put on sale, it'll be on the open market. There'll be other bidders than Wallop."

"Other developers, you mean?"

"No one's going to pay the kind of money we need without planning permission. It's Hobson's choice, Kee, the school or the Green. But I'm not Hobson. Even the parish council's not Hobson. It's the whole village, and that's who'll be making the choice at tomorrow night's meeting."

She walked on through the well-kept churchyard till they reached another arched gateway, this one with Guillemard arms and motto above it, marking the entrance to the family's own private route from Hall to church, known as Green Alley. A hundred years ago it had been a broad graveled path along which full-skirted ladies on the arms of full-bellied gents could stroll between banks of laurel and viburnum and lilac and rhododendron. But the cost of labor had gone up and the cost of irreligion had gone down and gradually Green Alley had shrunk to a muddy track scarcely wider than a sheeptrod.

Here she turned, the anger gone from her face, and reached out and touched her cool fingers against his hand.

"Larry, I'm sorry. I've no right to snap at you. Something's happening here—the school, the vicarage, the Green, the Hall—something that can run out of control unless we all stick together and use our heads. Forgive me?"

"Of course," he said. Her candid gaze, her wise smile, her understanding tone, the cool touch of her fingers, brought to him how much he admired and respected her. Several times in the past he had come close to opening his heart to her and confiding his feelings for Caddy. Something had always got in the way. But here and now seemed the ideal time, the ideal place.

He took a deep breath and closed his eyes.

"Kee," he said in a low voice. "I'm passionately, insanely, helplessly in love with Caddy."

He opened his eyes and found he was talking to Kee's retreating back. But having come so far he was not about to give up. Dauntless, he plunged after her along the narrow track till she reached a small clearing, where she paused and turned and said, "Sorry, Larry, were you saying something?"

"Yes," he said, keeping his eyes open this time. "I want to tell you that—"

"How very odd," said Kee.

"Odd? Why so?" demanded Lillingstone, assuming some kind of precognitive response to his proposed confession.

"The hat," she said.

He knew he wasn't wearing a hat. Nevertheless his hand flew to his head.

"There," she said impatiently.

He followed her pointing finger. The function of this clearing was easy to work out. Here those upper-class promenaders overcome by fatigue, devotion, or love had been able to rest awhile on a granite bench made for two. It was lichened and ivied almost to invisibility now, but its location was signposted by a marble faun strategically placed to leer encouragingly over the heads of bashful wooers.

A hundred years ago, who knows what ardent outbursts that prurient presence had provoked?

Today, however, it was a real turnoff. Laurence Lillingstone had not become a vicar without being able to recognize a sign when he saw one.

This, after all, was neither the time nor the place to confess an illicit love.

Not in the presence of a marble statue wearing a policeman's hat.

End of Volume 1

Volume the Second

PROLOGUE, being extracts
from the
JOURNAL of FRANCES GUILLEMARD

*August 29, 1931. After the school committee meeting this evening
Stanley asked me to stay behind to help with some correspondence. As
soon as we were alone he made a very stilted and stuttering proposal
of marriage! It was so unlike himself that I laughed and asked him if
he'd been reading Trollope, upon which he grabbed me in his arms
and kissed me so hard, I thought I would stifle, but I didn't want him to
stop. After that I would have stayed all night. As it was I got back very
late and expected a scolding (twenty-four and I still get scolded!) but it
turned out Selly had done something to draw all the fire and I was able
to slip upstairs hardly noticed.*

*All I wanted was to think about the evening and fill in my journal
but Guy appeared in his dressing gown, very put out because he'd
been sent to bed at nine for asking questions when the row started,
which he felt was considerably beneath the dignity of a young gent of
thirteen! He thought it had something to do with Agnes, the under-
maid, and said Father was in a tremendous paddy and talking, as he
always does when Selly gets in hot water, of sending him off to Uncle
Jack's "to grow up"! I got the feeling that, hurt pride apart, Guy
wouldn't be too displeased at the prospect of being left the sole son of
the house, with first pick of the horses and everything. But it probably
won't happen.*

*   *   *

August 30. *Went to Selly's room this morning and found him packing. This time it's true. He's spending a couple of weeks with Great Aunt Meg in Gilbert Street, then it's off to New Zealand to learn about sheep! As if there wasn't one thing we had an excess of in Eendale, which is sheep! He was very coy about the reason for his banishment, and in the end he got so pompous, we quarreled. What on earth do they feed them at school and college to make them believe a young idiot who's spent most of his time shut up with other young idiots knows more about life than any woman who isn't forty and formidable!*

Later I got it out of Mummy. Guy was right (he usually is, the little sneak) and Selly has been "misbehaving" with little Agnes Foote. Agnes has, of course, been sacked and sent back to her family in Byreford. I said it all seemed a bit extreme to me, Selly off to the antipodes and Agnes in disgrace all because of a bit of slap and tickle. Sharp intake of breath from Mummy at the expression! Said that the trouble was Selly was taking it too seriously and talking about being in love. Agnes was much more sensible (surprising how sensible servants have to be!) and I needn't worry about her. Didn't think it was a good moment to mention me and Stanley, knowing as I do that Father has already got him marked down as "modern," which is only one step above total decadence!

September 24. *This has been a dreadful day. I thought that since Selly sailed last week, I had observed a slight softening in Father, as if he relented his harshness to his son and heir, and, though too pigheaded to change his mind, was converted to a gentler, more rational regime in regard to the rest of us. So I told him about me and Stanley. Or rather, coward that I am, I told Mummy and let her pass on the news. I knew when I heard his cry of rage from the stables that I'd made a gross miscalculation! It was all Mummy could do to stop him from locking me in my room and heading down to the vicarage with a horsewhip. But at least it's done. I feel quite serene. Nothing will stop me from marrying Stanley now. It's silly, but I find the only thing that really worries me is that I can't see Stanley getting much help from Father in his efforts to rebuild the village school!*

October 26. *Today Stanley and I were married in St. Marks at Byreford! It was a disappointment not to have the ceremony in our own church but at least I was spared the threat of interruption from Father, who would have seen this as the ultimate provocation! I slipped up to the Hall this morning to see Mummy. She wept a lot and said that Father was implacable and wouldn't I change my mind even now! How little she understands. I bumped into Guy, who is home for half-term. He had the cheek to lecture me about disgracing the family by marrying an atheist socialist agitator! He really is the most obnoxious little snob. I have written to Selly baldly stating the facts. I hope he may be more sympathetic, though I know he'd never have the strength of will to stand up to Father. I thought of Selly later as I came out of church, and who should I see among the onlookers but little Agnes Foote, now Agnes Creed, for when I spoke to her she told me, blushing, that she'd married an old flame of hers from Byreford and by the look of her, he has not been long in doing his "progenitive duty." The euphemism is Mummy's. She spoke rarely of such things and always as a necessary pain. I hope I shall not think of it so. Soon I shall know. Stanley, who has stayed downstairs to smoke a pipe, has had time to burn a ton of tobacco by now! Shall I ring a bell to summon him to his "progenitive duty"? Then we would see how "modern" he is. But I think I hear him now.*

One

*Here I am once more in this scene of
dissipation and vice, and I begin
already to find my morals corrupted.*

Wield usually walked to work. It wasn't far and the exercise did him good. But these weren't the only reasons.

He lived his life in compartments and the bike did not belong in the same compartment as the job. There was no hard-and-fast rule. He'd use it if necessary. But why attract attention? He was "out" if being resolved never to deny his sexuality meant being out, but that didn't mean he had to wear a *Kiss-Me-Quick* T-shirt, did it? It was all perfectly reasonable.

Yet his mind, which could collate evidence, analyze statements, and parse PACE, with a speed and clarity beyond computer programming, knew that perfect reasoning is a perilous plan for living. Perfection has no safety net. One slip and it shatters.

When the job was going well, when he was fully involved with his work both on and off duty, he could imagine things were okay. Leisure in short bursts he could pack with his martial-arts classes, his Gilbert and Sullivan discs, his motorcycle maintenance, his Rider Haggard novels.

But when he had a full day off, or, worse, several full days, the truth came rushing up to meet him. These compartments were empty. There was no one to share them with. There had been no one for longer than he cared to remember. There was part of his life he hadn't just compartmentalized; he'd walled it off and plastered over the bricks.

It wasn't simply a matter of sex. A man could do without that and still function. Or if he couldn't, there were outlets of minimal risk.

But companionship, closeness, care; sorrow at parting and joy at reunion; planned trips and surprise treats; accusations, apologies, quibbles, quarrels, and quiet breathing; all the pain and pleasure of shared existence; this was what he'd walled himself off from, raising a dust of desolation which no amount of fresh spring air blasted over his face as he roared through the highways and byways of rural Yorkshire could blow away.

This time he'd been off for almost a week. If he'd made an issue of it he was probably entitled to more like a month. It had felt like a year. But now at last it was over, and precisely on the first stroke of twelve from the town hall clock, he passed through the imposing portals of Mid-Yorkshire Police HQ. He felt his heart leap, or at least lurch, as he smelled the dusty disinfected odor of the place, but it would have taken an ECG machine to detect the movement.

The last note of the hour was sounding as he reached the CID floor. Simultaneously a bulky figure stepped out of an office and a voice like a sports-day loudspeaker boomed, "My God, someone's rubbed the bottle and let the genie out! What time of day do you call this, Sergeant?"

And Wield knew he was back home.

"The time of day my holiday finishes, sir," he said.

"Holiday? I hope you've brought me a stick of rock, 'cos I know just the place to stick it!"

Judging the threat to be nonpersonal, Wield advanced to make his obeisance to the Head of Mid-Yorkshire CID and Master of All He Cared to Survey, Detective Superintendent Andrew Dalziel.

"Trouble, sir?"

"Owt or nowt. You know Sergeant Filmer?"

"Terry? Aye. Section sergeant out at Byreford, isn't he?"

"That's the bugger. Well, he reckons one of his plowboys has gone walkabout."

Plowboy was Dalziel's personal nomenclature for any uniformed officer stationed in the sticks. For decades the arrangement had been for each sizable village to have its own resident constable under the immediate supervision of a section office in some centrally placed small township. Economy disguised as efficiency was causing a radical shakeup of the system, and in the not-too-distant future the village bobby would vanish completely. Wield, like most thinking coppers, regretted his imminent demise. This was hands-on policing with good public relations, and the additional advantage that it provided a testing ground to see how promising youngsters coped with responsibility.

"If Sergeant Filmer says he's missing, he ought to know," said Wield.

"You reckon? Thing is, it's the lad's day off. He clocked off at noon yesterday and he's not due back on till eight tomorrow morning. Only, Filmer calls in at the police cottage first thing this morning—says there was a report he needed, but I reckon he just likes to stick his neb in, keep them on their toes—and there's no one there."

"But it's his day off."

"Makes no matter to Filmer. He uses his key to get inside, checks the bedroom, finds the bed's not been slept in."

"So he got up early and made the bed. Or found somewhere better to sleep last night."

"Against the rules. You don't sleep away from home without you inform your section office."

"You don't ring up at midnight and say, 'Hey, Sarge, I've struck lucky,' do you?" said Wield.

"My reaction, just. Not Filmer. He checks the wardrobe. If the lad did strike lucky, he went on the date wearing his uniform, 'cos it isn't there. Next he checks the car. It's alongside the cottage, badly parked, unlocked, with stains on the passenger seat."

"Bloodstains?"

"Strawberry jam for owt I know," growled Dalziel. "Now Filmer's right up in the air. Starts making what he calls discreet inquiries. I can hear him. *I've lost a constable, anyone seen him?*"

"And had anyone?"

"Not since yesterday afternoon. But first off he finds some old sod who reckons he saw our missing plowboy about teatime having a set-to with a Hell's Angel. . . ."

"In uniform? Or out?"

"In. So Filmer decides either there was an emergency which got him back in uniform, or mebbe this old boy, who's rising eighty and recovering from a stroke, is a bit confused. He keeps on asking, and, lo and behold, he finds himself another witness in the village who also recalls having a bit of bother yesterday with a Hell's Angel. Only, he got closer and he gives a description which makes this bugger sound

like a cross between King Kong and Rasputin. Now Filmer really
panics. First off he radios in a right alarmist report to the Mother
Superior, who naturally lobs the buck straight upstairs to Desperate
Dan, who can't find me 'cos I'm out doing some real police work, so
he drops it like a steaming hot turd right into the lad's lap. If I'd been
around it'd have got slung back with interest. Let Uniformed take care
of their own, say I!"

"So what's the state of play now, sir?" asked Wield, who had no
problem identifying the Mother Superior as Chief Superintendent
Almond, the new head of Uniformed Branch, while Desperate Dan
was of course Chief Constable Daniel Trimble, and "the lad" was
Wield's very good friend, Chief Inspector Peter Pascoe.

"You know Peter. Always a soft touch. Though to be fair, by the
time he gets landed, yon daft bugger Filmer has decided that he can
kill two birds with one stone by bringing in the plowboy's car for
Forensic to check the stain, and the witness to look at our Family
Album to try and spot King Kong."

"He put a witness in a car he wants Forensic to look at and drove
him here?" said Wield incredulously.

"See what I mean? Pete decides he'd best go and tiptoe through the
turnips himself, to see what damage has been done. Left me a note. He
can be a willful bugger when he wants."

Wield had a good face for hiding smiles, a capacity he used now.
"And Filmer?"

"He's in here with his star witness turning pages. You have a word
with him, Wieldy, come the old Sergeants' Union, see if he's got owt
sensible to say. I seem to make him nervous, can't think why."

Another smile was absorbed and Wield pushed open the door.

The shining bald head of Sergeant Filmer was bent alongside the
shining silver head of a man peering at a pageful of photographs.

At the sound of the door both heads turned.

Filmer's face registered relief as he recognized Wield.

The witness's face registered first surprise, then relief also.

And Wield's face for once allowed his feelings of disbelief, comprehension, and dismay to be printed clear.

"So you've got him!" cried Edwin Digweed, the Enscombe bookseller, jumping up. "Jolly good. Now perhaps you'll admit I wasn't
exaggerating when I said that here was a face marked for villainy if
ever I saw one."

"You what?" said Dalziel, who had followed Wield into the room.

"Is it Harold Bendish that's missing?" asked Wield.

"That's right. What's this old bugger on about?"

The old bugger looked ready to be offended, but as Wield advanced toward him, fear took over and he retreated till his legs caught the lip of the table and he could go no farther.

"For heaven's sake, someone!" he cried. "Shouldn't this man be under restraint?"

"It's all right, sir," said Wield soothingly. "There's been a mistake. I'm a detective."

"*What?*" Digweed looked from Wield to Filmer, saw no denial there, looked back to Wield, recovered both his balance and his aplomb, and said, very Lady Bracknellish, "A *detective? You?* That does indeed sound like a very great mistake. I still find it hard to believe. Superintendent . . . ?"

"This is Detective Sergeant Wield, one of my officers," said Dalziel in a dangerous voice. "Will someone tell me what's going off here?"

"I was in Enscombe yesterday, sir," said Wield. "I met Mr. Digweed, briefly. Then a bit later on, I— "

"You assaulted Constable Bendish!" interposed Digweed. "Excellent. To preserve your cover, isn't that the term? I presume that extraordinary costume you had on was some form of cover?"

"I spoke with Bendish, sir," said Wield stolidly, addressing himself to Dalziel.

"Oh, aye? And what did you say?"

Wield glanced doubtfully at Digweed, who said, "Yes, yes, of course. From being so vital a witness I have to be dragged from my place of business—which incidentally will be doing no business at all while I'm away—I have become an intrusive member of the general public who must on no account be allowed to overhear high-level police discussion. Excuse me, gentlemen, I shall return home where I will spend more of my valuable time penning a strong letter of complaint. You do, I presume, employ at least one token literate to read such letters? Never mind. I'll put it on tape also. Now I give you good day."

He strode out. It was a rather good, very English sort of exit.

Dalziel jerked his head at Filmer, who went in apologetic pursuit.

Then the Fat Man turned to Wield and fixed him with a gaze which would have frozen a Gorgon.

"Right, sunshine," he said with dreadful softness. "Now you can tell me what you were doing in fancy dress beating up PC Bendish!"

Two

*If I am a wild beast, I cannot
help it.*

Less than an hour's sensible driving from Mid-Yorkshire Police HQ, Enscombe is not remote by modern standards. But as the road began to narrow and the valley sides to steepen, Peter Pascoe felt a disproportionate sense of remoteness.

Everywhere there were signs of man's presence—the walls built out of stones painfully cleared from the green pastures alongside the shining river, the sheep grazing between them, the whitewashed farmhouses, the road itself—but nowhere was there anything to persuade of man's permanence. Good old heartless, witless nature seemed lurking everywhere, ready to rush back in the minute man dropped his guard.

Then he rounded a bend and beheld a Vision of Beauty.

He skidded to a halt and walked back to take a closer look. Beyond a pair of elegant wrought iron gates set in the thickest thorn hedge he'd ever seen, a graveled drive arrowed across a daffodilled lawn to a distant house which, though partially hidden by topiaried shrubs, looked as foreign to Yorkshire as a cockney Pearlie Queen in Barnsley market. No sturdy bield this, using nature's materials to resist nature's onslaughts. Here was Art, naked and unashamed. Built of red, no, almost pink brick, with hipped gables, battered chimney breasts, and a turquoise slated roof along which the creamy ridge tiles seemed to have been piped by a *pâtissier*, it stood as bold and as bright as a gay-rights demonstrator outside a rugby league ground.

He approached to stand near the gates, which were themselves worthy of close study. Into the flowing scrolled design were woven the word SCARLETTS and the initials J.H. He reached out a hand to caress the sinuous curves.

Next moment a black shape like a young bullock flung itself against the gates, setting the metal rattling, and Pascoe staggering back in terror, which was just as well, as a set of teeth like a ripsaw sliced the air where his fingers had been.

"Down, boy!" growled a harsh female voice, and a woman appeared from behind the thorn hedge.

"Bloody hell," gasped Pascoe. "That thing ought to be muzzled!"

"Muzzle's no use for keeping off trespassers," said the woman. She was gray-haired, of indeterminate age, with a hooked nose and unrelenting eyes.

"I wasn't trespassing," said Pascoe indignantly.

"You were touching," she said. "What's your business, mister?"

"I was just admiring the house."

"Admiring comes afore coveting," she grated. "I daresay you was *admiring* last night as well. Just bugger off or I'll mebbe let Fop out for a run."

Fop! If he couldn't get her under the Fighting Dog legislation, he could certainly have her under the Trades Description Act. But at the moment he could see little alternative to a dignified retreat.

He was moving away when a metallic aubergine cabriolet turned off the road and stopped in front of the gate. The driver stood up and peered over the windshield at him. He was at the turn of forty with a mobile, sensual face beneath an aureole of Titian hair. He wore a cordovan jacket which matched his car and around his neck was wound a shot-silk scarf just long enough when he drove at speed to give him something of Isadora Duncan's panache without risking sharing her fate.

In fact the first general impression Pascoe got was of a man who judged his effects carefully.

The second impression was that he knew him from somewhere.

"And what, pray, may your business be?"

The voice was light, educated, and redolent of the complacency of one who knows that if things of beauty are a joy forever, he's okay, mate.

"I'm a policeman," said Pascoe, taking the question literally. "DCI Pascoe, Mid-Yorks CID."

"Good Lord," said the man, leaping lightly (yet with a weighty awareness of his light leaping) out of the car. "You chaps *are* taking this seriously. I'm impressed."

Pascoe took the proffered hand but not the allusion. The shake was firm, warm, dry, and just the right length.

"As you doubtless know, I'm Justin Halavant. Bayle, the gates."

Bayle! The woman's name was as apt as the dog's wasn't! As for the man's, this confirmed his sense of recognition. This was Justin Halavant, who edited the *Post*'s arts page and frequently hosted TV's *North Light Show*.

"Leave your car," suggested Halavant as the gates rolled open. "Hop into mine."

Pascoe, feeling Fop's hungry eye upon him, hopped, and Halavant sent the car shooting up the drive at a speed which suggested he might be intending to enter the house without bothering to get out.

Happily, a deftly controlled skid brought them to a halt parallel to the façade. Pascoe, determined to show no reaction to these automotive histrionics, climbed out and said, "Some house! But not exactly the vernacular tradition, is it?"

"Hardly," said Halavant with a smile. "My great-grandfather had it built, partly to disoblige certain of his neighbors, partly to open up this part of darkest Yorkshire to the new light of taste. Basically it's a Morris design with a few exuberances added by the architect, who was a rather wayward pupil of Butterfield's."

"Butterfield? He did the parsonage at Hensall, didn't he?"

"You know about such things? Come inside and let me give you the quick tour."

He led the way through a series of rooms so full of goodies that Pascoe began to feel as he often did in great museums, that the total somehow came to less than the sum of the parts. The saving trick he had discovered was to focus on a single item and absorb all it had to offer, otherwise Art became Everest, bloody hard work, and essayed merely because it was there.

He paused in a long drawing room, blanked his mind, and trawled his gaze around the paintings which crowded the walls. It snagged on a small portrait whose narrow oval frame perfectly echoed the face of its subject. She was a young woman, not beautiful but full of character, with deep brown eyes, a rather long nose, and glowing skin tones. She met his gaze directly but demurely, yet he got a sense of fun, as though laughter were tugging at those modest lips, and wasn't there just a hint that her left eyelid was drooping in a cheeky wink? He looked closer and the impression was gone.

"This is nice," he said. "Does she have a name?"

"Probably, I don't recall. Some ancestor, eighteenth century, of course," said Halavant vaguely. "Are you specially interested in portraits, Inspector?"

"No. She just caught my eye. That serious, rather solemn posing expression, yet you get a sense she's amused, almost on the brink of a wink, so to speak."

"What?" Halavant came to stand alongside him. "Yes . . . yes . . . perhaps . . ."

He turned away abruptly and said, "You'll forgive me if I don't offer you any hospitality, but having just got back, I have things to do . . . so if we could get this business sorted . . ."

Clearly the tour was over. Time to be a policeman again.

"What business would that be, sir?" said Pascoe courteously.

"The false alarm last night, of course."

"Perhaps you could tell me about it, sir."

"What can I tell you that you don't know?" he said in some irritation, tugging at an old-fashioned bellpull by the fireplace. "I rang Mrs. Bayle last night to confirm what time I'd be back today, and she filled me in . . . ah, Mrs. Bayle. This incident last night. Tell us what happened."

The woman, who had appeared with silent speed and, to Pascoe's relief, without Fop, said, "Bell rang at nine o'clock. I looked through the peephole and when I saw it were him, I opened the door—"

"Him?" interjected Pascoe.

"Him. The constable. Mr. Bendish."

"Ah," said Pascoe noncommittally, but he felt Halavant's curious gaze on him and guessed he was beginning to suspect something odd here.

Mrs. Bayle took the *ah* as an instruction to proceed.

"I asked what he wanted and he said there'd been a report of a man hanging about, looking suspicious, and had I noticed anything. I said no I hadn't and good night. But he said he'd better take a look inside just to be sure as it were more than his job was worth, and likely mine, too, if Mr. Halavant came back and found something missing, and he'd been on the doorstep."

This sudden flood of words was, Pascoe guessed, a preemptive justification of having allowed someone across the threshold in her master's absence.

"What happened then?"

"He took a look around. Everything were in order, so he left."

"And you yourself felt no cause for concern?"

She hesitated and said, "Well, after he'd gone, I thought mebbe I heard summat outside, more like a nightbird than owt to worry about, but I sent Fop out for a run just in case."

Pascoe shuddered at the thought and Halavant came in with, "And naturally there was nothing. And if there had been, my extremely expensive, police-recommended state-of-the-art security system would have alerted the neighborhood. Mr. Pascoe, forgive me but I get a distinct impression that most of what you've just heard is new to you. Now, why should that be?"

It was time to come clean, or at least a little less muddied.

"You're right, sir," he said. "To tell the truth I only stopped to admire your lovely house, and things just went on from there."

Halavant smiled and said, "I wondered why such a senior officer was spending time on a false alarm. Are you in fact in the area on business . . . ?"

"I'm on my way to Enscombe to have a word with Constable Bendish, so no doubt I'll get the full story then," said Pascoe, seeing no reason to fuel rumor. "You know him, do you, sir? Settled in all right, has he? Old village communities can be difficult."

"I think you'll find Enscombe pretty unique," said Halavant ambiguously, as well as solecistically. "If your visit is in any sense an efficiency check, I would say from what I know of the young man, his devotion to duty has been puritanical, and his eye for the depth of a tire tread is phenomenal."

As he spoke he had been gently urging Pascoe to the front door. Pascoe's mind was full of interesting speculations, but as the door opened and he looked down the long length of unprotected driveway to the distant gates, they were all swept aside by the single basic question, was Fop loose?

He tried to find a way to phrase it that wouldn't make him sound like a quivering wimp, but the door clunked solidly shut before he could speak.

He set off at high speed, grew ashamed, forced himself to stop and admire a blossoming pear, then strolled to the safety of his car with studied ease.

Once seated and driving, normal service was renewed and all the speculations came flooding back. A puritanical devotion to duty, Halavant said. All the evidence certainly pointed that way. He came off duty at twelve noon yesterday. Twice since then—once when remonstrating with the Hell's Angel, and again last night at Scarletts—he had been seen in uniform doing his job. Curious.

He got Control on his radio, asking them to check with CID and with Filmer's section office whether there'd been any report last night of intruders in the grounds of Scarletts, then set off toward Enscombe once more.

His call sign crackled just as he reached the beginnings of the village and he pulled up in front of a steep-roofed single-story building inscribed VILLAGE HALL AND READING ROOM to acknowledge. Next moment Andrew Dalziel's voice filled the car like thunder.

"What's all this about an incident?"

Pascoe explained.

"Well, there's nowt on anyone's records," said Dalziel.

"That's a bit odd, don't you think, sir?"

"No, I don't. The lad's off duty, remember? Gets called out, finds it's a windup, he's not going to waste more of his own time putting in a report, is he? In fact, it probably decides him to make himself scarce for the rest of his time off. He'll likely turn up later, all apologetic about not letting Filmer know where he was. End of story."

"From what Halavant told me he sounds a lot more conscientious than that," said Pascoe. "What about the stains in the car?"

"Seems they're blood, all right, they're checking the group. But I can think of a dozen explanations, none of 'em sinister. And another thing. You can scratch the assault by the mad Hell's Angel. Wieldy'll tell you all about it. Try not to laugh."

"He's coming out here, too, is he?" said Pascoe, surprised.

"Someone had to ferry Filmer and Digweed back," said Dalziel defensively. "Any road, two heads should get this lot sorted out in no time, especially when one on 'em would frighten a confession out of a village pump. But take care, the pair of you. Don't stir things up. We'll look right Herberts if we blow this up into a dogs-and-divers job and it turns out young Bendish is banging the vicar's wife and has just shagged himself unconscious in the vestry!"

"Thank you for that, sir. Any other advice?" said Pascoe.

"Don't get on your high horse! Listen, you want local color, try Thomas Wapshare at the local. He'll talk your hind legs off if you let him. Knows how to keep a good pint, does Thomas, but be warned. His black pudding doesn't half make you fart!"

Interesting, thought Pascoe as he replaced the mike. Dalziel was obviously just a little bit more worried than he wanted to be.

Like a good cop he decided to take his superior's advice, though his motivation was mixed. Dalziel's intimate acquaintance with the hostelries of Yorkshire was famous and the Fat Man's recommendation of a beer was not to be missed. But where was the pub?

A cyclist had come down the High Street as Dalziel talked on the radio and was leaning his bike against the wall of a substantial granite built house directly opposite the village hall.

Pascoe wound down his window and called, "Excuse me, sir, can you tell me where the village pub is?"

The young man looked toward him. He had a pale, thin face, unshaven, though the resultant fuzz was more down than stubble, and amber eyes which gave an unsettling impression they were used for looking through rather than seeing with. Even more unsettlingly, his hands were occupied untying a shotgun from his crossbar and a gunny bag from his pillion. Something was dripping from the bag. It looked like blood.

Pascoe recalled Dalziel's warning about making himself look a right Herbert by stirring things up unnecessarily. On the other hand he would look a righter Herbert if he let this youngster pass unchallenged and it turned out he'd got Bendish's head in his gunny.

He got out of the car, glanced left and right to make sure he wasn't going to be knocked down by a speeding tractor or stampeding bullock, and when he looked back, the youngster had vanished. It was incredible. Perhaps the camouflage jacket the youth had been wearing was a new, advanced model! Then he saw the red droplets glistening up to the closed door.

Pascoe crossed the street. Above the door was a large wooden square which he'd registered vaguely as some form of weatherboarding. But closer, he realized here was a partial explanation of the strange nonresponse to his question. It was an inn sign, weathered almost to illegibility.

In fact, more than weathered. It looked as if at some time in its existence it had been assaulted with an ax and roasted over a bonfire. The once gilded lettering spelled out in the black of its own decay the

just readable words THE MORRIS MEN'S REST above the bubbled,
flaking portrait of a portly bearded gent, though identification was not
possible beyond his hairiness, as the best part of his face looked as if it
had been blown away with a blunderbuss.

Pascoe pushed the door. It swung open and he found himself in a
shadowy vestibule with four doors off. The spoor of blood led into the
second on the left.

He went through and found himself in a large farmhouse kitchen.
The young man had vanished, presumably through the open door
which led into a rear yard and garden. His gunny bag lay on a broad,
well-scrubbed table.

Seeing a chance to check without looking foolish, Pascoe moved
quickly forward, undid the lace around the bag's neck, and pulled it
open and peered inside.

A pair of big bright eyes peered back at him.

And a voice said, "Who the hell are you, then?"

Happily the voice didn't come from the bag. Unhappily, it came
from a broad-built man standing in the doorway and clutching a huge
bloodstained knife in his right hand.

Pascoe took two rapid steps back and another two sideways to put
the table between himself and the newcomer, who gestured with his
weapon and cried, "Watch it!"

Too late he recognized the words as a warning, not a threat. His shin
caught against a galvanized bucket half hidden under the table. Over it
went, spilling its contents all over the floor. He staggered, slipped, fell,
put his hands into something warm.

And when he held them up to look at them, they were as red and
sticky as the broad blade in the hand of the menacing figure looming
over him.

Three

They had a very rough passage, he
wd. not have ventured if he had
known how bad it wd. be.

The first half of Sergeant Wield's journey to Enscombe
passed in silence.

Wield would have liked to question Terry Filmer about
Harold Bendish, but as they were ferrying Edwin Digweed
back to Enscombe, he contented himself with letting Filmer
drive while he studied the printout he'd collected of the
constable's personal file.

Academically, he was very bright—bright enough, according to his headmaster, to have gone to university. Instead he'd opted to join the police in his native city of
Newcastle. The head, who couldn't keep out of his report his
feeling that this was a great waste of talent, put it down to
misguided adolescent idealism coupled with a belief that
universities were elitist, escapist, and effete.

Must have been talking to Fat Andy, thought Wield.

During training he had been outstanding on the theoreti-
cal and written areas of the course. But there'd been a bit of
a problem in the practical areas involving direct contact with
the public. Cutting through the jargon, Wield guessed that
what they'd got here was a case of that not uncommon
youthful arrogance which believes that if tried and tested
procedures don't seem to be working, it's the procedures that
are at fault, not the way they're being applied.

On attachment, however, the problems identified during
training had loomed larger, particularly his readiness to

argue the toss at all levels. Reading between the lines, Wield saw that things had come to a head and that while there was a marked reluctance to lose Constable Bendish (which said a great deal for the lad's potential), it was felt that if a new leaf were to be turned, it would be better to turn it elsewhere. So he'd been transferred to Mid-Yorkshire with the recommendation that before the village bobby system was finally phased out, this could be just the kind of job to help the youngster find his feet.

Things had come a long way even in the years since Wield had trained. They still had a long way to go (who knew it better than he?), but at least brassbound hearts and blinkered brains were no longer essential qualifications for rising to the top of the heap.

He was roused from his meditation by a sharp finger being driven into his shoulder blade.

"I've remembered something," said Digweed from the backseat. "Kee Scudamore, she runs the Eendale Gallery opposite my shop, she went up to Old Hall yesterday afternoon shortly after your departure, Sergeant. She took the shortcut along Green Alley, that's the old path which links the church to the Hall, quite overgrown since churchgoing went out of fashion among the gentry. We spoke when she got back and she told me in passing that somewhere along the alley she'd noticed a piece of statuary with a policeman's hat on it. Could this be significant?"

"A cap? And she left it there?" said Wield.

"Of course. Presumably someone had put it there as a joke. In villages you don't go around spoiling other people's fun. Not unless you're a policeman."

Wield glanced at Filmer, who said defensively, "I didn't see Miss Scudamore this morning, just her sister. She didn't say anything."

"The vicar saw it, too, evidently," said Digweed, as though his integrity was being called in doubt.

"Vicarage was the first place I went when I didn't find Bendish in Corpse Cottage," said Filmer. "But Mr. Lillingstone wasn't in."

"I thought the police house was called Church Cottage?" said Wield.

"It is, really. But Corpse Cottage is the name the locals use. The vicarage is the only house that overlooks it, so that's why I called there straight off. But like I say, the vicar was out."

Turning to Digweed, Wield said, "If the hat was put there as a bit of fun, sir, can you think of anyone who might enjoy that kind of joke?"

Digweed said, "Children, perhaps. Or the childlike mind. Tricks with policemen's helmets were, I recall, a favorite pastime of the Drones Club."

Wield, who had watched *Jeeves* on the telly, said, "Get a lot of Bertie Woosters in Enscombe, do you, sir?"

Digweed nodded a patronizing acknowledgment and said, "I suppose Guy Guillemard comes closest."

"Guy?" said Wield, his memory jogged. "The one your neighbor wouldn't serve yesterday? Who is he exactly?"

"Exactly, he is Squire Selwyn's great-nephew and, alas, heir, despite the superior claims of his granddaughter."

"So why doesn't she inherit?"

"Because," said Digweed, "Salic Law is one of the medieval practices still very popular in the upper reaches of Yorkshire society."

Wield turned back to the front and his file. If the old sod expected him to ask what Salic Law was, he was going to be disappointed.

They were only a couple of miles outside Enscombe now on the narrow, winding road Wield remembered from the day before, bounded by an ancient drystone wall on one side and a hedgerow not much younger on the other.

A post office van came up behind them, tailgated them for a while, then on the first not very long straight gave a warning peep on the horn and shot past.

"Bit chancy," said Wield.

"He's late for the lunchtime pickup," said Filmer. "Always late, is Ernie Paget. Except when he's early 'cos he doesn't want to be late somewhere else."

"At least he does move at speed when he has to," observed Digweed irritably. "Do we have to dawdle so? I have work to do, even if you don't!"

"More haste, less speed," observed Wield, which was not very original but proved almost immediately accurate. The red van had vanished around the next bend. Suddenly they heard a screech of brakes, a chorus of baa-ing, and a loud bang!

"Holy Mother!" exclaimed Filmer, hitting the brake hard.

They went around the bend in a fairly controlled skid, coming to a halt aslant the road with a jerk that threw Wield and Filmer against each other and flung Digweed forward with his arms wrapped around the front-seat head restraints.

The van hadn't been so fortunate. It was halfway through the hedge, straddling a narrow but deep drainage ditch, with steam jetting up from beneath the buckled bonnet.

Ahead, the road was packed with sheep, milling around in panic. A man was plowing through them, bellowing what sounded like abuse but turned out to be commands to a pair of Border collies.

"You both okay?" said Wield. Filmer grunted laconically but Digweed was no Spartan in either suffering or speech.

"*Okay?* Not content with depriving me of two hours of peaceful and profitable existence, you finally attempt to rob me of existence itself, and you ask if I am okay?"

He paused rhetorically, his face flushed with a rage which made him look a lot healthier than his usual scholarly pallor. He was, Wield decided, okay.

"Let's take a look at Ernie," said Filmer.

At this moment the door of the van opened and the driver staggered out. His face was covered in blood and he let out a terrible cry and slumped sideways as his feet touched the ground.

Fearing the worst, Wield got out and hurried forward.

"Don't move," he cried, recalling his emergency medical training.

The mask of blood turned toward him.

"Don't move? I've smashed me fucking van and broken me fucking nose and now I'm up to me hocks in freezing fucking water and you tell me don't move? Who the hell are you? Jeremy fucking Beadle? Gi's a hand out of here, it's sucking me down."

The farmer had arrived too. He was a man of medium height with a breadth of chest and shoulder which seemed to have bowed his legs. He had a shepherd's crook in his right hand, its handle carved from a ram's horn into a beautifully detailed hawk's head. He proffered this to the postman and hauled him onto the road.

"You've knackered that hedge, Ernie Paget," he said. "Who's going to fettle it, that's what I want to know."

"Sod your hedge. I were lucky it weren't your wall."

"Nay," said the farmer. "You'd likely have bounced off the wall. By gum, you're quick off the mark for once in your life, Terry Filmer. Last time I called police, they were an age coming. You going to arrest him for speeding?"

"You by yourself, George?" said Filmer. "You know the law when you've got stock on the highway. One man up front, one behind."

"Oh, aye? Happen I'm a bit shorthanded today. Like you lot, I hear!"

Wield noted the sarcasm, but was too busy checking Paget to try to follow it up. He couldn't find any damage apart from the nose and some bruised ribs, but it would take a proper hospital examination to check if there was anything broken.

"Let's get him into the car," he said to Filmer, "and you can call up some help."

"Hang about. I'll just sort these sheep, then you can come up to the house for a mug of tea," said the farmer.

He turned and began to bellow instructions again, rather unnecessarily, it seemed to Wield, as the dogs had been quite happily turning the flock through an open gate into the field beyond the wall. There was a cold wind blowing down the valley and Wield shivered. The farmer seemed unaffected, even though he was wearing only a short-sleeved tartan shirt and his close-cropped head was hatless. Wind and weather had cured his skin to the consistency of leather. His trousers, which were tied around his waist with baling twine and looked as if they could walk by themselves, were tucked into a pair of odd Wellies, the left black, the right green.

"I'm not going to hang around here any longer," declared Digweed, who had preserved an unnatural silence for the past couple of minutes. "I can be comfortable in my own house long before you get this lot sorted out."

"Do us a favor, Mr. Digweed," said the postman as Filmer helped him to the police car. "Tell Mr. Wylmot at the post office that I've been held up."

"Certainly," said Digweed. "I hope you'll be all right, Mr. Paget."

Wield felt, though he did not show, surprise at this faint glimmer of human feeling. He said, "Hold on, Mr. Digweed, and I'll walk into the village with you."

He followed Filmer to the car and said, "I'll leave you to sort this lot out. I'll be making for the Hall to meet Mr. Pascoe. Why don't we meet up at Church Cottage in about an hour?"

"Fine," said Filmer. "Try not to bleed on the seat, Ernie."

"This farmer, what's his name?"

"Creed. George Creed. He farms Crag End up there."

He pointed to a whitewashed farmhouse set like a solitary molar in the rocky jaw of land rising to the west. The track running up to it was steep and ungraveled. Wield hoped the postman's ribs, not to mention the car's springs, would survive the trip.

He said, "Owns it, does he?"

"Rents it from the Guillemard estate."

"They own most of the land around here, do they?"

"Did once. Lot of it had to go for death duties when the Squire inherited in the fifties. Since then the bottom's fell out of sheep, and there's only three working farms left on the estate and t'other two are in a bad way."

"But Creed makes a go of it?"

"Good farmer, George. Didn't just stick with sheep. Nice herd of cows too. And pigs. Best ham in the county comes from George's porkers."

"I noticed that he seemed to know all about Bendish going missing."

It wasn't intended as reproof, but Filmer seemed ready to take it as such.

"Most folk'll know by now," he said with some irritation. "It's not like the towns around here with no one bothering with their neighbors. And you've got to know how to talk to these folk. I don't know what your fat boss is playing at, sending a soft townie like that Pascoe out here. We'd have done better with a couple of dogs sniffing around the moor in case the lad's lying up there somewhere with a broken leg. Yon fancy-pants likely wouldn't know blood if he trod in it!"

"I'll pass your observations on, shall I, Terry?" said Wield. "And talking of blood and fancy-pants, Postman Pat's just dripped down your trousers."

And smiling to himself, he turned and hurried after the bookseller, who, forecastably, had been too impatient to wait.

Four

Which of all my important nothings
shall I tell you first?

At this moment Pascoe's pants were far from fancy, being of a bookmaker's check with enough spare room around the waist and buttocks to accommodate the bookic's runner.

The upside of things was that he was sitting in a bar lounge drinking the best beer he'd tasted in a long while.

The speed of his journey from horror to happiness was enough to give a philosopher pause. The menacing knifeman had dropped his weapon onto the table and helped him to his feet with expressions of concern and apology that had rapidly transformed him from Jack the Ripper to jolly Thomas Wapshare, landlord of the Morris Men's Rest. The bucket of blood, he explained, belonged to a pig and was the essential ingredient of the homemade black puddings for which he claimed a modest fame. And the eyes in the bag belonged to a large buck rabbit which, along with a couple of pigeons and a duck, were destined for t'other pillar of the pub's culinary reputation, Mrs. Wapshare's game pie.

Pascoe had started to explain who he was but, as at Scarletts, found himself treated as if expected. At this point Mrs. Wapshare appeared, looking just like her husband in drag, and expressing great concern at the state of Pascoe's trousers. Despite his modest protests she had them off him with a speed he hoped was honestly learned and took them away to be sponged while he climbed into a pair of Wapshare's colorful bags.

During this time the pale youth with the shotgun rematerialized in the kitchen and watched the debagging with that unnervingly unfocused stare. Pascoe felt he ought to ask him some questions but was inhibited by his own deshabille and also by some legal uncertainties. Game laws didn't play a large part in his detective life. Once he had known them but only as examination knowledge, which sparkles like the dew in the morning and has as brief a stay. He was pretty certain the pigeons and the rabbit were okay, but he couldn't swear to the duck. Wieldy would know. Wieldy knew everything despite never showing the slightest interest in promotion exams.

But at least he could check the gun license.

It was too late, he realized as he looked up from tucking his shirt into the trousers. The young man had vanished.

"Who was that?" he asked. "And where's he gone?"

"God knows, and He's not telling," said Wapshare. "Name of Toke. Jason Toke. Bit strange but he's harmless, and you'd have to walk a long mile to find a better shot. We buy a lot of stuff off him. He doesn't work—who does these days?—and the money helps him and his mam. But what are we hanging around here for, Chief Inspector? Come through into the bar and make yourself comfortable till your trousers are ready."

The bar was a delight, nicely proportioned and very user-friendly, with lots of old oak furniture well polished by much use, a huge fireplace with a log fire, walls completely free of horse-brass, and best of all, not a jukebox or fruit machine in sight. Wapshare drew a couple of pints before he got a potion which satisfied his critical gaze.

"There we are," he said, handing over a glass. "Clear as a nun's conscience."

Pascoe produced some money and when Wapshare looked ready to be offended, he placed the coins carefully on a ziggurat of copper and silver which towered up beside a notice saying SAVE OUR SCHOOL.

"Money trouble?" he said with the sympathy of a parent who spent so much time answering appeals that he sometimes suspected he'd been edged into private education without noticing it.

"Aye, but not just books and chalk. Worse than that. We need enough to pay a teacher, else they'll close the place down and bus our kids nine miles to Byreford."

"That's terrible," said Pascoe. "How's the appeal doing?"

"Okay, but not okay enough to provide an income. That takes real money. Only way we can get that is to sell something and we've nowt to sell except our Green. So, no school or no Green. It's what they call a double whammy, isn't it? But you've not come here to talk about schools, have you, sir? Not unless it's a school for scandal!"

"So what do you think I *have* come here to talk about?" asked Pascoe.

"At a guess I'd say . . . Constable Bendish!" He peered into Pascoe's face and let out his infectious laugh. "Nay, sir, don't look so glummered! There's no trick. Soon as it got around that Terry Filmer were getting his knickers in a twist about Dirty Harry going missing, I said to my good lady, five quid to a farthing some smart detective from the city'll stroll in here afore the day's out and start making discreet inquiries. So fire away, Mr. Pascoe."

Pascoe sipped his beer, decided that a man who kept ale as good as this was entitled to a bit of smart-assery, and said, "It's a fair cop. But no big deal. It's just that we need to get hold of Bendish, but it's his day off and no one seems to know where he's got to. Probably some simple explanation—"

"Like he's trapped under a fallen woman," said Wapshare with a grin. "Lucky devil!"

Wondering if this echo of Dalziel's theory sprang from local knowledge, Pascoe said, "Is that why you called him Dirty Harry just now?"

"No. That just slipped out. A kind of nickname some folk use," said Wapshare, hesitating before going on. "I might as well tell you, as you'll not be long finding out, your Constable Bendish didn't set out to make himself popular. For years we had old Chaz Barnwall, lovely man, and when he retired last back end, we gave him a party here that went on till milking time. Next night, dead on the stroke of eleven, the door opens and young Harold walks in. 'Welcome to Enscombe,' says I. 'You'll have a drink against the cold?' And he never cracks his face but says, 'No, I won't. For two reasons. One is my warrant, which doesn't allow me to drink on duty. The other is your license, which doesn't allow you to serve drink after eleven. Get supped up and shut up, landlord.' And he went outside and sat in his car in the car park, and the first lad who came out, he breathalyzed."

"New broom," said Pascoe. "Making his mark."

"He did that right enough. As well as the breathalyzing, he marked folk for road tax, tires, lights, MOT, leaving mud on the road, letting animals stray—you name it, if it's an offense, there's someone around here he's done for it! Can you wonder some folk took to calling him Dirty Harry!"

"So, a lot of people with grudges," said Pascoe. "You included?"

"Nay, takes more than that to cause a grudge around here. As for me, I were grateful to have an excuse to get to bed at a decent time. This pubbing takes up far too much fishing time as it is."

"I notice you don't exactly advertise," said Pascoe.

"Them as I want in here knows where it is," said Wapshare. "Plus a few discerning travelers like yourself, of course. But if it's the sign you mean, there's a story behind that."

A policeman in full possession of his trousers might have avoided the temptation and pressed on with official inquiries. But Pascoe felt himself in the grip of stronger forces than mere duty. He finished his beer and said, "A story, you say?"

"Aye. You'd like to hear it? Let me get you the other half. And what about summat to eat? Only take a tick to fry up some chips and a slice or two of my black pudding. Nay? You'll have a piece of cold pie, but? My good lady would never forgive me if I let you go without trying her game pie. That big enough for you? If not, there's plenty more. Now let me see. The sign. We've got to go back a few hundred years. . . ."

Pascoe began to feel this might have been a very serious mistake. But as he sank his teeth into the wedge of pie and found it matched in quality the superb ale, he comforted himself with the argument that this came under the heading of gathering local color.

"Thing is," began Wapshare, "there never used to be a pub here in Enscombe at all. There was no way we were going to get one without the approval of the Guillemards, and the Guillemards reckoned that the last thing working men needed was a pub to get bolshie in."

"The Guillemards? They're the family at Old Hall, right?" said Pascoe, recalling the brief briefing he'd received from Terry Filmer about the last sighting of Harry Bendish.

"That's right. Used to be a big bunch of them and right powerful."

"And now?"

"There's the old Squire; his granddaughter, Girlie; his great-nephew, Guy Guillemard, who's the heir; and little Franny Harding, the poor relation."

"I'm sorry?"

"Every posh family needs a poor relation to remind 'em how well they're doing. Only, in recent years they've not been doing so well. But way back, when I'm talking about, they were rotten rich, and they made sure Enscombe stayed dry till well into the last century."

"What happened then?"

"What happened? They were rude to Jake Halavant, that's what happened!"

"Halavant? Any relation to Justin Halavant at Scarletts?"

"You know Justin? Then mebbe you'll be surprised to learn that at the start of the last century the Halavants were nowt but a bunch of raggedy-arsed peasants who could hardly pronounce their own name, let alone spell it. The only one on 'em with enough brains to make a pudding was Jake. Good with his hands, too, carving, painting, owt of that. And a real artist with his tongue, by all accounts. So it didn't surprise anyone when he decided he'd had enough of living like a pig, and he upped and vanished. But everyone was knocked right back twenty years later when who should turn up in the village, looking, talking, and spending money like a gent, but young Jake!"

"How did people react?" wondered Pascoe.

"They were pleased, most on 'em. Enscombe folk like to see their own get on, so long as they don't forget who they are. Jake was a real Fancy Dan, but he was generous with all his old friends, and with what remained of his family, too, after the smallpox and the gallows had taken their share. Then one day he took it into his head to stroll up to Old Hall and send in his card. A bit provocative, maybe, but all they had to do was send word out they weren't at home."

"Oh, dear," said Pascoe. "I take it they didn't."

"No. They kept him waiting on the doorstep twenty minutes. Then the butler brought his card back with a message that if he cared to go around to the kitchen entry, the cook would be happy to extend the usual courtesy of the house to members of his family and dig out some scraps of food and old clothing for him. That was the biggest mistake they ever made."

"How so?" asked Pascoe, partly to hurry the story on but mainly because he wanted to know.

"Most folk reckon if they'd have been polite, after a while Jake would have headed back to London or wherever he'd come from. But instead what he did was this. He sniffed around and found that the Guillemards, who had a nasty habit of buying up local property at knockdown prices—which is to say, they knocked down anyone else interested in buying—were after this house and a parcel of land down the river alongside Scarletts Pool, which is the best fishing pool on the Een. At the last moment Jake nipped in and upped the ante and bought them both under the Guillemards' noses! If that weren't enough, next thing he gets himself engaged to a second cousin of the Finch-Hattons of Byreford who'd got tired of being a poor relation. The Finch-Hattons are proper Yorkshire gentry, and when they saw Jake had the brass, they were glad to get the lass off their accounts and onto his. Naturally they invited the Guillemards to the wedding, and they had to take a holiday out of the country to get out of going!"

"Game, set, and match to Jake," applauded Pascoe. "But how did this place become a pub?"

"I were coming to that. Jake set up house here, started a family, and in the fullness of time sent his eldest, Jeremy, to Oxford. Put a real polish on him, came back very arty crafty. When he got married, he wanted a place of his own and it was him as started building Scarletts on the bit of land his dad had bought by the river. Things had been quiet between the Halavants and Old Hall for a bit, but this set them going again. First off the Guillemards complained the builders were interfering with the fishing. Then when they realized what kind of house Jeremy was building, they played merry hell. Said it looked like a Chinese brothel and such outrages shouldn't be allowed in a God-fearing community like Eendale. Naturally that just egged Jeremy on to make it as bright and beautiful as possible."

"And how did the villagers feel?" asked Pascoe.

"Loved it," said Wapshare. "Not had so much fun since the Civil War. You see, we don't take sides here, Mr. Pascoe, we take seats and sit back to enjoy the show. But most folk thought things had gone too far when the Guillemards set fire to Jeremy's house when it were nearly done."

"Good Lord! But surely they couldn't get away with that?"

"Couldn't they just? Mind you, nothing were ever proved, but everyone knew," said Wapshare. "The Guillemards had to call in a lot of favors to get themselves clear, and that left them vulnerable to Jeremy's next move a year later when old Jake finally fell off the perch. This place were empty again. Most folk expected Jeremy to sell. Instead . . ."

"He turned it into a pub," completed Pascoe. "Brilliant! Do you think my trousers will be dry yet?"

"Nay, but your throat will be," said Wapshare, topping up his glass. "Naturally once word got to Old Hall what he was up to, hell broke loose again. The Guillemards opposed the license, but they were short on favors now, and getting short on money. Aye, I reckon even then the Guillemards' day was over, though they still couldn't tell twilight from noon. In the end they were left with nothing to fight about except the pub's name."

"Why? What did Jeremy want to call it?"

"He really tried it on! His first suggestion was the Guillotine and Basket! No one was very happy about that, and the Guillemards screamed loud enough to get his next two ideas vetoed too. These were the Cobden Arms and the Tolpuddle Martyrs. Politically provocative, said the Squire. And when Jeremy finally came up with the Morris Men's Rest, you'd have thought the Guillemards had won the battle of Waterloo!"

"Because they'd got something all feudal and pastoral instead of radical and provocative? I see their point," said Pascoe.

"Aye. And they saw Jeremy's when the sign went up," said Wapshare gleefully. "Not straightaway, I shouldn't think. Likely they were just puzzled when instead of a picture of daft buggers with bells on their knees dancing around a pole, what they got was a portly gent with a big beard. But finally it clicked."

He looked expectantly at Pascoe, who felt his detective credentials were at stake. He wrestled mentally, was ready to admit defeat, then it came, the click.

"Morris!" he said. "Not Morris dancers, but William Morris, the socialist. Good Lord, yes, that must have annoyed them. I presume the sign was a bit clearer then? It's a bit of a mess now."

"So would you be if you'd been shot at, attacked with an ax, tossed on a bonfire," retorted Wapshare. "The Guillemards put their people up to it, of course. But every time it happened, Jeremy just got his lads to put the sign up again, no repairs or anything, so everyone could see what silly asses the Guillemards were making of themselves."

It was a good story but even as local color he doubted if Dalziel would reckon it relevant to inquiries. Perhaps Mrs. Wapshare had been eavesdropping till her husband finished, for now the door opened and she appeared with Pascoe's trousers, cleaned and ironed and looking rather better than they had done when he put them on that morning.

He waited till she'd left before he started removing the borrowed bags.

"Mr. Halavant, Justin, does he own the pub now?"

"Aye. It's still his. Though for how much longer, I don't know."

Suddenly the merriment faded from Wapshare's voice.

"Why? Up for sale, is it? And would that affect your tenancy?"

"If Justin sells to who I think he's got in mind ... but it's still all hush-hush. We'll have to wait and see. We're good at that around here."

"I can imagine," said Pascoe, stepping out of the trousers, which he folded neatly and laid on the bar. "This feud between the Guillemards and the Halavants, does it still go on?"

"Not so's you'd notice. They don't exchange visits, but Justin and the old Squire are polite enough when they meet. Might be different when Master Guy inherits, though."

"Oh? Why's that?"

"He's a bit rumbustious, young Guy. Hadn't seen much of him for years, then he showed up a few weeks back. Seems he's started up some company that runs courses for executives and such; you know, where they run around the woods playing cowboys and Indians. Not the lot who camp out and sniff each other's bums, I don't think. Saw a program about them on the box. Yanks, of course. Tell you what, couple of pints of my best and a black pudding fry-up, and they'd not be so keen on bum sniffing!"

He roared his laugh and Pascoe smiled wanly.

"So he showed up," he prompted.

"Aye. Must have got wind of the development up at the Hall. This Health Park thing that Girlie, that's the Squire's granddaughter, is organizing. Well, Guy reckoned there was room for his lot to expand up here and use the Hall for his kids' games some weekends. Girlie didn't fancy the idea at all, and from what I hear, there was an almighty row."

"Wouldn't it be up to the Squire?" asked Pascoe.

"Oh, aye. So it were no contest. Guy's the heir, you see. Women don't come second with the Guillemards, they're not even entered for the race. He went off again soon after, but he came back yesterday with some mates to start setting things up. Funny-looking bunch. They got in here last night and made a bit of a row. Nothing I couldn't handle but I doubt if Justin would thole it. Doesn't care for noise when he's drinking, Justin, except if he's making it."

"Yes, I got the impression he liked the sound of his own voice," said Pascoe, testing how far employee loyalty went in the Morris.

It clearly didn't get in the way of a good gossip.

"Only one thing he likes better," said Wapshare.

"Art, you mean?" said Pascoe with deliberate naïveté.

"Aye, that comes into it," chuckled Wapshare. "Here, I'll tell you a story as'll make you laugh. It certainly brought the tears into Justin's eyes! There's this lass in the village, paints pictures, a real dish she is, outstanding, and, Justin, hello there, usual, is it?"

The transition was so smooth, Pascoe thought his hearing must be at fault.

Then a voice said, "I know most policemen are Freemasons, but surely there are subtler ways of indicating the fact, Chief Inspector."

And he realized simultaneously that Justin Halavant had come into the bar, and he had become so interested in Wapshare's reminiscences that he'd forgotten to put his trousers on.

Five

*The walk was very beautiful, as my
companion agreed whenever I made
the observation.*

Digweed had set off at such a cracking pace that he was
already passing the gate to Scarletts when Wield caught up
with him.

"Nice house," he said, determined to show he wasn't out
of breath.

"You think so?" said Digweed. "It is the home of our
local celebrity, Justin Halavant. He edits the *Post*'s art page.
You may have noticed his name as you flicked from the
sports to the comic section."

There was no answering that, at least not if he wanted to
remain a policeman.

They walked on in silence. Digweed was showing no sign
of fatigue, so presumably this cracking pace derived from
genuine fitness rather than just a desire to shake off an
unwelcome companion. Not that there'd been much chance
of that. Wield prided himself on his own fitness and he
found it invigorating to be stretching his legs in such sur-
roundings. The wind was gusting harder, sending sun and
shadow racing across the fields as the clouds scattered and
joined. In a fillet of blue so formed, Wield glimpsed a pair of
large birds, circling and soaring on broad rounded wings.

"Look," he said, pointing. "What are they?"

Digweed glanced up and said, "Buzzards."

"Buzzards?" echoed Wield, alert.

The bookseller gave one of his superior smiles and said,

"Let me guess. You have read a considerable number of pulp Westerns, and you were recalling that usually when Clint or Curly or Sundance sees buzzards circling, it means there's a body underneath. Right?"

"No," said Wield, unmoved. "I were just thinking how grand they looked. But out of interest, sir, if a man were lying up there dead or injured, would that attract buzzards?"

"Could do. They are carrion feeders. But that pair are rather too high to be actively engaged on anything but enjoying the weather."

"You reckon they do enjoy themselves, then?"

"It would be arrogant to believe they merely give delight, Sergeant. Though I suspect that like some human specimens, for instance bankers and estate agents and, dare I say it, certain kinds of policemen, they are unlikely to take delight in any other creature except insofar as it can be viewed as prey."

He smiled. Even though there was a lot of sneer in it, the smile came as close to a pleasant expression as Wield had seen on his face, and the sergeant, who had taken far worse crap than this, smiled back.

It was a mistake, probably coming across to the unaccustomed eye as a threatening grimace. Digweed's own smile vanished and he said irritably, "In any case you'd be ill advised to use buzzards as markers in your search for Bendish. Look."

At the top of one of their soaring circles the birds tipped their wings against the wind and slid down a shaft of sunlight in a stoop which probably covered a couple of ground miles in an instant.

The road was beginning to climb now as they approached the outskirts of the village. They passed a broad area of open meadow which bore a sign that by royal charter of Edward the Second this land was designated a Green to be held in common by the village of Enscombe. Adjacent to it was the village school, a sturdy granite building set a little above the road. A wooden post by the gate bore a placard which read SAVE OUR SCHOOL *Appeal Fund*, with a picture of a thermometer showing that £650 had so far been collected.

"What are they saving it from?" asked Wield.

"The Powers of Darkness," said Digweed. "Otherwise known as Her Majesty's Government. It has probably escaped your notice, concerned as you are with locking our young people up rather than educating them, but schools are now regarded as small businesses. They have a budget. Stray outside it, and the receivers move in."

"I'd heard parents were having to pay for books and trips and things," said Wield.

"Small beer," said Digweed. "Our situation is so dire that we may lose a teacher. In which case the Powers of Darkness' local representatives will do what they have been wanting to do these many years and close us down and bus all the children to Byreford. If you'll excuse me, I must have a word with Mrs. Pottinger."

A sturdy gray-haired woman had come out of the building and was organizing a group of children into a double line. Wield followed Digweed across the playground and studied an inscription carved in the granite lintel as the bookseller addressed the woman.

It read:

ENSCOMBE PRIMARY SCHOOL
Preserved and renewed by the efforts of the
Reverend Stanley Harding
and many of his parishioners September 1932
THANKS BE TO GOD.

Digweed and the woman were talking about a meeting to be held that evening in connection with the School Appeal. Digweed, he gathered, was on the Parish Council.

"And there's no other way?" said Mrs. Pottinger.

"We've always known the Green is our only asset. But of course nothing can be done without the accord of the whole village."

"And would it be enough?"

"With planning permission, perhaps. We've taken unofficial soundings," said Digweed.

"God help us, that it should have ever come to this," said Mrs. Pottinger, unhappily staring out across the Green.

The children were growing restless. A couple of little girls were giggling furiously at Wield. He recognized one of them as the child who'd run into his bike the previous day and winked at her, redoubling her giggles.

"Now, don't get silly," ordered the teacher, herself regarding Wield curiously.

"This is Sergeant Wield of the detective police," said Digweed ungraciously. "Mrs. Pottinger, our headmistress."

"Nothing wrong, I hope?" she asked.

"Just routine," said Wield. "The little blond girl, who is she?"

"Madge Hogbin. She lives with her grandparents up at Old Hall Lodge. Do you know her?"

"We bumped into each other once," said Wield vaguely. It would be interesting to have a chat with the child, but not here.

"Well, we must be off," announced Mrs. Pottinger. "We're going down to the river to see if we can spot the kingfisher. Have you seen it, Mr. Digweed? There have been several reports."

"Not yet. I daresay it will turn out to have been imported by Girlie Guillemard to guarantee the success of all these new ventures at the Hall."

"I wish there was something we could import to help us," said the woman. "All right, children. Move off now. And walk, don't run! Good-bye, Sergeant, Mr. Digweed. See you tonight."

"This Reverend Harding," said Wield as the crocodile moved off. "What did he do?"

"The school was in such a state of disrepair sixty years ago that the ancestors of our current Powers of Darkness were threatening even then to close it down and move all the kids to Byreford. Harding rebuilt the place almost singlehandedly and sent them scurrying back to their caves from which they have emerged, blinking and scratching their crotches, after all these years. But you don't want to stand here chattering about the mere future of a community when you've got the fate of one whole policeman to worry about, do you?"

He strode off, Wield meekly following, till very shortly they reached the village proper, marked on one side of the road by a village hall and the other by the Morris Men's Rest.

"Good pub?" said Wield, seeing no opening for a put-down here.

"Depends," said Digweed. "If your tastes run to heavy metal, flashing lights, and draft lager, then it's lousy."

Wrong again, thought Wield.

They continued up the High Street. Seen on foot the village was much more extensive than from even a slow-moving motorcycle, with frequent alleys running off between the front cottages into yards where a second range of buildings lurked. At the corner of one of these alleys stood the village post office and store, with an ornate sign advertising the proprietor as Dudley Wylmot, Esquire.

Digweed turned into the shop, with Wield following. Behind the counter a woman was sorting out some items of mail.

"Shouldn't bother with that, Daphne," said Digweed. "Our grand prix of a postman has run his van off the road."

"Oh, dear," said the woman in a voice that was upper class without being *refined.* "Is he all right?"

"He'll live to speed another day," said Digweed with a smile.

He actually *likes* her! thought Wield. She was certainly a good-looking woman, art having perfected what nature had well begun, her hair elegantly coiffed and subtly shaded, her face made up with that expertise in which liberality never spills over into excess. Nearer forty than thirty, judged Wield, whose own absence of beauty made him a connoisseur of it in others. And she'll probably look the same when she's nearer sixty than fifty. That at least we have in common!

"Something up, is there, dear? Hello, Edwin."

A man had risen from beneath the shop counter, clutching a tin of processed peas in either hand. He was not dressed for stacking shelves, unless a brass-buttoned blazer and spotted cravat were the recommended garb. He had a prominent nose over a pencil moustache and from the few words he had spoken Wield guessed that when he said *off* it would come out like *awf.*

"Oh, hello, Wylmot," said Digweed unenthusiastically. "I was just saying that 'Postman Pat' has had a smash."

Doesn't like *him,* but, thought Wield.

"Really?" said Wylmot. "He's all right, I hope?"

"Oh, yes. I think so. But they'll need to send someone else for the mail."

"Not today, they won't. Half day, or had you forgotten?" said Wylmot cheerfully. "We were just waiting for Paget before closing."

"But the mail ..." protested Digweed.

"It's all right. Nothing that can't wait till the morning."

"You think not?" said Digweed. "Does that mean you read all the mail posted here? If so, you must be a quick reader, as I myself brought in several packets this morning containing expensive and in most cases closely printed books. I might add that I paid first-class postage in expectation of a first-class service."

"You're always saying how these book-collecting chappies spend years chasing up a single volume," said Wylmot. "Another day won't make much difference. I say, something that could be important—Kee Scudamore was in earlier and she was saying that Girlie's starting up a shop at the Hall, postcards, stamps, souvenirs, that sort of thing. Have you heard about this?"

"Something," said Digweed.

"Well, I think it's a bit off." (Wield smiled invisibly. A definite *awf*.) "Don't want to tread on any toes, but give and take's the essence of village life, and it seems to me that the Guillemards are doing a bit too much taking."

"Then you'd better get yourself up there and make your point clear," said Digweed. "Daphne, my dear, nice to see you. Good-bye."

He looked at Wield as if expecting the door to be held open for him.

Wield said, "Excuse me, Mr. Wylmot, I'm a colleague of Constable Bendish. You've not seen him around, have you?"

"Can't recall last time I saw him. Never around when we were getting burgled, that's for sure!"

Mrs. Wylmot said, "He called in to settle his paper bill yesterday lunchtime."

"Didn't say anything about his plans for his day off, did he?"

"No. He bought a box of chocolate gingers, I recall, and seemed in a very good mood."

"He's probably just booked old Jocky Hogbin for jaywalking with his walker," said Digweed.

"Wouldn't surprise me," said Wylmot. "Little Madge used to pick up her granddad's black twist till Bendish threatened me with a summons for selling tobacco to a juvenile. What did he imagine she was going to do with it?"

"Chew it, probably," snorted Digweed.

On this rare note of unity they parted.

Outside, Wield said, "Mr. Wylmot is like yourself, I take it, sir?"

"Then you can just take it back," said Digweed indignantly.

"I only meant he's an off-comer, settled here by way of business."

Digweed said acidly, "Sergeant, my native woodnotes wild may have lost some of their sylvan resonance, but without wanting to make a chauvinist issue out of it, let me assure you I am born of good Yorkshire stock and that my family tree has its roots deep in this parish. I deeply resent being categorized with Mr. Dudley Wylmot, who is one of those pathetic souls who, having dreamt all his urban life of the joys of rustic retirement, has been foolish enough to pour his severance pay into realizing that dream."

"His wife seems a nice lady, but," prompted Wield.

"But, indeed. How such a creature came to marry Wylmot is a question at least as puzzling as what song the Sirens sang or what name Achilles assumed when he hid himself among women."

"Wouldn't know anything about that," said Wield. "Is that where I'll find the lady who saw the hat? The Eendale Gallery?"

They had reached the Tell-Tale Bookshop.

"Yes," said Digweed. "It is, by the way, Kee you want, the elder sister, the blonde."

"There's another, is there?"

"Yes. Caddy. She is, how shall I put it, artistic. In your pursuit of hard factual clarity you would be well advised to avoid converse with Caddy."

His tone was almost devoid of irony. I wonder why, thought Wield.

He let his gaze drift from Digweed's face to the sign above the Wayside Café.

"Creed," he said suddenly.

"Is that a request? A command? Or the beginnings of a conversation?" asked Digweed.

"It says up there the lady who runs the café is Dora Creed. Any relation of that farmer back there?"

"Brother and sister."

"Ah."

"Ah what?"

"I'd been wondering how a man up to his eyes in lambs could have heard so quick about Constable Bendish."

"And you conclude this is explained by his having a sister working in the center of the village? How beautifully logical, Sergeant. And how elegantly illustrative of the deficiencies of the detective process."

"Oh? Why's that?"

"Because Dora Speed stopped speaking to George yesterday lunchtime."

"I see," said Wield, who didn't. "And why was that?"

"Because of George's sin, Sergeant," said Digweed gravely. "Dora is a most religious lady. I myself regard religion as mostly pie in the sky, but if the pie is Dora Creed's apple, I may be a convert yet."

"And just what was this sin?" persisted Wield.

Digweed laughed his superior laugh and said, "That's where you could really impress with your detective skills. You see, no one has yet been able to find out. Sniff it out, Sergeant, sniff it out!"

I'd rather sniff out one of Dora's pies, thought Wield, his nose twitching at the delicious smells wafting from the café.

But duty called.

"I'll do my best, sir," he said to Digweed. "Thank you for your help."

And hoping, though doubting, that his courtesy might give the bookseller a brief frisson of shame, he headed for the Eendale Gallery.

Six

*Our Improvements have advanced
very well.*

In England, before the Great War destroyed the eternal
verities, for a noble family to stop "improving" their country seat was pretty clear evidence of financial difficulties.

In the years since, however, it has been the arrival of the
contractors which has signaled trouble, for no longer are
"improvements" made in the name of beauty, taste, or even
convenience, they are offerings on the altar of commerce.

Such thoughts ran through Peter Pascoe's mind as he
negotiated the driveway up to Old Hall and came to a halt
on a building site.

It was not a particularly large building site but typical of
the genus in that order was minimal and activity nonexistent. The work seemed centered on a building separate from
the main house and he guessed this was the stable block
which was going to house the Holistic Health practitioners.

Like many men who see the clouds of middle age on the
horizon, Pascoe's scientific skepticism about alternative
medicine cloaked a superstitious hope that some astounding
revelation would blow the clouds back before it was too late.
So it was with the reverence of a man entering a church that
he pushed open the stable door.

The smell that met him was just about right for a man in
search of a quasireligious experience. Thuriferously spicy,
malty, and leafy, it seemed to emanate from a column of
smoke. A burning bush perhaps. If so, it should speak.

It spoke. A warbling birdlike note, once repeated. Then a female voice. God after all was a woman.

"Yes, this is Girlie Guillemard. No, I do not see the point of checking again, but I shall do so. Wait."

Out of the smoke emerged a woman. Her tangle of ocherous hair was restrained by a fillet of baling twine. She wore a molting brocaded waistcoat over a once elegant silk blouse tucked into a pair of overlarge jeans, whose rolled-down waist underpinned her heavy breasts and whose rolled-up legs overhung a pair of Wellingtons, one green and one black. Her face was round, her eyes were gray, her nose was snub, her mouth too large, allowing plenty of room for both the meerschaum which was the source of the smoke and the mobile telephone into which she was speaking. She was incredibly attractive.

At sight of Pascoe she halted and said, "You from Wallop?" Or perhaps it was "You for wallop?" meaning some startling new therapy. But Pascoe knew he was fantasizing, having glimpsed the sign proclaiming that the mess outside was the responsibility of Philip Wallop (Contractor), Ltd.

He said, "No."

"Is there anyone out there?" she asked.

Assuming the question was neither theological nor thespian, he shook his head.

"There is no one here," she bellowed into the phone. "And as it is now past the hour when Mr. Wallop's employees start packing up when they *are* here, I doubt if anyone's coming today, wouldn't you agree? So just tell Mr. Wallop this when he finally emerges from his box of Transylvanian earth. Tomorrow lunchtime the whole village will be turning up here for my grandfather's annual Reckoning Feast, and if the area in front of the house isn't clean as a new penny by then, a new penny is a bloody sight more than Mr. sodding Wallop will get out of me. Got that, dearie? Good-bye!"

She switched the phone off and said, "Right. Now, who the hell are you? And what do you want?"

"I'm Detective Chief Inspector Peter Pascoe," he said winningly. "And I'd like to talk to you."

"Why? You found some little regulation I'm breaking?"

"Not my line, believe me," he said. "No, it's nothing to do with the Health Park."

"In that case what you want is the Squire," she said, setting off at a rapid pace through the door and across the building site toward the main entrance of the house.

Breathlessly Pascoe pursued her up some steps and through an imposing door into a sort of baronial hall. Compared to the acreage across which Errol Flynn swashbuckled with Basil Rathbone, this was small beer. Nevertheless, armed with one of the weapons festooning the wall and encouraged by the Korngold soundtrack his fertile imagination was conjuring up, Pascoe felt he could have buckled a fair swash in defense of Girlie Guillemard's honor.

Then the music swelled again and he realized he was confusing cause and effect. No ditty of no tone this, but a tape of virtuoso cello being played in a minstrel's gallery at the far end of the hall.

The volume faded again to be overlaid by a human voice chanting words roughly in time with the music.

> Then up spake Solomon Guillemard,
> A gradely man was he,
> "These nuns ye seek ha' ta'en their wealth
> And fled across the sea.
> I serve the king, the king serves God,
> The Church served God and king" —

"Grandfather!" bellowed Girlie.

The voice and music died together and slowly a figure arose in the gallery. It was an old man cloaked in a velvet curtain and made taller by a moth-eaten cossack hat.

"Who calls so loud? Can you not see I am in the throes of composition?"

"Tough tittie," said his granddaughter. "An inspector calls. You could be in trouble or a play. I'll put him in the study."

She was off again, a hard woman to keep up with but well worth the effort, Pascoe assured himself, puffing.

The study was an octagonal room, presumably fitting into one of the castellated towers (a nineteenth-century improvement?) flanking the Hall. It had the kind of wainscoting an extended family of mice could happily colonize and, from the holes at floor level, probably had. There were rows of dusty bookshelves but very few books, a rocking chair minus one rocker, a chesterfield which looked as inviting as a basking alligator, and where one might have expected to see a handsome old desk stood a rather battered kitchen table.

Pascoe touched its rough surface. It must have come across as a comment, for Girlie said, "Sorry it's so Spartan, but we had to realize a few assets. Banks are not so free with their money as once they were, not unless you're a Third World dictator or a crook in the City. The Squire should be along shortly. If not, just bellow. He sometimes gets sidetracked."

"Me too," said Pascoe as she made for the door. "Look, couldn't I just ask *you* a couple of questions, please? I'm looking for a policeman."

"Thought you were a policeman," she said.

"Constable Bendish. Your local bobby. That's who I want."

"Oh, him. Cheeky sod. Once asked me for a sample of my mix for analysis."

Pascoe, who had wondered himself about the possible presence of some illicit substance in the pipe, flushed gently and said, "It is certainly rather exotic."

"Herbal. I'm trying to wean myself off nicotine. Trouble is, I'm even more addicted to this stuff now. So you've lost Childe Harold?"

"I thought he was known as Dirty Harry."

"That's down in the Morris. Up here, as you've probably gathered, we're more into balladry."

Was he being sidetracked again?

Pascoe said, "Yes. What exactly is that all about?"

"Senility. It's our vices keep us going. You get too decrepit for the old ones, you've got to fill the gap with something new. Usually it's slanderous gossip or avarice. With the Squire it's a bad attack of history. The Guillemards are mentioned in one of the old northern ballads. Now the Squire's got it into his head to compose a whole ballad history of the family. Worse, he likes to give public performances. The WI got two hundred stanzas before Mrs. Hogbin had one of her turns. Fifty people rushed out to find a doctor. Two returned."

"That must have nipped his public career in the bud."

"No way. Around here you don't reject the Squire so lightly. He's got firm bookings for the Local History Society and the Workers' Educational Society creative writing group. He'd have been on *North Light* by now if that turd Halavant didn't run it. Here he comes. Ask him to give you a sample if you have an hour to spare! Bye!"

She was gone. Through the door came the Squire, now curtainless and hatless, these props (if props they were) resting in the arms of a young woman who hovered obscurely in the doorway, not quite in or out.

Even without the ermine extension the Squire was a good six foot
six, and he bore himself like a guardsman. Age had creased his face
like a cotton jacket after a long journey, but though his gait was
labored, his eyes showed no sign yet of being ready for the terminus.
"You are the police inspector?" he said magisterially. "How is it
that such tyros bear such titles?"

He seemed to be addressing his question to someone situated where
second slip would have been on a cricket field.

"Detective Chief Inspector, actually," said Pascoe.

The gaze adjusted to take him in.

"Just so. You have come about the unspeakable Bendish?"

"That's right," said Pascoe, marveling again at Enscombian pre-
science.

"Not before time. It is several weeks since I wrote to Tommy
Winter."

"Tommy . . . you mean Mr. Winter who used to be chief constable?"

"Used to be?" The eyes bored into him like a jeweler's drill.

"Yes, sir. He retired some while back. We have a new chief now.
Mr. Trimble. But he should have got your letter—"

"Why so? I marked it personal. You did not tell me of this Trimble."

This was directed at the slip fielder again. Pascoe decided it was
best not to let himself be tempted to flash his bat at any deliveries
swinging past him in that direction.

He said, "In that case, sir, it would probably be forwarded to Mr.
Winter in Barbados, where he's retired to. Could I ask you, sir, what it
was you wanted to consult Mr. Winter about?"

The eyes fixed him doubtfully, wandered to second slip questioningly.

The woman who was so unobtrusive that Pascoe had forgotten her
said, "Shall I order some tea, Uncle?"

She offered the suggestion meekly, almost inaudibly, but it recalled
the Squire to his hostly duties.

"Of course, my dear. Chief Inspector, do sit down."

Pascoe declined heavily onto the chesterfield and wished he hadn't.
The leather upholstery seemed to have been molded by generations of
men with more than the usual number of buttocks into something like
a relief map of Cumberland.

The woman had slipped out, leaving Pascoe with no impression other than that she was small and slight. This, he guessed, was Franny Harding, the poor relation, a guess confirmed when the Squire, balancing his length precariously on the deficient rocker, said, "Don't know what we'd do without Fran. Always there when you need her. And she eats next to nothing, you know."

Ignoring this tantalizing glimpse into the domestic economy of the upper classes, Pascoe, deciding that in this case ambiguity was the worse part of discretion, said bluntly, "Constable Bendish may have gone missing, sir."

"And you've come to spread the good news? That's what I call service."

Was he for real? wondered Pascoe.

He said, "So could you please tell me why you wrote to Mr. Winter? What had Bendish done? Booked you for speeding, something like that?"

"Speeding? What's the fellow talking about?" (This to the slip.) "I haven't sped for twenty years or more. Anyway, that's what you people get paid for, isn't it? Booking chaps for speeding, that sort of thing. Sneaky kind of work, I give you that. But it's in your job description, and I wouldn't whinge about a fellow doing what he gets paid for. But *striking*, that's something else. Conduct unbecoming, get my drift?"

"Striking?" said Pascoe, a whole new area of explanation for Bendish's absence opening up. "You mean Bendish went on strike? He wasn't doing his job?"

"Of course he was doing his job. Is the fellow brain dead or what?" (To the slip.) "Look here, I'm not complaining about the fellow's work. Zealous he was, by all accounts. But this other business. Striking. Not the thing, you know. But a delicate matter, with ladies in the house. So I thought, a word in Winter's ear. Barbados, did you say? Thought only crooks made enough to retire to Barbados. Have you checked your pension fund?"

"This *striking*, sir," said Pascoe, determined not to be diverted again. "Are you sure you've got it right . . . ?"

"That's what they call it on *Test Match Special*. Seem to think it's a bit of fun, but I don't know. Had none of it when I was a yonker. Not so bad when it's a girl, I suppose, but more often than not it's a fellow. And what happens if they harm the wicket, eh?"

"*Streaking*," said Pascoe. "You mean streaking."

"That's the chap."

"And you say that Constable Bendish is a streaker?"

"Certainly. Saw him myself. There I was in the conservatory potting my pelargoniums, and I looked up, and there *he* was, running along the wall around the walled garden, naked as the day he was born."

"Good Lord," said Pascoe. "Are you sure?"

"Of course I'm sure. Couldn't be surer. Hung like a bull he was. Prize bull at that."

"This walled garden, could I take a look?"

"Sorry, it's a bit inconvenient at the moment. Lost the key after old Hogbin had his stroke. Not much to see so early in the year anyway. You interested in gardening? Young men should have an interest. Old men too. Mine's family history. Did you know I was working on a ballad chronicle of the Guillemards? Perhaps he'd care for a few stanzas?"

The question was addressed to slip, but this time Pascoe, scenting danger, flashed his bat in an attempt at interception.

"I'm sorry, sir, but I don't have much time. . . ."

"In a hurry? Quite understand. I'm very busy myself. Fran, you there?"

The young woman was, standing in the doorway with a tea tray in her hands.

"The inspector hasn't got time for tea after all. Leave the tray here, my dear, and show him out. Good day to you, Inspector. Give my regards to Tommy Winter."

And Pascoe found himself being steered out of the room with the uncomfortable feeling that by concentrating so hard on the outswinger, he had allowed himself to be comprehensively yorked.

Seven

*Mary and I . . . went to the
Liverpool Museum & the British
Gallery, & I had some amusement
at each, tho' my preference for Men
& Women always inclines me to
attend more to the company than
the sight.*

Caddy Scudamore was all eye. What she looked at she saw
totally, and much of what reached her through the other
senses was translated visually also. For her the baking
smells of Dora Creed's oven filled the street between with
golden threads, and birdsong was a drift of blossom on the
bright spring air.

Naturally because God is fair, and fairy godmothers always reserve some gifts from the cradle, there were compen-
sating deficiencies.

In conversation she only heard what she wanted to hear;
in kindness she only gave what she knew she could spare;
and in morality she was pleasantly surprised at the regularity
with which the justifiable and the convenient coincided.

"All that is needed to raise her to the top rank of artists,"
opined Justin Halavant in his *Evening Post* preview of her
last one-woman show, "is a deep distress to humanize her
soul."

It was presumably in a spirit of pure artistic altruism that
after the show's opening, he had ambushed her on the studio
stairs and wrestled her to the ground with breathless assur-
ances of eternal love and a rave review.

Caddy, however, was not yet ready for quite so deep a
distress, so she had responded by kneeing him in the balls.

Whether this distress humanized *his* soul is difficult to
say, but it certainly hospitalized his body, and no review of

any kind appeared in the *Post*, just a note to say that the arts-page editor was convalescing after, appropriately enough, "a bad fall."

Up to this point there had been a close and generally mutually beneficient connection between Scarletts and the Eendale Gallery. The Scudamores were regular ornaments of the artistic soirées Halavant held for his metropolitan friends, and he always brought his house-guests to the gallery, urging them to buy cheap what the soaring wheel of the art market would soon render dear. His patronizing possessiveness sometimes got up Kee's nose, but money in the till is a potent decongestant, and had he been able to accept his testicular rebuff in the spirit in which it was given, that is, necessary but no big deal, then as things had been they might have remained.

Unhappily Halavant's hurt went straight through his prostate to his pride. It was inconceivable to him that the Scudamores would not dine out on the story, so he set about getting his retaliation in first.

One evening Kee walked into the Morris bar just as Thomas Wapshare said, "I never read any review in the *Post* of young Caddy's latest show. Did I miss it?"

Halavant, who was sitting with his back to the door, shook his head sadly and, raising his voice so the whole room could hear, replied, "No, Thomas. There was no review. As you know, I've long been a patron of Caddy's work. More, I may say I've been a guide and counselor to the girl. But in this latest show I felt she had gone down a blind alley. As a friend I offered this criticism constructively and privately. And I promised her there would be no adverse review. Alas, her response was distressingly immature, causing a rift which I hope time will mend. The child has indisputable talent. Let's hope she grows up before she fritters it all away on such meretricious daubs."

He paused, modestly awaiting the applause due to such a display of selfless forbearance, but his audience's gaze was focused over his shoulder. He turned his head slowly and Kee advanced, smiling.

"Justin, I'm so glad I've caught you. I want to apologize for my sister's behavior. After all you've done for her, I really don't know how she had the gall to resent your attempts to grope her. But as you say, she's very young. Probably it was just a knee-jerk reaction. Talking of knee jerks, how are your privates? Has the bruising gone? I believe they were dreadfully swollen, though in your case, that's not a totally unusual condition, is it?"

Thus the rift betwixt salon and gallery became a schism, though the usual good sense of interested Enscombians prevented it from hardening into trench warfare. Why take sides when with a bit of nimble footwork, you can move quite happily between the lines?

Sergeant Wield as yet knew none of this as he entered the Eendale Gallery and saw the now familiar expression of half recognition touch the face of the slim, elegant blond woman working with a calculator at an open ledger.

"Miss Scudamore?" he said. "Miss Kee Scudamore?"

"That's right. Can I help you?"

He showed her his ID and said, "I were looking for Constable Bendish. You haven't seen him around, have you?"

"No. Sorry. He used to come in regularly on Sundays to check I wasn't selling anything which would contravene the terms of the Sunday Trading Act, but thankfully he gave that up for Lent."

Wield smiled and said, "What about his hat?"

"I'm sorry?"

"I understand you observed a policeman's hat on a statue."

"What?" Her eyes turned from his face to the window as she looked across at the bookshop. "Ah, you've been talking to Edwin Digweed."

"Listening," said Wield, and was rewarded with an understanding smile. "He said you'd mentioned it to him. Didn't seem like a secret, so he passed it on to me for what it's worth."

"Quite right too," she said. "I'd probably have mentioned it myself when Sergeant Filmer got around to me."

Wield, not too impressed by this sudden display of civic dutifulness, said, "So you'd heard the sergeant was asking questions?"

"It's a small place," she said.

"Depends if you count the moors," said Wield. "Now about this hat—"

"*Oh, my God!* That's incredible! Don't let him go!"

The outburst came from a young woman in a paint-stained smock who'd appeared at an interior door. Wield just had time to register full parted lips and huge dark eyes under a torrent of richly black hair before she turned away and he heard footsteps racing up a flight of stairs.

"My sister, Caddy," said Kee. "You must excuse her. She doesn't waste much time on social niceties."

The footsteps returned cut by half, as she took the stairs two or three at a time. Then she was back in the gallery clutching a sketching pad and a pencil.

"I've got to have your face, do you mind? It's amazing. Do you live around here? I'd love to do a portrait, would you be interested?"

All the time the pencil was speeding over the paper.

"Caddy, for heaven's sake!" said Kee in that tone of reproof underpinned with pride that parents use when their kids are being intrusively precocious. "This is Sergeant Wield. It seems PC Bendish has gone missing."

"Probably off chasing rustlers or something. Sergeant, okay, if you're hot on a scent, I can see how sittings could be a problem, but if I could take a few pics? I can work off photos, not the same, of course, but at least they don't want to talk or pick their noses. Okay? Great, don't go away."

The flying footstep routine was repeated.

"Sorry again," said Kee. "Don't let her bother you if you'd rather not. But she is good."

"These hers?" said Wield, studying a selection of watercolors. "Very nice. She's good on sheep, isn't she?"

"No, not those," said Kee. "They're Beryl Pottinger's, our school head teacher. They sell surprisingly well. Tourists like a nice view of somewhere they've been. Those are Caddy's up there."

Wield looked and said, "Oh, aye," which was the nearest his natural courtesy as well as his native reticence would let him come to "Bloody hell!" From Mrs. Pottinger's placid pastorals to Caddy Scudamore's lurid landscapes was perhaps a small step for an artist, but it was a mighty leap over a high cliff for a man whose walls were hung with Victorian prints of Gilbert and Sullivan characters.

Caddy was back with a camera which seemed to have a will of its own, clicking and winking and winding itself on with minimal outside interference. Wield began to feel uneasy. Both privately and professionally his instinct had long been to keep himself in the background, and this degree of attention was without doubt threatening. When the camera was replaced with a camcorder, he felt it was time to retreat.

"This statue. You couldn't show me where it is, could you?" he said pleadingly to Kee.

She looked at the ledger, looked at his face, took pity, switched off the calculator, and said, "Why not?"

"I'll come too," said Caddy. "I need to get him in motion."

"Oh, no, you won't," said her sister firmly. "This is a place of business, remember?"

"You could have fooled me," said Caddy sulkily. She was, observed Wield with a critically neutral eye, one of those rare women on whom sulkiness is becoming. When she pouted, her full lips rounded into a moist pink funnel a hetero could pour his soul into.

"Oh, well, I'd better get these developed, then," she said, and vanished up the stairs once more.

"Caddy, you will listen for the doorbell, won't you?" called Kee after her, but got no reply.

"I might as well give up," she said to Wield with the resignation of use. "Once she gets in that darkroom, she doesn't hear a thing."

"She develops her own, does she?" said Wield.

"Oh, yes. Don't be deceived by the impression she gives of chaos on the hoof. Like a lot of kids nowadays she manages to have one foot in Bohemia and the other in high tech without showing any sign of doing the splits."

The pride was there again, strong and unmistakable. You needed to be a pretty well-balanced character and have a firm sense of your own worth, to tolerate the demands of wayward talent in a younger sister, thought Wield.

As they left the gallery the young cyclist Wield had noticed the day before came to a silent halt before them.

"Hello, Jason," said Kee neutrally. "Do you want something?"

"Caddy. Got something for her."

"I'm afraid she's too busy now," said Kee.

The youth regarded her with strangely unfocused eyes. She returned his gaze as steadily and stood her ground in front of the door.

Wield, whose eyes had been taking in the young man's submilitary garb and the shotgun clipped to his crossbar, said, "You got a license for that gun, lad?"

"Yes," said Toke without looking at him. "Later, then."

He moved swiftly away.

Wield said, "Hold on—!" but Kee interrupted, "It's okay, Sergeant. He does have a license. In fact he's probably got a license for all the weapons he's got."

"All . . . ? How many does he have, then?"

"A whole armory, according to local rumor. But I've never seen them, so don't take what I say as gospel."

"You don't like the lad, but?"

She shrugged and said, "He's a bit weird. And he's got a thing about Caddy. I don't like weird men having a thing about my kid sister."

They set off at a brisk pace up the High Street.

As the hill began to climb she pointed to a narrow driveway off to the right just below the church.

"That takes you round to Corpse Cottage, where Mr. Bendish lives. Then it climbs up the hill to the vicarage."

"Is that right," said Wield, pausing. "It's well hidden."

"Do you want to take a look? We can carry on up to the vicarage and get into the churchyard that way."

"The vicarage is around there, too, is it?"

"Higher up, on the same level as the church."

Wield said, "No, we'll just go the regular way. I'll leave the cottage till later."

When I've not got a sharp-eyed civilian in tow, he added mentally, and then caught those sharp eyes smiling at him as though he'd spoken aloud.

They climbed the hill till they drew level with the war memorial.

Wield paused. It was in the form of a Celtic cross with the simple inscription FOR THE FALLEN OF THE PARISH OF ENSCOMBE with two lists of names, alphabetical and without rank, one for 1914–18, the other for 1939–45.

"You had some bother last Armistice Day," he said.

"Yes. When they gathered for the service, they found someone had spilled blood over the cross. Animal blood. You were asking about Jason Toke. It was Jason that did it. Everyone knew."

"Toke?" said Wield. "He's a funny-looking antiwar protester."

"How very observant of you," said Kee. "He is, as he looks, quite obsessed with things military. Just like his brother."

"There's another?"

"Was. Warren. A couple of years older than Jason. A year ago last Christmas he got blown up in Northern Ireland. That's when Jason started turning weird. One symptom was he wanted the Parish Council to put Warren's name on the war memorial. He got extremely upset when they wouldn't."

Wield ran his eye down the list of names.

"There's a Toke there already. Two."

"Oh, yes. They're all here if you look. Tokes and Wapshares, Hogbins and Guillemards, Digweeds and Halavants, all the old local families. A roll of honor or a testament to futility, depending how you look at it."

"No question how Toke looked at it," said Wield. "How come he hasn't joined up?"

"Perhaps even the army draws a line. No, that's unfair. It's just as likely to be a reluctance to leave his mother alone. They're very close."

"That's all right, then," said Wield. "So your only real objection to Toke is he fancies your sister? Can't blame him for that."

He spoke sincerely. Even lacking the equipment tuned to that particular wavelength, he had no trouble picking up the signal.

"Yes," she said, not without pride. "Caddy's very attractive."

"So you don't really think Toke could be positively dangerous?" he pressed.

She said, "Who knows what anyone is capable of if pushed in the wrong direction, Sergeant? Even a policeman."

They had walked up the hill and now they entered the churchyard. It was extremely well kept, grass razed, weeds trimmed, moss and lichen carefully removed from the headstones to leave even the oldest inscriptions legible.

"Someone works hard," Wield observed.

"We know how to take care of our dead," said Kee.

The same names he'd seen on the war memorial were repeated here, though the democracy of its alphabetic listing was absent, with Tokes and Hogbins packed close together under simple slabs radiating away from the marble mass of the Guillemard mausoleum, over which brooded an intricately carved version of the bird he'd noticed on their coat of arms.

"What is that thing?" he asked.

"Heraldically it's a halcyon, which in mythology guaranteed calm seas when it was brooding on its floating nest. Its real-life equivalent is the kingfisher. According to tradition, i.e., Guillemard propaganda, there were kingfishers nesting along the Een when the first Guillemards settled here in ten sixty something, and as long as they continue there, the family will enjoy halcyon days."

"Must be pleased there's one here at the moment," said Wield, recalling Mrs. Pottinger.

"My, what sharp eyes and ears you have, Sergeant," she said, smiling.

Wield smiled back, thinking how nice it was to get information without having to suffer Digweed's savage put-downs.

When they reached the entrance to Green Alley he pointed to the lintel and asked, "What's *Fuctata non perfecta* mean?"

"Depends who you ask. *Fuctata* means painted or rouged, and by extension forged or counterfeit. It's either feminine singular or neuter plural. Thus the family will tell you it means either, Things which are painted cannot be perfect, or, A rouged woman has got something to hide. In either case the implication is that the Guillemards play by the rules, what you see is what you get."

"What if I ask in the village?"

"There are some who might go along with the Guillemards' claim to honesty by assuring you it means, We're not perfect, we're a bunch of phonies!"

"And you, miss?"

"At the moment I'm rather in sympathy with the answer you'd get from the habitués of the Morris just before closing time."

"Which is?"

"*Fuctata non perfecta* means, Fuck you, Jack, we're all right! Ah, here we are."

She led the way into a small clearing. The fitful wind twitched the clouds and let a meager ration of spring sunshine filter through the arching shrubs to light up the blossom of an old laurestinus leaning rather wearily against a little stone bench.

"How very odd," murmured Kee, letting her gaze drift all around the glade. "I'm afraid it's gone."

"What? The hat?" said Wield.

"Not just the hat. The whole dashed statue!"

Eight

Miss H. is an elegant pleasing pretty-looking girl, about nineteen, I suppose, or nineteen and a half, or nineteen and a quarter, with flowers in her head and music at her finger ends.

Frances Harding, having escorted Pascoe to the door, looked ready to flee back into the house. The sun happening to break through the clouds at this moment touched her face, letting Pascoe see clearly what before he'd only got a vague impression of. Unsure and self-effacing she might be, but now it struck him as the uncertainty of spring, and he guessed there was a definite self here to efface. Her eyes when not cast modestly down were bright with intelligence and blue as the ribbon which tied back her hair. For a moment he was reminded of someone. Girlie, perhaps? Or the Squire? He didn't think so.

He said, "Could you show me where the walled garden is?"

She started as if he'd made an immoral suggestion and said quickly, "I must go back in. Grunk's rehearsing."

"Grunk?"

"The Squire," she said. "Great-uncle . . . it's my name . . . look, I have to go, he hates to be without music."

"Surely he can press a switch himself?"

The incomprehension on her face sparked comprehension on his.

"I'm sorry. What a twit. It was you playing, wasn't it? I thought it was Casals or someone on tape!"

Her pale face flushed with pleasure, turning from snow drop to almond blossom. A man might spend his time less profitably than striving to induce this effect, thought Pascoe.

"Look," he said. "It would just take a minute. And he's got to drink his tea. My tea too! If I go myself, heaven knows where I'll end up!"

For a second longer she hesitated, wrinkling her nose like some young rabbit sniffing the air outside the family burrow, then she said, "All right."

She moved with unobtrusive speed and Pascoe found he had to make an effort to keep up. They went around the side of the house past a Victorian cast-iron conservatory, which looked to be held up by a rampant vine growing within.

"That's the walled garden over there," said the girl, pointing toward a rough-hewn granite wall rising eight or nine feet above the unkempt lawn and looking as if it might have been built to keep the natives out rather than a garden in.

Distance away was about sixty yards, judged Pascoe, wondering how good the Squire's eyes were. As he approached, it became apparent there would be no problem about anyone running around its rampart, which from the density of the grassy fringe growing out of it looked to be at least a couple of feet wide. The entrance door, which faced away from the Hall, was solid oak and firmly locked.

"How long since the key was lost?" asked Pascoe.

"A little while," said Fran vaguely. "In fact I don't think anyone's seen it since Mr. Hogbin went."

"Hogbin?" said Pascoe, recalling this was the name of the old man who'd reported the altercation between Bendish and the Hell's Angel.

"He lives at the Lodge. He looked after the gardens till he had a stroke before Christmas."

"And nobody's wanted to get in here since then?"

"There's not a lot to do in the winter. And Girlie says it's hard enough looking after what you can see!"

Pascoe, looking around, took her point. There was a large tract of formal lawn bounded by outcrops of shrubbery, with farther afield the blossom of orchards, the spring green of woodland, and above all the brooding brownness of the naked moor.

"Not much point in taking too much care if you're going to have your cousin Guy's skirmishers trampling all over the place," he said lightly. "Interesting mix that, a Health Park and a battlefield."

She shook her head so vigorously, the blue ribbon came loose, allowing her hair to veil her face, preventing him from reading the emotion there.

"I've got to get back to Grunk," she said.

She set off but after a few paces paused and waited.

So I'm not trusted to wander at will, thought Pascoe.

Back at the house he said, "Thanks, Miss Harding. I hope I get the chance to hear you play again. When's the Squire's next performance?"

"Tomorrow at the Reckoning," she said. "That's when everyone comes to pay their rents. But I'm sure you won't need to stay in Enscombe that long."

"I hope you're right," said Pascoe, realizing too late the accidental rudeness, but it didn't matter anyway, as she'd already vanished into the house.

He turned away to see Sergeant Wield coming down the drive accompanied by a classically beautiful blonde. Beauty and the Beast, thought Pascoe. Dalziel would have said it. Does that make me any better than the Fat Man?

"Afternoon, sir," said Wield formally. "This is Miss Scudamore, who runs the gallery in the High Street. Thought you might be interested in what she's got to say."

The woman gave a brief and lucid account of her sighting of the hat.

"And now you say this statue's vanished?"

"The sergeant needed to see the hole in the ground where it had been standing before he was convinced," said Kee. "Makes you wonder if Doubting Thomas was a policeman."

She smiled to show there was no malice in her frivolity.

Wouldn't have made any difference, thought Pascoe. Wield was no princess to be bruised by peas.

"I'd not be surprised," said the sergeant. "Thanks for your help, miss."

"My pleasure. Call again before you leave. My sister's a fast worker when divine inspiration descends."

With a cool nod at Pascoe she walked away.

"What was that about divine inspiration?" asked Pascoe, thinking he detected a reaction to this apparently innocuous parting shot.

"Nowt," said Wield. "You got anything yet?"

"I'm not sure. Funny place. Nice pub. Did you get in?"

"No, I didn't," said Wield with emphasis. "Didn't get into the Wayside Café either. Thought you had to be a superintendent before you could spend time in them places."

"Whoops," said Pascoe. "Well, if you've not been eating and

drinking, just what have you been up to? And Fat Andy said you'd fill me in on this Hell's Angel."

Pascoe seemed disproportionately entertained to learn that Wield had been the villainous biker, but he listened with close attention to everything else the sergeant told him. He had great respect for Wield's powers of observation and reasoning. Also it was important to his own self-esteem to keep his end up. Wield had been a sergeant while he was still a constable. Now promotion had taken him several steps beyond the older man and in some ways it was much more important to convince Wield that his advancement was justified than Dalziel. Correction. Nothing was more important than keeping Dalziel sweet. But it was terror that motivated him there while with Wield it was affection.

They walked up the drive as they talked till they reached the scene of Wield's encounter with Bendish.

"Of course all this is less important now that we've got the much later sighting at Scarletts," said Pascoe. "But this thing about the hat intrigues me. This little girl . . ."

"Madge Hogbin. She lives in the Lodge with her grandparents."

"One of whom is old Mr. Hogbin, who had a stroke, lost the key to the garden, and was watching out of his window when you met Bendish," said Pascoe, not to be outdone in local knowledge.

"Aye. And he's still watching," said Wield.

"So he is. Let's go and have a chat, shall we?"

The door was opened by Mrs. Hogbin, whose "turn," Pascoe recollected, had saved the WI from further exposure to the Squire's balladry. Her bright eyes and rosy cheeks suggested that the "turn" might well have been theatrical rather than medical.

She waved aside Pascoe's attempts at explanation with the unflattering assertion, "Makes no matter who you are. He doesn't get far with the walker, so I push in anyone who comes a-calling. Witnesses, travelers, insurance men, he don't mind so long as he gets a bit of gossip."

Mr. Hogbin was standing in the shallow window bay, leaning into his aluminum walking frame as if it were a pulpit, and peering down at the nodding daffodils with all the noble intensity of Doctor Donne about to say something striking about bells. He didn't move or turn his head even when his wife said, "Here's someone to see you, luv. Bobbies, they say they are."

"Mr. Hogbin," said Pascoe, "I'm Chief Inspector Pascoe and this is

Detective Sergeant Wield. We're trying to get hold of Constable Bendish and I gather you saw him yesterday afternoon."

"Aye. I told Sergeant Filmer all about it."

His voice was strong and slow, with a discernible pause between words, though whether this was an aftermath of the stroke or just a natural habit wasn't easy to say.

"Can you tell us, please?"

The old man turned his head now. He looked at Wield without recognition, which probably meant his long sight was good enough for action but not for detail.

He said, "I saw our Madge come running out of the bushes slap bang into this motorcycle."

"Oh, dear, that must have been a shock," said Pascoe.

"Nay. Fellow were hardly moving. It were her own fault and I could see she weren't hurt. So she runs on into the house. Then Mr. Bendish appears—"

"How? I mean, where did he come from?"

"Out of the shrubbery," said Hogbin.

"The same bit as your Madge comes out of?"

"Aye. Likely she'd been up to some mischief and he were chasing her. They're good chums mainly, but she can be a cheeky little monkey when she wants."

"So you saw the constable and this motorcyclist talking. . . ."

"Aye. I got the impression Mr. Bendish were giving him a rollicking."

Pascoe smiled and said, "He probably deserved it. And what happened then?"

"I got called for me tea."

"So you didn't see the end of this . . . discussion?"

"No, but likely it came to nowt. Not like in old Chaz Barnwall's day. Clip a kid's ear just for looking cheeky, would old Chaz. As for someone taking a swing at him, he'd have parted their hair with his truncheon!"

Pascoe exchanged a puzzled glance with Wield, then said, "What makes you think PC Bendish wouldn't defend himself?"

"Saw him, didn't I? Not long back. Bang! Down he goes, hits the ground, gets up, all bleeding. And what's he do? Goes off meek as a lamb, doesn't even look back."

"Where was this? Who hit him?" asked Pascoe.

But the old man's only response was to shut his lips tight and shake his head, and his wife came forward, saying, "Now, don't overtax yourself, Jocky. I think he's had enough for now, gets tired easy, you shouldn't pay too much heed to what he says, past and present gets all mixed up. . . ."

On this tide of words the two detectives found themselves washed out into the kitchen, a pleasant, light room full of spicy baking smells and with its walls lined with childish pictures.

"Did Madge do these?" guessed Wield.

"That's right. Always painting and drawing, our Madge. They do a lot of art at school. Mrs. Pottinger's a right good painter herself, so I reckon she thinks it's important."

"But you don't?" said Pascoe, smiling.

"So long as it doesn't interfere with spelling and arithmetic, I suppose there's no harm in it. But such odd things she paints. That's one she did herself last evening. Now, what's that meant to be, I ask you?"

Pascoe looked at the painting Wield was peering at. To his eye it looked like two figures clad in blue having a fight.

"A wrestling match?" he guessed. "What do you think, Wieldy?"

But Wield said nothing. He was recalling his gently lustful thoughts as he watched Harold Bendish strutting his stuff around the motorcycle yesterday, and wondering if little Madge Hogbin was gifted with ESP. For to his guilty eye the painting showed quite clearly two policemen locked in a passionate embrace!

Refusing Mrs. Hogbin's offer of a cup of tea, the detectives left.

Outside, Pascoe said, "What do you make of that? How confused is the old boy?"

"Not much, I'd say, and his missus even less," said Wield. "It 'ud explain Bendish's bruise and cut hand if he'd been in a ruck."

"But his hard-man image doesn't make it sound likely he'd back down."

"Depends how in the wrong he was," said Wield.

"Maybe. But it still sounds out of character. Like this flashing. From the sound of things, the only flashing this fellow is likely to do is with his roof light when he flags down some mum for pushing her pram too fast—bloody hell!"

It wasn't a pram that came speeding up behind them but a Land Rover, horn blaring, driver grinning broadly as he sent the two policemen tumbling into the lower reaches of a rhododendron bush.

"Who the hell was that?" cried Pascoe as the vehicle swept out of sight down the drive with no diminution of speed.

"Guy the Heir, I think," said Wield, standing up gingerly and testing his limbs and trousers for damage.

"Right. Let's go and talk to the lunatic," said Pascoe grimly.

They found the Land Rover in front of the Hall. Three young men and a green-haired girl had got out and were busy unloading boxes of equipment. Identifying their leader as the athletically slim man wearing a Barbour jacket and a superior air, Pascoe approached him and said, "Excuse me, sir, could I see your driving license?"

Guy Guillemard looked him up and down insolently and said, "Are you selling brushes or have you brought your chum for the cure? Don't think we do plastic surgery."

His acolytes laughed appreciatively.

"You might care to look at this, sir," said Pascoe, holding his warrant before the man's eyes. "Now, your license, please."

Guillemard examined the warrant with mock awe, then he said, "No, I don't think I want one, so why don't you just piss off?"

Taken aback, Pascoe checked to make sure he hadn't pulled out his library card by mistake. He hadn't.

"Perhaps you can't read," he said. "The name's Pascoe. Detective Chief Inspector Peter Pascoe."

"You were one of the oiks littering the drive, right?"

"I was one of the pedestrians you almost ran over."

"Can't hit gold every time, can we? But if you are a cop, you ought to be aware that as this driveway is not a public highway but private property, whatever breach of the road traffic regulations you are alleging doesn't apply. I could be a one-eyed epileptic fifteen-year-old, and drunk as a skunk to boot, and you couldn't touch me. So why not give it a rest, Sherlock, and if you want to block the traffic, go and do it on a busy motorway."

Pascoe looked at the smiling, self-assured face and felt an almost irresistible impulse to punch the man's nose through the back of his neck. Worse, he found he did not wish to resist the impulse. In front of all these witnesses to cut through the knotted ambiguities of his attitude to his career with a single blow! To exit not with a whimper but a bang! It had all the allure of simplicity.

A cloud of smoke had formed in the doorway of the Hall. Out of it emerged Girlie Guillemard. She advanced toward them, saying, "There you are, Guy."

The man turned, opened his arms as if in anticipation of an embrace, and said, "Girlie, my sweet. What does a thirsty man have to do to get a drink around here?"

The woman hit him full in the face, an opened-handed smack which sent him staggering back against Pascoe.

"You watch your manners for a start," she said mildly. "Your let's-pretend fights are fine for consenting adults, but not when you start picking on folk who can't fight back."

Pascoe was so close, he could see the muscles on the back of Guy's neck clench like a fist. Then Girlie kissed him lightly on the cheek and said, "By the way, I thought you were staying last night. What happened?"

Slowly the neck muscles relaxed.

"Sorry, I got held up, in a manner of speaking. I did try to ring, got the engaged signal, then I got cut off altogether. That thing of yours must be on the blink."

Girlie looked at the mobile phone around her neck and said, "You were probably too drunk to dial the right number. I need to talk to you, Guy. After you've finished with Mr. Pascoe, that is."

His face now composed to rue, the man swung around, reached into one of his many pockets, and pulled out a wallet from which he took a driver's license.

"There you are, Inspector. Sorry to have been an arsehole. And sorry if I got a bit close on the drive. Will take more care next time. Sorry."

The smile was no longer superior but almost childishly appealing. Now might be an even better time to punch it off, thought Pascoe. He resisted the temptation. Or missed the opportunity.

Studying the license he said, "This your vehicle, sir?"

"Indeed. Well, the business's really. You'll find everything in order. Taxed, tested, and insured. What brings you here, anyway, Chief Inspector? You don't look like a traffic man to me."

"One of their constables is missing," said Girlie.

This sounded like an irresistible cue for laughter, but Guy the Heir kept his face straight and said, "Not the estimable Bendish, I hope?"

"You know PC Bendish, sir?"

"Oh, yes. We've had contact." His lips twitched momentarily, then he became serious again as he said, "Look, if it comes to beating the

moors or anything like that, give us a yell. This baby can go anywhere, and so can the ugly buggers who travel in her."

Now they all laughed and the atmosphere eased enough for Pascoe
to feel able to withdraw with dignity.

He said, "I hope it won't come to that, but thanks for the offer. And
in future try to observe your own speed limit."

The warning went unheard or at least unacknowledged. At some
point Frances Harding had appeared on the scene. Guy headed toward
her crying, "There she is, my little celandine! Fran, have you heard?
Dear Constable Bendish has taken French leave and can't be found
anywhere. We must all keep our eyes open for him, mustn't we? In
case he comes to harm."

He reached her and aimed a kiss at her lips, but she ducked her head
evasively and inadvertently dealt him the painful blow with her brow
that Pascoe had been tempted to with his fist. At least he assumed it
was inadvertence, though the color flooding her pale cheeks seemed
this time to have more of the cranberry of wrath in it than the apricot
of embarrassment.

He looked toward her. Their eyes met. He smiled and she looked
away.

"Time to be off, Wieldy," said Pascoe. "Let's get down to Church
Cottage. Could be our wandering boy's home now."

"Could be," said the sergeant.

"You don't sound optimistic. What's up? Got a bad feeling about
this place?"

Wield's forte was facts, so if he started getting bad vibes it was
unusual enough to be worth noticing.

"I don't know. If it's bad, I mean. I've certainly got a feeling
that something has happened . . . or is happening . . . or is going to
happen here . . . something big. Mebbe I should book in at this Health
Park!"

"I certainly shouldn't mention it to Fat Andy," said Pascoe. "He'd
likely dose you with cod liver oil."

He spoke lightly, reluctant to admit that Wield's premonition
chimed with his own sense of atmospheric disturbance. Such presenti-
ment on an Adriatic beach sent the attendants scurrying to furl the
parasols, though to the holiday visitor they brought merely a thrill of
pleasure at the storm to come. It all really came down to how he saw
his function here. Was he an involved attendant or just an idle tourist?

Wield looked as if he'd chosen the latter role, standing by the car door, rubbernecking the northern sky like it was the dome of St. Mark's. He let his own gaze drift upward. At first he could see nothing but the wind-torn clouds above the lowering moor. Then he caught a movement.

A bird . . . no, two birds . . . very high . . . circling, circling . . .

Nine

I like him very much. I am sure he is
clever & a Man of Taste.—very
smiling, with an exceedingly good
address & readiness of language—I
am rather in love with him.—I dare
say he is ambitious & Insincere.

As he shaved in the morning, or saw his elegant profile on
the arts page of the *Evening News,* or played a video of one
of his TV shows, Justin Halavant usually congratulated himself on being Justin Halavant.

Best of all he liked to see himself mirrored in the envious
eyes of his acolytes, those who, for a mere tithe of his wit,
looks, style, taste, and success with women, would have
traded their sister's virtue, which he'd probably already had
gratis anyway.

But there were times when he had to acknowledge that,
though what he had, he had perfectly, he did not have
everything.

For instance he had no talent for burglary.

It had started well enough. Getting into Corpse Cottage was
surprisingly easy. He turned the door handle and it opened.

Just for the show of the thing, he called, "I say. Constable
Bendish!" twice. Then he stepped inside.

Now the trouble started. A burglar would presumably
know where to start looking. He opted for the deep alcoves
found by the chimney breast which Bendish clearly used as
his office. Here was a bureau with all the necessary forms of
his business carefully pigeonholed. But the drawers were
locked, and the cupboards beneath also, and though in tele-
fiction such things burst open at the touch of a nail file, in
real life they proved much more obdurate.

In any case it was surely a waste of time searching in an office for what all the evidence suggested had remained unofficial?

He went upstairs. Bedrooms were the opposite of offices. Here a man was at his most private. Here he would hide what touched him most closely.

But where? No locked drawers here, but nothing in them save socks and shirts and vests and pants. The shelves of the wardrobe were no more productive. He lifted the pillows off the bed, then in desperation raised the mattress to check beneath.

It was while he was thus occupied that he heard the car pull up outside.

Had he shut the front door? He couldn't recall. In any case it made no matter; what he had done, anyone could do. Car doors opened, slammed. Voices floated upward. He had to act, but action belonged to another world than this. He was a figure in a painting, caught on canvas forever, the raised mattress in his hands. The *whence* and *whither* others must decide as they shuffled past in judgment with their catalogs at the high port.

Then he was seized from behind, the mattress fell back on the bed, and he on top of it with his attacker straddling him. Rape! Oh, God! Was this what it felt like? Had Caddy perhaps felt like this as he flung her down on the stairs in the Gallery?

This rare pang of guilt was immediately rewarded with the idea of dealing with his attacker as she had dealt with hers. But to do this he needed to twist around to bring his knee into play and his assailant had a lock on his neck which held him helpless.

Then he heard footsteps on the stairs and felt rather than saw other men racing into the room.

"What the hell's going on here?" demanded Peter Pascoe.

In strict terms what was going on was clear for all to see. A man dressed as a vicar was pinning Justin Halavant to the bed with what looked like a professional wrestling hold.

"Who are you?" demanded the holy wrestler, turning to look at them.

"Police," said Pascoe. "Do you mind standing up?"

The vicar relaxed his hold. Immediately the underling twisted around and brought his knee up in what would have been a vicious assault on the clerical crotch had not its owner slipped easily off the bed before contact was made.

"Good Lord," he said as he saw his victim's face. "Mr. Halavant."

And equally amazed, the now supine man said, "Lillingstone! What the hell are you playing at?"

"A better question might be, what are you both playing at?" said Pascoe sternly. "This house is police property. Would you mind explaining what you're doing here?"

"In my case, that's very easy," said Lillingstone. "I'm doing what I imagine is your job. I was coming down the drive from the vicarage when I saw a movement up here. I'd heard about Mr. Bendish's absence, so naturally I was suspicious. I came in—"

"How?" interjected Pascoe.

"Through the front door. It was ajar," said the vicar. "I came upstairs and saw what I thought was a burglar stooping over the bed lifting up the mattress. So I performed a citizen's arrest."

"Very civic minded of you," said Pascoe. "And you, Mr. Halavant. How was it for you?"

"An outrage!" said Halavant, standing up and checking his body for damage, his clothes for disarray. "I had come in search of Constable Bendish. Finding the door open, I came in and called his name. There was no reply but I thought I heard a noise upstairs, so I came up."

"Why?" asked Pascoe.

"In case the constable was in trouble. He may have had a fit or a fall. It was my duty."

"Enscombe is positively awash with civic concern," murmured Pascoe. "And you were raising the mattress in case the constable had somehow slipped beneath it during his fall or his fit?"

"I thought he might have rolled beneath the bed."

"In that case, wouldn't it have been easier simply to stoop and look?"

"I choose never to stoop," said Halavant. "I'm puzzled why you should be so puzzled by *my* concern when you yourself are clearly concerned enough to bring in reinforcements to investigate your constable's absence."

He smiled at Wield, who gave him in return what Dalziel called his senna-pod tea look.

"That's because I'm puzzled why you came here looking for Bendish when you know he's missing," said Pascoe gently.

Momentarily nonplussed, but quickly recovering, Halavant replied, "I hardly took that rumor seriously, Inspector. I mean, I hadn't realized till now that you'd actually formed a posse. All I wanted was a word about the report of an intruder at Scarletts last night."

The vicar, perhaps overcome by a sense of feeling foolish, sat heavily on the bed.

"Fair enough, sir," said Pascoe. "As soon as we contact Bendish we'll ask him to get in touch with you. Sergeant . . ."

Wield held open the door for Halavant to pass through.

Lillingstone rose as if to follow, but Pascoe said, "No, sir. If you could just spare a moment of your time . . ."

"Of course. How flattering."

"How so?"

"I get the chief inspector while our local celebrity has to make do with the sergeant."

Pascoe said, "That's because you're the more interesting case, sir."

"How's that?" said the vicar uncertainly.

"Mr. Halavant is a journalist and media man," said Pascoe. "So it must be almost second nature for him to bend the truth. But when someone in your line of country starts telling lies, *that* I find really interesting."

"What on earth do you mean?" said Lillingstone, flushing.

"This room is on the wrong side of the house for you to see any movement in it on your way down the vicarage drive. Also if your story were true, we'd have been in time to see you entering the house as we drove up. No, it seems to me much more likely you were here already when Mr. Halavant came in. You hid, hoping to slip away as soon as you got the chance. Then you heard our car. Reckoning the chances of two intruders going undetected weren't good, you decided to put yourself firmly on the side of the angels by apprehending your fellow burglar."

"I resent the term *burglar*," said Lillingstone indignantly.

"You'd be surprised how many burglars do," said Pascoe. "But indignation without explanation doesn't get you jelly for your tea. So what's the gospel reading for today, Vicar?"

"I'm sorry," said the man wretchedly. "You're quite right, of course. No excuse. Just sheer vulgar curiosity. I'd heard about Harold and I thought that maybe in the cottage there'd be some clue. . . ."

Pascoe, who didn't believe a word said, "Okay. So let's have the key. And don't say, 'Which key?' The door wasn't forced. We know Sergeant Filmer left it locked this morning. So, the key, please. And perhaps you would like to tell me where you got it?"

The vicar put his hand in his pocket and produced a rusty old latchkey.

"There's an old keyboard in the vicarage," said Lillingstone. "Full of old keys, some of them labeled. Church Cottage was one of them."

"Why on earth should there be a key to a police house in the vicarage?" asked Pascoe.

"The cottage used to belong to the church," said Lillingstone. "The Hogbin family rented it for generations, but finally they decided they'd had enough and moved out, and my financial masters put the cottage on the market. That's when your people bought it as a police house."

"What was it the Hogbins had had enough of?" asked Pascoe.

Lillingstone smiled the relieved smile of someone being invited to leap out of the hot seat of interrogation into the saddle of his hobby-horse and said, "Being haunted, of course. It's a good story. Would you like to hear it?"

Another diversion into the past! thought Pascoe. He really had to start resisting them. Yet he was getting a sense, which he wouldn't care to have to explain to Dalziel, that whatever was going on in Enscombe would only be understood by reference to history.

He said, "Only if you've worked on it long enough to make it short."

"Fear not. It's part of my address to the Local History Association. The parlor's the best place to tell it. Can we go downstairs?"

Am I imagining it, or is he keen to get out of this bedroom? wondered Pascoe. They made their way downstairs, meeting Wield on the way up.

"Why don't you take a look around up there?" suggested Pascoe.

Wield was the best systematic searcher of premises he'd met, though if you knew what you were looking for, there was no one to beat Andy Dalziel. No system, but he had a nose for going straight to the spot. As for himself, Pascoe acknowledged a deep-rooted distaste for this hands-on invasion of privacy which rendered his searches pain-giving as well as painstaking. Dalziel had once remarked, "Pete, lad, I'll always know if you've been searching my room, 'cos you'll leave it tidier than you found it!"

The sergeant continued upstairs. Pascoe and the vicar went into the living room and Lillingstone took up a public speaker's stance in front of the fireplace.

"You probably remarked as you approached the cottage that this wall behind me is in fact built right into the hillside," the vicar began. "Beyond that wall, Mr. Pascoe, lies my graveyard."

He paused for effect. Pascoe looked at his watch, also for effect. Lillingstone grinned and hurried on.

"I'd like to take you back to Lammas 1787. That was the third day of the longest uninterrupted period of rain ever recorded even in these damp climes. It was also the day when the Hogbin clan gathered to bury Susannah, their matriarch, who had ruled them with a rod of iron for more than three decades. Alas, it was as true then as it is now, that the longer you are feared, the less you will be mourned, and the relief the Hogbins felt at getting out of the deluge and into this house was redoubled by their realization that the dreaded Susannah was gone for good. They ate the funeral meats and drank the funeral ale, and the gathering got merrier and merrier, so that even the sound of the incessant rain beating against the windows only increased their merriment.

"Quips and jokes flew thick and fast, and frequent repetition of the best only served to make them the funnier. And the most brilliant shaft of all has been saved for us in the written record of Silas Hogbin, then a youngster of nine or ten, who was sitting crouched here, in the alcove behind the chimney breast, drinking in the wild talk of his elders as children love to do.

"His own father had just repeated it for the umpteenth time, 'Aye, but didsta see t'ole? Fuller o' watter than Daft Jimmy's heed! T'owld lass weren't *buried*. She were *launched*!' And for the umpteenth time the Hogbins fell about with laughter.

"But this time it was not the sound of mirth alone which followed the joke. Another noise intruded, at first scarcely distinguishable through the laughter, but eventually causing it to still as the mourners strained their ears to identify its source."

Lillingstone paused dramatically. Right on cue came a groaning, creaking noise, which seemed to come out of thin air. Pascoe gave a little start, then grimaced as he realized it was only Wield moving something upstairs.

"Get a move on, will you?" he said with the brusqueness of embarrassment.

"It was at this moment," resumed the vicar, "that young Silas had a strange experience. In his own words it was as if a great finger jabbed into his back and started to push him forward into the room. He looked around to check the cause.

" 'Hey, Dad,' he called. 'This wall's starting to bulge—'

"And simultaneous with his warning the stones of this very wall flew asunder to admit a great tide of earth and rocks and water. You can imagine the panic. Screaming and praying, the Hogbins went scrambling for the doors and windows with scant regard for the precedence due to sex or age. Nor was it just natural fear for their lives which set them fleeing. It was also the supernatural terror caused by the violent entry on this muddy tide of a still bright-handled coffin, which burst asunder on this very floor to reveal the pallid face and wide accusing eyes of the founder of their feast, Susannah!"

He stopped speaking and stood with his fingers pointing dramatically downward.

It was a bit over the top, thought Pascoe. He wondered if his sermons were like this.

He said, "Sounds a bit of a tall story to me, Vicar."

"What? It's well documented, I assure you," said Lillingstone, looking hurt. "It was the same cloudburst that caused the tower to take its final lurch sideways and washed out the foundations of the old vicarage, making it too dangerous to live in. The vicar had to bed down at Old Hall till the parish raised enough money to build the fine old vicarage I now inhabit, so it's all down in black and white in the records."

"Very generous parishioners you have around here," said Pascoe.

"Indeed they are," said Lillingstone, as if suspecting a slight. "They practiced self-help here long before it became a euphemism for governmental meanness and insensitivity."

"And Church Cottage became Corpse Cottage. Was Bendish bothered by ghosts, that you heard?"

"Young Harry? No!" laughed Lillingstone. "Far too sensible to believe in ghosts."

Pascoe noted "young Harry," the first nondeprecatory reference to Bendish he'd heard. Christian charity? Law-and-order solidarity? Or genuine liking?

He said, "But the Hogbins weren't sensible?"

Lillingstone laughed again and said, "I believe the Hogbins would still be here if the Squire hadn't offered them the lodge rent free and a sharecropping deal in return for Jocky taking care of the Hall gardens.

But it made a better story for them to be haunted out than hired out. Most Yorkshiremen love facts, Mr. Pascoe, and they like them penny plain. Enscombians are something else. They go for tuppence-colored every time."

Wield's head appeared around the door and looked significantly at Pascoe.

Lillingstone said, "I'll be on my way, then, if there's nothing else?"

"Not unless you've decided to tell me your real reason for being here," said Pascoe. "Vicars should stick to penny plain, even in Enscombe, wouldn't you agree? So come to confession when you're ready."

Lillingstone left, looking seriously discomfited.

"Doubt if you'll be getting an invite to the Sunday School treat this year," said Wield.

"I'll survive. You found something, have you, Wieldy?"

"Could be owt or nowt. Everything's in order. Hard to say what's missing without knowing what was here to start with. But at least we can be sure he wasn't dressed for duty when he took off, which is a relief."

He had led the way upstairs into the bedroom. The wardrobe door was open. He pointed to a black garbage bag lying inside. Pascoe stooped and opened it.

It contained two police uniforms, fresh back from the dry cleaners by the look of them.

Or rather, one and a half police uniforms, for Wield's sharper eye had spotted a discrepancy. He picked up one pair of trousers, looked at the label, and said, "We're not using Marks and Sparks as a supplier now, are we?"

"Seems unlikely. Why?"

"That's where these came from. Right color, and just about the same material. Would get by a casual glance, maybe, but not a real inspection."

Pascoe shrugged and said, "So he spilled paint on the originals and didn't want to have to explain himself to Filmer. Who incidentally needs a kick up the backside for missing this lot."

"Probably just thought it was dirty washing," said Wield defensively.

"Whereas it is in fact very clean washing," said Pascoe thoughtfully. "Odd. Bendish was wearing one of these uniforms at Scarletts last night. And I've not noticed an all-night dry cleaners in the village, have you?"

Before Wield could riddle this riddle, an all-too-familiar voice
came drifting up the stairs.

"Is there anybody there?"

Pascoe went out onto the tiny landing and looked down into the
hallway.

"Only us listeners," he said. "Can I help you, Mr. Digweed?"

"That depends," said the bookseller, frowning. "We met at the
station earlier, didn't we? I've forgotten your name. . . ."

"Pascoe. Chief Inspector."

"Just so. And from the sound of it you are perhaps also the token
literate in our benighted constabulary. Or did my question merely stir
up some childhood memory of rote-learned verse? I daresay even the
worthy Sergeant Wield knows de la Mare's *Traveller*."

Here we go again, thought Wield as he descended the stairs behind
Pascoe, wondering if his boss could resist the temptation to take the
old fart on.

He couldn't.

"De la Mare's 'Listeners,' I think you mean," he said courteously.
"His *Traveller* is, of course, something else. But what urgent business
brings you here, Mr. Digweed?"

"Who said anything about urgency?" said the bookseller, somewhat piqued.

"A self there is that listens in the heart / To what is past the range
of human speech, / Which yet has urgent tidings to impart," said
Pascoe.

Digweed regarded him, frowning. Yet it did not seem to Wield that
it was merely being capped in this arty-farty quotation game that
made him frown.

Then the bookseller said, "Of course, you're quite right. And I'm
sorry if I spoke boorishly. Think of it as a protective bitterness, like
painting the nails with alum, causing more discomfort to the biter than
anyone who happens to get scratched."

Wield, assuming cynically that his thick skin was excluded from
this apology, was surprised when Digweed filtered a frosty smile in his
direction also.

Then the bookseller's expression turned businesslike.

"And, yes, Mr. Pascoe, it is a matter of urgency that brings me
here hoping to find Sergeant Filmer and your good Sergeant Wield
at their rendezvous. My shop has been broken into. I have been
robbed."

"I'm sorry to hear that, sir," said Pascoe. "What's been taken?"

Digweed rolled his eyes upward and said, "I run a bookshop, Chief Inspector, a shop for selling books. So why don't you hazard a guess?"

And Wield grinned to himself at this evidence that not even quotation itself kept a man safe from scratching.

Ten

*You distress me cruelly by your
request about Books; I cannot think
of any to bring with me, nor have I
any idea of our wanting them.*

The bookshop had a musty, dusty smell which Pascoe
drank in like mountain air. To Wield's nose, however, it
wasn't a million miles removed from the pong of a damp
cardboard box used as a cot by some unfortunate in the
shopping precinct.

Digweed took them into a back room and showed them a
window from which a circle of glass had been removed.

"How could they do that?" asked Digweed.

"Stick a sucker on the glass, an ordinary drain plunger
would do," said Wield. "Whip around it with a glass cutter
and pull. Then reach in and unlock the window. I'd get onto
the glazier right away, sir. Don't want to put temptation in
folks' way."

"I am quite capable of cutting a piece of glass and opening a tin of putty myself," said Digweed acidly. "Country
life teaches you self-sufficiency. Indeed I begin to wonder if
we might not be better off policing ourselves."

"What seems to be missing?" interrupted Pascoe, who
had been examining the shelves more like a bibliophile than
an investigator.

"As far as I can make out from the gaps, a rather eclectic
selection. To wit, a modern edition of Thorburn's *Birds,* a
nineteenth-century history of the warrior, and a catalog of
the Renoir exhibition at the Hayward in 1985."

"So, a Renaissance burglar," said Pascoe. "Worth much?"

"Not a lot. The *Warrior* was rarish and nicely bound, but not in much demand. Fifty, sixty pounds the lot, I suppose."

Wield, peering through the lozenged glass of a locked cabinet, said, "These in here would be more valuable, would they, sir?"

"Indeed, but as the cabinet is locked and every inch of shelf space is full, I would hazard a guess that nothing has been removed."

He spoke in the tone of voice used by primary teachers and party political broadcasters, provoking Wield to a dull obduracy.

"He could have used a picklock, taken some valuable stuff, wrapped the covers around them other books, and put them back in the cabinet so's you'd not notice."

He saw he'd said something daft as well as dull, because even Pascoe was smiling. But at least he got between Wield and Digweed's more savage mockery by quickly saying, "Not very likely, Wieldy, as having the original dust jacket usually quadruples a book's value. Right, Mr. Digweed?"

"At the very least."

"Nevertheless, it might be as well to check," said Pascoe loyally.

With a long-suffering sigh Digweed produced a key and unlocked the cabinet. He ran his eyes and one finger lightly along the book spines and said, "No, they have not been touched."

Wield reached by him and plucked out a volume, not realizing till he did so that this might seem to imply a doubt of Digweed's judgment, and not caring when he did realize. What had caught his eye was the author. It was a copy of *Lysbeth* by his much loved Rider Haggard. The flimsy, rather soiled jacket was buff-colored with nothing on it but the full title, *Lysbeth, A Tale of the Dutch,* the author's name, and that of the publisher, Longman's & Co., on the spine in blue.

Digweed was hovering anxiously as if he feared Wield might be about to tear the volume in half like a circus strongman.

"May I take that, Sergeant?" he said. "Unless of course you were thinking of purchasing it."

"No," said Wield. "I've got it already."

"Really? Not, I think, this particular edition," said Digweed with his best patronizing smile.

"Oh, yes," said Wield. "Just the same, except mine's in a lot better nick. Published 1901, wasn't it?"

He opened the volume to check, saw he was right, saw also the typed insert containing a description and price.

"Bloody hell!" he exclaimed.

Digweed removed the book from his fingers. He was no longer smiling.

He said, "If indeed you do have a copy of this edition, perhaps we could do business, Sergeant."

"No, thanks," said Wield. "Sentimental value. They were my auntie's. And besides, I like to read them."

"They? Them?"

Pascoe, who had been enjoying this, said, "Oh, yes. Sergeant Wield's got what must be a full set of Haggards, isn't that right, Wieldy?"

"Of first editions?" said Digweed faintly.

"I don't rightly know," said Wield. "I've never bothered to look."

"And dust jackets?"

"Oh, aye. They've all got wrappers, stops 'em getting mucky. That's what they're for, isn't it?"

"Oh, yes." Digweed replaced the book. "All finished here? Good." He smiled at Wield as he relocked the cabinet and said, "Forgive me if I seemed brusque before, Sergeant. You were quite right. You cannot tell a book by its cover. And you, Mr. Pascoe, are you also a collector? An incunabulist, perhaps?"

Wield could see that Pascoe knew what this meant.

"Far from it," he said, smiling. "About four hundred years, in fact. If I collect anything, it is, for my sins, detective novels. Like Sergeant Wield, I inherited a few first editions. From my grandmother. Her tastes, alas, ran to crime rather than Rider Haggard. She had a good collection of prewar Christie. I suspect she probably had the lot at some stage, but she bought to read, not to collect, and I get a mild pleasure out of filling the gaps, usually without jackets, I hasten to add."

"Yes, they can be very expensive," said Digweed, regarding Pascoe sourly. Perhaps he didn't approve of collecting crime!

"Back to business," said Pascoe briskly. "You live on the premises?"

"I have a flat upstairs."

"And did you come in here when you got up this morning?"

"No, I didn't. I don't open till ten, and as I unlocked the door Sergeant Filmer came hotfoot from the café, where Mrs. Creed had assured him I would be able to give a first-class description of the horrendous Hell's Angel who had kidnapped PC Bendish."

He flashed a shared-joke smile at Wield. Funny what a few old first editions will do, thought the sergeant.

"Since that time, as you will know, I have not had a minute which I could call my own."

"In other words, we don't know if the break-in took place last night or this morning," said Pascoe.

"No. I suppose we don't. Does it matter?"

"If it was this morning with the place empty, he might have gone upstairs to see if there was any cash or valuables lying around," said Pascoe. "Did you check up there, sir?"

"No. I just spotted that some books had gone and, following the popular trend, went straight out in search of a policeman."

"Shall we look now?" suggested Pascoe.

They followed Digweed upstairs.

It was not the easiest of journeys, as the narrow treads were rendered even narrower by piles of books which reared into tall stacks when they reached the landing and spread to fill all but the narrowest channels of floor space in the first room they entered.

A desk was just visible under a Manhattan skyline of Waverley Novels. Digweed pulled open its drawers and said, "All in order as far as I can see."

The next door on the landing stood ajar to reveal a bedroom. The single bed was unmade. Above the bed hung a handsome charcoal sketch of a tree-sheltered river pond with the initials *R.D.* in one corner. The floor space was crowded with books also.

"Do your customers come up here to browse?" asked Wield, unable to keep the wonderment from his voice.

"Of course not," snapped Digweed. "In fact browsers form a relatively small part of my custom. The specialized and commercially viable end of my business is done through the mail."

Then, as if recalling his be-nice-to-the-sergeant policy, he added ruefully, "But I see your point. Fond as I am of books I have no desire to end up crushed to death in my own bed by the sheer weight of literature. I am seriously considering a shift to new premises."

"For the books?" said Pascoe.

"Oh, no. The books have their home here. For me. In fact if the rumor I hear that your policy on rural policing is changing and Corpse Cottage might soon be on the market, that could suit me very well."

He paused, considered, then added, "Oh, dear. That must sound rather crass in the circumstances, concerned as you are about your missing colleague."

"*Possibly* missing colleague," said Pascoe.

"Whatever. I apologize. Back to our crime. No, I can see no evidence that our burglar has been up here."

Pascoe wondered what, in the midst of such chaos, such evidence might look like. But as he looked down at the book-lined stairs his mind was filled not with the regret of a detective that in all this confusion he might be missing a clue, but of a book junkie that he might be missing a bargain.

The shop doorbell rang and a voice called, "Anyone there?"

Next moment Sergeant Filmer appeared at the foot of the stairs.

"Thought you'd got lost," said Pascoe accusingly.

"Sorry, sir. But the ambulance took an age. Saw your note at the cottage. You said you'd found something there. . . ."

Pascoe gave a God-help-us glance at Wield, then said, "You finish off here, Sergeant," and clattered down the stairs.

Digweed said, "Curious how whenever one of you seems about to say something interesting, my presence becomes de trop."

"We'll be just as discreet about your little bit of bother, sir," said Wield.

"My *what?*" said Digweed with indignation. And something else?

"The break-in, sir. Better check in here while we're at it."

Without waiting for a reply he pushed open the one remaining door and peered in with surprise. It still wasn't tidy, but compared with what lay behind, it was like walking into a police box and finding yourself in a spaceship. He saw a couple of computers, a printer, a copier, a binder, and various other bits of equipment. There were piles of books here, too, but not the dusty derelicts crowding the landing and stairs. These were sparkling new; indeed some of them were still only half born.

"He didn't get in here, Sergeant," said Digweed irritatedly. "I can see everything's in order."

"Just as well. Worth a bob or two, this stuff," said Wield. "You do your own publishing as well, do you?"

"In a modest way. Now can we—"

"This is nice," said Wield, picking up a slim volume entitled *On the Banks of the Een—A Naturalist's Year*. The author was Ralph Digweed.

"A relative, sir?"

"How perceptive," said Digweed. "It was published privately in 1914. I thought it worth offering to a wider readership."

Wield's mind went back to the war memorial. There had been an R. Digweed on it, died in 1918, aged fifty-eight. Presumably it was not only the young who lied about their age. He opened the book.

March 21, 1913. Last night we celebrated the birth of the Squire's heir. The wags recalled that four years ago when we celebrated Miss Frances's arrival, the ale ran out before midnight. Strange how the Guillemards at birth value so cheap what at marriage they will declare so far beyond common purchase! But the birth of a son naturally turned the flagons of Old Hall into Widows' Cruses and the revels went on into the early hours with promise that they would be renewed in a couple of days at the Reckoning. Not for this, however, was I going to neglect my custom these many years of welcoming the first day of spring by Scarletts Pool, so I sat in the parlor, chuckling over little Edwin's present of The Card **till dawn pinked the sky, when I made my way down to the river.**

Wield looked up to find Digweed watching him closely.

"Sorry," he said. "Got carried away. Real interesting. This Edwin . . ."

"No," said the bookseller. "Despite my foxed and faded cover I am not little Edwin."

"Didn't think you were," said Wield. "Your father, right? And Ralph was your grandfather? I were looking at the war memorial earlier. . . ."

"Yes. The war. Ironically, on the first day of spring five years later he was still waiting for dawn on the misty bank of a river. It was the Oise. But the only light he saw in the east was the flame of the German guns as Ludendorff's army began their last big push which almost won them the war. An hour later he was dead. That copy of *The Card* he mentions was in his effects which were returned home. Later I inherited it in turn. It was my first valuable first edition. In a sense it set me off on the path which brought me here, so perhaps the Great War wasn't a total waste after all."

He spoke in his usual dry, faintly mocking tone, but Wield had no difficulty in detecting the current of pain and anger beneath, nor in sympathizing with it as he thought of that other Digweed letting his mind wander to the peace of Enscombe and the clear waters of the Een as he stood in a cold, dank trench, waiting for his death.

But sympathy was a dangerous dish to offer the bookseller. His eye caught a pile of unbound title pages bearing a striking design of a woman stepping through an archway entwined with flowers and the words *The Journal of Frances Guillemard Harding: A Selection.*

His mind made connections.

"This Frances he talks about . . ." he said, holding up the *Naturalist's Year.*

"The same. Our Squire Selwyn's big sister."

"And what relation is she of that little lass up at the Hall?"

"Ah, you've met young Fran? Her grandmother, who married the local vicar back in the thirties."

"That's why she's coming out of Green Alley into the churchyard, is it?"

Digweed's eyebrows shot up.

"You recognize the arch? Well spotted. They may make a detective of you yet."

"It doesn't have any flowers around it, but," said Wield.

"The flowers are dear Caddy's version of the pathetic fallacy, and a peculiarly apt conceit, I would say. By her own account the day Frances swapped the Hall for the vicarage was the day she started to bloom. Not that her family saw it like that, of course. Thus time brings in his revenges."

Wield said, "You say Caddy, the Scudamore lass, did this?"

"That's right."

"But the illustrations in your granddad's book are his own."

"Indeed. He was a competent amateur—a talent which, regretfully, has not descended to me. Caddy is something very different. She has a truly formidable talent and is always eager to try her hand at something new. She's produced some fascinating sketches to go in Lillingstone's parish history when it's completed."

Digweed was sorting through a pile of drawings as he spoke, then it seemed to occur to him that such enthusiasm was not something he wanted to share with a mere policeman and he suddenly thrust them out of sight saying, "But how boring you must find all this, Sergeant. You must be dying to rejoin your colleagues and catch up on all their new clues."

"Yes, sir. Can't wait, sir."

Digweed gave him a sharp glance, then smiled and said, "It's no use reverting to your PC Plod mode, Mr. Wield. I am no longer deceived. I can see your Mr. Pascoe thinks highly of you and he does not strike me as a man to suffer fools gladly."

"Because he can spot a quote?" ventured Wield.

"*Quotation*, I assume you mean? Yes, that was . . . revealing. Incidentally, does he have a wife? I seem to recall the name from somewhere. A Ms., rather than a Mrs., Eleanor Pascoe, was it?"

"Ellie. If you'd met her, you'd not forget her," said Wield with the fervor of an acolyte.

"Then I haven't met her, unless it was on my catalog mailing list. Perhaps I can add your name, Sergeant?"

"My shelves are pretty full," said Wield. "But I'd like to buy one of these if I may."

He held up the *Naturalist's Year*.

"Really?" Digweed almost looked pleased. "I'll be putting the dust jackets on them later. I daresay you'll be around for some little time?"

"I daresay. Don't I get it for less without the jacket?" said Wield.

"What? Ah, a joke! No, that's only old books, Sergeant. Don't worry. If there's a rush, I'll save one for you."

He ushered Wield out of the room, locking the door behind him. Downstairs they found Pascoe and Filmer. Neither looked pleased.

"So how's our dear postman?" asked Digweed.

"No worse than a broken nose and a cracked rib," said Filmer.

"Good. And is the Post Office sending a relief van?"

"Pointless, seeing as the shop's shut this afternoon. But it'll all go first lift tomorrow, so it won't make much difference."

"Indeed not? What's a few hours when the normal service can take days? Now, about my burglar, Mr. Pascoe . . ."

"Sergeant Filmer will take care of it. This is his patch," said Pascoe rather acidly. "Looks to me like whoever it was got scared, grabbed what he could, and ran."

"That's it? Oh, good. Another case solved. Well, I'll go and repair the window so that no one will even notice there's been a crime, and that way we'll all be happy, won't we?"

He went into the rear room, banging the door.

"Is he always like that?" wondered Pascoe.

"Bark's worse than his bite," said Filmer defensively. "He's well liked by the locals. It's just a question of knowing what's what."

"Indeed," said Pascoe. "Perhaps from time to time you might care to share these arcana with me. For now you'd better hurry in there to make sure you've completed your observations before Mr. Digweed starts his repairs. And once you've finished here, you might care to head back to Church Cottage to make sure there's nothing else you've missed."

He made for the door.

And Wield, pausing only to murmur, "He's well liked by the locals," followed.

Eleven

*I suppose you see the corpse? How
does it appear?*

Outside, he found Pascoe breathing deep of Enscombe's fresh spring air and the fragrant baking smells from the Wayside Café.

Hope and his digestive juices rose, making his stomach rumble.

"Bit hard on old Terry, weren't you?" he said conversationally.

"All he had to do was say, 'Whoops, sorry, I didn't think of looking for uniforms in the bottom of the wardrobe.' Instead he went stroppy on me."

Wield smiled. He knew a lot of people who'd found out the hard way that Pascoe's mild manner was not an invitation to take liberties. You didn't survive long in Andy Dalziel's chocolate box if you had a soft center.

He said, "Thirsty work, being in a bad temper, but."

Instead of taking the hint Pascoe was staring across the street.

"Are my flies open, Wieldy?" he asked. "There's a young woman across there can't take her eyes off me."

Wield turned. Standing at the window of the Eendale Gallery was Caddy Scudamore. Seeing that she had his attention she raised her hand and waved. Or was she beckoning? He looked away.

"Dammit, it's you she's after, Wieldy," said Pascoe with mock regret. "Friend of yours?"

"That's Caddy Scudamore," said Wield. "She's a painter. Any chance of a cup of tea and a bite to eat? I'm clemmed."

"Later, I promise," said Pascoe. "Didn't your mother ever tell you it was rude to keep a lady waiting?"

And with many a longing backward glance Wield let himself be led across the street and into the gallery, where Caddy Scudamore was waiting with undisguised impatience.

Close up, Pascoe's first thought was What a marvel it is that a small place like Enscombe should be so full of extremely attractive women. And his second was What a shame it is that none of them seems the least bit interested in me!

Caddy Scudamore had seized Wield's sleeve and was pulling him through an inner doorway leading to a flight of stairs.

"Can you spare just a moment, please," she said. "It's the coloring and shadows. They just don't come out right on film. Honestly, it won't take a minute."

Pascoe was interested to observe that being gay didn't seem to make it any easier to resist being dragged upstairs by a gorgeous girl.

He followed uninvited and stopped in the studio doorway to cope with a triple surprise.

First there was the studio's size, much bigger than he'd expected and full of light. Second there was the chaos. The floor was littered with discarded sketches, half-finished paintings, jars full of brushes, hi-tech equipment, rainbow-colored palettes, newspapers, books, mugs, plates . . . he'd seen rooms left tidier by a bunch of vandalizing burglars!

And third, dragging his attention from the surrounding chaos, there was the huge crucifixion scene.

Caddy had guided Wield across the floor with surefooted ease and stood him by an easel. With one hand she explored his features while the other transferred lines and shapes onto a sheet of paper. Wield showed no emotion, but the sight of those paint-stained fingers pushing themselves against his tight-closed lips gave Pascoe a voyeuristic charge.

He dragged his eyes away, tiptoed across the room, and examined the crucifixion more closely.

The Enscombe background teemed with three-dimensional life. Not only was every inch of canvas crowded but much had been painted over, not so much to obliterate it as to relegate it to a kind of misty otherworld where it still continued to exert its existence, even its simultaneity. Beneath trees heavy with both blossom and fruit lay an Adam and Eve couple, their faces pressed too close for identification. But Digweed was recognizable, slinking furtively down the High Street clutching what looked like a pile of drawings rather than books. Outside the Hall a column of smoke veiled but did not conceal Girlie Guillemard. The inn sign outside the Morris had a tiny but identifiable sketch of Justin Halavant clutching his crotch, and everywhere there were bushes and shadows which concealed or even grew into the slim but menacing figure of Jason Toke.

He shook his head to clear away these disturbing images and glanced at his watch. *Ars longa* but enough was enough.

"Time to be on our way, Sergeant," he said sternly.

She was onto colors now, using fingers as much as brushes, the paint staining her hair as she pushed it back from her brow to stare with fierce concentration at Wield's face.

"It's like granite," she said. "You'd think nothing but grays at a glance, then you get closer and suddenly there's the whole spectrum . . . and such textures too. . . ."

Granite was right, thought Pascoe. Wield looked completely petrified. Then from below came the sound of a door slamming and Kee Scudamore's voice raised in anger.

"What do you think you're doing there? Caddy, where the hell are you?"

The spell was broken. Wield and Pascoe set off simultaneously for the door, but Caddy, whose feet clearly had a built-in memory of the studio's minefield, was down the stairs ahead of them.

"There you are," said her sister. "How many times have I told you not to leave the till unattended?"

"I'm not here to steal," protested the figure standing on the wrong side of the till counter.

It was Jason Toke, at once furtive and defiant. He was carrying two bags, one the bloodstained gunny, the other a plastic carrier.

"What *are* you here for?" enquired Pascoe gently.

"Brought something for Caddy," said the boy, regarding Pascoe uneasily.

Definitely not Bendish's head, decided Pascoe. Another dead rabbit, perhaps? The carrier looked as if it held something fairly heavy, but too square for a dead animal. Suddenly Toke plunged his hand into the gunny and brought out a bird. Even Pascoe, who was no ornithologist, knew at once what it was. Or had been. A kingfisher. Death had not dulled the brilliant blue of its wings, which shone with such intensity, it seemed they might still beat the air and send the dangling creature arrowing from Toke's careless grasp.

"Said you wanted to see old kingy," said the youth, proffering the corpse to Caddy. "For the colors. That's what you said."

"Oh, Jase," whispered the girl. "But not dead."

"Colors is the same," protested Toke. Some impression of the shock felt by all those in the room seemed to have got through. He tossed the corpse onto the desk. It fell so they could see the hole in its breast.

"Colors is the same," he repeated. "And it's a sight easier to paint, I'd say. You see him move, too fast to photo let alone paint. Any road, couldn't just leave him lie. You take him if you want. No use grieving over what's done. That's no way to survive. Take and make, that's the way. Take and make."

This spate of words took them all by surprise. Then he turned with that deceptive speed Pascoe had noticed before and was through the door before anyone could try to hinder him.

"Something needs to be done," said Kee, looking at the dead bird. "This is going too far."

"It's my fault," said Caddy in a low voice. "I never meant . . ."

"You can't blame yourself, darling," said her sister, putting her arm around the younger woman's shoulders. "Could one of you please dispose of this thing?"

Wield reached to pick up the dead bird.

Caddy said, "Oh, can't I keep it? Those colors are incredible. . . . I know that killing it was wrong. . . ."

Wield said, "More than wrong. Illegal. Protection of Birds Act."

Pascoe nodded vigorously, delighted at this confirmation of the avian expertise he'd ascribed to the sergeant on his first encounter with Toke's dead birds.

"Yes, and we'll need the corpse as evidence," he said. "Young Toke's got some answering to do."

"Make sure you ask the right questions," said Kee.

"I've heard about the war memorial," said Pascoe, regarding her curiously. "But Sergeant Wield here got the impression you didn't think there was too much to worry about. Have you changed your mind?"

She looked uneasily at her sister, who was still regarding the dead bird greedily, and said, "I think he's ticking, Mr. Pascoe. I don't know whether he's a bomb, a clock, or a death-watch beetle. But I think perhaps someone should find out, don't you?"

It was, strictly speaking, another job for Filmer. There couldn't be any connection with the missing constable. Could there?

"You'd better tell us where he lives," he said.

"Intake Cottage, it's set well back from the road just beyond the Morris. They rent it from the Hall estate, but Jason looks after the upkeep himself."

"They?" said Wield.

"He lives with Elsie, his mother."

"And what do you mean, he looks after the upkeep?" asked Pascoe, sensing an overemphasis.

Kee half smiled and said, "Why spoil a surprise? You can see that for yourselves!"

A few minutes later Pascoe and Wield were seeing for themselves. It was certainly a surprise.

For a start, Intake Cottage had a dilapidated look at odds with the well-tended appearance of most of Enscombe. Once painted white, its now graying walls were streaked with water and mud from the leaky gutters, giving the building the air of a leprous zebra which had limped away from the herd to die. The roof, with several slates askew and a couple missing, was the breeding ground for some interesting lichens which looked as if they might have crawled up there to escape the Great War battlefield beneath. Once it might have been a prototypical cottage garden, all hollyhocks and delphiniums, goldenrod and old moss roses, but someone had gone to work with chainsaw and strimmer, razing all vegetation within a radius of twenty feet of the house.

"What's this got to do with the hunt for Bendish?" wondered Pascoe, holding up the dead kingfisher in a plastic evidence bag.

"Search me," said Wield sulkily. "If we'd gone into the caff, we'd never have seen it."

"It's our next port of call, I promise," said Pascoe. "But look at it this way, if you hadn't gone when Caddy called, she might have sent Jason looking for you too!"

When they walked up the weed-crazed path to the door, they were faced with another oddity. It wasn't the decaying mouse-gnawed raft of planks which might have been expected in such a dilapidated structure, but a solid aluminum slab with two mortise locks and a security peephole. As Pascoe waited for a reply to his knock, he observed that the windows, too, were metal framed and double glazed. Interesting priorities.

The peephole darkened as an inward eye checked him out, then the door opened on a chain and both eyes, screwed up myopically against the light, peered out at about third rib level.

"Yes?" said a voice, soft as moleskin.

"Mrs. Elsie Toke?"

"Yes?"

"Is Jason in, Mrs. Toke?"

"No."

The door began to close.

"Mrs. Toke, hold on," said Pascoe, hastily holding his ID up to the crack and introducing himself. "Can we come in a moment?"

The door closed. There was a long moment when it looked as if it might stay that way, then it swung silently open.

"Come in," said Mrs. Toke.

She was a tiny woman who must have needed to stretch on tiptoe to get her eye up to the peephole, but for some reason her size was less remarkable than it might have been. Pascoe found himself thinking the odd thought that you did not expect an elf to be large, and there was certainly something elfin about her. Faces like this had peered out through ferns in his infant storybooks, anxious and curious and above all otherworldly. She stood still as he passed by her into the low-beamed living room, yet she gave an impression of constant movement, like a wood sorrel in a spring breeze.

"He is a good boy," she said, "though he finds it hard to understand the world."

Pascoe sat down in a soft and pleasantly body-embracing armchair. If she was going to telepath his questions, he might as well telepath her offer of hospitality.

Mrs. Toke was regarding him with a gaze which seemed to rely as much on sound as light.

He said, "There are things which *have* to be understood, Mrs. Toke. Like the law, for instance."

He held up the kingfisher in the plastic evidence bag.

She leaned forward to look close and said, "Oh, the lovely thing."

"Lovely indeed. And protected," said Pascoe.

"And you think my Jason killed it?" she said. "You're wrong. He'd not do that. Not to old kingy."

She spoke with absolute conviction, but Pascoe was unimpressed. In

his experience ninety-nine out of a hundred mothers confronted by a
video of their offspring robbing a bank or ramraiding a warehouse or
even just jumping a red light would say, "No, not my Tom or Dick or
Clint. He'd never do a thing like that." He was looking forward to
meeting the hundredth who'd say, "Yes, that's the little toe-rag. Why
don't you bang him up forever?"

"But he does shoot birds, doesn't he?" he said.

"Oh, yes. For the pot. Only for the pot. What reason would he have
to shoot old kingy?"

Best reason in the world, thought Pascoe. Love, sweet love.

He said, "Could we take a look at Jason's room while we're here?"

It would be interesting to see if it did contain the secret arsenal Kee
Scudamore suspected.

"No," said the woman.

Pascoe was only slightly surprised by the finality of her tone. She
didn't look the type to make a fuss about legal rights and search
warrants, but these days the telly made everyone a barracks-room
lawyer.

He said, "Not to worry. I'm sure Jason will be back soon. Mr. Toke,
Jason's father, is he still . . . here?"

He glanced significantly at Wield as he spoke.

"All right if I use your lavvy?" said the sergeant, rising.

"First left up the stairs," said Mrs. Toke. "Jason's room is next one
along."

So even the little people knew the interesting ways of coppers,
thought Pascoe, amused.

"You were asking about Toke," continued the woman. "Dead these
ten years. Police killed him."

"What?"

"Chasing a stolen car, they said. Knocked him off his bike. He were
out looking for work. Used to be a keeper up at Old Hall but got laid
off when they started cutting back. Crowner said it were an accident,
no one to blame."

"I'm sorry," said Pascoe helplessly.

"Not your fault. And he's happier now. Find it all right?"

Wield had reappeared in the doorway.

He said, "Yes, thanks. Got a moment, sir?"

Pascoe moved quickly before the woman could complain. The stairs
were dark, narrow, and creaky, the landing the same. But some things
had changed in the last hundred years. One of them was the door next to

the bathroom. It was the same breed as the main entrance, tight fitting, metallic, with a peephole but no keyhole, just an electronic number pad.

"Without the code you'd need a bazooka to get in there," said Wield.

"Perhaps bazookas are what he keeps in there," said Pascoe.

"Something else odd," said Wield. "Outside, this place looks semi-derelict. Inside, but, it's right cumfy. Not fancy but everything well tended and spick and span."

Pascoe had registered this, but not registered that it might be significant.

He said, "So?"

"So it's good to keep people out," said Wield, rapping on the solid metal door. "But it's best if you don't have them wanting to get in in the first place."

Pascoe pondered this as he returned to the living room, where the woman was sitting with the evidence bag in her hand.

He said, "I see why you said no when I asked if I could see Jason's room. You meant you couldn't open it. Doesn't that bother you, Mrs. Toke? Doesn't it make you wonder what he's got in there?"

"I know what's in there," she said, mildly puzzled. "And of course I can open it. No point otherwise."

"Point?"

"Having a secure room if I can't make myself secure in it too. Jason can't be home all the time."

She was losing him but not Wield, who said, "Being secure matters a lot to Jason, does it? That's why he won't bother with the outside of the cottage?"

"He says that when they come they'll go for the rich-looking places first."

Pascoe was beginning to think that Kee Scudamore was if anything an optimist.

He said, "Doesn't it bother you, Mrs. Toke? I mean, you must know there's no one coming."

"Must I?" she said, smiling a sad, fey smile. "May not happen what Jason thinks, but there's something coming the likes of which Enscombe's never seen before. I can smell it."

"And what's it smell like, missus?" asked Wield.

"Blood," said the woman. "It smells like blood."

End of Volume 2

Volume the Third

June 13, 1886. Edwina has asked me to paint her portrait. I told her I doubted if my poor skills were up to the subject, meaning I could not, as she desires, hope to produce anything which could stand comparison with that ancestral portrait from the last age which, if I am not mistaken, shows the hand of a true master. She, however, took this as a compliment to herself, the kind of compliment which to tell truth I have long been tempted to give, but have always lacked courage. Now she blushed, and looked modestly down, then looked up again straightaway, with such bright eyes and so pleasing a smile that I could not but hope perhaps she nursed for me something of the deep feeling I have long felt for her. So I have been bold by accident!

When I told Jeremy of this, he laughed and said I was a booby and it is my shy diffidence which has forced Edwina into this subterfuge to throw us together! I can hardly believe this, but he assures me that in these matters, particularly where there is a difference of fortune, young ladies of the most unquestionable modesty are permitted by instinct and custom to drop an encouraging hint. So I have agreed to do the painting unless, as seems likely, her parents forbid it.

June 15. Her father, it seems, offers no objection! When I marveled at this, Jeremy replied a trifle sardonically that the Squire would see no objection to indulging Edwina in this silly whim of wanting her portrait done so long as he didn't have to pay a real artist, and in addition he could not imagine one so self-effacing and deferential as myself would ever dare aspire to his daughter's hand.

This was a mixed comfort to me! And I still have grave doubts as to my ability to perform the task as I would like. Edwina has sent the other portrait from the Hall to my studio so that I might better imitate the style and my heart sinks as I study it. I could see that Jeremy, too, had misgivings when he saw the painting for the first time, saying he had not thought it would be of so high a standard. But he has made a suggestion which may lessen the comparison that if both the portraits are set in matching frames, this outward similarity may divert the uncritical eye from the differences of artistic quality! Edwina offers no objection, and Jeremy has undertaken to use his connections to find a fine framer, though I have not mentioned his name to Edwina. Not that she would object, but her father still flies into a fury at the name of Halavant!

July 2. The portrait is finished! To tell the truth it might have been finished a good week or more earlier had I not been so reluctant to lose this excuse for being so often in my love's sweet company. For now at last I have the right to call her my love. This forenoon prompted by her own expression of regret that soon my task would be over, I made my declaration and she almost fell into my arms. I am the happiest of men. But this confirmed that these sittings must cease, for while love unspoken must take what chance it can get of proximity, once a man has declared and been accepted, it would be un-gentlemanly to continue in a situation which takes advantage of her parents' ignorance. Therefore the portraits have been given to Jeremy for dispatch to the framers, and Edwina and I have agreed that I shall use the occasion of their delivery to the Hall to seek the necessary interview with her father.

I find that I am more pleased with my own painting than I had hoped. Though it is far beneath the transcendent quality of the older portrait, and though I cannot come close to catching the perfection of my loved one's inward beauty, yet I think that what true love and deep devotion can do has been done, and if this shows through, then I need not feel ashamed to see my effort hung alongside the other.

July 30. Four weeks since the pictures went to be framed. I have never known time to pass so slowly! But Jeremy says that such work as these deserve may only be obtained in London. And he added, with a kind of sad knowingness, that perhaps I would not thank him for hurrying the framer, for now, though I do not yet possess my love, I may at least continue to dream of her possession. I suspect he fears that my suit will be rejected by the Squire. Yet why so? I am not rich, it is true. But my family have been gentlemen as long as the Guillemards, and Yorkshire-men a lot longer!

August 4. *It is over. The pictures are hung, and so might as well I be. Jeremy was right beyond my worse fears. There was no raging rejection, just a terrible coldness. "It will not do," said the Squire. And I was shown the door, all so smooth and swift that I found myself walking down the drive with scarce any awareness of how I got there. And Edwina, I learn, is sent away to some old connection of the family in Wales.*

Jeremy has urged me to pursue her and persuade her to come away with me. Would she agree? I think she might. But what right have I to tempt her to a course which will separate her from her family, probably forever? As Jeremy well knows, the Guillemards do not easily forgive. Nor are my own prospects so sure that I can, unaided, offer her anything but deprivation and hardship. Jeremy has offered to loan me money but I cannot take it. I will, however, accept his invitation to join him on the tour he proposes through Italy to Asia Minor as his aide-de-camp and secretary. I would go to the wastes of Lapland rather than remain in reach of such sights as rend my heart with sad remembrance here in my beloved Enscombe.

One

What is your opinion?—I say
nothing & am ready to agree with
anybody.

"**B**lood," said the woman. "Human. Group O. Recent. And enough of it to suggest a good-sized wound."

"Shit," said Andrew Dalziel.

"Just blood," said the woman.

Dalziel looked at the phone and wondered if the creature behind this cool, detached, scientific voice was pulling his leg. He decided to give her the benefit of the doubt.

"Sorry, luv," he said. "It's just that Bendish's group is O."

"A peculiarity he shares with forty-six percent of the population," she said.

"Aye," he said. "Owt else?"

"Perhaps."

"What's that mean? Didn't think you lot did perhapses."

"It means, perhaps there is something else," she said. "Our tests continue. Will continue. Soon as I get off this phone."

"Well, don't let me keep you," grunted Dalziel.

He heard the phone at the other end being gently replaced, but he held on to his own. Desperate Dan could be back from lunch now and already dialing Dalziel's number to ask for an update on the missing plowboy. Normally Dan Trimble was a cautious man, fully aware that the path to whatever dizzy constabulary heights he still hoped to scale was littered with the bones of men who'd tried to take it at a rush. But after lunch, with the last brandy still hot in his gob and the news from Forensic hot in his ears, he might be tempted to do something daft, like contradict his head of CID.

Leaving the phone dangling over the edge of his desk, Dalziel headed for the car park.

An hour later, as he drove into Enscombe, his car slowed like an old milk horse as it passed the Morris Men's Rest. Nobly Dalziel resisted the temptation. He wanted to talk to Pascoe and Wield before he set that dedicated rumor-monger Thomas Wapshare's tongue wagging even more rapidly than it probably was already.

And there they were, ahead of him, getting out of Pascoe's car and heading into the Wayside Café.

He gave a blast on his horn and wound down his window as he came to a halt.

"Look who's here," he said. "The Lone Ranger and Tonto! Why don't you hop inside and tell me what wrongs you've been righting today?"

Dora Creed appeared in the doorway, attracted by the blast or the bellow. Wield, assailed by the Tantulean smells thus released, hesitated and Dalziel called, "Sorry, missus, but these lads have got more important things on their mind than grub."

Dora Creed said, " 'Whether therefore ye eat or drink, or whatsoever ye do, do all to the glory of God.' "

"Don't fret yourself, lass," said Dalziel. "I'll keep them on the straight and narrow."

Once in the car, Wield put all thought of food out of his mind as he and Pascoe related their adventures. Dalziel gave no prizes for details remembered later.

When they'd finished Dalziel said, "So what's your verdict? Should we be worried or is it all a waste of time caused by yon dopey ha'porth Filmer not knowing better than to bother his lads on their day off?"

"There are certain oddities," said Pascoe slowly. "But whether they add up to a cause for real alarm I'm not sure."

"That's a don't-know from the Lone Ranger," said Dalziel. "What says Tonto?"

Wield said, "It's a funny place, Enscombe."

"And that's it? I'd have been better off asking Silver!" said Dalziel in disgust.

This provoked Pascoe into retorting, "There's certainly one very real cause for concern, sir. You're here!"

"I'm not sure how to take that, lad," said Dalziel.

"I mean, something must have come up. From Bendish's car, is it?"

"Who's a clever bugger, then?" said Dalziel. "But you're right. The stain in the car is blood and it's recent and it's the same group as Bendish. Still means nowt. I can think of half a dozen explanations, none of which involves thuggery, buggery, or skullduggery. But it does mean we need to be certain from the start we're missing nowt. So let's go back to the beginning, which seems to mean Old Hall. This old sod who saw someone knock Bendish down lives up there, right? And it was there you met him prancing around baht 'at, right? And it was there the Squire spotted him flashing, right?"

"Right," said Pascoe. "But we've been there and asked the questions—"

"Oh, aye? All on 'em? Like, was he erect?"

"Sorry?"

"Bendish, on the garden wall. Did he have a hard-on, or was he just trying to pick up an all-over tan?"

"I didn't ask," admitted Pascoe. "Though the Squire did seem to think he was very well endowed."

"Then we'd best find out. One thing we shouldn't forget is we're in foreign parts here, where likely they play tiggy with hammers and dole out justice with a pruning hook. Looked at from a tabloid viewpoint, what we've got here is a missing cop who's a flasher, chases around after kids, and did something once that he got duffed up for but didn't dare fight back. So let's get up to Old Hall and see if we can't get this lot sorted!"

When they reached the Hall they found the main door open and the sound of angry voices coming from within. Dalziel led them inside with the eagerness of a sports fan who has arrived after the kickoff. There they discovered Guy and Girlie Guillemard, their recent truce annihilated, having a high-class row.

"I want it back, Guy," the woman was yelling. "You had no right to take it. I want it back or I'll treat you like any other thief!"

"Who the hell do you think you're talking to?" demanded Guy. "Perhaps you need reminding—"

"That one day all this will be yours?" she interrupted mockingly.

"Well, till it is perhaps you should remember that while the Squire's alive, I'm the factor here, which means I call the shots and you grin and bear it!"

Like a Wimbledon audience the three policemen turned their eyes to the man and awaited his riposte. But Guy, who at least had the wit to know when he was outmatched, was looking for an easier opponent to vent his wrath on.

"What the fuck do you want?" he screamed.

For a second Wield thought the question was aimed over the man's shoulder at them, till he realized Guy's gaze was directed upward to the minstrels' gallery, over which leaned George Creed.

"Brought a ham for the Reckoning," said Creed equably. "Office were empty, so I've been wandering around looking for someone."

"In future you bloody well wait outside till you're asked in," snarled Guy. "Not that you're worth asking in, the rent you pay. It wouldn't keep me on condoms. When did it last go up?"

"That's for you to know and us to guess," said Creed, grinning broadly.

"George's rent is estate business," said Girlie. "Which isn't yet yours, Guy."

"Oh, but it will be," he said evilly. "You'd better both believe that."

He strode toward the door, spotting the detective trio for the first time.

"Christ, it's the Keystone Kops. Step inside, gents. It's Liberty Hall. For the time being!"

He pushed by them, or at least shouldered Pascoe and Wield aside, but bounced off Dalziel, who watched him go with the calm indifference of a grizzly to a gnat.

"Gentlemen, how can I help you?" asked Girlie, relighting her pipe.

Pascoe said, "This is Superintendent Dalziel, Miss Guillemard."

Dalziel said, "How do, missus. Any chance of a word with your granddad?"

"What for?" she asked, puffing a jet of smoke in his face.

Pascoe waited expectantly. The presence of the queen mother herself wouldn't inhibit Dalziel from introducing the topic of Bendish's putative erection if he felt like it.

He didn't. Sucking in her smoke like an extinguished dragon, he said, "Just wanted to ask permission to take a look around the policies."

"The grounds, you mean? Be my guest."

"That'll be all right, will it?" said Dalziel with a frown. "I mean, you've got authority . . . ?"

But she was not for winding up.

She said, "The way you lot pussyfoot around the laws of trespass, anyone's got authority. But if you'd like a chitty, I'll be happy to sign one."

Creed appeared in the room, carrying a leg of ham. He nodded recognition of Wield, who said, "Things quietened down in the lambing shed, have they?"

"Not so's you'd notice, but when t'Quality snaps its fingers, what choice has a poor farmer got but to come running?"

He spoke in a bantering tone, which seemed to amuse rather than irritate Girlie.

"George," she said, "if you'd like to fetch that ham to the kitchen. Gentlemen, I'm sure I'll see you later."

Dalziel watched them go thoughtfully, then slapped his hands together and said, "Right, where's this walled garden, then?"

Pascoe led the way around the side of the house, pointing out the conservatory en route.

"So it was from here the Squire saw Dirty Harry flashing the family jewels."

"So he claims. But like a lot of folk around here, he seems to inhabit more than one world at the same time," said Pascoe.

"He were sure enough to write to Tommy Winter about it," said Dalziel. "Where's the door?"

"Around the side, but you can't get in. They lost the key when old Mr. Hogbin had his stroke."

"Oh, aye? Let's take a look anyway."

When they reached the door Dalziel tried the handle, shaking it vigorously to confirm it was locked.

"Want me to climb over, sir?" asked Wield, confident in his multi-gym agility.

"No need for that, Tarzan," said Dalziel, taking from his pocket what looked like a fountain pen but unscrewed to reveal a bouquet of instruments like old-fashioned buttonhooks.

Pascoe, who had seen it before, groaned and looked away, as he still averted his eyes from the television screen when something particularly unpleasant or embarrassing seemed imminent.

When he looked back the door was open.

"Right. In we go," said the Fat Man.

This was not, Pascoe realized, the secret garden of the old children's story, with shrubs and flowers allowed to rampage into weedy ruin. This was a garden which earned its keep, with bean rows and asparagus beds, cold frames and compost pits. Not that there was any lack of color. The inner walls were lined with fruit trees all in various stages and hues of blossom, while over the narrow gravel paths red and black currant bushes draped their flowered festoons. Nor did it have a much neglected air. There was work to be done, certainly, but it's an indefatigable worker whose garden doesn't have a slightly unkempt look after a long, damp winter. To Pascoe's not very expert eye it looked as if someone had been keeping things ticking over, which—considering that the key had been allegedly lost since last autumn—was yet another probably meaningless oddity to add to the rest.

Dalziel was moving purposefully toward a long lean-to shed built against the southernmost wall, presumably because here it stole least sunlight. Warmth was of the essence in this moorland setting, which was why the walled garden had been built in the first place. Pascoe had felt a distinct rise in temperature as soon as he stepped inside and when he touched the mortar holding the big granite slabs together, he found it held the albeit slight heat from this still dispassionate vernal sun.

The shed was locked, this time with a padlocked bolt. Dalziel seemed merely to glower at it and the door flew open.

"Sergeants first," said the Fat Man, stepping aside. "Just in case there's a mad axman lurking."

Wield would have liked to be convinced this was a joke. He slowly advanced, blinking as he adjusted to the limited light seeping through the single-paned window, which weather on the outside and spiders on the in had rendered almost opaque.

His foot hit something loose and metallic, and he stooped to look closer. "Bloody hell," he said.

"What?"

Wield turned to the opening.

"Half right, sir," he said to Dalziel. "All we want is the man."

In his hands he held a small ax.

Now the other two followed. Dalziel produced another pseudo fountain pen from his inner pocket. This one turned out to be a flashlight. Bet he's got everything an old-fashioned cop needs in there, thought Pascoe. From a corkscrew to a cattle prod.

But he was glad of the thin beam of light which the Fat Man sent slicing through the shadows.

It was basically a store shed containing most gardening implements both ancient and modern, ranging from graip and dibber to chainsaw and strimmer. There was a musty, peaty, earthy smell distantly and not too pungently underpinned by something vaguely stercoraceous. A double row of shelves bowed under the weight of various tins and bottles containing stuff to kill and stuff to quicken.

"Here, sir," said Wield.

He was standing at the point farthest from the door looking down at a tweedy traveling rug which had been laid over three or four bags of peat and commercial compost to form a rough bed with the imprint of a human figure still visible in it.

Dalziel squatted down with an ease surprising in a man of his shape and let the flashlight beam move slowly across the rug. The light brought out all its rich colors—and brought out, too, some darker flecks and several quite large stains.

"Blood?" said Pascoe.

"Could be," said Dalziel. "One way to find out."

He produced a pair of scissors and a plastic bag from his portmanteau pocket and snipped a small area of stained fibers from the rug.

"Why not take the whole thing?" wondered Pascoe.

"Because this is the nearest we've got to a scene of the crime so far," said Dalziel. "Not very near, if you ask me, but scenes of crime are like bathrooms, lad. Always leave 'em the way you'd like Forensic to find 'em, did no one ever tell you that?"

Pascoe, who had seen Dalziel leave a scene-of-the-crime like a rose garden invaded by a billy goat, and heard him opine that Forensic couldn't find turds in a cesspit, held his peace.

Wield said, "So you don't reckon there's much chance this has got owt to do with Bendish, sir?"

"Didn't say that," said Dalziel. "But ask yourself: you've met some odd buggers around here by the sound of it, but are any on 'em really odd enough to assault a police officer and keep him locked in a garden shed?"

He paused expectantly, awaiting his answer. And answer there came, but not from Wield.

The shed door was suddenly slammed with great force. They heard the hasp being rammed home. And before they could move or even utter their outrage, the grimy windowpane was shattered, admitting a flood of dazzling daylight, the barrel of a shotgun and the somewhat paradoxical series of commands, "Now listen in, you blighters, down on the ground, hands in the air, and don't move a finger or I'll blow your heads off!"

Two

*I feel happy in having a friend to
save me from the ill effect of such a
blunder.*

Their rescue came almost as quickly as the attack, which
was perhaps just as well for the future of civilization as
Pascoe knew it, or at least that part represented by Squire
Guillemard.

Dalziel had fallen sideways as if in obedience to the first
clause of the paralogical command, but once out of sight of
the person at the window he bounced up silently and mur-
derously with the wood ax in his hand, clearly intent on
severing the gun barrel from its stock, and as much of its
owner's arms from his torso as he could manage.

After that Pascoe did not doubt but that the Fat Man
would have run through the wooden wall of the shed to
complete the amputative process.

As it was, a sharply upraised female voice crying,
"Grunk! What are you doing?" was followed by the immediate withdrawal of the gun and the almost simultaneous
opening of the door.

Pascoe, recognizing the voice, was the first to step cautiously into the sunlight. A few feet away he saw Frances
Harding with one restraining arm around Selwyn
Guillemard's waist and the other forcing the shotgun barrel
downward.

The weapon jerked spasmodically as Dalziel emerged and
it took all the girl's strength to maintain it at a safe angle. On
the whole Pascoe found his sympathies with Selwyn here,

for the sight of Dalziel furioso, or perhaps more precisely furiosant, for there was certainly more of the mad bull than the enraged hero in his looks, was enough to set a conchie reaching for his rifle.

"You!" he snarled, striding toward the old man. "Put that gun on the ground, else I'll chop it in half!"

"Steady on," protested the Squire. "It's a Purdey."

"I don't care if it's Prince Philip's prick, put it down in one piece, else I'll put it down in two."

Perhaps feeling that one capable of such lèse-majesté was not going to show much respect for the person of a mere country squire, the old man carefully laid the weapon on the grass.

Dalziel hurled the ax between Guillemard's feet with a force that buried the head several inches into the turf, scooped up the shotgun, and broke it in a single movement.

It was unloaded.

"He wasn't going to fire it," protested Fran Harding indignantly, then rather weakened her moral position by adding, "We don't let him have any cartridges."

Pascoe decided it was time for introductions.

"Sir," he said, "this is Mr. Selwyn Guillemard, who owns Old Hall. And this is Miss Harding, his great-niece. Squire, this is Detective Superintendent Dalziel of the Mid-Yorkshire CID."

The Squire, though giving the general impression of being shorter of marbles than the Parthenon, had no difficulty in taking this in.

"Oh, Lord. Bobbies," he said. "Met you before, haven't I?"

"Yes, sir," said Pascoe. "I called earlier."

"Yes. Thought you looked a bit familiar when I saw you breaking in, but after Aunt Edwina, my mind was very much on burglars. And that bleeding fellow's one of yours, too, is he?"

This seemed an unnecessarily rude way of referring to Wield until Pascoe glanced around. A sliver of flying glass must have caught the sergeant's left earlobe, which was gushing like a punctured wineskin.

"Wieldy, you all right?" asked Pascoe anxiously.

"Fine," said Wield phlegmatically, applying an already sodden handkerchief.

"We really ought to stop that bleeding," said Frances.

"Nay, lass, a good bloodletting never harmed anyone," said Dalziel dismissively. "And he's not lost as much as 'ud make a good black pudding."

But Frances Harding was not to be overfaced.

"Will you be all right, Grunk?" she said to her great-uncle.

"Of course, my dear. You run along and stitch the fellow's ear back on. Can't have the place looking like Gethsemane."

The girl offered the Squire's arm to Pascoe, who gingerly took it. Then she went to Wield and after a brief examination of the cut urged him toward the house despite his evident reluctance.

"Trained nurse, you know," said the Squire with proprietorial pride. "And eats like a sparrow."

So. Another surprise from the passerine Miss Harding. Or perhaps not. Even when they ate like birds, poor relatives were probably expected to sing a varied repertoire for their supper.

"Now, sir," said Dalziel, whose rage had vanished like a politician's principles in the face of altered circumstances. "I'd like a quick word if I may. We'll let the other matter go, shall we? Genuine misunderstanding."

The Squire shot a glance to second slip as if in search of guidance.

"Very well," he said. "I shan't bring any charges. But you really ought to get permission before you start breaking into a fellow's property."

Pascoe watched to see if this legal one-upmanship would continue, but Dalziel was not a man to lose sight of the main object for long. A patient man, he reckoned that once you'd got what you'd come for, there'd still be a lot of time to kick the other bugger in the balls.

"Sorry about that," he said. "But you weren't about. I believe you are a chum of Tommy Winter's, sir."

"That's right. You know him, do you? Yes, I suppose you would. Run off to the West Indies with the mess funds, your chappie here was telling me."

"Was he, now," said Dalziel. "Well, we like to keep these little upsets in the family. What I wanted to talk about was this letter you wrote to Tommy. About Constable Bendish."

"He did get it, then? Good. Took his time about replying, I must say. So what are you going to do? Sweep it under the carpet, eh?"

"We take the matter very seriously, sir, believe me," said Dalziel. "So you'll understand if I ask you a few questions, just to make sure we've got the facts straight."

"Help with inquiries sort of thing, you mean? I'm with you. Fire away."

Pascoe closed his eyes and wondered how in a world full of politicians, prelates, insurance salesmen, alternative comedians, and
Dalziel, evolution had failed to come up with a closable ear.

"Right. First off, what was the weather like?"

Pascoe opened his eyes.

"Weather? Let me see. Yes, I've got it. Sunny—I recall he was
silhouetted against the sun. Had to squint a bit to make out who it
was."

"Yes, I see. Excuse me, sir, but I wonder, could you tell me what
kind of bird that is? Sorry to change the subject, but it's an interest of
mine."

Dalziel pointed upward. Pascoe strained his eyes to glimpse the
object of this hitherto unsuspected ornithological interest circling high
to the north.

The Squire said, "Buzzard. Useful Johnny for clearing up carrion.
Excellent eyesight. Like mine. That satisfy you, Dalziel?"

Stark bonkers he might be, but he was no fool, this Squire.

"Thank you, Squire," said Dalziel, inflecting the word ambiguously so that it fell between feudal address and saloon-bar familiarity.
"Warm sun, was it?"

"Hardly, man. It was the middle of winter. Sharp wind coming over
the moor, if I recall."

"What we used to call crinkle-ball weather, eh?"

"Long time since I heard that. But, yes. Only, in this case . . ."

"Yes, sir?" prompted Dalziel.

"Fellow didn't seem to be very crinkled to me. On the contrary.
Rigid above and swinging free. Lots of it too. No shortage of coupons
when he got his meat ration. Is any of this significant? I mean, are
these clues or something?"

"Could be," said Dalziel. "So what happened?"

"He jumped down out of sight."

"And what did you do, sir?"

"Me?"

"Yes, sir. Today when you saw what you thought were odd goings-
on around your walled garden, you came belting over here like the
Fifth Cavalry."

"Well, I didn't do that for three very good reasons. One, I was in the
conservatory and by the time I got me woollies on, he would probably
have been long gone. Two, even if he wasn't, what could I say? You

chaps probably go on courses which tell you how to deal with fellows flaunting their tackle, but I've led a sheltered life."

"You said there were three reasons?"

"Oh, yes. It was time for me tea. But I got to thinking about it, and I thought, It's not on, this fellow exposing himself all over the place. Could give that little girl of Hogbin's down at the lodge a nasty turn. Or even young Fran."

"I thought you said Miss Harding had trained as a nurse, sir?"

"What? Oh, yes. Take your meaning. But it's not the same when it's in the line of duty. Like a wife. Bound to get the odd glimpse but doesn't want the thing flaunted at the breakfast table. So I sat down and wrote to Winter. Thought he should know what his troops were up to."

"And you were quite right, sir," said Dalziel unctuously. "Now you just leave it to us. You said something about being worried by burglars earlier."

"Did I? Wouldn't surprise me."

"About your aunt Edwina, I think it was. She's been having bother, has she?"

The old man laughed, putting Pascoe in mind of those eerie fragmentary bugle notes Mahler was so fond of.

"Can't say what kind of bother Edwina's having, but I doubt it's from burglars. Must be nigh on sixty years since she got carried down Green Alley. It's her picture I meant."

"And it's been stolen?"

"Thought it had. Noticed the gap. Took me a bit of time to get used to not noticing it if you know what I mean, so I noticed it all the more because it's not long since I got used to noticing it wasn't there anymore. You with me?"

Is he putting us on? wondered Pascoe. If so, he was doing it too well for Dalziel to risk a confrontation.

"If you could mebbe be just a little clearer?" said the Fat Man.

The Squire said, "It's simple, really. Girlie said Fran needed a sitting room of her own. Funny ideas these women get. And I said, all right, because she was a nice child, and very hardy considering the size of her, hardly ever needed a fire lit. So Girlie gave her Frances's old room."

"Another Frances?"

"My sister. Fran's grandmother. She moved out, you know, to

marry the vicar. Took her pictures. They were her own, not the family's. Edwina had left them to her, you see. So she was entitled even though they did leave gaps."

"The gaps you got used to?"

"That's right. Till Edwina came back."

For a moment Pascoe thought they were deep in Corpse Cottage country.

"Her portrait, you mean," said Dalziel.

"That's right. That blighter Halavant . . . do you know the man? You chaps ought to take a close look at him. Peasant family, ne'er-do-wells, not two pennies to rub together, then suddenly they're rolling in the stuff. Can't have got it honestly, that stands to reason. But he acted decently here, I must say. His father, Job, had got hold of Edwina somehow and said on his deathbed she had to go back, so Halavant sent her around. No great loss to him or gain to young Fran, really. She was no oil painting, not even when she was, if you follow me."

"And this was the painting you thought was stolen?" asked Pascoe.

"Haven't I just told 'em that?" said the Squire, glancing toward second slip in exasperation. "I popped in to see Fran on my way to bed last night, only she wasn't there. And nor was Edwina. I thought, hello, you were gone when I came back—"

"Back?" said Pascoe. "From where?"

"New Zealand, of course. Thirty-two or three. Frances had gone off with the vicar by then—I thought I explained all this!"

"Ignore the lad, sir," advised Dalziel. "He's a bit slow."

"Know the type. Good NCO material, but no grasp of strategy. Where was I? Oh, yes. Edwina. I thought . . . then you came back by yourself—"

"By herself?" said Pascoe faintly.

"Yes," said the Squire as if to an idiot child. "Not with Frances."

"There was another picture? Of your sister?"

"Don't be an ass! Great-great-something Frances. Now, she was a bobby-dazzler. Probably gave Edwina the idea of having herself done. Thought a bit of nifty brushwork could make up for what nature left out. Never works. If God had wanted us perfect, we'd have all been manufactured in Japan!"

Dalziel's stomach rumbled like an underground train.

"You hungry?" said the Squire. "Pop around to the kitchen, say I said you could have some scraps."

Dalziel smiled a saurian smile.

"Kind of you, sir. Just to get this sorted first, you didn't report it to the local police by any chance, did you?"

"To young thingie with the dong? Didn't want him back up here, did I? No, I went to bed. Mentioned it to Girlie at breakfast this morning. She went off to look, came back, and said Edwina was still there where she'd always been, except when she wasn't of course. So there you are, all a dream, I expect. Can't hang around here all day talking about dreams, can I? Work to do. Get some of my best ideas on the move. Wordsworth was the same, you know, used to walk around composing."

He picked up the Purdey and, using it as a walking stick, tottered off toward the woods which lined the river.

"What do you make of that, sir?" asked Pascoe.

"Composing, he says? Looks more like decomposing to me," said Dalziel. "But nice neat little feet these Guillemard men have got, haven't they?"

Uncertain whether the reference was to prosody or cordwainery, Pascoe didn't reply.

"Not to worry," said Dalziel. "Let's go and see about these kitchen scraps, shall we?"

Three

*I daresay she was nothing but an
innocent Country Girl.*

"**I**t really needs a stitch," said Fran Harding.

"Does it? Well, it'll have to wait," said Wield.

"I could do it," the girl offered diffidently. "It's okay.
I wouldn't be using a sewing kit, I've got the proper
gear."

"Have you, now? How come?"

"After I finished my training, jobs were hard to find
where I wanted them and Girlie said, why didn't I stay on
here to look after the Squire?"

"The old gent seems like he can look after himself," said
Wield dryly.

"He's frailer than he looks, and he's got ... various
things wrong with him. He doesn't need a full-time nurse by
any means, but having one on the spot puts off the time
when he will need one, if you follow. At least that's what
Girlie said. And I said yes, because I love it here. Anyway
the point is, I've got my own medical store with everything
for emergencies. So I can put a stitch in if you like. You'd
need to see a doctor about antitetanus, though."

"That's all right. My jabs are up to date," said Wield.
"Okay, luv. Go ahead."

She led him upstairs to a small sitting room comfortably
furnished with a couple of old armchairs, a writing bureau,
and a few pictures on the walls. She left him here and went
off into an adjacent room, returning with a well-stocked

medical bag. The stitch took a few seconds to put in, hardly hurt at all, and looked a neat, efficient job.

"That's grand," said Wield. "Right professional."

"Thank you," she said, smiling with pleasure.

He smiled back and said, "I were looking at your grandma's journal before."

Her expression changed to one of such alarm, he hastily added, "No, it were more Caddy Scudamore's picture I were looking at," but that didn't seem to improve matters either.

"Sorry," he said. "I wasn't prying but I happened to notice it when I was round at Mr. Digweed's, and I know it's not out yet, but it is going to be published, isn't it?"

"What? Oh, yes. Of course. Just some extracts. It was Larry, that's the vicar, who found it when he was sorting out some old papers in the vicarage. Grandma used to live there, you know, she married Mr. Harding, and the journal must have got left behind when they went abroad. . . ."

Something—relief, perhaps, though for what?—was making her garrulous. First rule of interrogation was, if you get 'em talking, go with the flow, whatever direction it takes. This wasn't an interrogation, but the principle held.

"Abroad? Where was that?"

"Africa. That's where my mother was born."

"Africa? You mean, like missionaries? That must have been a change from Enscombe!"

"I suppose so. But they couldn't stay on here . . . well, the family didn't approve of the marriage, and in those days if there was a row between the church and the Hall, it was the vicar who went."

"When your mum were born, didn't that help mend matters?"

"If it had been a boy, it might have done, I suppose. But they didn't rate girls."

"Not unless they wanted to marry someone from the hoi polloi," said Wield. "How did the present Squire react? He must have been your gran's brother?"

"He wasn't around when it all blew up. I think he was in New Zealand or somewhere and by the time he came home, they'd gone out to Africa. His younger brother, Guy, was here, but he seems to have taken the family line."

"That 'ud be the present Guy's grandfather?"

"Yes."

"Ah," said Wield noncommittally, but not so much so that there wasn't a moment's silent sympathy between them.

"And did your gran ever get back here?" he resumed.

"No. She died in Africa. They both did."

"And your mum?"

"She was sixteen or seventeen, she wrote to tell them back here what had happened. There was no reply. The Squire, our Squire, found the letter a couple of years later when he inherited, and he wrote off straightaway, but she'd moved on by then and by the time the letter finally caught up with her, she was having too good a time in London in the sixties to pay it any heed."

"So how did you get here?" he asked.

"Mum was in her thirties when she had me. A mistake, maybe. Or maybe she wanted something a bit more permanent than anything else she'd got out of the past few years. I never knew who my father was. I'm not sure if she did. But she looked after me as best she could, which was a lot better than she looked after herself. When I was nine she knew she was dying of cancer. She wrote a letter to the Squire saying I would be arriving on such and such a train, packed my things, took me to the station, put me aboard, and kissed me good-bye. Girlie met me at the other end. By the time they traced Mum to the hospital she'd been admitted to, she was dead."

It was a moving story, and though Wield found himself stumped for a response, it certainly deserved a better one than it got, which was the eruption of Dalziel into the room saying, "Now then, take my eyes off him for a second and he's off upstairs with the prettiest lass in the house. By God, that's neat, Sergeant. Have you ever thought of an earring?"

"We've been looking for the kitchen," said Pascoe apologetically. "The Squire offered some refreshment."

"Aye, scraps from the gentry's table are a feast to us common folk," said Dalziel. "Which is Aunt Edwina, then?"

There wasn't much contest, as there was only one portrait amid a host of watercolor landscapes. It was a competent rather than striking painting of a lively rather than beautiful woman, in a handsome oval frame, and signed with the initials *R.D.* at one side.

The three detectives stood before it and studied it with the judicious interest of a Royal Academy selection committee.

Pascoe was struck by an odd sense of familiarity. Wield was musing on the initials. Dalziel was concentrating on the wall.

Fran said, "Look, if you're really hungry, I'm sure we could rustle up something."

As she spoke she ushered them firmly toward the door.

Wield, unfed since breakfast, was far from loath. Pascoe, recalling how the tea he'd been offered earlier had been snatched from his lips, was cautiously hopeful. Only Dalziel, usually a tiger on the trail of food, was uncharacteristically reluctant.

But even he was unable to resist the gentle pressure applied by the girl to get them out of her room.

But as they descended the stairs they were greeted by Girlie, who said, "Don't know if it concerns any of you lot, but there's a car talking to itself out there."

They went outside and found Dalziel's radio crackling his call sign impatiently.

The Fat Man slid into the driver's seat and admitted his presence. He was told the chief constable would appreciate a phone call from him. He looked at his watch. It was past four. Plenty of time for Desperate Dan's macho brandy to have been diluted by Mid-Yorkshire's notoriously bromide tea.

"Right," he said.

He got out of the car. Girlie was standing in the doorway, presumably in the hope of seeing them off the premises. He went toward her and said, "Is that a phone around your neck, luv, or do you make your own jewelry?"

Without a word she unhooked the instrument and handed it over. He walked away from them all, dialing, but if this was in the interest of confidentiality, he'd have needed to walk for another ten minutes to render his side of the conversation inaudible.

"Hello, sir . . . Aye, it's me. . . . What? . . . Oh, that. Group O? Forty-six percent of the population, nosebleed, gave a lift to a kiddy that had cut its knee, hundred explanations. . . . That's why I came out myself, to be sure. . . . Aye, I've not forgotten the area liaison meeting tonight . . . on my way back now. . . . Mr. Pascoe too . . . No, Sergeant Wield's spending the night here . . . at the cottage. . . . The lad's not due on duty till eight in the morning . . . likely he'll turn up right as a trivet, and the sergeant'll be there to greet him. . . . Well, if he doesn't, we'll have to think again, won't we? . . . Bye now."

He returned and handed back the phone to Girlie.

"Thanks, luv," he said, and to Fran standing behind her cousin, "Sorry we can't stay for that grub. Some other time mebbe?"

The two women withdrew into the house.

"Right," said Dalziel. "Peter, you hop in and we'll pick up your car on our way through the village. Wield, you can walk down to the cottage. Do you good, a bit of exercise. You look to me like you've been eating too much."

"Yes, sir. Sir, why precisely am I spending the night at Corpse Cottage?"

"What's up? You've not got something better to do? Don't answer that. Nay, lad, it's just that I'm not sure what's going off around here, but if owt else happens, I'd like to think there were someone handy who's not completely doolally. Right?"

"Right," said Wield unenthusiastically.

"One thing, but," said Dalziel through the car window.

"Yes?"

"Gets dark about half six at this time of year, doesn't it? I'd make sure you were locked up indoors with a cross around your neck and a clove of garlic up your jacksie! Take care!"

And with his laughter echoing back from the ivied front of Old Hall, Dalziel sent the car lurching out of sight around the curve of the bosky drive, and left the village to darkness and to Wield.

Four

You are now collecting your People
delightfully, getting them into such
a spot as is the delight of my life;—
3 or 4 Families in a Country Village
is the very thing to work on.

So dusk stole down on Enscombe.

Crag End Farm, tucked under the western wall of the valley, felt its shadow first. George Creed washed his Wellingtons under the yard pump and laughed as he saw the mud slide off their rubbery blackness. Life was good apart from that silly quarrel with his sister, but that would soon be put to rights. Would have been put to rights already if her daft Scripture quoting hadn't driven him to a matching obduracy. Tomorrow would see things sorted, one way or another. He sat on the bench under the kitchen window and lit a pipe. Time for a smoke before he went into the village for the Save Our School meeting. His old dog, sensing his master's contented mood, settled with his head on the damp rubber boot, and together they watched the shadows which already embraced them reach out to cover Scarletts and the winding river.

At Scarletts, too, the inmates acknowledged the approach of night in their different ways. Mrs. Bayle set about checking her defenses. Fop sniffed the air with hopeful anticipation. And Justin Halavant poured himself a glass of Bâtard-Montrachet, which some Frog had claimed was the best wine in the world for getting philosophical on.

So far the test was inconclusive.

He took a careful sip and once more examined the situation.

Looked at positively he was no worse off.

Looked at legally he had lost nothing that he could really complain about losing.

Looked at morally a problem had been solved, a wrong righted, a dying wish fulfilled.

But neither these considerations, nor yet the wine, prevented him from feeling robbed, cheated, and humiliated.

Ultimately it was all down to that ungrateful child, Caddy. True, his approach had been less than subtle; in fact memory of his gaucherie was almost as painful as memory of its consequences; but there had been no need for that sister of hers, the Ice Queen, to share his humiliation with the whole village. And any guilt he had felt about Caddy herself had been washed away by his detection of her part in this latest outrage. Presumably the whole village knew about that too. Therefore it was meet that his revenge should be taken against the village as a whole. And what better wine than the Bâtard to appetize revenge? But not tonight. Tomorrow was the Day of Reckoning. Quite soon enough to draw on himself the hatred of all his neighbors. He rose and went to the door and shouted, "Mrs. Bayle!"

"Yes?"

"If Mr. Philip Wallop calls, tell him I'm out. Ask him to call again tomorrow."

"Oh, yes? Going to the school meeting, are you?"

The meeting? Yes, why not? That's how it had all started. So why not!

On the edge of the village as the shadows stretched to consume the wilderness he had created out of Intake Cottage's once lovely garden, Jason Toke, too, was thinking of Caddy. He had nothing so positive as hope; what he did have was a certainty that without that ghost of a dream of a possibility which was his mainstay, something cataclysmic would happen in his life, sending him shooting off irresistibly in some new and unforecastable direction. To Jason the best thing that had happened in recent times was the story of Halavant's rejection. Justin had wealth, power, influence, yet Caddy had rejected him. So what did she want?

And that ghost of a dream of a possibility came again to haunt the boy's mind as his supple, intelligent fingers dismantled and oiled his guns.

Higher up the valley where the sun lingers longer to gild the lead of the church roof and flood the vicarage windows with fire, thoughts of

Caddy filled Larry Lillingstone's mind also as he sat at his desk over his neglected papers. He had known it was a mistake from the start. As soon as he felt those longings, he should have gone straight around to the bishop and told him he couldn't stay in Enscombe. What matter if he looked foolish? Anything was better than this mess he had got himself into. Yet was it such a mess? Was it not an occupational hazard of his calling since time began for a poor priest to find himself teetering astride the perilous gap between the state's laws and his flock's needs? His famous predecessor Stanley Harding hadn't hesitated to defy convention or the law in his efforts to save Enscombe school.

But Harding's motives had been pure! Whereas he had thrown up his hands in firm refusal till he had learned of Caddy's involvement. . . . Oh, Caddy, Caddy, Caddy. Would she be at the meeting tonight? Did he want her to be or not? Perhaps the best thing would be to stay away himself? After all, nothing would be certain till tomorrow. Perhaps it would turn out to be an empty dream after all and things could be put back to what they were?

There was a tapping at the window. He rose and peered out into the dusk. Standing on the lawn, looking as insubstantial as the light vapors rising from the damp grass, was the figure of a woman. For a long moment he regarded the pale oval of her face without speaking or moving. Then with a deep sigh he began to open the French window.

Only one building stands higher in Enscombe than the church, and that is Old Hall. Nor is this an entirely fortuitous symbolism. The Hall was built on the site of, and out of the stones of (and, some whispered, with the wealth of), the old priory of St. Margaret. When Thomas Cromwell's team of dissolvers reached this remote part of Yorkshire, all they found was a smoking ruin. The lady prioress, so they were assured by the local justice of the peace and lord of the manor, one Solomon Guillemard, having received advance warning of the king's just wrath, had fled to the popish Netherlands, taking with her all her followers and, what was worse, all their valuables. On word of this the loyal peasantry of Enscombe had risen up in righteous indignation and not stood down again till the priory was reduced to the present worthless ruin, which, nonetheless, out of patriotic love and feudal duty Solomon Guillemard was willing to take off the state's hands for a very small consideration. The men from London, having learned the hard way that it rarely paid to argue with a Yorkshireman, accepted the offer and hurried on to their next port of call, hoping to find better pickings at Jervaulx or Rievaulx.

All this Squire Selwyn had put into his ballad, but as he sat at his writing desk that evening, his thoughts, like Lillingstone's, were not on the papers before him but on a woman.

Girlie had said she had something she wanted to talk over with him, and from her manner he knew it was no light matter. He feared the worst. Had she turned out to be one of those feckless fluttering kinds of girl he recalled from his youth, there'd have been no problem. She'd probably have gone off long since and got herself married. Instead she had taken on the Hall and all it involved, including looking after young Fran and himself—no easy task, that! And what was more, she'd made a first-rate job of it, dragging the estate back from the brink of ruin and now planning for its future survival with the help of this damn Health Park. If anyone deserved to inherit, it was Girlie.

But she couldn't. Not a matter of law. Male inheritance was no longer the hard-and-fast thing it had once been. But that in his view made it all the more important. His study of the family history had taught him this if nothing else, that tradition had to come before personal whim. How many squires of the past must have wished they could redirect the inheritance? His own father had never concealed his preference for his younger son, Guy. But *Fuctata non perfecta*. You didn't fiddle with the natural state of things, and he'd inherited. Now it was only proper, pain though he was, that the present Guy should inherit in his turn.

He had told Girlie this, said he would leave her what was his personally to leave (which wasn't much), and added (which was less), that he would urge upon Guy his family duty to see that Girlie and Fran kept a roof over their heads. His own recommendation was that Girlie should not rely on her cousin's kindness but, while she was still young, divert her undoubted talents for making money for the estate to making money for herself.

She had listened politely, said thank you, and gone about her business.

And now he was filled with a foreboding that she was coming to tell him she had taken his advice and was leaving.

He couldn't blame her. But, oh, God, how he would miss her.

That was her now, tapping on the door. He straightened himself up and prepared for bad news.

It was both better and worse than he expected.

When she had finished, a silence fell between them, stretching out as if to fill the space left by the receding light.

She hadn't asked for a decision but he knew one was expected of him.

"Tomorrow," he said finally. "Leave it with me till the Reckoning. I'll make up my mind by then."

Five

I was as civil to them as their bad breath would allow me.

Dusk descended, too, on Enscombe's newest inhabitant, but brought with it nothing heavier than the realization that he hadn't eaten for ten hours and was bloody hungry!

Wield went into the kitchen at Corpse Cottage, opened the fridge, and stepped back with a shudder. He'd seen more inviting scenes-of-crime. Kids today were a primitive tribe, eating stuff which would put most Western tourists on their back for a fortnight.

Nothing for it but the Morris. Both his superiors had recommended it, so it was almost a dereliction of duty not to sample its wares.

He stepped out of the front door. It was a surprisingly remote situation despite its village setting. Up against the churchyard wall with the High Street just out of sight downhill and the vicarage just visible uphill, Corpse Cottage was well placed to be haunted. Yet he felt nothing but an almost proprietorial pleasure as he stood on the step.

Whistling "When the Night Wind Howls in the Chimney Cowls," he set off to the pub.

Two things surprised him as he pushed open the barroom door. The first was how full the place was so early in the evening. The second was that his arrival didn't provoke that moment of speculative silence any newcomer might expect in a country pub. In fact he got a few welcoming nods from one or two of the faces he recognized.

At the bar a man he presumed was the landlord said, "Pint of the best, Sergeant?" already drawing the ale as he spoke.

"Thanks," said Wield, reaching into his pocket.

"First's on the house. I'll make my profit out of you later," said Wapshare. "Any news of the happy wanderer?"

"Not yet," admitted Wield.

"Not to worry. Happen he'll turn up. And you're spending the night at Corpse Cottage to welcome him? That's friendly!"

The man knows everything, Pascoe had warned. But was he telling everything he knew? Wield tasted the beer and, like Pascoe before him, decided that allowances could be made.

"You do a good trade for early on a midweek night," he commented.

"Nay, it's not always like this," said Wapshare. "They're just getting primed for the meeting."

He nodded at the Save Our School pyramid of coins, against which rested a notice advertising a progress-report meeting in the village hall at eight P.M.

"I hope there's good news," said Wield. "Any chance of a bite to eat?"

"Aye. Slice of game pie do you for starters? Sit yourself down and I'll bring it over."

He took his pint to a small table by the window. Wapshare soon followed with a tray laden with pickles, chutney, tomatoes, bread, and a hunk of pie like a lumberjack's wedge.

"Give us a shout when you're done and I'll fry you up a slice or two of my black pudding," said the landlord. "Oh, Lord, here comes the cabaret."

The door had opened on a wave of noise to admit Guy Guillemard and his friends. They made for the bar, where the Heir sat on a stool and viewed the other customers with a droit-de-seigneurish air. Most got on with their drinking. Only Dudley Wylmot from the post office, sitting with the remains of several large gin-and-tonics before him, showed any eagerness to catch the seignorial eye. His sycophancy was counterbalanced by the look of glacial indifference his wife gave the new arrivals before concentrating on her spritzer.

Guy nodded condescendingly at Wylmot, then his eye fell on Wield and a smile like a toothpaste ad spread across his face. He came across to his table and sat down.

"Evening, Sergeant. Left you to guard us overnight, have they?"

"Something like that, sir," said Wield.

"That chap on the drive with you, the one who seemed to think I was trying to zap him. He's your superior, right? Yet he looks rather younger than you. Now, why is that, I ask myself."

"Mebbe because he were born a few years after me," said Wield.

"What? Ah, a joke. Which confirms what I suspect. You're one of the good old breed of British bobby, conscientious, clever even, but not wanting the hassle of promotion, content to stay a sergeant so you can devote more time to your wife and family—three kids, little house in a leafy suburb, couple of cats, and a cross-breed terrier—likes a jar with the lads, goes to the match on Saturday, but is always glad to get home to the little woman and the animals. Am I right or am I right?"

Wield nodded, not in agreement but at a connection he had never made before between *prat* and *prattle*. If this was the best that an expensive education could do for a lad, then why did folk like Ellie Pascoe get agitated if rich fools demanded the right to subject their progeny to it?

"I knew it," said Guillemard with a patronizing smugness which made Wield long for the Dalzielesque chutzpah to say, "Nay, lad, I'm as queer as a clockwork orange, so why don't you shut your big fat mouth and give your tight little arse a chance?"

"You're the one who knows what's what, not that jumped-up squirt pretending to be a gentleman, and certainly not that grotesque who showed up later. So, tell me, Sergeant, you who know your place and have so determinedly kept it, wouldn't this be advice you'd give to all young bobbies?"

He leaned across the table to give Wield the full benefit of his wisdom and smile. Early though the hour was, he'd already wined and dined well on something garlicky washed down with cognac, if the pungent waft from his mouth was a true messenger. His friends, too, sounded a lot livelier than could be put down to a single draft of even Mr. Wapshare's good ale. How indiscreet might the drink make him? wondered Wield.

He shifted slightly to avoid the reek and said, "You wouldn't have anyone in particular in mind, sir?"

"For instance?" said Guy, helping himself to a pickled onion.

"Constable Bendish, for instance," said Wield, for whom a little obliquery went a long long way. "He was seen having a dust-up with someone fitting your description."

"Really," said Guy, unbothered by this exaggeration. "Put it in a report, did he?"

"No, sir. Still a serious matter, but."

"Not what I call serious, Sergeant. I've met more resistance in a Bangkok brothel."

"So you admit to assaulting a police officer?" said Wield.

"No, I bloody don't. I admit to the justifiable chastisement of an erk who'd stepped out of line. He knew he had it coming, otherwise he'd have fitted me up on an attempted murder charge, wouldn't he?"

"Why are you telling me this?" asked Wield.

"To save public expense and police effort. I told the erk next time I came to Enscombe, I'd finish the job properly. I came back yesterday. So my advice to you is work out how far a frightened rabbit can run in twenty-four hours, and start looking there! What the hell's Wapshare getting his knickers in a twist about?"

There had been a huge crash from the bar followed by an explosion of laughter and voices, loudest among them the landlord's crying, "Right, that's it. Out, you lot. You're barred!"

Guillemard made for the bar, his arms spread in what he probably thought was a placatory gesture. Wield could see that the initial crash had been caused by the toppling of the Save Our School ziggurat.

"Wappy, what's the problem?" said Guy in his best talking-to-the-toddlers voice.

"No problem, and the name's Wapshare, Mr. Guillemard," said the landlord. "I'm just exercising my legal right to refuse service and order this lot off my premises."

"Of course you are, and it's understandable, but let's not overreact, shall we? It's just an excess of high spirits for which they're truly sorry, isn't that right, boys and girls? You're truly sorry."

"Yes, Guy, we're truly sorry," they echoed in mock contrition.

"There you are. Any damage, we'll pay. And they'll build your pyramid again, only a lot higher this time. Won't you, children?"

"Yes, Guy, a lot higher this time," chorused his friends, enjoying this new game.

"So what do you say, Mr. Wapshare? Forgive and forget?"

Wapshare spoke very slowly.

"I say, I don't want their money and I don't want their company. I want them out of here, and I don't want to see them back."

"Oh, dear," said Guillemard. "If they go, then I'll have to go, you do understand that?"

"Understand it? I bloody insist on it!" roared Wapshare.

Wield felt like cheering.

Guy the Heir looked around the room, his face still smiling but the smile now thinly stretched over fury.

"If that's the way you feel, Wappy. Your loss, not ours. I mean, it's not what you'd call lively, is it? My ancestors needn't have bothered about trying to close you down, the place died naturally a long time back and it's just that no one's bothered to bury it. Come on, boys. Let's leave this mausoleum before the dust chokes us."

He made for the door. The others trooped after him.

Wapshare's face relaxed to its customary benevolence.

"Right," he said. "Who's good at picking up money?"

There was a general laugh, almost immediately echoed and drowned by a cheer from outside and a crash as though something had been hurled against the pub wall.

Wield half rose, looking inquiringly at Wapshare, who shook his head.

"Don't interrupt your meal, Sergeant. They'll just be taking it out on the sign. Guillemards have been doing that for a hundred years, and we're none the worse for it yet!"

Outside an engine roared into life and Wield looked out of the window to see the Gung Ho! Land Rover heading up the High Street, presumably to continue the merrymaking at the Hall. Most of the customers were bending to pick up the fallen coins. Wylmot, eager to demonstrate how much he belonged, was foremost among them, but the gins had taken their toll and when he stooped he would have gone right over if his wife hadn't grabbed his arm.

"Come on, Dud," said Wapshare, emerging from behind the bar and taking the other arm. "We'll find you a nice comfortable seat at the back. Sergeant, I'll be closing for a while till the meeting's over, but don't rush your grub. Help yourself to owt you need, and if you leave afore I'm back, just pull the door shut behind you."

Five minutes later Wield found himself completely alone. Dalziel's dream of heaven, he thought, just as Pascoe's was probably to be left alone in the Tell-Tale Bookshop for a couple of hours.

And his own dream of heaven? He tried to fantasize but found he couldn't. So, a man without a dream. He ought to be unhappy, but, rather to his surprise, he found he wasn't.

He finished his food, went behind the bar, and drew himself another half of bitter, as much for the pleasure of doing it as need of a drink. The place looked different from this side of the counter. He knew a lot of cops who'd taken their pensions and gone in for a pub. He didn't fancy it himself. What did he fancy? A packet of pork scratchings! He helped himself, checked the price list for food and drink, was pleasantly surprised, left his money neatly on top of the till, dropped another couple of pound coins on the reconstituted Save Our School pile, now more Pyrenees than pyramid, and went out into the night.

It would have been pitch-black if the uncurtained window of the village hall hadn't laid a causeway of light across the road. He walked along it till he was close enough to hear as well as see the meeting within.

The vicar was on his feet. He had a good pulpit voice but he didn't seem to be bringing tidings of great joy.

"The Appeal has done well," he was saying. "But as we always knew, there is little chance of getting close to the very large sum we need to guarantee the school's future—"

"Then we have to sell the Green," yelled someone. "Isn't Phil Wallop interested? We could do with some new houses for the young ones—"

"Don't kid yourself our young 'uns 'ud be able to afford owt that Wallop built," interjected someone else. "And don't imagine he'd hire local workmen, either, if that's what you're thinking—"

"Please!" cried the vicar above the resultant hubbub. "Look, what I suggest is we postpone any decision. . . . Yes, I know I said it had to be tonight, but . . . look, I don't want to raise hopes, but there's a faint chance that a sum of money, a reasonably large sum might . . . I can't say more. I'll be able to tell you definitely tomorrow . . . at the Reckoning. . . ."

A man offering a ray of hope ought to try to look happy, thought Wield. But the vicar's expression was more like what you don't want to see on your doctor's face as he examines the X rays.

Wield turned away. This was a private meeting, a family affair, and he wasn't a member of the family. It was a rather melancholy thought. Perhaps he should have stayed a bit longer in the Morris and got merry or really miserable. He looked across the road to the pub. In the light from the window behind him he could see the sign above the front door. Pascoe had told him its history. But maybe *history* was the wrong word.

People don't change, thought Wield. They just do the same things differently.

From the burnt, battered, and blasted bosom of William Morris there now protruded a short, dully gleaming rod of steel.

Six

We had a beautiful night for our
frisks.

The High Street was quiet as a deserted film set as Wield strolled back to Corpse Cottage. Not much given to flights of the imagination, he found himself conjuring up pictures of how it must have been a hundred, two hundred, three hundred years ago!

Back at the cottage he switched on the tiny telly and checked whether Bendish's unappetizing larder ran to a pot of tea. It did, and a good brew at that. The lad might live off junk food but at least he hadn't sunk to instant tea.

But what might he have sunk to?

The thought hit him hard. Here he was, mocking the youngster's eating habits, making himself comfortable in his house, while all the time . . .

All the time what?

He didn't know. Perhaps there was nothing to know, or nothing more than would result in a lot of rolled eyeballs at the waywardness of youth and a right rollocking for the returned prodigal.

Time to drop a shutter. He sat with his tea on the ancient but very comfortable sofa and concentrated as much of his attention as was necessary on an alternative comedy show. It was certainly alternative, dispensing with all the old detritus of the past, such as laughs. After a while he decided that, attention-wise, it didn't require both eyes and ears, so he closed the former. And eventually God, who is merciful even to undesert, cupped His divine hands over the latter, and he fell asleep.

He was awoken by a scratching, tapping noise. For a moment he had no idea where he was. Even when awareness of location struggled through, enough confusion remained for him to mislocate the source of the noise in the fireplace wall through which Susannah Hogbin's coffin was alleged to have burst. Interestingly, instead of terror this filled him with a strangely passive curiosity. Everyone deserved at least one small personal otherworldly experience before the big general one. He settled back to enjoy his, and was rather disappointed when the noise was repeated, this time indisputably from the window.

He flung back the curtain and discovered that truth long known to doctors, that the living are much more frightening than the dead.

Edwin Digweed's fine-boned face was pressed close against the glass. Seeing Wield, he gestured imperiously toward the front door.

Rubbing the sleep from his eyes, Wield opened it.

"May I come in?" said the bookseller, stepping past the sergeant. "Despite appearances to the contrary I am not a door-to-door salesman."

The appearance to the contrary consisted of a zipped leather bag, which he set down beside him. Wield switched off the TV, on which an etiolated, exophthalmic epicene who looked as if a good woman would crack him like a stick was explaining his admiration for Renoir's *Baigneuses*.

"What can I do for you, sir?" he asked unenthusiastically, hoping that his presence in Corpse Cottage wasn't going to have half the village treating him like the local bobby.

"For a start you can accept my apologies."

"Eh?"

"It occurred to me after our last encounter that it might be that, to someone unfamiliar with my ways, one or two of my mannerisms could have come across as, how shall I put it, discourtesies."

Wield, who could think of other ways to put it, said nothing and Digweed resumed. "So when I heard after the school meeting that you were spending the night here, I got to thinking of you alone in a strange house, not knowing what has happened to your young colleague, though I'm sure nothing untoward has happened to him, nevertheless I thought, as a peace offering and a belated token of welcome to our village . . ."

He unzipped the bag and pulled out a jacketed copy of *On the Banks of the Een*. The cover illustration had been taken from the painting of Scarletts Pool over Digweed's bed, with his grandfather's initials *R.D.* still visible though much reduced.

"That's right kind," said Wield, taken aback. "How much . . . ?"

"No, no, a welcome gift, I say. Also I wondered if I could tempt you to join me in a drink?"

This time it was a bottle of Jim Beam that came out of the bag.

"I am, I fear, a traitor to my continent. Let others sing of single malts and fine French brandies. For me this is the true Hippocrene, the real Spiritus Sacer."

He was rattling on a bit even by his standards, but Wield didn't mind. This much he had learned from Dalziel. Man offer you a drink, get it down quick, then ask about his motives. And besides, he'd never tasted bourbon.

"I'll get some glasses," he said.

"No need," said Digweed. "Doubting if young Bendish has reached the age where he can either value or afford decent glassware, I took the precaution and the liberty . . ."

He came up with a pair of ornately cut barrel tumblers in golden crystal, which caught the light as if filled with sunshine.

Wield, a lover of plain glass, thought them a bit over the top, but so almost was the measure Digweed poured, and when he tasted the sweet smoothness of the liquor, he was able to say without hypocrisy, "That's smashing."

The bookseller smiled and topped up his glass once more. Wield settled back comfortably. Sooner or later they'd get to the man's real motives. With nectar like this on tap he could wait.

"Those Rider Haggards you mentioned," said Digweed.

"Oh, aye?" said Wield, disappointed they'd got there so quickly.

He must have given away more than he intended, for Digweed added hastily, "No, I'm not trying to persuade you to sell them, but I should love sometime to see them. A complete set of Haggard firsts in dust wrappers. It would be like . . ."

For once he seemed lost for words. Perhaps the poor old sod didn't find owt exciting except books.

"But no more of books. I cannot have you suspecting my motives."

"Comes with the job," said Wield lightly.

"I suppose so. Have you always been a policeman?"

"I were a kiddie for a bit."

Digweed laughed, genuinely, not his superior putting-down snort, encouraging Wield to a cautious opening-up.

"I started out as a draftsman's apprentice, but it didn't take. So I joined the force," he said.

Age seventeen; panicking at the awareness of his sexuality roused by the attentions of his perceptive boss; making a macho statement.

"A draftsman?" mused Digweed. "Do you still draw?"

"Not like your granddad," said Wield, touching the book. "Only scene-of-the-crime diagrams. How about you? Did you have a real job afore you retired?"

Oops! His desire to turn the conversation away from himself had made him uncharacteristically clumsy. This stuff took a quick hold!

Digweed raised his eyebrows and tipped the bottle.

"I'm sure there must be questions about the police which contain as many offensive assumptions," he said dryly. "Selling books is a real job, believe me. In fact, I, too, trained for the law, as a solicitor. But as I lived abroad for much of my life, opportunities to practice were limited. I came back to the UK about ten years ago, intending to find myself a niche in the business world. Instead, I found things in such a state, and such a ghastly gang of blinkered jackasses running things, that I was ready to leave again in a sixmonth. Happily, I visited the scenes of my birth and upbringing first, partly out of sentiment, partly to sort out some family property. And when I realized that here in Enscombe at least, things remained much as they had been, I decided to settle and follow the line of business I had always fancied, selling old books."

Wield drank some more and said, "You talk like this place were special, I mean, really special. Almost like, perfect."

"Good Lord, no! Enscombe is very much *fuctatus* rather than *perfectus,* I'm glad to say. Perfection is unnatural, Sergeant, because it implies the absence of either development or decline. Haven't you noticed it's the political parties and the religions with the clearest notions of the perfect society that cause the most harm? Once admit the notion of human perfectibility, and the end can be made to justify any amount of pain and suffering along the way. Besides, it would put us both out of work. No crime in the perfect society, and no desire to read about the imperfect past either! So here's to imperfection!"

They both drank deep.

"So to get back to your question, Sergeant, I am certainly not retired. I suspect my argent locks as well as my profession have misled you. Blossom can be white as well as snow. How old do you take me for?"

"Nay, you're not catching me like that," said Wield.

"I think a man would have to rise early to catch you, Sergeant. Fifty-seven. You are blessed with a face that gives little away, but I bet you had me closer to sixty-seven?"

Wield, who'd never heard his face called a blessing, nodded confession.

"Don't let it bother you. I wish I could tell some winter's tale to explain that my hair turned white in a single night, but it was a gradual process, starting surprisingly early. No coffins came through the wall to accelerate matters. Talking of which, it doesn't bother you staying alone in a place like this?"

"No. Not even afore I started supping this stuff," said Wield. "In fact I've felt right at home from the start. Some spots have a nice feel to them."

"I know what you mean. I feel the same."

"Well, that's one thing we've got in common," said Wield.

"Two," said the bookseller, holding up the bottle and topping up their glasses. "Do I get an impression that you find it surprising we have any common ground at all?"

"Common ground's easy enough to find, sir, except that when you find it, like this Green of yours, it's often just summat else to quarrel about."

Digweed frowned and said, "If we're going to quarrel, I'd prefer you stopped calling me sir. It gives you such an advantage."

"Never fret," said Wield. "In the Force it's usually the only term of abuse a poor cop can aim at his superiors."

"Do I come across as so superior, then? I don't intend to."

"That makes it worse."

"I suppose it does. I'm sorry. If it helps, the Digweeds, too, have been looked down upon in their time."

"By the Guillemards, you mean? Your granddad, was it?"

"Good Lord! Are you clairvoyant?"

"Just a detective," said Wield, not unsmugly. "The way he talked about the birthday treats at the start of his journal. Very acid. Reminded me a bit of you."

"I'll take that as a compliment," said Digweed. "But do go on. Strut your stuff, as they say."

Thus challenged, Wield delayed a moment by sipping his drink, his mind racing. He found himself handling *The Naturalist's Year* as though, like a medium, he might pick up some helpful vibration from it. Then his eyes fastened on the jacket illustration.

"R.D.?" he said. "Same initials on that picture of the Squire's aunt Edwina, right? Your granddad painted it. When he were a lot younger . . . and he fancied Edwina. But he got choked off. . . . Not by Edwina. By the family. Thought he weren't good enough. . . . That's why he's so sarky about the way they value their womenfolk. . . . Eventually he married someone else, late on in life, he must have been in his late forties when your dad were born. . . . But he never forgot, and that's why he called your dad Edwin, after his old love!"

He could see from the bookseller's expression that this soaring flight of fancy, larklike, had never diverted from its factual base. Bloody hell, he thought, emptying his glass. If I'd discovered this stuff sooner, I could have been chief constable by now!

"Truly remarkable!" exclaimed Digweed. "You're sure it wasn't you who burgled my shop in order to read my grandfather's earlier journals?"

"I'm right, then?" said Wield.

"With the very slight addition that Edwina fancied him with an equal passion. It was she who got them thrown together by discovering in herself this longing to have her portrait painted to match one she already had of some ancestor. But though a gentleman, Ralph was held to be below the salt as (a) being poor, (b) being an artist, and (c) being a close friend of the younger Halavant, Jeremy, the one who built Scarletts. Once the family realized what was going on, that was that. Poor Ralph."

"Poor Edwina, more like it. At least he still had choices he could make," said Wield.

"Yes, poor Edwina too. But don't feel too sorry for her, she wouldn't have thanked you. A pliant child she may have been, but she grew into a feisty old lady. And she got her revenges. Though she did not quite live to see it, she it was by all accounts who instilled in her great-niece, Frances, that sense of self-worth and independent spirit which gave her the strength to walk out on the family and marry Stanley Harding."

"Good for her!" proclaimed Wield. "Here's to both on 'em!"

They clinked their glasses together with most melodious chime and drank a deep toast.

"So there we are," said Digweed. "Something else in common. Go on like this and we could find we're twin brothers, separated at birth!"

He laughed at the absurdity of his own fancy and Wield, with a sudden revival of all his old feelings, thought, Patronizing prat! He thinks he's doing me favors!

He said, "Wouldn't go as far as that, sir."

Digweed regarded him quizzically and said, "Oh, dear, it's that *sir* again! You are clearly determined to quarrel. Tell you what, if we *are* going to fall out, let it be over things we dislike, rather than spoil the things we like with arguing about them. In fact, it supports my antiperfection principle that when a politician wants to really unite the electorate, he looks for a common hatred rather than a common enthusiasm. So what is it turns you off?"

Wield thought, then said with a slow emphasis, "Snobs. I don't like snobs. How's that for starters?"

"Excellent. No quarrel there. My turn. Little Hitlers. People who turn a molehill of authority into a mountain of obstructionism."

"Fair enough. Politicians."

"Spot on. Undertakers."

"They're only doing a job," said Wield defensively.

"Of course. But do you like them?"

"No," admitted Wield. "Beer that's too cold."

"Beer that's too warm."

"People that don't care about beer."

"People that go on too much about beer."

"Motorway service stations."

"Airport lounges."

"Game shows."

"Soaps."

Wield sipped his bourbon thoughtfully and queried, "No exceptions?"

"Well, I used to be quite taken with *Eastenders*. And of course being of everyday country folk, I adore *The Archers*," admitted Digweed anxiously.

"That's fine, then," said Wield with a grin, and suddenly found he was enjoying himself immensely. "People who, when you're

out walking, know the names of all the hills and insist on telling
you."

"People who send family newsletters at Christmas."

"Drivers who open doors in front of motorcyclists."

"Drivers who park where they shouldn't," said Digweed, one eye-
brow raised quizzically.

"Banks."

"People who turn down book pages."

"People who think they're right all the time."

"Vivisectionists."

"Exclusive clubs."

"People who persecute minorities."

"Hypocrites!"

"Fascists!"

They realized that the exchange had gathered pace and volume,
regarded each other in faintly flushed embarrassment, then relaxed
and started to laugh.

"People who leave heel-taps," said Digweed, leaning over to fill up
Wield's glass.

"Hey, leave some for yourself," protested the sergeant, looking at
the almost empty bottle.

"You forget. I have to rise and make my way home. As a respected
parish councilor, I try not to fall on my face in the High Street more
than once a month."

"And you've had your ration for this month?"

"If only I could remember," said Digweed solemnly. He rose and
extended his hand.

"Good night, Sergeant Wield. A duty that turns into a pleasure is a
pleasure indeed."

Wield took the offered hand and tried to stand up, but Digweed
urged him gently back onto the sofa.

"I can see myself out. Sleep well. And I hope your wandering boy
returns. I hope all lost and wandering boys everywhere find their way
home. Good night."

He went out, his back straight, his gait steady. Wield heard the door
bang shut and let himself sink back into the cushions.

"Am I on duty?" he asked himself. " 'Cos, if I am, having downed
a good half bottle of bourbon, I am definitely drunk on duty, which is
or used to be a hanging offense."

He looked into his glass. It was empty again. On the floor before him Digweed had placed the bottle with about half an inch in the bottom.

"Thank you, Mr. Digweed," said Wield, reaching down for it. "But you're still not getting my Hider Raggards."

And he fell back in a paroxysm of giggles which finally moderated to a grunting chuckle, and eventually to a steady snore.

Seven

*The Wylmots being robbed must
be an amusing thing to their
acquaintance, & I hope it is as
much their pleasure as it seems their
avocation to be subjects of general
Entertainment.*

Wield woke to the sound of bells.

He listened for the voice of God in them till they diminished to the trill of a telephone, whereupon he rolled off the sofa and went crawling in search of the instrument, certain that it would be the voice of God on it, full of wrath at being kept waiting.

He was right about the wrath, but it was Dudley Wylmot's, not Dalziel's.

"About time," he said petulantly. "Can you get down here right away! We've been broken into again."

Wield looked at his watch. It was ten to six. He thought of telling Wylmot to sod "awf," dismissed the idea, thought of advising him to ring Filmer at the section office, or to ring HQ in town, or to—

"Hello? Hello? You still there?" demanded Wylmot.

"Sod awf," said Wield.

Even as he said it he couldn't believe he was saying it. He, Wield, the master of control, the man who let it all hang in.

"I'm sorry? I missed that. My wife was speaking. What did you say?"

Wield drew in a huge lungful of air to service a long sigh of relief.

He said, "I'll get down there soon as I can, sir."

He rang off, then dialed the section number.

A yawning constable answered. Wield identified himself,

explained the situation, then went on, "Ask Sergeant Filmer to get over here soon as he can, will you? I'll take a look, but I don't want to be away too long."

He went into the bathroom and immersed his head in a basinful of cold water, rubbed some toothpaste on his teeth with his fingertip, and rinsed it out.

It wasn't till he was walking out of the bathroom that it registered, there was toothpaste but no toothbrush.

Outside, he drank in the cool air of a fine spring morning. The sun was up, but nobbut just, and the final coda of the dawn chorus still filled the air, plus the dull roar of a distant tractor reminding him that Enscombe was a working village and a farmer's day still ran with the sun.

Walking was a little shaky at first, but by the time he reached the High Street he was beginning to feel more like a pulse in nature and less like a wrench in the works.

He met a couple of farmworkers, who greeted him as casually as if they'd been doing it for fifty years. Perhaps his stubbled chin and rumpled clothes made him merge with the background.

At the post office he found Wylmot in a state of hangover which made his own condition positively healthy. He recalled remarking the speed with which the man had been sinking the gin-and-tonics. Foolish fellow. Now, if he'd stuck to pure old bourbon . . .

Complacently he said, "Show me."

Entry had been through a kitchen window, using the same technique as the Tell-Tale Bookshop the day before. The difference was that here there was an alarm system.

Wield checked it. The main switch was off.

"What happened, sir? Forget to switch it on?"

"I must have done," said Wylmot. "I was rather . . . tired last night. Usually it's something I do automatically. Oh, shit. I hope the insurance won't make a fuss. We had it fitted after the last time and there was a discount on the premium."

"These things happen, sir," said Wield. "What time did you discover the break-in?"

"About half an hour ago. It wasn't me. It was my wife."

"Have you any idea what's missing?"

"From the shop, yes. They don't seem to have touched anything in here."

Here was the sitting room cum dining room through which they went on their way to the shop. Wield paused at the connecting door and said, "Would this have been locked?"

"That? No. I mean, if they got that far, they'd be in, wouldn't they? So what's the point of giving them something else to damage?"

To Wield the natural end of this logic was to pack all your valuables into a suitcase and leave them on the kitchen table.

He went into the post office.

The place was in a bit of a mess, but it was mainly papers which had been scattered around, nothing which would have made a lot of noise.

He said, "Where's your bedroom, sir?"

"Right above," said Wylmot.

From the look of him it would have taken the massed bands of the Grenadier Guards playing reveille to waken Wylmot, but perhaps his wife had heard something.

Wylmot went on, "It's mainly mail they took, so far as I can see. The old safe we had you could get into with a hairpin, but this new one, you'd need gelignite. And I'm very careful to lock everything of value away. The tills were empty, of course. So I reckon they went for a lucky dip in the mailbag. It was rather fuller than usual, as there was no collection yesterday."

"Oh, yes, the postman's accident. Any chance you can remember what was actually in the bag? Can't have been too much, not from a small place like Enscombe."

"We do a surprising amount of business," retorted Wylmot. "If we didn't they'd soon close us down, believe me. Oh, there you are, dear."

Daphne Wylmot had appeared in the doorway. She wore a green-and-gold silk dressing gown, which ran liquescently over the curves of her body. Her shoulder-length hair had been brushed till it shone like the gown and she had applied just enough makeup to give life and color to her morning face. Her feet were bare and her magenta-nailed toes flexed prehensilely on the cool tiled floor.

Wield viewed her with the dispassionate approval of an art lover, and her green eyes returned his gaze with the puzzled speculation of a beautiful woman not getting the response she expects, even at this time in the morning.

"Hello, Mrs. Wylmot," said Wield. "Detective Sergeant Wield. We met yesterday. I believe you discovered the break-in?"

"That's right, Sergeant. I felt the draft as soon as I opened the kitchen door."

"You were up early," said Wield. "Did something disturb you?"

"I don't think so. Should it have?"

"No, I meant, sleeping directly above the shop . . ."

She smiled and said, "I wasn't, not last night. Dudley was a little . . . indisposed when we got home so I thought it best to let him have our double bed to toss and turn in. I went into the spare room, which isn't above the shop. No, I simply woke up, felt like a cup of tea, and came down. It wasn't all that early, not for us. Someone has to be around to receive the newspapers about six forty-five, and I didn't anticipate Dudley being well enough."

"I see," said Wield. He looked at her husband, who was staring into a mailbag like a nervous air passenger about to be very sick. "Perhaps you could help Mr. Wylmot work out what's missing. But try to touch as little as you can."

He went back into the living room and let his eye run slowly over the route the burglar must have taken from the kitchen, then broadened the field of search. He was acting more out of habit than hope. Clues detectable by the human eye were rarer in life than in literature. But there was something. Under a table, a piece of gray-brown clay almost invisible on the heather-mix carpet. It bore the imprint of the deep tread of a shoe or boot and was set hard.

Carefully he carried it through into the kitchen, helped himself to a freezer bag off a roll on the wall, and slipped it in. Then he opened the kitchen door. It led onto a small porch which housed a washing machine and was also the dumping ground for a couple of pairs of Wellingtons and a pair of men's walking boots. He checked their treads. None was deep enough to match the piece of clay.

He went through the outside door into a small yard, prettified by a couple of tubs bright with the flowers that bloom in the spring. The walls were about six feet, no obstacle to an active man, and in any case warpage had shifted the position of the solitary bolt on the yard door so that it touched but could not enter the hole drilled in the post to receive it, and the door swung open when he pulled at it.

He returned to examining the walls just in case his man had come over the top, but found no sign. The only odd thing his sagacious eye did observe was that in one of the flower tubs, a group of Poeticus Narcissi was a flower short. The stem had been snapped in half quite recently and there was no sign of the white-petaled flower with red-and-yellow cup either in the tub or on the ground.

He made a note, but didn't bother to underline it. The flowers that bloomed in the spring tra-la were unlikely to have anything to do with this case.

Whistling the tune he reentered the cottage, just as Filmer arrived.

"You sound happy," said the uniformed sergeant.

"It's this early rising. You should try it."

"No need to be cocky just 'cos you were sleeping on the spot," said Filmer. "Any word of young Bendish yet?"

"No," said Wield, glancing at his watch. "But there's still time. I'd best get back to Corpse Cottage. You take over here, Terry."

"That's right, run like hell before fat Dalziel finds out you're missing," mocked Filmer. "God, he's got you buggers scared witless, hasn't he?"

"Don't be daft," said Wield. "He's just a big cuddly bear and we all love him."

He passed on what he'd gathered, both information and material, then left without speaking to Wylmot again. The man was quite capable of complaining at being fobbed off with Filmer, and Wield, alert to what he thought of as the Enscombe effect, didn't want to risk being tempted to a second *sod awf*.

As he walked past the Wayside Café, his nose caught the smell of fresh baking and his stomach gave a low, pleading rumble. He tried the door. It was locked but the noise of the handle brought Dora Creed out of her kitchen. She did not look welcoming as she unlocked the door.

"Sorry, but I were passing and I've not had any breakfast and I could smell your baking. . . ."

"I'm getting things done for the Squire's Reckoning," she said. "This is a very busy morning for me."

"Aye, it will be. Sorry to trouble you. . . ."

"You spent the night in Corpse Cottage, did you? You're up early."

"There was a break-in at the post office," he said.

"Another? 'Woe unto them that call evil good, and good evil.' Just wait here a moment, Sergeant."

She vanished into her kitchen, leaving Wield reflecting that she didn't seem much surprised at this new evidence of man's depravity. A couple of minutes later she returned carrying a plastic bag containing a foil-wrapped packet.

"Thanks a lot," said Wield. "How much do I owe—"

"No need for money or thanks, Sergeant. 'I was an hungered and ye gave me meat. I was a stranger, and ye took me in.' My duty and my pleasure."

It was enough to turn a man religious, thought Wield, and his conversion was confirmed when he opened the foil parcel and discovered a feast of fresh-baked rolls filled with crisp hot bacon. He washed them down with a mug of Bendish's good tea and felt for a while that all was right with the world.

But as the minutes ticked by his worries about the fate of Bendish returned and with them his old conviction that while bacon butties were a strong plea in mitigation, God stood convicted of at least willful neglect in the way He managed the world.

At eight on the dot the phone rang. He snatched it up, praying it would be the young man ringing in with apologies for being late . . . except, of course, he would hardly ring his own cottage!

Andy Dalziel said, "Morning, sunshine. Anything happening?"

"No, sir. Except there was a break-in at the post office."

"Oh, aye? Any connection?"

"Doubt it. What now, sir?"

"What do you recommend? The circus?"

It was a straight question. Dalziel liked straight answers.

He said, "If it were up to me, I'd say not. At least, not yet."

"Any particular reason?"

"It just doesn't feel like a spot where something nasty's happened," said Wield reluctantly.

"I'd like to see Desperate Dan's face when I try that out on him!" said Dalziel. "But you're the man on the spot, Wieldy. For now. I'll be out later with the lad to take a look for myself. Try not to go completely native till then, eh? And I'll tell you one thing, Wieldy . . ."

"Yes, sir?"

"If young Bendish is still alive when we find him, I'll mebbe kill the bastard myself!"

End of Volume 3

Volume the Fourth

PROLOGUE, being an extract
from the
JOURNAL OF FRANCES HARDING
(née GUILLEMARD)

February 18, 1932. *What a mixed day this has been. The morning was gray and gloomy. At ten Stanley went to the Palace to see the new bishop. He expected a reproof for his campaign to improve the school, and though he knew that he came close to breaching the law by his encouragement to parents to keep their children away from school till such time as the fabric of the building and the insanitary washrooms, etc., should have been put to rights, he hoped that he might at least engage the bishop's sympathies. I remained at home, receiving and setting out the items for the sale in the vicarage by which we hoped to boost our fabric fund. When Stanley returned I saw he had received something far worse than a reproof. We are to move, or rather be moved! I see my father's hand unmistakably in this. He has been unrelenting in his opposition to Stanley. He even makes the whole household drive to Byreford twice on Sundays to worship! And of course his influence in the county is so great that he can bring pressure to bear on a young and inexperienced bishop that even a more experienced man might find hard to bear.*

"Where shall we go?" I asked Stanley.

"Nowhere that they want us to go," he exclaimed. "The bishop thinks I am bribable with some comfortable suburban parsonage. I

*told him that if I left it would be to somewhere that needed me more
than a Yorkshire suburb. Like Africa."*

*The idea both frightens and excites me. But we had no time for
discussion because people started to arrive for the sale. Things were
going rather slowly, till who should turn up but Job Halavant? He is
no churchgoer, but God moves in a mysterious way, and I suspect my
father's withdrawal from church life, and in particular his steadfast
refusal to give any help or support to Stanley's school campaign, has
inspired a contrary interest in Job! He bought several pieces of old
furniture which Stanley had put up for sale, and he bought Aunt
Edwina's pictures too. I was sorry to see them go. Stanley didn't want
me to sell them, as they were all I brought with me from the Hall, but it
was precisely for that reason I insisted. He was willing to part with
everything of his own, so how could I do less? Job payed an excellent
price, then on top of that he added five hundred pounds for the fund.
Stanley said if we went on like this, we would be able to do what really
ought to be done, which is rebuild the school from scratch. He was
half joking, but lo and behold! two hours later Job Halavant returned.
He had been on the phone and said that he had persuaded Theo Finch-
Hatton to supply stone from his quarry at cost, which Job himself
would defray. Likewise Joe Nibb's building firm was going to loan us
digging and building equipment free, charging only for labor, which
again Job was willing to undertake, which meant work could start
almost straightaway!*

*Whatever his motives are, this is God's hand at work. Likewise, if we
do go to Africa, it will not be the malice of my father in Old Hall that
sends us there but the mercy of Our Father in Heaven.*

One

*It was a Prince of days—everybody
was out and talking of Spring.*

Wield stood with a cup of tea in his hand and looked out
of the window. Spring sunshine on a cottage garden. Color
here a-plenty already with the tulips and daffs and a golden
torrent of forsythia, and the promise of so much more to
come, lilies and delphiniums, roses and red-hot pokers. It
needed a bit of work now the growing season was under
way, but by the start of May it would be a picture. And the
whole village too. A picture.

Wield was no sentimentalist. If this business required the
full police circus—police transports crowding the High
Street, an army of bobbies beating across the moors, the
village hall turned into an incident room, Post Office vans
laying extra lines, helicopters quartering the skies, diggers
and divers disturbing badgers and fish in their search for
what no one wanted to find, house-to-house inquiries, the
media mob, the bar of the Morris loud with urban oaths, the
floor of the Wayside Café muddied with wallies' Wellies—
if that's what it took to find out what had become of Harold
Bendish, so be it.

On the other hand, to do that to a place like this if it
wasn't necessary was so much tactical bombing; no permanent physical damage, of course, but places could be traumatized as well as people.

He rinsed his cup and then with great care washed Digweed's glasses too. They were probably worth a fortune and

breaking them would be ill return for what was probably the man's one good deed of the year.

No, that was unfair. Digweed was obviously well thought of locally and willing to spend time and energy on the common weal. Last night he had called a truce. Wield was happy to let peace break out in its train. He began to whistle "The Flowers That Bloom in the Spring Tra-la" as he dried the glasses.

Behind him someone coughed and he turned to see Filmer viewing this domestic scene with a lip-curl that prompted him to ask frivolously, "Solved the Great Post Office Mystery yet, Terry?"

"Funny," growled Filmer. "One thing for sure, he won't be flying down to Rio on the proceeds."

"Or *she,*" said Wield. "Mustn't be sexist. What's the damage?"

"A cardigan Mrs. Stacey got from a catalog but it didn't fit, a couple of Mr. Digweed's mail-order books, and an herb pudding."

"A what?"

"Mrs. Hogbin's herb pudding. It's famous. Whenever she makes one, she sends a slice to her nephew in Wimbledon. Those were the packets so far as the Wylmots can recall. Some letters, too, they think. I've checked with the packet senders. The cardigan cost twenty pounds, the books were worth about fifty, and the pudding about seven and six."

"Seven and six?"

"They still count in old money among themselves around here," said Filmer.

"So. Any ideas?"

"Incomers," said Filmer with a countryman's certainty.

"Oh, aye? Up the motorway from the big city, hit the target, and off, all for some books and an herb pudding?" mocked Wield.

"You got any better ideas? Going to run around with this like Prince Charming after Cinderella, perhaps?"

He produced an evidence bag containing the sole cast Wield had found and tossed it onto the table with such force, the cast broke in two.

"Careful," remonstrated Wield, carefully picking up the bag. Broken, the cast showed even more clearly what it consisted of. Sand, earth, cement, gravel . . . It occurred to him he knew exactly where he could find such a combination underfoot. Before he could share his revelation, Filmer said, "Fat-arse and fancy-pants still stinking in their pits, are they? When are they going to start taking young Bendish's disappearance seriously?"

"Oh, soon," said Wield vaguely. Filmer's genuine concern about his missing lad was touching, but that didn't make his griping any less irritating. "You hold the fort here, will you, Terry? I've just got to pop up to Old Hall."

He made his way into the High Street and turned up the hill past the war memorial. As he entered the churchyard he glimpsed a figure moving rapidly between the tombstones before vanishing through the arch into Green Alley. He couldn't be certain, but it looked like Franny Harding, clutching her cello case. She had been coming from the direction of the vicarage and on impulse he went to the arch leading into the vicarage garden and peered through.

In the morning dew a single line of small footprints led from the French window across the lawn. None went the other way, which meant either she'd gone into the vicarage via the drive up past Corpse Cottage. Or she'd been there all night. Giving encores?

He caught a movement behind a bedroom window and, ashamed, he turned away and hurried into Green Alley.

So deeply immersed in thought was he that he almost walked through the little glade without noticing. Then he did a classic double take. The faun's statue was back.

Odder still, as he looked at it, its head fell off.

And oddest of all, it spoke.

"I didn't break it!"

He advanced and peered over the marble bench. Crouched behind it was little Madge Hogbin.

"Hello, luv," he said. "Shouldn't you be getting ready for school?"

"Don't go to school on Reckoning Day," she said.

"That's nice. Did you see who brought the statue back?"

She shook her head violently and repeated, "I didn't break it."

"Didn't think you did," he said, picking up the head and wedging it into place. "Did you see it with a hat on the other day?"

"Yes."

"And who put it there? Mr. Bendish, was it? Harry?"

"No."

"No? Who, then?"

"The other one."

"The other one what?"

"The other policeman, silly!"

"The other policeman? There were two policemen? And what were they doing?"

She put her fist to her mouth and giggled bubbily.

"I'm sorry, luv. I didn't hear you. What were they doing?"

The fist came out.

"Kissing!" she shouted. Then she was away through the bushes, trailing laughter behind her.

Wield resumed his walk and his musings. This time they were almost fatal, for he stepped off the path onto the drive without slowing down and had to step back extremely quickly as a battered yellow VW Beetle raced by, heading for the main gate. He just had time to glimpse Fran Harding's diminutive figure crouching at the wheel, and leaning against the passenger seat her cello case.

Behind her she had left a scene of frantic activity with half a dozen workmen cleaning up the mess left by their renovation of the stable block. This display of energy was explained by the supervisory presence of Girlie, pipe at full steam, standing on the entrance steps and occasionally issuing a fumarolic exhortation to greater effort.

As Wield went slowly toward her, studying the ground in the hope of spotting a matching print to confirm his theory about the post office cast, Guy the Heir came striding across the garden to join his cousin on the steps. They exchanged what didn't seem like very cousinly words, then he headed away toward the Land Rover parked around the side of the house.

Wield went up the steps and joined Girlie.

"Young Fran seemed in a hurry," he said.

"Not another near miss, I hope! Don't know what's got into that girl. She'd better be in just as much of a hurry to get back here. It's the Squire's Reckoning today, and I need all hands to man the pumps."

"At least you've got the weather for it," said Wield.

"Sun always shines on Reckoning Day," said Girlie. "Anything I can do for you, Sergeant, as long as it doesn't involve taking my eye off these layabouts?"

But Wield was not listening. Rapt as Crusoe on that fatal Friday, he was looking down at a damp print on the age-smoothed granite which, in pattern and dimension, looked a precise match for the post office cast.

He looked at Girlie's feet. They seemed the right size but she was wearing a pair of green Wellies, not sneakers, and besides there was no reason for her feet to be damp.

He heard the roar of the Land Rover's engine bursting into life and the vehicle came slowly toward them. Wield raised his hand in an effort to signal it to stop, but Guy the Heir, either ignoring or mistaking the gesture, responded by raising his hand to his gray forage cap in mock salute.

The gesture confirmed what Wield had deduced. The flowers that bloomed in the spring tra-la did after all have something to do with this case, for in the crease of the cap, at the point where Guy's fingers mockingly touched it, was tucked a drooping, fading narcissus.

Two

*. . . and then for Candor & Comfort
& Coffee & . . .*

"Couldn't you at least drive me up to the door?" pleaded
Pascoe.

"Don't be daft! It's nobbut a step and you'll have to walk
into the village afterward anyway," said Dalziel. "See you
later."

He'd brought it on himself by speculating as they drove
along on who had rung Bendish with the report of someone
hanging around Scarletts. Was the idea to get him there, or
just to get him out of the way? Maybe no one rang. . . .
Maybe it was word of mouth. . . .

At which point Dalziel said, "Seems to me like you left a
few gaps, lad."

"Not really. Not what I'd call gaps. . . ."

"Aye. Big enough for a horse to crap through. We'll be
passing yon fancy house soon. Good chance to fill 'em."

"And you, sir . . . ?"

"Not me. No good with these arty-farties. I think I'll have
a word with that Dora Creed at the café."

"Miss Creed? But what's she got to do with anything?"

"Don't know. But she's got nice little feet. And there was
a bloody good smell coming out of her caff yesterday. Here
we are. Out you get!"

And here he was faced with what seemed like a mile of
Fop-patrolled garden to get across.

If it were a mile, he broke the world record and practically fell through the door when at last it opened to his urgent knock.

It was only as the door closed behind him that he realized, like the cowardly prince in the legend, that his flight had brought him face-to-face with what he most feared. There at the foot of the stairs, like Anubis guarding the entrance to a pharaoh's tomb, sat Fop.

Slowly the beast arose, slowly advanced, and slowly took a long, reflective sniff at his crotch. Then scornfully it turned away and vanished into the kitchen.

Some test had been passed, for Mrs. Bayle said, "I'll tell him you're here."

"I'd like a word with you first. Please."

She led him into a laundry room, where she resumed her task of ironing sheets. There was a warm, comfortable smell, reminding him of childhood. Ellie was not big on ironing sheets.

"It's about the night Mr. Bendish called," he began. "Can you remember exactly what he said?"

"He said there'd been a report of someone suspicious hanging around the house."

"Did he say someone had phoned him with this report? Or told him direct? Or what?"

She regarded him stonily and said, "You asked what he said exactly and I've told you. Nowt about phones or owt like that, just there'd been a report."

"Fine, good, excellent," said Pascoe. "So you let him in to look around."

"He insisted."

"And what did he say when he came in?"

"First off, he asked me if the alarm system was on. I said aye, it were always on, and he said would I switch it off, and I said what for? And he said so's he wouldn't set it off when he was checking, and I said he could check without touching, and he said his mate who was checking outside would likely try the windows to make sure they were fast—"

"Hold on," said Pascoe, reluctant to interrupt this unprecedented flow but in need of clarification. "His mate? What do you mean?"

"I mean his mate. T'other bobby in the car."

"You mean there were two of them?"

"No wonder you lose track, mister, when you don't know how many you've got in the first place!" she said in exasperation.

"This other policeman, did you know him?"

"No. Not that I saw much of him, but the only other bobby I've ever seen with young Bendish is yon Sergeant Filmer and it weren't him."

"How do you know?"

"Not big enough. Sat there with his hat on and there were still plenty of space above, not like yon awkward-length Filmer."

Pascoe recalled Dalziel's words. Gaps big enough for a horse to crap through. And shuddered at the thought of the Fat Man's reaction to this extraordinary new information.

But that was for the future. Here and now he'd better devote all his energies to making sure he didn't leave a crack a mite could crawl through.

"What happened then?"

"We went around the house, him picking things up and fiddling with things when all he had to do was ask me if owt had been interfered with and I'd have soon told him. He opened the curtains and checked the windows—"

"Did you see anything of this other policeman, the one who was supposed to be checking outside?"

"Aye, I got a glimpse, but it's no use asking if I recognized him. It were dark out there and I'd switched the security lights off with the rest of the system. Is this going to take much longer? I've got the lunch to be getting on with."

Pascoe, who did not relish the thought of a transfer to the kitchen where Fop was demolishing bones, said hastily, "Not long. Just tell me what else happened."

"Happened? Nowt. No, I tell a lie. We got to the drawing room—"

"That's the long room, the one with many pictures?"

"Aye, that's the one. And while we were in there the phone rang, and I went out into the hall to answer it."

"What was the constable doing then?"

"Same as other places, fiddling with the window, I think."

"Who was it on the phone?" asked Pascoe.

"I don't see that's any of your business," she said.

"Well, if it's a secret . . ."

"No secret," she said. "It were some lass from the television wanting to talk to Mr. Halavant about his next program. She said he'd gone through it with his producer but he'd managed to mislay his notes or summat and there were some things he needed to check."

"Did she keep you talking long?" asked Pascoe.

"Long enough and all for nowt. I told her he weren't home, but she insisted I took down all the bits they needed to know about running order and inserts and that stuff."

Beneath her scorn was a certain pride at being au fait with such matters. Even the Mrs. Bayles of this world were not impervious to the seductive charms of the telly.

"But in the end it were all for nowt," she concluded, all scorn now. "She suddenly announces the producer is signaling he's found his notes after all, so thank you and good night!"

"So you didn't need to bother Mr. Halavant with this?"

"No, but I told him just the same."

"Why was that?"

"Because like you, he asked. Just after you'd been yesterday. Just the same, question after question. I told him I went back to the constable and I showed him out and I watched him get in the car—"

"His colleague was back in the passenger seat?"

"Aye. And I saw them go down the drive and out of the gate. And I made sure they shut it behind them. Then I went back inside and checked around for myself. And then I thought I heard a noise—"

"Like a bird, I think you said?"

"Aye, but not like any bird I know," she replied. "Truth is, I don't hear high sounds so well anymore. Doesn't bother me, got a special bell fitted to the phone so I don't miss none of his calls. So this noise, it was more like I knew it was there than really heard it."

She glared at him, defying him to comment on this admission of weakness.

"So you let Fop out? Did he find anything, do you think?"

"Came back in licking his chops, which is usually a sign, but it could've just been a rabbit. Now I reckon, if you've any more questions, you'd best ask the master! He's in the long sitting room."

The master was discovered on a chaise longue, wearing a dressing gown which looked as if it had been bought in a Noël Coward memorabilia sale and staring moodily into space across a demitasse of bitterly aromatic coffee.

He frowned at Pascoe and said, "You'll take a cup?"

"No, thanks," said Pascoe, hearing the door close behind him with an emphasis which said, He'll fetch his own cup if he does!

"In that case, state your business," said Halavant.

Unflustered by this brusqueness Pascoe studied the walls.

There was a gap where the pretty lady with the hint of a wink had been.

He said, "What happened to your ancestor, sir?"

Halavant said, "Oh, I took it down. For cleaning."

"Really? Not because it turned out to be a forgery?"

"What the devil do you mean?" demanded Halavant, pale, though not, it seemed to Pascoe, with indignation.

There was the distant clangor of a very loud telephone. A few moments later Mrs. Bayle appeared at the door.

"It's that Mr. Wallop," she said unceremoniously. "What shall I tell him?"

"Tell him? Tell him? You may tell him ... to go to hell! Mr. Pascoe, you haven't answered my question."

"Nor you mine," said Pascoe, seating himself on the edge of a high wingchair. "Now, which of us shall go first, do you think?"

Three

I have been listening to dreadful Insanity.

"No," said Girlie Guillemard. "I've no idea where Guy has gone, like I've no idea where Franny's gone. All I know is I'm up to my eyes in work, and everyone I might expect to help me goes bunking off as soon as I turn my back!"

She was clearly on the edge of her nerves, yet Wield sensed it was more than a mere organizational crisis which had brought her here. He got the impression she could have supervised the building of a pyramid without breaking sweat.

He said, "I see your statue's back. The faun."

"Oh, is he? Good," she said indifferently. "Nice to know Guy takes notice sometimes."

"Its head's broken off, but," he added. That got her.

"What? Shit!" she exclaimed angrily. "Useless wanker! George, there you are. Come to help with the furniture, have you?"

Wield turned to see George Creed approaching.

"What? Oh, aye, that's right," said the farmer. "Morning, Sergeant."

This was a very obliging farmer indeed, thought Wield, ready to drop everything in the middle of lambing to come up here to do some furniture removal.

He must also be a very strong farmer, added Wield when it became apparent that the furniture in question was the long oak refectory table in the main hallway.

"Sergeant, I wonder, could you . . . ?"

It was beyond the strength of even two of them and Girlie had to press a couple of Wallop's reluctant workmen before they could maneuver it through the doorway and out onto the lawn. At this point a lorry turned up laden with trestles and folding chairs from the village hall, which a quartet of muscular youths started to unload and arrange over the grass. It would have made more sense, thought Wield, to wait for this lot to appear before attempting to move the big table. He gave a hand for a while till he noticed that Creed seemed to be excused from duties after his initial efforts, and Girlie, too, had abandoned her supervisory position to go into a close confabulation with the farmer around the side of the house. After a while Creed nodded and turned away and headed toward the woods. Girlie returned to harangue the workmen for an alleged slackening of effort and Wield took the opportunity to slip away.

The farmer was out of sight, so Wield pressed on along the gravel track he'd taken through the neglected formal garden, which merged without boundary into a mixed orchard whose buds the warm spring sunshine was exploding into pink and white blossom. Soon the path greened from gravel to moss and the fruit trees were replaced by beech and oak and ash in which birds piped and chattered their warning of intrusion. Then, with a suddenness that surprised him, this, too, was drowned in the sound of rushing water and he found himself at the edge of a steep gorge looking down at the turbulent Een.

"Can't see him," said a voice. "Must be down at Scarletts Pool."

He turned to see the Squire with a pair of field glasses in his hand, resting against and blending in with a silver birch.

"What must?" asked Wield.

"Kingfisher, of course. Unbroken record since the Middle Ages. That surprises you, eh? Got him in my ballad. Like to hear?"

Wield nodded, thinking of the bright limp body in Jason Toke's hand. The Squire cleared his throat, raised his head, and began to recite.

Kingfisher wears the heavenly blue
Of Mary, Heaven's Queen,
And bears a heavenly message, too,
Along the banks of Een.

Though popes may pine and kings decline
Though thrones and fiefdoms fall,
While I still rule o'er rock and pool,
A Guillemard holds the Hall.

He finished and regarded Wield complacently.

"That were grand," said Wield.

"Fellow thinks it was grand," said the Squire with mild surprise, looking toward second slip. Then the bright eyes returned to Wield.

"Tradition, you see. Got to go with it, even if it doesn't seem to make sense. You must find this in your line of business. Apply the rules even when they strike you personally as a load of bollocks, right?"

"Aye, more or less," agreed Wield.

"There you are, then. *Fuctata non perfecta*. Know what it means, Sergeant? I'll tell you. *Life can be a bastard*. Loose translation, but very apt. Oh, yes, apt indeed. Excuse me. Chap I've got to see."

He moved away and Wield saw that it was no euphemistic excuse. George Creed had appeared some distance away and as he watched, the Squire went to join him. The two men stood regarding each other for a moment, then they moved out of sight into the trees.

Wield was about to start back toward the house when a movement downstream caught his eye. Someone was crouching on the riverbank, staring down into the water. He walked along till he was directly above and could see that it was Jason Toke. Wield started to climb down the steep bank, clinging to bushes and rocks to stop his descent from turning into a fall. He made a lot of noise but the sound of the water must have covered it. Or else the youth, Narcissus-like, was too rapt to admit distraction.

"Morning, Jason," said Wield.

The youth shot upright and spun around, poised for flight. Curiously, when he saw who it was, he visibly relaxed.

"What are you doing?" asked Wield. "Looking for another kingfisher to kill?"

"Didn't kill him," said Toke with a lack of passion which was, curiously, more convincing than indignation.

"No. So what are you doing?"

"Watching."

"What?"

"Water."

It came out as simple fact rather than studied insolence.

"Not got your gun?"

"No. Didn't want it today. Sometimes it's better without it."

"Why's that, Jason?" asked Wield gently.

He raised those disconcerting eyes and said, "Sometimes it's better. If you don't want to use it."

"I see," said Wield, hoping he didn't. "So it's at home, is it? I'd like to take a look at where you keep it, Jason. Shall we go now?"

"If you like," said the boy indifferently.

Wield prepared to scramble back up the side of the gorge, but when Toke set off along the bank downstream, he bowed to local knowledge and followed. Eventually they came out of the gorge and after a quarter mile or so the youth led him across a field into a lane which brought them behind the Morris and alongside Intake Cottage. Neither spoke till they were on the narrow path through the ravaged garden.

"Why'd you cut everything down, Jason?" asked Wield.

"Cordon sanitaire," said Toke, pronouncing it right. "Don't want cover right up to house."

"Cover for what?"

"Them, when they come."

"When who comes?"

"Makes no matter who," said Toke, rapping a rapid five-beat pattern on the door.

Mrs. Toke opened it almost immediately, acknowledged Wield's attempt at explanation with her usual myopic stare, and retired to the living room. Toke led the way upstairs, ran his fingers lightly over the code panel on his bedroom door, and pushed it open.

Wield, half expecting some kind of hi-tech armory, was rather taken aback to find himself in what looked like any teenager's bedroom.

It was untidy, with magazines strewn over the floor and posters blue-tacked to the walls. The most hi-tech thing in sight was a cassette deck and a pair of low-grade speakers.

A closer look was slightly more disconcerting. The magazines were all combat and survival journals. And the posters featured portraits of people like Mao and Che and Castro and Guzmán. A student trying for radical credibility might have collected such a gallery, but Wield couldn't see Toke wanting to impress anybody.

He said, "Heroes of yours, are they, Jason?"

"Heroes?" the boy echoed as if the word meant nothing.

"Yes. I mean, you admire what they stand for?"

"Don't know what they *stand* for. Just know they could all take care of themselves, live off the land, survive."

"Survive? But not forever, eh?"

"No one survives forever."

This was getting philosophical.

Wield said, "Do you think there's someone out there after you?"

"Don't you?" said Toke.

"Well, yes. Sometimes," admitted Wield. "But not so that I need protection."

"Don't need what you got. You're a cop. People shout at you, you don't go away."

"Whereas you do?"

"Farmer shouts at a fox, old bushy goes away. But he's got to come back. Got to feed, hasn't he?"

"Even if the farmer's waiting with his gun?"

Toke nodded vigorously, as if pleased he'd at last got through.

"And sometimes farmer don't wait. He comes after old bushy with his horses and his dogs."

"But that's a fox we're talking about, Jason," said Wield gently. "Not a human being."

"Humans too," said Toke with the certainty of faith. "You watch that old telly, you see it every night. All that shooting and chasing. All them folk sitting around starving 'cos there's no one looking out for them and they don't know how to look out for themselves."

"But this is England, Jason," insisted Wield. "Surely you don't need to put up all these defenses here in Enscombe."

"Yeah, Enscombe's all right, mostly. But there's people come in from outside. There's always people coming. You've got to watch out or they'll have you afore you know it."

"Like the police, you mean? Was Constable Bendish one of the ones you had to watch out for?" asked Wield.

For a few moments the youth's face had been animated by what for him was probably a rare desire to communicate. But now the old blankness was back.

"Don't know nowt about that one," he said.

"But he came up here to check where you keep your gun, didn't he?"

"Yeah. Said it were all right."

"I'm sure he did. Now I'd like to see."

Toke opened the ancient mahogany wardrobe which almost filled one wall. There weren't many clothes hanging there, which was just as well, for a large part of the interior was filled with a steel gun cabinet. Toke produced a set of keys from inside his shirt and opened it. There were two shotguns inside. One was a traditional side-by-side twelve-gauge. The other had a shorter single barrel and a slide action. Wield regarded them both with distaste. The old truism that it wasn't the guns that caused trouble but the people who used them cut little ice. Guns were like cars. There was no telling how a man would react to having control of one. He felt the seductive pull of the longer, more elegant double-barreled weapon now, though he knew the crook out for trouble would opt for the uglier slide-action gun with its superior fire-power.

"Of course you've got all the necessary certification?" he said.

Toke pulled out a wallet that looked as if he'd recently shot it and extracted some creased and stained papers. They all looked in order.

Wield returned them. As Toke relocked the gun cabinet, the sergeant stooped to take a closer look at magazines on the floor and noticed the corner of a leather-bound book protruding from under the bed. He pulled it out and examined it.

It was *The Warrior: An Illustrated History*. A piece of newspaper acted as a marker. He opened the book and read, *At one end of the scale stands the professional soldier, prepared through conditioning and training to cope with almost any combat situation. He works in a team, accepts his superiors' orders unquestioningly, and expects the orders he gives to his subordinates to be accepted in the same manner. At the other end stands the berserker, or baresark, the individual warrior par excellence, who, finding himself pushed to the last extremity either by external forces or internal pressures, throws caution to the winds and runs amuck among his enemies, heedless alike of the wounds he receives and the terrible dole he deals. It has often been the case, when circumstances shift the soldier from his professional calm to the berserker state, that Victoria Crosses are won.*

"That's private," said Toke, turning from the cabinet and seeing what Wield was doing. "Give it here."

"Hold your horses, son," said Wield. "Interesting book, this. Had it long?"

"Long enough," he said defiantly.

"And this one?" said Wield, pulling Thorburn's *Birds* from under the bed. "You had this one long enough too? Where's the other? Can't see it here."

"What other?"

"Book of paintings, Mr. Digweed said."

Now the youth looked alarmed.

"That one's a present," he protested with an almost touching illogicality. "Thought she might take heed of me if I gave her that."

"Caddy, you mean?" said Wield gently. "You were going to give it yesterday till you saw us there, right? So you gave the kingfisher instead."

"Didn't harm him, but," asserted Toke once more. "She likes colors and pictures and things. Thought she might like me if I gave her that book with all the paintings in it."

"And these?" said Wield, hefting the two volumes in his hand.

For the first time Toke looked guilty.

"Them's for me," he admitted. "No one wanted them. They was always there!"

"You could have bought them," suggested Wield.

"What with? Think I'm made of brass?"

"Must have taken a lot of money to do up this house."

"That were needed. And there were nowt left over."

"From what?"

"From Warren's money."

Warren . . . the elder brother, the one killed in Ireland but not thought qualified for the war memorial.

"Warren left you some money, did he?"

"What he saved. And there was some from the army."

"And you spent it making the cottage secure?" said Wield.

"Wouldn't have been needful if Warren had come back!" cried Toke. "Warren knew how to look out for us."

His face was twisted with remembered grief. Wield, frightened at the emotions he'd tapped, reached out a comforting hand, but the youngster ducked as if from a blow and, pausing only to grab a carrier bag from behind the door, shot through the door and down the stairs. By the time Wield followed, there was no sign of him except the open front door.

He went back upstairs and did a thorough search. There was no sign of any weapons other than those safely locked in the steel cabinet.

Mrs. Toke was standing in the lobby when he came back downstairs. She looked at the books he was carrying and said, "It's that lass, mister. You're lucky. Lass like her makes some men do strange things. Doesn't mean it, but that makes it worse."

Ignoring the curious reference to his invulnerability, Wield said, "Couldn't you persuade him it's hopeless?"

"He needs hope, Jason. Put it all in his brother, and when that went, look what followed. Take this away, could be summat else 'ud take its place, but could be it's the end of things."

The phrase, quietly spoken, fell from her lips like a sentence of death.

"Do you think he could harm anyone, luv?" asked Wield gently.

"When living's a pit of blackness, what's harm?" she answered. "I'll watch him, never fear. And tell Mr. Digweed I'll make it right."

"That mightn't be enough," said Wield. "He might still want to prosecute."

"Nay, tell him I'll see he gets all he wants," she urged.

"Now, that sounds like an offer he'd be mad to refuse," said Wield with a smile.

Four

*I have a very good eye at an
Adulteress.*

It was midmorning when Andy Dalziel, ignoring a CLOSED sign, pushed open the door of the Wayside Café.

The tables were crowded with trays laden down with good things. There were pies and pastries and bread rolls and sausage rolls and plate cakes and cupcakes and trifles and custards and Bakewells and sponges and—

"We're shut," said Dora Creed, emerging from the kitchen with another tray. "Can you not read?"

"Aye, can I. The Good Book," said Dalziel. " 'And he said, Son of man, cause thy belly to eat, and fill thy bowels with this roll I give thee.' "

He helped himself to a sausage roll and thrust it into his mouth.

Dora said, "Ezekiel, three, three."

"I love a holy woman!" said Dalziel, swallowing. " 'Then did I eat it and it was in my mouth as honey for sweetness.' I'll have another of them."

She said, "You're that policeman, aren't you?"

"Superintendent Dalziel," he said. "Andy to my friends. And you're Dora Creed, the best baker in Yorkshire. My dad were a baker, you know. Came down from Glasgow in the Depression, got taken on at Ebor's, they've been taken over by some supermarket long since and it's all done by computers now. I'd almost forgot what real baking smelled like till I came in here."

"We're still shut," said Dora, less positively. "I'm getting stuff ready to be picked up for the Squire's Feast."

"You mean all this lot's going up to the Hall?"

"Aye, it's traditional. He feeds everyone who turns up for the Reckoning."

"Does he, now?" said Dalziel speculatively. "I'll tell you what, luv. You carry on, and I'll just fit in the odd question as you go by."

"Well, if it's official," she said, weakening.

"If it were any more official, it 'ud be wearing pinstripes," he assured her. "In fact, why don't I give you a hand with these trays while we're talking."

"And yourself a hand with my grub, I don't doubt," she said sharply.

" 'Thou shalt not muzzle the ox when he treadeth out the corn,' " said Dalziel. "Deuteronomy."

"I know where it's from," she said. "I'm just amazed where it's got to."

"You and I are going to understand each other very well," laughed Andrew Dalziel. "Is that an apple pie? My favorite."

"Aye, but it's not cut."

"Cut? You're not expecting it to do more than one, are you?"

She began to laugh and Dalziel would have laughed with her if his mother hadn't taught him that it was rude to laugh with your mouth full.

When Wield arrived ten minutes later he found the two well-upholstered figures sitting at one of the tables, their heads almost meeting across a somewhat diminished trayful of confections, with Dora Creed doing most of the talking, a predominance maintained by the fact that the sight of Dalziel's open mouth clearly affected her like a fledgling's gape and she couldn't resist popping something into it.

Wield had been making for Digweed's shop with the recovered books till the sight of Dalziel's car diverted him. Now he wondered if it were wise to break up such an intimate tableau and thought of withdrawing, but the Fat Man looked up and said, " 'Watchman, what of the night?' "

"Isaiah twenty-one ten," said Dora.

"Eleven, I think you'll find, luv," said Dalziel. "Why don't you go and look it up while I talk with Shadrach here?"

Obediently, nay, gladly, the woman rose and left. What would have been her attitude if Dalziel had turned up in leathers on a bike?

wondered Wield. Probably the same. You didn't apply human rules to a force of nature.

He sat down and brought the Fat Man up to date.

While not expecting fulsome praise, he had hopes of an acknowledgment that his morning had not been in vain.

"So you reckon you've solved both these break-ins? Bloody hell, Wieldy, I left you here so's you could find this missing plowboy, not do his sodding job!"

"Is that right, sir?" said Wield, stung. "And what have you found, apart from the quality of Miss Creed's pastry?"

"Me?" Dalziel's left eyelid drooped in a knowing wink. "I've found out what George Creed's sin was. Have a custard tart. They're lovely! And stop sulking. It spoils your baby looks!"

What indiscreet reply Wield, in the grip of his Enscombe-inspired openness, might have made was never known, for at that moment an ancient pickup rattled to a halt outside and a pair of young farmworkers appeared in the doorway.

"Miss Creed!" yelled one of them. "We've come for the grub."

Dora emerged from the kitchen and said apologetically to Dalziel, "I'm sorry, but I've got to get this stuff up to the Hall."

"Nay, lass, we'll help you load it," said the Fat Man gallantly. "Won't we, Sergeant?"

And for the second time that day Wield found himself acting as an unpaid laborer for the Guillemards.

As he staggered out weighed down by one of Dora's trays, he saw Digweed emerge from the bookshop. He glanced Wield's way and the sergeant opened his mouth, but before he could speak the bookseller's glance slid over him dismissively and the lean, patrician figure moved swiftly across the street and vanished into the gallery.

Sod you too! thought Wield. But any further brooding on the snub was prevented by the arrival of Pascoe, chauffered by Justin Halavant.

Pascoe looked with mild amazement on the scene before him, but Halavant's gaze was on the gallery door through which Digweed had just vanished.

He said, "Look, I need to pop into the Morris and set Thomas's mind at rest."

"No, hang on," said Pascoe, who'd got out. "I think Mr. Dalziel—"

"I am not about to flee the country, Chief Inspector," said Halavant acidly. "But I have better things to do than sit around while your colleagues moonlight as removal men."

He gunned the engine, swung the wheel hard over, and managed a U-turn with millimeters to spare.

"What was that all about?" asked Dalziel.

"I don't know. Cold feet, maybe," said Pascoe. "It's not good news, sir. What it looks like is, the night before last young Harold Bendish conned his way into Scarletts in order to steal a painting. He had an accomplice also dressed as a cop, probably in his spare uniform. While Mrs. Bayle was out of the room answering a fake phone call, Bendish removed the painting, passed it through the window, took in a copy, and hung that in its place."

"Desperate Dan's going to love this," said the Fat Man. "But if you've got it right, lad, why's yon prancing pillock not running around screaming blue murder and threatening to write to his MP?"

"I'm not sure. It's almost like he's treading water. He didn't argue with anything I said . . . it was like he knew it all already. I mean, he'd taken the picture, the copy, if I'm right, off the wall already."

"But he hadn't come running to us to make a complaint?"

"No, sir. And another thing. The original was an eighteenth-century painting of a fashionable young lady. Halavant said it was one of his ancestors. But according to local history, during the eighteenth century, and well into the nineteenth, the Halavants were still, to quote, a bunch of raggedy-arsed peasants!"

"So he's ashamed of his family origins," said Dalziel. "No crime in that. Where's he off to now?"

"The Morris. You know he owns it? Well, evidently he was thinking of selling but after our little chat he's changed his mind for some reason, so he's keen to let Wapshare know."

The Fat Man's eyes lit up.

"So it'll be celebration time down there. It's time I looked in, else Thomas will be thinking he's offended me. I should've gone there first off, anyway. Yon bugger misses nowt that goes on in Enscombe."

"Excuse me, sir," said Wield. "I think we're in business."

He pointed down the High Street to where a Land Rover had just pulled up outside the post office.

"Returning to the scene of the crime, you reckon?" said Dalziel as they watched Guy the Heir get out and go inside the shop. "All right, we'll have a word as we go on past to the pub."

He turned and shouted to Dora Creed. "Thanks for the grub, luv. I'll mebbe see you up at the Hall later. Keep smiling!"

" 'A merry heart maketh a cheerful countenance,' " she called.

" 'And he that is of a merry heart hath a continual feast,' " capped Dalziel.

Where the hell does he get all this scriptural knowledge from? wondered Wield as he and Pascoe fell into step on either side of the Fat Man, who was striding purposefully down the middle of the street.

Doc Holliday and the Earp Brothers on their way to the OK Corral, thought Pascoe. All it needed was a good soundtrack. Dalziel broke wind. Not *My Darling Clementine* after all, but *Blazing Saddles*, amended Pascoe wryly.

They stopped outside the post office. Through the window they could see Guy Guillemard talking to Daphne Wylmot. He was full of animation, she markedly less so.

"Full marks for nerve," said Wield grimly. "Shall we go in, sir?"

"Just hold your horses," said Dalziel thoughtfully.

Inside, Guy had picked up Daphne's hand from the counter. She glanced toward the window, saw the watching trio, and said something to the man, who turned to look at them and roared with laughter; then, blowing the woman a kiss, he came out of the shop.

"If it's not the Keystones!" he mocked. "Who said silent comedy was dead?"

He climbed into the Land Rover. Wield looked urgently at Dalziel, who stepped forward and said, "Mind you belt up, sir."

"Thank you kindly," said Guy. "Mustn't be breaking the law, must we? Ciao!"

The vehicle pulled away.

Wield turned incredulously to the Fat Man but before he could speak, Dalziel patted him on the head almost paternally and said, "Usually it makes no difference, Wieldy, but sometimes having the wrong aerial really mucks up your reception. Hang on here a tick while I have a quiet word."

He went into the shop, leaving the door open so that his "quiet word" came booming out.

"Morning, missus," he said. "Superintendent Dalziel, CID."

"Good morning. If it's about the break-in I'm afraid my husband isn't here."

"No matter," said Dalziel. "You can pass on owt you think he ought to know, luv. It's just a sort of confirmation, really, as the bishop said to the choirboy. First off, you and Guy Guillemard are having it off, right?"

"What?" The woman's voice rose disbelievingly. "What do you mean . . . ?"

"Well, like, you're having a fling, screwing, humping, shagging . . ."

It would have been semasiologically interesting to see where Dalziel's search for the *mot juste* led him, but the woman lacked the true scientific spirit.

"How dare you talk to me like this?" she interrupted angrily.

"Sorry, luv," said Dalziel penitently. "Does that mean you'd rather we waited for Mr. Wylmot? I'm not in a hurry."

Sometimes Pascoe thought Dalziel was a sadist. Sometimes he thought he was just a man who liked to cut through crap. Always he knew that with the Fat Man you got a choice. Either you did things his way now, or you did them his way a little later.

Daphne Wylmot read the runes and said in a voice which was suddenly as calm as a summer sea, "That won't be necessary. Yes, Guy and I are lovers. Please go on."

"And last night Guy Guillemard came around here after your husband had gone to sleep."

"Yes, he did."

"Bit chancy that, wasn't it, luv?"

Daphne laughed musically.

"No, I don't take chances, Superintendent. Dudley can't hold his drink. When he's had a skinful, he falls into bed and that's it for at least six hours."

Wield, recalling her spritzer and Dudley's large gin-and-tonics, thought grimly that she certainly didn't take chances.

"So you switched off the alarm and opened the back door and let Guy in. And when he'd finished, you let him out and forgot to put the alarm back on."

"I didn't forget. I was rather . . . tired myself when we finished, so I just told him to let himself out. I knew I'd be up first and I meant to lock the door and switch the alarm on then. But when I saw we'd been burgled, I thought it would be foolish to touch the alarm."

"Very wise," said Dalziel, beaming. "There, it hardly hurt at all, did it, missus? Thanks for your cooperation."

"And thank you in advance for your discretion," she replied.

"You can bank on it," said Dalziel gallantly. "Good-looking lass like you, but. I reckon you could do a lot better for yourself than yon bag of wind."

"Really? You've fucked Guy, too, have you?" she asked with wide-eyed interest.

It was a rare pleasure to see Dalziel put down beyond riposte, but they knew better than to let it show.

He glowered at them suspiciously as he came out of the shop and said, "So that's only one of the two crimes-of-the-century you've solved, Wieldy. Mebbe you'd better check them books really did come from Digweed's shop before you start crowing about the other."

He nodded up the street to where Digweed had just emerged from the gallery. The bookseller glanced in their direction, then hurried into his shop.

"I'll see you in the pub, then," said Wield, glad of a chance to escape.

"Poor old Wieldy!" laughed Pascoe, watching him hurry away.

"You were ready to go along, weren't you?" growled Dalziel. "And you've not got his excuse. So let's be getting on down to the Morris, shall we? And see what kind of cock-up you've managed to make!"

And suddenly Pascoe felt all his newfound certainties crumbling like Dora Creed's shortcrust pastry.

Five

*How soon the difference of temper
in Children appears!*

Kee Scudamore had been sitting by the till when Digweed entered the gallery.

"You're looking very pensive," he said. "I didn't think you found finance so enthralling."

"It's money that makes the world go around," she said. "I should have thought last night's meeting made that quite clear. This windfall Larry hinted at, have you any idea what it might be?"

"I should have thought you were more likely to be his confidante than I," he answered, smiling.

"What's that supposed to mean?" she asked angrily.

"Whoops. Sorry. You seem to be fond of his company, that was all I meant. Forgive me if I strayed into an impertinence."

"A misconception, certainly," she said rather bitterly. "I can assure you that it isn't me he's got his eyes on."

"Ah, you've noticed, then?"

"Hasn't everyone?"

"Indeed. Has he said anything?"

"Not in so many words, or rather, so far I've avoided hearing them."

"I see. Or rather I don't. Why should he speak to you rather than Caddy herself? I know you are in some ways in loco parentis, but surely such old-fashioned notions hardly apply in this day and age, not even in clerical circles?"

"Can't say. You'll need to ask Larry."

"Perhaps not," he said, regarding her thoughtfully. "Here's that deed of his, by the way. Very interesting notion of yours but, as I forecast, far beyond the reach of my own rusty law. I faxed it off to a chum of mine who's better equipped to pronounce on such things. I'll let you know as soon as I hear. Of course, Larry might be well ahead of you in all this. Could be that this is what he was getting at last night."

"Yes. Perhaps." The idea seemed to please her. "I think I'll take this back to him now and drop a hint."

He said gently, "Kee, you will take care."

"I'm sorry?"

"I'm very fond of you, that's all. Look, sometimes it seems better to plunge in, take risks, get your pain over. But pick your moment. You've got to carry on living afterward, whatever happens."

"What on earth are you talking about, Edwin?" she asked, very controlled.

"Oh, I don't know. Finance perhaps. Investment. That's what makes the world go around, didn't you say? Is Caddy above?"

"Yes. You want to see her? You might tell her I'll be out for a while. Not that it makes the slightest difference!"

"No. I don't suppose it does," said Digweed.

He ran lightly up the stairs and went straight into the studio without knocking. Caddy was standing in front of her portrait of Wield, studying it critically.

"Good Lord," said Digweed. "Is that who I think it is? Of course it is, there can't be two like that!"

"Hi, Edwin," she said. "There's something missing."

"Indeed. And from your crucifixion still, I see. Have you decided whose face is going to plug that gap?"

"Whoever fits," she said vaguely. "Was there something special you wanted?"

"Just to say, that cover business, it's all finished now. All loose ends tied up. Okay?"

"If you say so," she said indifferently.

"I do. Caddy, exactly what is it you're trying to paint here?"

His gaze had moved from the oval blank above the shapely torso to the background. By a trick of compression Scarletts had been relocated just below the school. Halavant, accompanied by Fop, from whose jaws dangled a scrap of bloodstained cloth, was looking toward the Green, where the builder Phil Wallop, previously imaged standing triumphantly next to a cement mixer, had been overpainted to a pale shadow, but his check-trousered legs could now be seen bright and fresh waving from the mixer's mouth.

"What I see," she said. "Or maybe time. The way one thing takes the place of another, but nothing ever really goes away. Not here, anyway. But it's not right either. It's so easy to miss things, isn't it?"

She was back in front of Wield's portrait.

Digweed said encouragingly, "Honestly, it's fine. Such a strange face. God, I'd not like to play poker with him!"

"Yes, I think he's a man who uses silences like you use words. . . ."

She let the sentence hang, then began to laugh.

"That's it. Of course. Thank you, Edwin."

"For what?" he asked. Then bewilderment turned to incredulity as he looked from her face to Wield's and back again.

"Caddy, if you're saying what I think, well, that's absurd. . . ."

"Of course, but isn't everything? So that's all right."

She picked up her brush and palette and approached the painting. Her foot kicked over a half-full mug of cold coffee, but she didn't notice as she began to attack Wield's eyes.

Digweed left. There was little point in staying. As he crossed the street he noticed the three policemen gathered outside the post office. Perhaps, he thought uncharitably, they'd caught Wylmot fiddling the postal orders.

He hurried into his shop and up the stairs into the computer room. Hardly had he entered when the bell on the shop door sounded.

"Damn," he said, going out onto the landing and looking down the stairs.

"Morning," said Wield. "No, don't come down. I'll come up. I've got something for you."

He mounted the steep stairs two at a time. On the landing he paused and sniffed. There was a pleasantly pungent, rather spicy smell in the air.

"Not interrupting a meal, am I?" he said.

"As you've just seen me come in, and as it's only eleven o'clock in the morning, it's hardly likely," said Digweed with all his old acidity. Then immediately relenting, he added in a friendlier tone, "It's that tiny kitchen of mine. Cooking smells seem to hang around forever. Come in here."

He led the way into the computer room and threw open a window.

"There. Now we can smell the spring. Isn't it a lovely day? Always is for the Reckoning, of course. Now, how can I help you?"

"You can confirm that these are yours," said Wield, handing over the books.

"Yes, indeed, these are they. Well done. Where did you find them?"

"In Jason Toke's bedroom," said Wield.

"Ah, yes. That poor boy. I'd begun to wonder. . . . I'd seen him in here looking at *The Warrior* and other military books. The Thorburn too . . . but it was the Renoir catalog that threw me. Where is it, by the way?"

"Still in his possession, I'm afraid. It wasn't for himself. He stole it to give to Caddy Scudamore."

"Of course. He's besotted. The poor child."

"Him or her?"

"Jason, of course. I think on closer acquaintance you'll find it hardly a description which applies to Caddy. Look, Sergeant, I really don't want to burden the lad with more trouble than his own mind creates for him. I shall not be pressing charges."

Wield frowned and said, "You may not be doing him a favor. Court appearance could put these obsessions of his in striking distance of a psychiatrist."

"You think he needs treatment? For being in love and reckoning that Britain in the nineties is a dangerously uncivilized place to live? Tut, man. By those criteria I suspect fifty percent of the population are sick!"

"Fifty percent of the population aren't obsessed with guns and survival techniques," said Wield. "But you must make your own mind up. I doubt if we tie him in with the post office job, Mr. Wylmot will feel so generous."

"Jason and the post office? But that's simply absurd!" protested Digweed.

"Why do you say that?" asked Wield.

"Well, I don't know, it just seems so. I mean, you didn't find anything at Intake Cottage to suggest a connection, did you?"

"No," admitted Wield. "Same MO, but. Any road, sir, no need to bother you with that. Oh, by the way, thanks again for last night. The book, the bourbon, the thought. It were right kind. I really enjoyed it."

"Me too," said Digweed, offering, rather to Wield's surprise, his hand. Mebbe this was how the middle classes acknowledged you weren't a yob all the way through. His hand was cool and dry, his grip firm.

"Sergeant . . ."

"Yes?"

"Perhaps I could call and collect my glasses later?"

"Sorry, I forgot all about them. Yes, sure. Or I'll bring them down here."

He went out onto the landing. The spicy smell seemed stronger than ever. The door into the tiny kitchen was ajar, but the smell didn't seem to emanate from there. And it was surely more herby than spicy.

Wield's nose was twitching in a very odd direction, both olfactorily and metaphorically.

He said, "Okay if I use your lav?"

And without waiting for an answer he went through the half-open door of the bathroom. He knew he was right straightaway. This was the source of the herbal smell; more precisely a tall wall cupboard.

He pulled its door open. It housed the hot water cylinder with a couple of shelves for airing clothes. He pushed aside a pile of underpants.

There it was, hard against the side of the hot tank, the source of the telltale aroma, a small parcel bearing a Wimbledon address and almost certainly containing the slice of herb pudding Mrs. Hogbin sent to her nephew regularly. There was a packet addressed to a mail-order firm, that would be Mrs. Stacey's cardigan. And two harder packets clearly containing books. And half a dozen envelopes.

Why should Digweed have turned burglar to retrieve his own books? Then one of the names on the book packets jumped up and hit him in the eye.

Mrs. Ellie Pascoe.

He turned with the packages in his hands.

"I think I'd better see if I can find some more bourbon," said Edwin Digweed.

Six

I tell you everything, and it is
unknown the Mysteries you conceal
from me.

Larry Lillingstone sat with his dusty records strewn all before him, but his inward eye was focused on the annals of his own pastorship, and the result was far from blissful.

"Larry, one of these days I'm going to catch you doing something deeply embarrassing," said Kee from the open French window.

"Kee, I'm sorry. I was miles away."

"Metaphysically, I presume?"

"Physically, too, soon. I don't think it'll be long before Enscombe and I part company."

"Good Lord. I think I'd better sit down."

She came forward with her easy grace, slipped into a wheelback chair, and regarded him expectantly.

"I've asked to see the bishop next week," he said. "I think it's time I moved on."

"But you've only been here two minutes."

"I suppose in Enscombe terms that's all that six months amounts to," he said. "But man proposes, God disposes. Kee, I was just going to have a coffee. Let me get you one."

"No, really, I'd rather . . ." But Lillingstone was already out of the room. She heard his footsteps go down the flagged corridor into the kitchen, then emerge and run lightly up the stairs. Perhaps he really needed to go to the loo and some clerical modesty forbade him from saying so. But there was no distant flushing of water as the footsteps descended like a

Goon Show sound effect, diminishing into the kitchen once more, and finally crescendoing back to the study.

"Coffee," he said, handing her a mug. "Was there something special you wanted to see me about?"

"No. Just to return this," she said, laying the deed of gift on the table. "But while I'm here . . . What you said last night at the meeting, about perhaps something coming up which could save the school—it didn't have anything to do with the vicarage, did it?"

"What do you mean?" he asked almost angrily.

"Just that with the vicarage being up for sale—"

"Oh, you don't imagine you'll get any money out of the church commissioners, do you?" he mocked. "They've got the cost accountants in too."

"No, it wasn't that, it was something quite different. But it will keep. As, apparently, will your ray of hope."

She made to rise and he said abruptly, "It's Caddy."

"I'm sorry? You mean Caddy is going to save the school? Or Caddy is your reason for leaving?"

He laughed a little wildly and said, "Both, perhaps. Or neither."

She regarded him with irritation, herself with more. She didn't want to talk about his feelings for Caddy, had consciously avoided his previous attempt to broach the subject. Left to himself he would probably make his play, get brushed off with that indifference which was more hurtful than dislike, be brokenhearted, then recover. But the idiot wanted an audience! It was Kee's belief that there is no obstacle to intimacy greater than a shared secret. And she wanted to be intimate with this man. Upstairs, downstairs, indoors, outdoors, in sickness and in health intimate!

She ought to get out now.

He said, "Kee, I need to talk about Caddy. . . ."

She fixed him with her wide, candid gaze and said, "No need, Larry. I've seen Caddy drive enough men to irrational behavior to recognize the symptoms."

"Men. Which men?" he asked indignantly.

Time to bring him down from his romantic heights.

She said, "Justin Halavant, for instance."

"I'd have thought assaulting young women was far from irrational in his scheme of things," said the vicar contemptuously.

"Champagne, silk sheets, and a light scatter of rose petals are more in his line than a quick bonk on a drafty staircase next to a roomful of people whose good opinion he values," said Kee.

Surprise made him consider this unexpected defense, and for the first time since he'd heard the story of Halavant's repulse, Lillingstone felt a tendril of sympathy trail across his mind.

He brushed it aside and said heavily, "I love her."

"Oh, *love*," she said, smiling faintly. "Where does that leave us? For some reason you haven't declared your passion (nice word that, both exact and euphemistic), perhaps because you have very reasonable doubts whether Caddy would make a satisfactory clerical helpmeet, or perhaps because you've got a mad first wife already locked up in the attic."

She glanced up at the ceiling in mock suspicion, and down at Lillingstone in mock surprise as with perfect timing a floorboard creaked.

"I love the way old houses join in conversations," she said, trying to lighten things.

"We are talking about your sister," he said, unresponsively.

"So we are." Time to take the plunge. "Larry, your comfort, if comfort there can be, must be that you're right if you think Caddy wouldn't make a satisfactory wife for a vicar. Nor for almost anyone. Nor, incidentally, a satisfactory live-in or live-out mistress, if your thoughts stray in that direction."

"You're very blunt," he said coldly. "Frightened of losing a sister, or a meal ticket, I wonder?"

"Oh, dear, it's bad enough for rudeness, is it?" said Kee. "I only wish there were anything I could do which might be of comfort to you. All I can give is that coldest of advice, that you should exert yourself to forget her. I'm sorry."

"Exert myself?" he cried, spiraling into melodrama in an effort to hide the true depth of his feelings. "How easy for those who have no sorrow of their own to talk of exertion! But as I've told you, I shall probably be exerting myself out of Enscombe in the very near future. I hope that will satisfy you."

"No, I didn't come here in search of any such satisfaction," she said, rising. "And to tell the truth, I'm not all that keen to hear you rabbiting on about your feelings for my sister. Thanks for the coffee, which incidentally was cold."

"Oh, shit," said Lillingstone. "Kee, I'm sorry. I'm a pompous twerp, aren't I? And that crack about a meal ticket was unforgivable. We all know how much Caddy relies on you to give her space to work. I'm sorry. Forgive me?"

"Forgiving's easy. It's understanding that's hard," she said. "You say that man proposes, God disposes. So why don't you carry out your part of the arrangement? Go and see Caddy and propose to her— marriage, anything you will! That way, at least, you'll get your pain over and I won't find myself having to present my sister as some kind of monster."

He shook his head and said helplessly, "I wish it was so easy."

"I can't see how it can be any easier unless you do it by fax," she said.

"The point is I can't do it at all," he said. "The thing is, I've taken a vow of celibacy."

He spoke with a rather defiant pride, deriving from his sense that while a pact with the Deity certainly demanded a modicum of reverential awe, it also had about it an inescapable whiff of absurdity.

Kee looked neither awestruck nor amused, merely puzzled.

"Good Lord," she said. "Does this mean you're a closet Catholic or something?"

"No," he said. "Just an Anglican who may have bitten off more than he can chew."

"In that case, can't you get out of it? The papers seem full of priests who've jilted the pope in favor of a good woman."

"It's probably easier when you're taking on a whole system," said Lillingstone glumly.

"Ah, I see. In your case it's your own conscience you're up against and that carries a lot more weight than a mere trifle like the authority of the Holy Catholic Church!"

"Now, hold on," he said, growing angry. "This is my faith we're talking about—"

"I don't think so. I think it's your ego," said Kee, angry in her turn. "Makes you feel good, does it? More perfect than the rest of us? But you can't stop feeling randy, so you decide, if you can't have Caddy, next best thing is a little heart-to-heart with me. Vicarious sex, how apt! But I'm not into that game, Larry. What you need is another chap in a skirt on the other side of a grille."

She made for the window. He went after her, saying, "Please Kee, don't go like this. I don't know where I am, I need to talk—"

"Then talk to your Leader up there!" cried Kee, pointing satirically at the ceiling.

And once again with perfect timing there came a noise. But no creaking board this time. A distinct crash, as something fell and shattered, and a voice letting out an angry, "Oh, bug—" hastily cut off.

"There's someone up there," said Kee. "All this talk of vows and celibacy, and you've got someone stowed away up in your bedroom!"

"No, really, it's not . . . it's no one—"

"No one? This I just have to see."

Before he could stop her, she was past him, out of the room, and racing up the stairs.

He followed, protesting, but there was no chance of catching her. By the time he reached the landing she was flinging open the bedroom door. And stopping dead in her tracks.

She didn't know what she expected, she only knew this was far, far worse.

<u>Seven</u>

*Now, it will gradually all come
out—your Crimes & your
Miseries—how often you were on
the point of hanging yourself—
restrained only . . . by the want of a
Tree.*

Digweed said, "In a sense it was my own property I was
stealing."

"Oh, aye? In what sense does Mrs. Hogbin's herb pudding or Mrs. Stacey's cardigan belong to you?" asked Wield.

"I wasn't going to keep them," protested the bookseller.
"I would have left them at the GPO in town."

"That might save you six months," said Wield dryly. "So
what made you decide to steal your own property?"

"It was a foolish impulse," said Digweed. "I realized I
had packed the wrong book in one of my parcels. I could, of
course, have retrieved it from the Post Office this morning,
but last night as I returned home, my judgment clouded by
alcohol—you recall we drank a considerable quantity together, Sergeant—the notion came into my head of picking
up the parcel there and then, so to speak. I think I must have
been influenced by the discovery of Toke's burglary of my
shop. *Traumatized* is I think the cant term. I deeply regret
my action and will of course make full restitution."

"Bollocks," said Wield.

"I beg your pardon?"

"That 'ud be a better line," said Wield. "You try the other
load of bollocks out in court and you'll get five years. Let
me take you through it slowly. You didn't do it on the way
home, you did it in the early hours of the morning. You
weren't traumatized by Toke's break-in, but it did give you

the idea of how to set about it. You didn't ask Wylmot for the parcel back because you knew, him being a by-the-rule-book kind of gent, he was unlikely to break regulations and hand back an item of mail that had been accepted. And of course, once you'd asked for it and been refused, any subsequent theft might have put you in the frame."

He paused and admired Digweed's attempts to look indignant.

"And as for your judgment being clouded by alcohol, I reckon you were sober as a judge. And don't give me any crap about yon bourbon you so generously brought along in case I was feeling lonely. All you wanted to do was make sure the one cop left in the village was in no fit state to be snooping around in the middle of the night!"

"Now, that's outrageous!" protested Digweed, flushing.

"Is it? You even brought them fancy glasses so's I'd not notice how much I was drinking compared with you!"

The flush remained but it had more of shame in it now than indignation.

"All right, Sergeant, I admit it. Such was my intention. But I don't want you to think . . . look, all right, I was not predisposed to like you. But it will not do. In vain have I struggled. I do not say this in hope of influencing you in your official capacity, but my feelings will not be repressed. Already before last night I was beginning to realize there was more to you than meets the eye. Last night, I admit it, I came because I wanted to get you drunk. But I stayed because I found that, despite all the differences between us, I was enjoying myself."

He ground to a halt. Wield regarded him with astonishment, then burst out, "Well, thanks a lot, sir. That'll really keep me warm in the geriatric ward, recalling how a gent like you once took a shine to a common or garden copper like me."

For some reason the reaction seemed to please Digweed, who smiled as he replied, "Hurt your feelings, have I, Sergeant? Or are you perhaps just a teeny bit ashamed to think that you actually enjoyed a night's drinking with a tedious old intellectual like me?"

Wield fought back an inclination to return the smile and said, "So let's see what all the fuss was about, shall we?"

He took the parcel addressed to Ellie Pascoe and started to rip it open.

"I told you, I realized I'd packed the wrong book," said Digweed, alarmed. "And it wasn't that packet anyway—"

"You don't give up, do you?" said Wield. "Of course it was this packet. Soon as you realized our Mr. Pascoe might be related to your

Mrs. Pascoe, you got worried, and you didn't let up till you'd checked they were one and the same. So what is it you don't want to fall into the hands of a copper's wife?"

He didn't have an answer ready himself, apart from porn or a terrorist handbook, neither of which seemed very likely. But what came out was a well-used copy in a slightly tatty dust jacket of Agatha Christie's *Murder on the Orient Express*. He opened the accompanying letter.

Dear Mrs. Pascoe,
Here is the copy of *Murder on the Orient Express* we talked about on the phone. I hope it is to your satisfaction and that your husband finds it a suitable ornament to his collection. I enclose my invoice in the sum of £295 as agreed.

"Bit hefty for an old thriller, isn't it?" said Wield.

"It's a first edition, with dust wrapper," said Digweed. "In better condition I could get four hundred. At that price it's a bargain."

"No, it's not," said Wield. "It's dodgy, else you'd not have wanted to get it back when you discovered it was intended for a cop. Is it a forgery?"

"Hardly," said the bookseller. "That would cost more than the book's worth!"

"Then it's the jacket! What was it you said yesterday—a jacket could bump the price up by four times or more?"

He saw by Digweed's face that he'd hit on the truth.

"But why?" he asked. "I mean, okay, so you make a hundred quid or so, it's not going to make you rich, is it? And it's a fellow book lover you're ripping off."

The accusation hit Digweed where it hurt. He said, "Look, it's not as bad as it seems. . . . Well, yes, it is, and I'm ashamed, but my motives . . . What happened was I happened to get two inquiries from the States on the very same day for this volume, and I knew where I could lay my hands on one. I already had on my shelves a couple of copies without wrappers—"

"Worth?" interposed Wield.

"Oh, thirty, forty pounds," said Digweed. "But that wasn't the point. I had to disappoint one of my American customers, and I was wondering which when . . . a friend said, why disappoint either? and a few days later came up with this superb copy of the wrapper design.

Well, I did the jacket copy, I mean the writing—it was a sort of challenge—and in the end I had something only a truly expert and scientific examination could distinguish from the original. It all took time and money, you understand. In fact by the time I finished—"

"You were working for nothing, yes, yes," said Wield impatiently. "So you sent one of the Americans a copy . . . no, in the end you sent them both a copy, didn't you?"

"I didn't want to play favorites," said Digweed. "Then coincidentally—these things always go in threes, don't they?—there came this query from Mrs. Pascoe. It was for an anniversary present, and she'd set her heart on getting him this, and I was her last hope. . . . I couldn't resist."

Wield nodded in amused recognition. One of the many things he admired about Ellie Pascoe was that in matters of commerce she didn't let her feminism inhibit her from using her femininity.

"This friend who copied the design, it was Caddy Scudamore?"

"I never said that," said Digweed. "I shall never say that."

"Very noble," said Wield. "But you're better at bitchy. Man should follow his natural bent."

"Talking of which," said Digweed abruptly, "I presume my particulars will be fed into some know-it-all computer? So perhaps I should preemptively admit I have a record."

"You what? You're not really the Pink Panther?" said Wield, smiling.

"No, though in retrospect my trial seems more comic than tragic. Here are the facts. About thirty years ago a certain gentleman who later became an ornament of the House of Lords was discovered in a Brighton hotel committing what was called an act of gross indecency with his solicitor. It caused great mirth. The lord-in-waiting got six months, suspended. The young solicitor was adjudged to have been led astray by a man his superior in age and social standing, so he got let off with a hefty fine, which he could scarcely afford. And he was also debarred from practicing law by his professional council. No prizes for guessing his name. It will all be there in your records, I do not doubt."

Long before Digweed finished talking, Wield had reached his own conclusion.

He knows about me. He can't do, but he does. It's nothing I've done or said, I'm sure of that. So someone's told him. Who? Pascoe? Never. Dalziel? Not unless he saw something in it for himself! Which left . . .

no one. Maybe he was being neurotic and Digweed had pressed his button without being aware of it. Such things happened sometimes in interrogations, and the suspect coughed to crimes he wasn't even suspected of, when all he had to do was look blank.

But meeting the bookseller's gaze full on and seeing the ironically interrogative arch of those hispid eyebrows, he knew that this time he was got bang to rights.

He said quietly, "Mebbe I should warn you, attempting to influence a public officer by blackmail or intimidation gets you far more than burglary."

Digweed's irony rounded into puzzlement, then exploded into disgust.

"Good God, man, what do you think I am? Some young shit tried that on me once. I told him to publish and be damned. Then, seeing from his oikish expression that he did not grasp the reference, I kicked him in the crotch. He certainly grasped that!"

Wield said, "Assault as well as burglary? You're a man of hidden talents."

"Not so well hidden as yours, if you don't mind me saying so," said Digweed.

Wield considered this, found he didn't mind, and said, "All right. I'm sorry I misunderstood. Trouble with you is, the stick's got so many wrong ends, it's a hard job finding the right one. So nothing's changed, then. I know you're gay. You know I am. I'm still a cop, you're still a crook."

"So what happens now?"

Wield said, "I'm thinking. Care to tell me how you clocked me?"

"I didn't. Retrospectively I see indicators, of course, such as a strange reluctance to despise you as much as you clearly deserved. But, no, it was Caddy. Don't be surprised. She has a true artist's eye and sees behind most masks."

"So she knows about you?"

"Good Lord, everyone in Enscombe knows about me!" laughed Digweed. "And knew about me long before our worthy constabulary did me the favor of 'outing' me all those years ago."

"A favor, you say? And you're not thinking of returning the favor?"

"By outing you? How many times do I have to tell you, I'm neither a blackmailer nor a radical."

"So why let me know you know?"

"Just to be sure. I'd have tried to check you out even if this unfortunate business hadn't come up. So let's forget it, shall we, and carry on regardless. What now?"

"How often have you done this?"

"I've told you. The two Americans and Mrs. Pascoe. She was the last. If it wasn't that Cad—that my friend had done me three jackets and I still had one left, I wouldn't have dreamt of it. In fact I spoke with my friend just after our first encounter and told her that was it. I must have subconsciously penetrated your disguise even then!"

"And your friend?"

"She—or he—had no more interest in my case. All that concerned her was the technique involved. For an artist copying is part of the learning process, whether it's an old master or a book design."

"But you've still got the genuine jacket, I take it?"

"Yes, I have. But why . . . ?"

"I think Mrs. Pascoe deserves it. In fact," added Wield, removing the forged jacket and slowly tearing it up, "I think she's going to get it, don't you?"

"Yes, of course," said Digweed, regarding him with an expression in which bewilderment warred with hope.

"Good. Just to be on the safe side, I'd run a duster over the rest of the mail, the bits you shouldn't have touched. And wear gloves when you take them into town to repost them."

The bookseller fell to with a will. . . .

What the hell am I doing? Wield asked himself. I must be mad! But before his introspection could go farther, Digweed stopped in his task of rubbing his prints off envelopes and said, "Sergeant, I didn't pay any heed to these before, but now I look closer . . . well, there's a couple here I think you ought to see."

He passed over two identical buff envelopes.

Wield took them and studied the addresses.

"I think we've got a problem," he said.

Eight

When are calculations ever right?—
Nobody ever feels or acts, suffers or
enjoys, as one expects.

Dalziel's entry into the Morris was like the prodigal's return home.

"Thomas, it's been a long time!" boomed the Fat Man.

"Should have been sooner," said a beaming Wapshare. "When I heard you were in the village yesterday, I drew a pint straight off 'cos I thought, Any moment now he'll be here! When you didn't show up, I thought, Mebbe he's got religion!"

"Shortage of time, Thomas, that's all. But I'll have it now, long as it's not the same one. Where's Halavant? Isn't that his car out front?"

"Oh, he was here, but he nipped out the back as you came in the front," said Wapshare. "Owes you money, does he?"

"He's just driving away," said Pascoe, looking out of the window. "Shall I go after him?"

"Nay, I doubt you'd catch him on foot, lad. He'll keep. He owns this place, doesn't he?"

"Thinking of selling, didn't you say, Mr. Wapshare?" said Pascoe.

"He was, but he seems to have changed his mind. That's what he popped in to tell me," said Wapshare. "Andy, will you have a piece of pie to go with that beer? Don't have time to do you a black pudding, I'm afraid. I'm off up to the Hall shortly for the Reckoning Feast."

"Might just join you," said Dalziel. "Yon Creed lass knows her way around a bakery, doesn't she?"

"Aye, and there'll be some of her brother's ham to go with it," said Wapshare, smacking his lips at the prospect.

"Been around a long time, these Creeds?" asked Dalziel after downing two thirds of a pint.

"Oh, aye. Used to be shepherds on the estate, when there were an estate. Then way back before the war, old Sam Creed, that's Dora and George's granddad, took a step up in the world, married little Agnes Foote who was lady's maid to the Squire's wife, and a bit later when the tenancy of Crag End came up, Sam applied and beat the field. Creeds have been there ever since, and bloody good farmers they are too."

Pascoe watched with interest to see if Dalziel would be any better than he'd been at stanching this flow of history, but the Fat Man seemed content to fill his mouth with pie and listen.

"Talking of Halavant," said Dalziel as Wapshare refilled his glass, "weren't there something about a picture, the Squire's auntie or summat . . ."

"That's right," said Wapshare. "Worth a bit, by all accounts."

"What makes you say that?" asked Pascoe, thinking of the rather dull painting he'd seen on Fran's wall. Not even love had been able to raise Ralph Digweed above an honest competence.

"Just the fuss old Job made about giving it back," said Wapshare. "Hetty Bayle told me about it one night when she'd had a drop too much of the genevas. She were there at the deathbed, you see, ready for the laying out. Best layer-out in these parts is Hetty Bayle. Turns out a corpse fit for a Whitsun wedding, my old mother always used to say."

Mrs. Bayle as layer-out did not present a more gruesome picture to Pascoe's mind than Mrs. Bayle made confidential by a surfeit of gin. He shuddered and asked, "What did Job—that was Justin's father, right?—say exactly?"

"Just that young Fran had to have her grandmother's picture back. Must have been weighing on his conscience. He wasn't a man to let himself be bothered by trifles, wasn't Job."

"How had he got it in the first place?"

"Well, it was when the vicar, Mr. Harding, the one Frances from the Hall got married to and fell out with the family over, it was when he was running around like mad, raising money to save the school back in the thirties. You see, there wasn't much help forthcoming from the Hall 'cos he'd married Frances and the old Squire wasn't going to do owt that might help the vicar! Anyway, Mr. Harding had a bit of a sale at the vicarage, and Job went along and bought a few sticks of furniture and also these pictures that were his wife's. Didn't want her to sell them by all accounts, but she was determined she were going to do her bit. Got a decent price from Job, and a bit later when the fund were still short, Job chipped in a big lump more to make it up. Everyone reckoned at the time he just wanted to show the Hall lot up for a lot of mean bastards. But looking back, it seems likely now that his conscience were bothering him 'cos that picture of Edwina were worth a lot more than he said."

"Pictures. You said he bought some pictures. Plural," said Pascoe.

"Aye, I believe there were another, but the one the fuss was about, the one Job told Justin to give back, was old Edwina," said Wapshare confidently. "He were a hard bugger, but with eternity staring him in the face he thought it best to set the record straight."

But eternity hadn't been staring Justin in the face, thought Pascoe. When old Job whispered with his dying breath, *Give Fran her grandmother's picture* he left his son a choice, not a real choice perhaps, but one by which a man obsessed by artistic beauty might be able to salve his filial conscience.

"All right, lad, spit it out," said Dalziel. "When you start standing there like a hen with the gapes, it means you've had an idea."

"Just a thought, really," said Pascoe, glancing uneasily at Wapshare.

"Nay, it's all right," said Dalziel, taking his meaning. "You can talk in front of Thomas. Sooner or later he hears every bloody thing that's said around here. Only, he knows if it's said to me, or by me, and he passes it on without my say-so, he'll end up in one of his own black puddings. Right, Thomas?"

"You know me, Andy. Soul of discretion."

"Arse 'ole more like," said Dalziel. "Peter?"

Pascoe explained, concluding, "So if there were some doubt about the provenance of this painting, that would explain why Halavant's been so coy about reporting its theft."

"And you say you found him rooting around Corpse Cottage?"

"Actually he was lying on the bed with the vicar on top of him," said Pascoe. "But I suspect he went there to search in the first place."

"So, he's a bloody sight sharper than some folk I could mention."

"He had all the facts," protested Pascoe.

"That's what we get paid for, Peter. Getting there without the facts," said Dalziel pontifically. "This picture, how much might it be worth?"

"I don't know," said Pascoe. "I'm no expert and what I saw was only a copy. But if it was by someone really big like Reynolds, say, the sky's the limit. There are a lot of other important portraitists in the eighteenth century who would fetch a small fortune."

"So," said Dalziel with satisfaction. "Enough to make a poor cop think it worth taking a risk, eh?"

"But it can't have seemed all that much of a risk," offered Pascoe. "With the copy in place, and with Halavant reluctant to report it missing if and when he noticed . . ."

"So why's young Bendish not around toughing it out?" demanded Dalziel, glaring at the door as if he expected the answer to come bursting in.

It opened, and Wield stepped inside. He was carrying a plastic supermarket bag.

"Well, bugger me," said Dalziel. "Here's some of us working our fingers to the bone, and others have got time to bunk off and do their weekend shopping!"

Wield's gaze took in the pint pot and the half-eaten pie.

"Sorry to interrupt, sir," he said. "But you know you left your car outside the caff? Well, the radio were bleeping, so I opened the door and I found this dumped on the seat."

He upended the bag on the bar and tipped out the stolen packets and letters.

"Don't tell me. You've solved the post office break-in again!" said Dalziel. "Who's in the frame this time? Me?"

"You shouldn't leave your car unlocked," said Wield mildly. "No, I reckon someone got cold feet and just decided to give the stuff back. But there is something here you should look at."

"Aye, well, first things first. What did Control want?"

"Message for you to get in touch with Mr. Trimble, sir. But I really think you ought to see these first."

He placed the two brown envelopes in front of Dalziel.

"I saw Bendish's writing on the notice board in the cottage," he said. "This looks like it."

One of the envelopes was addressed to Sergeant Filmer at the Byreford section office. The other was addressed to Chief Constable Daniel Trimble.

Dalziel weighed them delicately in his hand as though attempting to access their contents by ESP. Then with sudden decision he inserted his forefinger under the topmost flap and ripped the envelope open.

"Sir," said Pascoe anxiously, "should you be doing that?"

"Could be a bomb," said Dalziel. "Any road, likely they were open when you found 'em, eh, Wieldy? Now let the dog see the rabbit."

He pulled out the single sheet in the envelope addressed to Trimble, read it without any visible reaction, then turned his attention to the much longer missive addressed to Sergeant Filmer. Now, like Belshazar's dining-room wall, those slablike features began to show a message.

And when he finished he said, as Belshazar himself probably said in some vernacular translation, "Well, fuck me rigid with a wooden truncheon!"

"Sir?" said Pascoe.

"Want to read them now they're open, do you?" observed Dalziel scornfully. "Here, then, take a look. Thomas, I need a phone."

"In the kitchen, Andy. Help yourself."

"And, Thomas, me nerves are shattered. I think I'd better have a large medicinal malt to stick 'em back together again!"

Nine

*You write so even, so clear both in
style & Penmanship, so much to
the point & give so much real
intelligence that it is enough to kill
one.*

Pascoe read the shorter letter first. It was dated two days
earlier, the day of Wield's visit to Enscombe.

Dear Mr. Trimble,
    I am writing this to let you know my intention to
resign from the Force with immediate effect. I am
sorry not to give more notice but I hope you will
agree that once an officer has decided that he is not
cut out for police work, the best thing is for him to
go as quick as possible. Also I have quite a lot of my
annual leave entitlement unused, so I hope this will
do instead of whatever notice I should have given.
    I apologize if this has caused any inconvenience,
but as the post of village constable in Enscombe is
due to disappear soon anyway, I hope it will not be
very much.
        Yours respectfully,
        Harold Bendish (Police Constable 79H8)

He passed it over to Wield and turned to the other letter,
which had the same date.

Dear Sarge,
    I'm writing to say that I'm resigning from the
Force. No point trying to do anything about it, be-

cause by the time you get this I'll be long gone and in any
case I've written to Mr. Trimble, too, so there's no point
thinking you can keep it quiet and talk me out of it. But I
wanted to write and tell you personally because in your own
way you've tried to help me and because I'd like someone in
the Force to know what's what and I reckon I know you as
well as anyone. That should have told me something about
myself a long time back. I mean the way I never seemed able
to make any real friends in the job. So you've got elected to
listen and if you think there's anyone up there who'll give a
toss why I've gone, feel free to show him this too.

I joined the police because everywhere I looked, every time
I switched the telly on or opened a paper, I was told the
world was full of crap, and why didn't I drink the right beer
or wear the right clothes or use the right aftershave and
things would be all right. I thought, I've got to do something
about this or else I'll go off my trolley. I thought of politics
but it didn't take long to suss out that this was where ninety
percent of the crap started. Social work looked a better bet
except it was as full of weirdos as politics was of wankers and
I reckoned you'd have to become a fully paid-up member
before they let you anywhere near real decisions, and then it
would be too late. Then it came to me, what about the police?
The way I looked at it, the job gave you something important
to do at every stage from the bottom up, and there were real
chances to get somewhere pretty quick where you could start
influencing the way things were run. In a funny way it was
the lousy press the Force has been getting recently which
made up my mind. I thought, there's a window here, while
they're washing all their dirty linen and before things have
got quiet enough for them to start muckying the next lot, for
someone like me to step in and get a quick bunk up as the
acceptable face of policing.

Well, it didn't quite work out like that. I tried showing the
acceptable face up in Newcastle and I got nutted for my
pains, and back at the station I got rollocked and bollocked
and told to get a grip. I came close to jacking it all in then but
instead I accepted a transfer down here, though when I first
got a look at Enscombe I thought, Harry boy, this is the
biggest mistake you ever made! I mean, what had a tiny little

isolated spot like this to do with all those things in the real world which had got me into the police in the first place? It was you that got me to give it a try, Sarge, though I don't suppose you knew how close I was to bunking off. You said that just because it all looked so peaceful I shouldn't think that Enscombe was a cushy billet. Folks round here would be sizing me up and comparing me with old Chaz Barnwall who'd been here for donkey's years. You told me not to try to get too friendly too quick, but if I stuck to the rules and showed I was here to keep the Law I'd soon find my feet. You finished by saying that looking after a village area like this was the best chance a young bobby had of showing what he was made of. Then, as you were leaving that first time, you hesitated and said, "Enscombe's not like other places, son. Not even like other places in Yorkshire. Keep your guard up, else it'll have you!"

That's what really caught my attention. So I gave it a try and I thought, If playing by the book is the way to get promoted somewhere I can start doing some real good in, so be it, and I came on really hard. And all the time, it was all still going on in the papers and on the telly, the crap, the crime, and here I was, making sure the Morris shut on time and tractors didn't leave too much mud on the roads. Also I was lonely, I admit it. I sat in Corpse Cottage some nights and stared at the wall and almost wished old Susannah Hogbig would come bursting through in her coffin just to give me someone to talk to. I even used to look forward to you coming around to check up on me. Sometimes you told me I was doing okay, and I wanted to ask, Yes, but what am I doing okay? And sometimes you tore a strip off me because I'd not filled in a report properly or I was late in calling in. And sometimes you'd talk about the old times, and how different things were now, and how you couldn't thole the idea of working in a big town anymore, and how it had all once been such a lot better because people trusted each other. And I'd try to tell you how I wanted to see things in the future, and you'd look as if you were listening, but I suppose it was just in the same way I used to look like I was listening to you, when really neither of us had much idea what the other was talking about.

Then one day . . . well, I won't go into details, but one day I
realized it didn't really matter, any of it, not your nostalgia
or my dreams. The one thing they had in common was they
both drew a ring around the present, the here and now which
is the only really important thing because it's the only thing
we can be sure of. I'm not explaining this too well, but I
suppose what I'm really saying is, I let my guard down, and
like you warned me could happen, Enscombe got me! I think
it's because in this place for some reason past and future are
part of the here and now so you don't always have to be
staring forward or peering back. Or put it another way,
whatever was wrong with me when I came here is cured now.
I mean, the world still stinks, and I've not given up on saying
it. But policing is for other people, not for me. Don't misun-
derstand me, Sarge, I'm not knocking the job, though you've
got to admit there's a lot of right bastards in it who quite
frankly shouldn't be let loose with a tuning fork, let alone a
truncheon. But they're not all like that, and I can only hope
the ones who are all right in the end get the others sorted.
Me, I've got myself sorted, or maybe I should say Enscombe's got me sorted, and I can see now that policing's no
way forward for me. So I'm off. I'll just catch the post if I
hurry, so you should get this tomorrow morning so you'll
have a day to get someone else out here. Or maybe the brass
won't think it's worth it with the job schedule to be axed so
soon. They could be wise. Enscombe's not a safe place for a
growing lad!
      Take care. And thanks for . . . well, just thanks.

                                              Best wishes,
                                              Harry

Handing over the letter to Wield, Pascoe said, "If he posted these
when he said, why didn't they get delivered yesterday morning?"
      Wapshare, who'd been following events with a lively interest, said,
"It's easy to miss the post around here. If he's in a hurry, Ernie Paget's
as likely to be half an hour early as half an hour late. Says it keeps up
the average."
      "And if he missed the post day afore yesterday, it wouldn't have
gone yesterday because Paget had his accident," interposed Wield
without looking up from his reading.

"Sod's law," said Pascoe.

"Someone talking about me?" said Dalziel, coming back into the bar.

"I was just saying if we'd got these letters when Bendish intended, they'd have saved us all a lot of angst," said Pascoe.

"Angst? You don't know the meaning of the word," said Dalziel. "Come to that, neither do I! Gi's them letters, Wieldy. Desperate Dan's given me permission to open them."

He took the letters and the whisky Wapshare had poured for him and returned to the kitchen.

Pascoe, who had less trust than Dalziel in his ability to intimidate Thomas Wapshare into silence, moved across to the window with Wield and said in a low voice, "What do you think?"

"I'm not sure if it's getting better or worse," said Wield. "Get anything from Big Ears there?"

He glanced toward Wapshare, who smiled back.

Succinctly Pascoe filled Wield in with his theories about the paintings.

"Aye, the one he gave back, Aunt Edwina's portrait, were by Digweed's granddad, Ralph," said Wield, and explained things in his turn.

"So, not worth a lot. But why did it go missing again, according to the Squire?"

"They needed the frame for the copy?" suggested Wield. "When she got herself painted by Ralph, Edwina wanted the picture to match the one of eighteenth-century Frances. So she got Ralph to put them both, his and the old one, in matching frames."

"Thirsty work, this talking," said Wapshare, who had stolen silently upon them carrying two pints. "I reckon you lads deserve a drink."

"You know, I reckon we do!" said Pascoe.

"Bloody hell," said Dalziel, coming into the room a moment later. "Turn me back for a moment and it's piss-up time. Where's mine, Thomas?"

"What's the chief say, sir?" asked Pascoe.

"He says, as far as he's concerned, Bendish's resignation is effective from the date of these letters."

Pascoe took this in and said, "Clever. So anything he might have done from then on, he did as a civilian."

"That's right. Dan's got ambitions and bent cops leave a smell around that top brass don't like. This way he hopes there won't be any need for Special Investigations to come crawling all over us. I reckon he'll be lucky."

"Why?" asked Pascoe. "Look, whatever Bendish has been up to, he clearly wanted to distance himself from the Force before he got up to it."

"Don't be naïve, lad," said the Fat Man. "He hoped this job at Scarletts would pass unnoticed, but he wasn't about to hang around with his fingers crossed. On the other hand, just to do a runner would raise a lot of dust—the way it has, in fact. So he wrote these letters in a pathetic attempt to cover up his disappearance."

"Maybe," said Pascoe stubbornly. "But I, for one, am glad to know he's probably alive and well."

"Forgetting the blood in the car, are you?" said Dalziel.

"And in the garden shed," added Wield.

"Oh, aye. But that's something else," said Dalziel. "I've been on to Forensic. There *was* blood on that bit of rug I sent 'em. But Group A, not O. And several weeks old. And mixed up with traces of semen and vaginal fluid. So forget about some bleeding prisoner. The only thing to get banged up in there was some lucky virgin a few weeks back. Mebbe just about the time our Constable Bendish was seen trawling his tackle around the garden wall!"

"So you think that he—"

"Was banging that quiet little maiden who's got you all fooled? Aye, do I!"

"But Franny's not the only possibility," protested Pascoe. "It needn't have been anyone from the Hall at all. Or there's Girlie."

"Nay, she's otherwise engaged. Saw it straight off first time I clapped eyes on 'em."

"On who?"

"Her and George Creed, of course," said Dalziel in exasperation. "Got their Wellies mixed, hadn't they? Which means they put 'em on in a hell of a hurry. Which means likely someone caught 'em at it!"

"George Creed's sin," said Wield, recalling Digweed's mocking comment.

"Sin? Aye, that's about the strength of it. It were a right shock for Dora, walking in on them like that, her being so religious and all. . . ."

"She told you this?" said Pascoe, amazed.

" 'I cried unto the Lord with my voice. . . . I poured out my complaint before him; I showed him my trouble,' " said Dalziel complacently. "Once she knew that I knew, she weren't slow to tell me. So Girlie's out. Got herself a man she's got a lot in common with. . . ."

"Such as?"

Dalziel glanced at Wapshare and winked.

"Same Wellie size, for a start. No, it's little Miss Muffet. . . . What's up with you, Wieldy?"

And Wield, recalling a trail of footsteps in the morning dew, and a trail of false suspicions across his mind, said, "I think I might know where Harry Bendish is."

Ten

Who can understand a young Lady?

"**I** thought the body was unfamiliar," said Justin Halavant. "And now I recognize the face, I see why."

He was peering at the crucifixion. The naked woman now had a head. It was unmistakably Fran Harding's. And it was wearing a policeman's helmet.

"Oh, hello, Justin," said Caddy, turning from her easel. "What do you think?"

"I think," he said, scanning the triptych judiciously, "that perhaps like most good ideas, it has outlived its usefulness."

"Scrap it, you mean?"

"One does not scrap a scrapbook," he reported. "These are working notes. Trying things out here has taught you invaluable things. Light has been easy since the Impressionists, but you have learned to master darkness. The head, though, is merely jocular. Worse, it is perhaps confessional."

"I know you're right," she said rather sadly. "I just needed you to tell me. It's over. I hoped for a masterpiece, but you always knew it was just a doodle. Shit."

"Don't be too hot for perfection, Caddy," said Halavant. "It is, in human terms, a form of stasis, the inevitable precursor of decay. Wherefore resist it, distrust it, if necessary destroy it. My God. How dare I preach to you! I turn my back for a moment and you make a leap forward like this!"

He was looking at the Wield portrait.

"It's okay, you think?"

"It's magnificent," said Halavant simply. "They'll mark the start of your first truly mature period from this."

"I don't know if I like the thought of being truly mature," said Caddy, looking directly at him for the first time. "How are your balls, by the way?"

"No permanent damage," he said. "But they are not the motivation of my visit. This is."

He unwrapped an oval parcel he had placed by the door on entry to reveal the forged portrait of the first Frances Guillemard.

"Oh, dear. I'm afraid I can't change it for the real one, I haven't got it."

"Don't be silly. I don't want it changed, I want it signed. Painted from memory of what—half a dozen viewings? It's a splendid piece of work."

"But not good enough to fool you?"

"Oh, yes. At least for some time, if that nice policeman, the almost normal one, hadn't drawn my attention to it. Once I looked closely and caught that hint of a mocking wink, I knew!"

"Made you mad, did it?" she said, grinning.

"A little," he admitted. "I worked out what had happened and went around to Corpse Cottage to try and retrieve the original. Like many of my moves lately it rapidly degenerated into farce."

"Why not just tell the police?"

"Because it was quite clear to me who had painted this and I had no desire to involve the country's best young artist in a forgery scandal at the outset of her career."

She regarded him skeptically.

"But now they know."

"They worked it out for themselves. One should never underestimate the pedestrian mind. It's walking slowly that gives you the best view of the countryside. However, merely sign your name to this and it (a) ceases to be a forgery and (b) increases its potential value to me."

"But what about the original? Don't you want it back?"

"No. It's Fran's by right. She should have had it last year when Daddy died. Was that someone downstairs?"

Caddy went to the door and called, "Hello?"

There was no answer and she said, "No, just the boards warming up in this sunshine."

"Yes, it does ease old joints rather, doesn't it? Where's Kee? She wasn't downstairs, so I came straight up."

"She went up to the vicarage."

"Really? Interesting but worrying. To embrace religion is a definite step on the path to spinsterhood."

"I don't think it's religion she's after embracing," said Caddy with her wicked grin.

"What? You mean His Reverence? I got the impression from Mrs. Bayle, the Hecate of Enscombe who gathers weekly reports from all the weird sisterhood, that Larry our pastoral lamb was bleating after you."

"He'll get over it," she said with the confidence of one not unfamiliar with the recuperative powers of suitors brought to the edge of death by her indifference. "Kee's far better at that sort of thing than me."

"And she's told you that she loves him?"

"Of course not. Kee never tells me anything she thinks might make me worry about the future."

"And would her marrying the vicar make you worry?"

"Not really. I'm sure they'd come up with some ingenious scheme for letting me paint in the vestry. But it would cause Kee a lot of problems. She may not know it, but she's the kind who'd like a houseful of kids. *That* she might feel she's got to give up because looking after me is a full-time maternal job."

"But why not tell her you can look after yourself?"

She laughed joyously.

"Come on, Justin! After Kee you know me better than anyone. In fact, artistically speaking, you know me best of all. So you know that after six months of looking after myself I'd have either died of food poisoning or been arrested for nonpayment of bills. No, I'll need to be taken into care if Kee is going to have any chance of the life she deserves."

She was looking at him expectantly.

He said, "I'm not sure what you're getting at...."

"Last time we met I was pretty sure what you were getting at."

"Caddy, yes, that was an aberration, compounded, I fear, by my egotistical reaction—"

"Hold on. Are you saying you really didn't want to screw me?"

"No, I mean, yes, of course, but no, not so brutally—"

"You mean that really, deep down, you respect me?" she mocked.

"Yes. In fact, I do."

"I believe you," she said. "That's always been what's made you bearable under the crap, Justin. You know what I'm about, sometimes you're way ahead of me. But that doesn't stop my tits from turning you horny. Look, you have to understand, that stuff doesn't mean all that much to me. Maybe someday, but not yet. Which doesn't mean to say that I simply lie back and think of England. But this would always come first. Anytime and every time. Are you with me?"

She made a gesture which took in her studio and all that was in it.

"I think so," he said cautiously. "You'd like me to act as, er, your patron . . . ?"

"Patron? Hell, no. I don't want to be patronized. I want to be cosseted, comforted, guided, encouraged. Could you manage that, Justin?"

"I believe so," he said. He looked again at the portrait of Wield. "In fact it would be a privilege."

"And one privilege deserves another," said Caddy.

She crossed her hands on the bottom hem of her long, loose smock and in a single swift movement pulled it overhead to leave herself naked from the waist up. The zip on her jeans seemed to fly open of its own volition and she peeled them easily off her strong brown legs.

Halavant's mouth fell open and he did a little involuntary skip backward.

"No time for dancing, Justin," she said. "This is a workshop, not a preview. If Kee doesn't have her wicked way with the vicar, she could be back any moment."

For a moment Halavant hesitated, but only for a moment. There is a tide, and his was so close to neaping, there was no time to waste. Rapidly he stripped off his elegant clothes. There was of course nowhere to hang them, so, trying to miss the more obviously damp patches, he dropped them on the floor. From here on in, life, he guessed, would be full of such sacrifices. But full too of, oh, such rewards!

"You look almost ready to start without me!" she mocked. "Will it be all right here, or do you have a thing about doing it on the stairs?"

She flung open the door as she spoke.

Jason Toke, crouched on the narrow landing, leapt to his feet like a beast of the forest startled by the beater's drums. For a moment he stared at the naked figures before him, then with a cry so high-pitched as to be almost inaudible, he fled down the stairs and out of the gallery. On the landing floor lay the Renoir catalog.

"What the hell did he want?" cried Halavant.

"Nothing," said Caddy. "Just to give me a present. I don't think he'll be back."

"You're sure?"

"Does it matter?"

"Not in the least."

"Then what are we waiting for?" said Caddy Scudamore.

Eleven

The Complaint I find is not considered Incurable nowadays, provided the Patient be young enough not to have the Head hardened.

As Dalziel and his two subordinates strode back up the High Street, they saw the door of the Eendale Gallery burst open and Jason Toke come hurtling out.

Wield called, "Jason!" but the youth went running by, his pale, wild face giving no sign that he either saw or heard the policeman.

Wield halted and said, "Shall I go after him?"

"What the hell for?" growled Dalziel. "Didn't you just say yon blabbermouth Digweed doesn't want to press charges?"

"There's still the kingfisher," said Pascoe.

"Oh, aye. Crime of the sodding century. That reminds me. This Toke's a gun freak, isn't he? Well, Forensic said to pass a message to whichever of you two buggers gave them the bird, it weren't shot with a bullet but summat more like an arrow. So it's not Toke you want, it's the ancient fucking mariner! Let's just concentrate on our wandering plowboy, shall we?"

They reached Dalziel's car, still parked outside the café. Pascoe looked across at the gallery, noted the aubergine cabriolet parked there, and murmured, "I wonder what he was running from? Perhaps we should take a look."

Without waiting for the Fat Man's approval he crossed over and stepped through the still-open door of the gallery. The door behind the counter was open, too, and he could hear noises on the stairway. He listened carefully for a few seconds, then retreated, closing the door behind him very quietly.

"Everything okay?" said Dalziel sarcastically. "No blood on the walls?"

"No, sir. Everything seemed tickety-boo," said Pascoe.

"Grand. Get in. You too, Sergeant, pardon me for breaking your trance."

"I were just thinking about that arrow, sir . . . yes, sir, I'm getting in!"

His nearest and dearest knew that when Dalziel let out a certain kind of Minotaurine roar, discussion was useless and delay might be fatal. As Wield slipped into the backseat of the car he glanced up and glimpsed Digweed's narrow figure at the bookshop's upper window. Their gazes met, momentarily engaged, then the car was moving and Wield was struggling to close the door.

Digweed had watched their approach up the street with considerable unease. Wield's precise motives for covering up his crime were not all that clear, yet he did not anticipate he would change his mind. On the other hand, that ton of lard he worked under looked capable of sniffing out irregularities like a pig after truffles. So it was with some relief he saw the car move off.

With fear of imminent arrest removed, he was able to let his thoughts once more refocus on what had happened that morning. No, *focus* was the wrong word. There was nothing so sharp happening in his mind, just a turbulence of puzzlement, hope, trepidation, anticipation, and downright fear.

He heard the phone ring in the computer room, then the tone to signal the fax machine was engaged.

He allowed the sounds to toll him back from these perilous seas to the real world, though in what sense words fed into a machine many miles away and somehow spewed out into his office should be realer than his own deepest hopes and fears, he couldn't say.

Wield, too, meditated on the implications of the cover-up as Dalziel turned into the lane that ran past Corpse Cottage to the vicarage.

He tried to soothe his dyspeptic conscience with the Fat Man's frequent assertion that, the way the CPS threw out perfectly good cases that had cost overworked detectives many sleepless hours, it made more sense morally, socially, and legally to leave justice in the hands of a rational, informed intelligence such as his own.

Dalziel's precise words were "Them wankers couldn't spot a bishop in a brothel. You get more sense from a pissed parrot."

But even in the vernacular this oracular utterance brought little comfort. There was in Wield a strong streak of Puritanism which did not take kindly to the feeling that, however you dressed them up, his motives had been personal, private, and self-indulgent. All right, the goods had been recovered, no real harm done, Digweed wasn't going to reoffend, and so on, and so on.

But beneath all this he knew that if Digweed hadn't been gay—no, even that was an evasion, making himself out to be some brave crusader for gay rights; this was far more personal—if he hadn't surprised in himself an inexplicable liking for the man, he'd have fingered his collar, and let Andy Dalziel and the CPS decide what happened next.

According to the trick cyclists such an admission or recognition ought to have been cathartic. It wasn't.

They paused briefly at Corpse Cottage but found it deserted.

"Where's that useless bugger Filmer?" demanded Dalziel.

Pascoe, who was beginning to suspect he had been less than just to the section sergeant, said, "He has got rather a lot on his plate, sir."

"Aye, that figures for a bugger who wouldn't know kippers from custard," said Dalziel. "Let's not hang about. If Sherlock here's right, it's murder at the vicarage after all."

"Hardly murder, sir," objected Pascoe mildly.

"We'll see about that," said Dalziel with a promissory snarl.

But when they reached the vicarage, it, too, was deserted, or at least there was no reply to their urgent assault on the front door.

Wield led the way around the side and Dalziel was about to work the same rough magic on the French window as he'd done on the walled garden door when Wield said, "Sir!"

"What?" said the Fat Man. "Jesus, he's got lift-off!"

The sergeant had reached up into an old beech tree and swung himself with gymnastic agility onto a low bough to give himself a view over the churchyard wall.

Moving through the gray forest of memorial stone he glimpsed three figures, one female, two male, and one of the males had bright red hair.

"There they are," he said. "Stop in the name of the law!"

He dropped lightly to the ground to be met by the amazed stares of the other two.

"I don't believe this," said Dalziel. "Did he really shout that?"

"Wieldy, are you all right?" said Pascoe anxiously.

"Never better. It's just something I've always wanted to say," said Wield. "Sorry. Are we going after them?"

"Aye, we are," said Dalziel, setting off across the lawn.

It occurred to Pascoe that if Bendish sought sanctuary in the church, like Thomas à Beckett, he was in for a big surprise. But Wield pointed to the open door leading into Green Alley and they plunged into that shadowy tunnel, which the sudden surge of vernal sun seemed to have rendered even more luxuriant. Drooping boughs brushed their new fingers of leaf and blossom against Wield's face as he raced along. Pascoe was not far behind, but Dalziel, who, though surprisingly fast over a short distance, was no marathon man, had slowed considerably.

Now the path broadened into the little restful glade, and Wield stopped so suddenly that Pascoe ran into him.

Sitting on the bench under the mocking eye of the marble faun was a young man dressed in gray slacks and a white shirt, above which flamed a mop of bright red hair. Against his left leg, like a symbol of office, rested a chestnut walking stick with a bone handle carved in the shape of an eagle's head.

"Hello, lad," said Wield. "Still baht 'at, I see."

Pascoe, who had been rather impressed by the young man's letter, smiled reassuringly and said, "Hello. It's good to see you're okay."

And now Dalziel arrived, moving at the measured pace of the high priest approaching the sacrificial altar.

"Harold Bendish?" he said. "There's a lot of folk that'll be glad to hear you're still alive. By the time thee and me's finished, I'll be surprised if you're still among them."

Twelve

What a trifle it is in all its Bearings
to the really important points of
one's existence even in this World!

It was, thought Pascoe later as he ran his mental video of the scene, less like a suspect being interrogated than a young king, Alexander, say, dealing patiently with the complaints of his disaffected satraps.

Wield, anticipating they would move off, said, "On your feet, lad," and Bendish rose willingly enough but winced as he put weight on his left foot and leaned on the ornate walking stick.

"What's up? Sore leg?"

"It's a bit stiff," admitted the young man.

"Let's have a look," said Wield.

Obediently Bendish pulled up his left trouser to reveal a neatly repaired jagged gash in his calf.

"I recognize them stitches," said Wield, fingering his ear.

"I recognize those teeth marks," said Pascoe, shuddering. "Fop?"

"That's right."

The two younger policeman glanced inquiringly at Dalziel, who said, "All right, sit down, lad. We can get the formalities over here as easy as anywhere."

It was not intended as a kindness. PACE required that a suspect should be interrogated as soon as was humanly possible under properly controlled conditions with a tape recorder running. But Dalziel liked, when he could, to get his script edited well in advance.

So the young man sat down again and as there was only room for one on the bench unless their purpose was amatory, the others stayed standing.

"You've not had my letters, then?" said Bendish. "I thought you can't have had, from what Larry was saying."

Dalziel, looking irritated to have the initiative wrested from him, said, "We've seen them now, lad. Only difference they make is whether you're a bent cop, or were just masquerading as a cop when you committed your crimes. Either way, it's worth an extra five stretch."

Pascoe rolled his eyes at this exaggeration, but Bendish seemed unaffected by it. He said, "I'm sorry that people have been put to a lot of trouble because my letters were delayed. But apart from searching for me to make sure I'm all right, what else are you after, sir?"

Dalziel said, "Okay, son. You want to play it that way, fine. Let's get down to cases. Harold Bendish, did you two nights ago by making a false report of a possible intruder gain entrance to Scarletts?"

"It wasn't exactly a false report," said Bendish. "There was an intruder."

"Eh?"

"Yes," said the youth, grinning broadly. "Me."

Wield and Pascoe looked expectantly at the Fat Man, waiting for the thunderbolts, but he merely passed a huge hand across his face and went on, "While you were inside, you persuaded Mrs. Bayle to turn off the alarms, and then your accomplice diverted Mrs. Bayle with a telephone call from a mobile phone?"

Bendish considered, nodded, said, "Yes."

"And while Mrs. Bayle was out of the room, you removed a painting from the wall, passed it through the window to your accomplice, took in a copy which you had had prepared, and hung it up in place of the original. Right?"

"Yes."

"And this accomplice was Miss Frances Harding of Old Hall?"

Bendish hesitated, and that hesitation confirmed what Pascoe already knew, that the young man was deeply in love. His only line of defense against these charges was that the painting was Fran's anyway, and he could hardly advance that without naming the girl. Yet when it came to the point, he found it hard.

He said, "It was all my idea. . . ."

"Oh, aye? And she's little Miss Innocent, is she? Come on, lad. We

know all about you two banging away in the garden shed!" said
Dalziel with provocative coarseness.

Bendish flushed the lovely color Wield recalled from their first
encounter and his fingers whitened around his stick. Quickly Pascoe
said, "She left the phone under the window, didn't she? And you went
back for it. And it started ringing"—that would have been Guy the
Heir trying to call Girlie—"and Mrs. Bayle let Fop out. . . ."

"He got me as I was going over the gate," said Bendish, wincing at
the memory. "There was blood everywhere and my trousers were
ruined. Fran was marvelous. She drove us back to the village and then
we . . ."

His voice trailed off. He was still worried about mentioning names,
Pascoe realized. Not ratting was as much a problem for cops as for
crooks.

"You went to Corpse Cottage," he said. "Because that's where
you'd arranged to meet Caddy to hand over the painting so she could
remove it from the frame and put Aunt Edwina back in."

It was obvious when you thought about it, though Bendish was
regarding him with awe and even Dalziel and Wield looked impressed.

Encouraged, he pressed on. "Fran probably wanted to take you to
hospital, but that was going to need far too much explanation. So you
said she could patch you up, she had the training and the equipment,
and you'd recently updated your tetanus jabs and were still taking a
course of antibiotics as a result of your run-in with Guy the Heir."

"Have you been talking to Fran?" demanded the youth. "Or
Caddy? That's it. Caddy!"

"No need. But you needed somewhere to lie up. You couldn't stay
in the cottage, it was too dangerous to smuggle you into the Hall,
so . . ."

He paused. To his audience it may have seemed a rhetorical flourish. In fact it was simply a drying-up. They'd gone to the vicarage, that
was clear. But why in the name of God had Lillingstone allowed
himself to be sucked into this crazy and criminous business?

God, who is sometimes amused to take the profane use of His name
as genuine prayer, decided to take Pascoe off the hook, and gave
Harold Bendish a nudge.

"It was Caddy who suggested the vicar," he said. "Larry . . . well,
Larry's got this thing about her. Everybody knows, only he thinks they
don't. So once she explained all about the school and everything . . .

and I think it helped that it was one in the eye for Justin Halavant, as the vicar's been a bit narked with him ever since word got out about the pass he made at Caddy—"

"Hang about!" commanded Dalziel. "The school and everything . . . ?"

"Oh, aye," said Wield, who saw no reason why Pascoe should grab all the detective kudos. "They were stealing the picture so they could sell it and get enough money to save the school. I thought everyone knew that. I expect the idea started when the vicar gave young Fran her gran's journal and she read about Job Halavant picking the painting up cheap. And I expect it were Caddy who spotted it at Scarletts—"

"It was the frame," said Bendish. "She was in Fran's room one day talking about the illustrations she were doing for Mr. Digweed's edition of the journal, and she looked at Aunt Edwina and said she knew where there was a frame exactly the same as that, only the picture in it looked to be worth a hell of a lot more. One thing led to another—"

"And you all ended up in a conspiracy to rob," said Dalziel, eager to bring proceedings back down to earth and start arresting people. "Grand. Mr Pascoe, would you care to—?"

But Pascoe, with *i*'s still to dot and *t*'s to cross, took the enormous risk of ignoring him.

He said, "The next morning Mr. Lillingstone took the uniforms, or at least one and a half uniforms, to the dry cleaners in town, popped into Marks and bought a pair of trousers of the same color to replace the torn ones, and went to Corpse Cottage to put them in the wardrobe. Only, he didn't realize that not only was the hunt already up for you, Harry, but also Halavant had spotted the substitution and worked out who must have taken it. Lillingstone lied quite well for a vicar. Funny what a man will do for love, isn't it, Harry? I mean, that's what got you into this mess, isn't it? Love? All for love?"

He spoke gently, almost sadly, not at all mockingly.

Dalziel made a noise like a dog trying to bring up a bit of bone that had got stuck in its throat.

Bendish gave him a look which was composed equally of scorn and pity.

He said seriously, "If you've read my letters I thought you'd have understood. Of course I love Fran so much I'd do anything for her. But I hope I'd have done this anyway, because it needed doing. It was too important not to do."

"For crying out loud!" exclaimed Dalziel. "You stole a sodding picture, you didn't stop World War Three!"

"I don't know about that," said Bendish. "I did something to help the village keep its school without having to sell the Green. Maybe ultimately that'll help tip the balance, one more kid getting a decent education, one more place keeping out the concrete. I don't know. All I know is that if things are perfectible, if things really can get better, then we've all got to start where we're at. I tried to give myself a bit of lift-off by joining the police. It seemed to make sense. If you want to influence society, go where there's a chance of getting a bit of clout. I should have learned up in Newcastle. It didn't work out there, but I just blamed myself."

"Whereas it's actually the police force's fault?" said Pascoe, interested.

"No. Not as such. Look, I gave it another try down here. I tried to be what everyone told me a good cop should be, so that ultimately I could fit in and really help. Enscombe seemed so together, so very much itself, that I felt I should be able to make it work here if I could make it work anywhere. But after a while it began to feel just like it felt up in Newcastle. I was going nowhere, nothing was happening, and that's when you start wondering if maybe the reason there's so much crap in the world is that that's the natural state of things, and you begin to suspect that even in a place like this, if you probe too far beneath the surface, you'll find it bubbling around down there, the old unchangeable primeval crap we all came from and we're all going back to. I got very depressed. Then I met Fran, and that changed things completely for me personally. I knew I had to leave the force, of course. It was the wrong place for me. I saw then that in a perfect world we wouldn't need the police, so there was no way I could work toward that perfection while I was actually part of one of the main symbols of imperfection, was there?"

"You know," said Dalziel, "could be I'm wrong about you, lad. You spout that stuff in court and mebbe you won't get banged up in jail for five years, they'll just throw you into a psycho ward for life! Now, Chief Inspector Pascoe, this being your case, strictly speaking, if you haven't forgotten the words, would you like to arrest Mr. Bendish, or shall I?"

"Don't you think we ought to talk to the others concerned?" said Pascoe. "I mean, Mr. Halavant hasn't yet made a formal complaint. And if in fact this picture does indeed really belong to Fran . . ."

Wield, seeing that the Fat Man was getting close to apoplexy, looked at his watch and said, "They'll likely all be at the Squire's Reckoning, sir. I get the impression no one in these parts misses out on a free feast, not when Miss Creed's been doing the baking."

The angry blood hesitated, hung in suspense, then began to retreat from Dalziel's face.

"I'm glad there's still one of you can talk some sense," he said. "On your feet, lad. Let's go and see if this Reckoning's all it's cracked up to be!"

End of Volume 4

Volume the Fifth

PROLOGUE, being an extract from the draft of an
uncompleted
HISTORY OF ENSCOMBE PARISH
by the
Reverend Charles Fabian Cage, D.D. (deceased)

*To a casual eye Enscombe may appear the prototypical English vil-
lage, with its setting, its architecture, its antiquities, its society, its
economy, all combining to offer something like that pastoral perfection
of which the poets dream. Yet a closer examination reveals much about
the place which is deceptive if not downright deceitful!*

*Take the name. No problem here, one would think. The village in the
combe or valley of the River Een. Yet a little pause may make one
wonder what on earth a* combe *is doing in this county of dales?
Combes or coombes are commonplace in the West Country and (as
cwms) in Wales, yet I cannot readily think of another example in
Yorkshire. Enscombe is the kind of name someone might invent who
had never been farther north than, say, Hampshire! Toponymists typ-
ically offer a puzzling variety of alternative derivations, such as
Enna's Combe and Eanna's Combe, the first suggesting a connection
with the Sicilian vale where Proserpine, gathering flowers, herself a
fairer flower, by gloomy Dis was gathered; the second implying that
the Irish Saint Enda, or Eanna, rested here while on his way from
Galloway (where he trained as a monk) to Rome to be ordained.
Neither suggestion deals with the intrusive* combe, *but together they*

are interesting in the choice they offer between the Christian and the pagan worlds.

Less attractive to the scholars but much more persuasive to a native is the theory advanced by the well-known Yorkshire folklorist P. N. Walker. He refers to a legend that at some time in the mythic past a monstrous Grendel-type creature appeared in the northlands, bringing death and destruction wherever it went. Only one isolated hamlet, by foresight and cunning, managed to avoid the creature's depredations, and this became known as the village that escaped "the monstrous visitor," which is in Old English entisc cuma, *eventually reduced to Enscombe.*

Unconvincing? Well, I like it. But what's in a name anyway? A date, now, is something different. We ought to be able to trust a date. We find the year 1508 carved all over Old Hall. Yet researches show that the building was completed sometime in the 1560s. It appears that Solomon Guillemard, the then squire, having appropriated much of the wealth of the dissolved priory of St. Margaret to himself and bought the land and remnants of the priory at a knockdown price, determined to confuse any subsequent investigation by naming his new manor Old Hall and predating it by half a century! Interestingly this accords very well with considerable backdating which has occurred in regard to the Guillemards' arrival in England. They were certainly not among the first wave of Norman nobility who conquered with the Conqueror. Rather they appear to have been part of that great invasion of "carpet-baggers" which customarily sweeps in behind a victorious army.

I pointed this out to the squire when he honored me with the opening stanzas of his ballad history which describes his ancestors' deeds of derring-do at Hastings. I also mentioned that I could find no reference to this curious myth of the talismanic kingfisher before a court case of 1661 when, after twisting and turning throughout the period of the Civil War and the Commonwealth in a manner which made the Vicar of Bray look like the Rock of Ages, Squire Gabriel Guillemard was claiming back land along the Een which he alleged had been stolen from him by the Parliamentarians. Running out of legal argument and factual evidence, he suddenly produced this myth of the kingfisher plus a dozen witnesses to swear they had seen it fly to the precise boundary of the claimed land, then turn and fly upstream once more. Nobody has ever lost money by overestimating the superstitious credulity of an English jury, and the case was won.

Selwyn clearly knew all this. He remarked not unjustly that it ill behoved anyone in my line of business to insist on literal truth, and gave me another dozen quatrains for my pains!

I do not tell these stories to accuse the deviousness of the Guillemards, but rather to suggest that such a leading family is exactly what one would expect Enscombe to have chosen. Not chosen in any electoral democratic sense, of course, but by that process of natural selection which is how all living organisms contrive to survive. And Enscombe is a living organism, make no mistake about that, and an incredibly adaptable one, too, androgynously apotropaic, ready to be anything in the expectation of being ever, accepting change as the price of unchange, an Artful Dodger of a village making one demand only of its inhabitants, which is unquestioning love. Fuctata non perfecta—*which, incidentally, was the coinage of one Cuthbert Guillemard, who, after some misguided expressions of sympathy for Mary Stuart, decided after her execution that the family's old French motto* Sanz loy sanz foy, *or Lawless and faithless, was capable of misinterpretation*—Fuctata non perfecta *really means, It's better to be painted than perfect.*

And so it is. For the monster is loose again, and has been these past several years, roaming free and ravaging the land. It, too, has the gift of disguise, now appearing as a wild-eyed woman, now as a vacantly smiling man. But always it gives itself away by the reek of greed and corruption that hangs about it.

Let us pray that when it reaches Enscombe it will not recognize us under our paint, but pass us by.

One

*The truth is that the Secret has
spread so far as to be scarcely the
Shadow of a secret now.*

So at last the villagers of Enscombe gathered for their
Reckoning.

The spring sun had not flattered to deceive but floated at
its zenith in a cornflower-blue sky, shedding the warmth of a
pleasant midsummer day. A gentle breeze flicked the hems
of the white tablecloths but threatened no greater mischief,
so heavily were they weighted down with the fruit of Dora
Creed's labors. Here were pies and pastries, turnovers and
tarts, ham-bulging rolls and butter-oozing baps, sponges so
light, a real March wind might have carried them away, and
fruit cakes so dense, it required two hands to set them in
their place.

All that stood between the villagers and this feast was the
collection of the Squire's rents, once a tedious business with
the line of tenants winding away across the lawn and vanishing into the shrubbery, but now, in these lean and efficient
times, scarcely enough to form a queue. So they mingled,
and exchanged greetings and gossip, and salivated content-
edly in the expectation of plenty, with never a thought for
what other strange dishes their frolicsome Yorkshire god
might have put on the menu. Only Elsie Toke might have
had some forebodings, but she was too concerned in looking
around anxiously for a glimpse of her son to turn her eyes
inward.

For Wield, as he led the way out of Green Alley onto the

drive, there came one of those I-have-been-here-before experiences, as a battered yellow Beetle nearly clipped his toes. It skidded to a halt in front of the Hall and Fran Harding jumped out. Lillingstone and Kee Scudamore were standing on the steps and she ran up to them, her voice, usually so soft, rendered loud by worry.

"Larry, what's happened? I've been to the vicarage, there's nobody there."

"It was time to come into the open," said the vicar. "I talked with Kee—"

"Kee? But Caddy said—"

"Not to tell me anything in case I disagreed?" said Kee. "She was quite right. Of course I'd have disagreed with anything which was likely to put my sister in the dock! As it happens, I've found out for myself. As the police are clearly doing."

"The police? But Harry's letters—"

"Don't seem to have arrived. Once Harry realized that, he knew it was time to put in an appearance."

"Then where is he?"

The two on the steps didn't reply. They were looking over her head to where the quartet from Green Alley, moving at Bendish's slow pace, were coming toward the house.

Fran turned, saw, and came running toward them, calling, "Harry! What are you doing? Are you all right?"

Then she was in his arms, pressing herself to him as if she wanted to fuse their bodies together. It was sexier than any porn film Pascoe's duties had obliged him to see, and he looked away in embarrassment.

Dalziel said, "All right, luv. Leave some for old Tom's breakfast."

Eyes blazing, she turned on him and cried, "Whose idea is this? He shouldn't be walking, it could open up his wound."

"Nay, lass, it's nowt to do wi' me," said the Fat Man. "He were wandering loose when we found him. But talking of wounds, the BMA might be interested to see your license to practice medicine."

She gave him a glance of scorn that would have frizzled a lesser man, then slid down to her knees in front of Bendish. For a terrible moment Pascoe thought she was going to indulge in some even more intimate form of embrace, but all she did was roll up his trouser and examine the gash.

"Come and sit down," she said. "Before you do yourself any more harm."

She led him gently to the steps and urged him to sit on the bottom one. He looked up at her with proud adoration. It was a scene to touch a Tartar's heart. Dalziel said, "Pity your sister's not here as well, Miss Scudamore."

"Why's that?" asked Kee.

"Then I'd not have to repeat myself after I've arrested these three."

The blond woman looked unimpressed and said, "If you'd care to hang on a minute I think she's here now."

Halavant's cabriolet was coming sedately down the drive. In the center of the rear seat, looking like a head of state showing himself to the people, was the patrician figure of Edwin Digweed. But it was Caddy Scudamore in the passenger seat who drew most eyes. Her wind-touseled hair, the glimpse of brown thigh as she vaulted over the car door, the fullness of her lips, the glow of her skin, the untrammeled motion of her body beneath her paint-stained smock, and perhaps above all her total lack of self-consciousness about her beauty, acted on the other two women like sunlight on candle flames.

Digweed got out too. He had a piece of paper in his hand and to Wield's assessing eye he looked full of news. But as he took in the composition of the scene before him, he clearly decided it could wait.

Halavant had walked around the front of the car and held out his hand to Caddy. She put out her tongue, but took it, and swinging their hands between them like children, they advanced to the steps.

"Good day to you all," said Justin brightly. "Harry, there you are. How nice to see you."

And Caddy, looking straight at her sister, said, "We're going to be married."

Lillingstone turned pale and swayed. Kee seized his elbow and held it tight.

Dalziel said, "Congratulations. You'll let us know if you're honeymooning abroad?"

"Will I?" said Halavant. "Why so?"

"Don't want a trial with our star witness and one of the defendants out of the country, do we?"

"What trial would that be?" said Halavant courteously.

"The trial of Mr. Bendish and Miss Harding for stealing your painting. The trial of Mr. Lillingstone for harboring Mr. Bendish, knowing him to have stolen your painting. And the trial of Miss Scudamore, for forging a copy of your painting knowing it was to be used in furtherance of a felony."

He was having a bad day in his efforts to shock.

Halavant merely smiled and said, "I fear you may have been misinformed, Superintendent. It's true my fiancée did make a copy of a painting that used to be in my possession. I have it here, as a matter of fact."

He opened the trunk of his car and produced the picture in its oval frame that Pascoe had last seen on his wall.

"A marvelous copy, you must agree, fit to fool any but the most expert eye. Fortunately, as you can see, my talented fiancée has signed it, so no confusion is possible."

Proudly he pointed to the flowing signature.

"And the original, sir?" asked Pascoe, seeing that Dalziel might be on the point of saying something Dan Trimble would regret.

"Why, the original is, I believe, in the possession of its rightful owner. I was merely the fortunate borrower of it for a while."

He smiled pleasantly at Fran Harding, inviting her to share in their mutual triumph over the forces of law and order. But the girl wasn't smiling back.

"You bastard," she said.

Now there was evidence on Halavant's face, if not of shock, at least of mild surprise.

"Perhaps I haven't made myself clear, Fran," he said. "I renounce all claim to the painting. I acknowledge you have full title in it. I believe your purpose is to sell it and donate the proceeds to saving the school. If it is what I believe it may be, it should fetch enough not only for that admirable project but to provide you with a considerable dowry beside—"

"If it's what you believe . . . ! Hypocritical bastard!"

The young woman's face was mature with anger.

Kee said, "Fran, what's the matter?"

"This is the matter!" cried Fran Harding, going to her Beetle and pulling her cello case out. She flicked its catches open, raised the lid, and pulled out an oval of canvas which she flourished in Halavant's face.

"I've been to town this morning to see an expert from Sotheby's. He had come all the way up from London, and you know what, he wasn't pleased. Not to come all that way to see a fake!"

"I don't understand," said Lillingstone, whose color had slowly returned. "I thought this was the forgery?"

"That's right," said Caddy, clutching the framed portrait protectively.

"The copy, she means," said Halavant. "No, Fran, you're so-called expert's got it wrong. . . ."

"I don't think so," said Fran. "When did you sell it, Justin? What happened to the money?"

Everyone looked at Halavant. He was either innocent or a tremendous actor.

He said helplessly. "I'm sorry, I can't explain. . . ."

Digweed, like the three policemen, had been reduced to the role of neutral spectator. Now he coughed dryly. He may not have practiced for long, but to Wield it sounded like a true solicitor's cough, bringing the family at war over a will to order.

"If I may . . . ?" he said. "Fran, what precisely did your disappointed expert say?"

"He said that it was definitely not eighteenth century but a very competent nineteenth-century portrait in the manner of Reynolds. It could possibly fetch between eight and fifteen hundred at auction—"

"That puts me in the clear, I think," interrupted Halavant. "I may look antique to a child like Franny, but I was not around in the nineteenth century to commission forgeries!"

Fran looked ready to dispute this, but Digweed said, "It occurs to me that the original portrait was out of the hands of the owner, Edwina Guillemard, for a lengthy period in the eighteen eighties. This was when my grandfather Ralph was painting her portrait to match the one of Frances Guillemard she already had."

"Edwin! You're not saying that your grandfather—"

"No, of course not," said Digweed indignantly. "Anyone who's seen his picture of Edwina can see that while he was a reasonably competent oil painter, he was far from possessing the skills necessary to fool all the sharp-eyed people who've been fooled since."

"What then?" said Halavant.

"There were two reasons Ralph needed the portrait. One, to help him in his task of painting Edwina. Two, in order to get both portraits put in matching frames. I know from his journal that he used a friend in the art business to do this, and he became rather concerned at the length of time it took to get the frames prepared."

There was a moment of puzzled silence, broken by Wield, who said,

"This friend of your granddad's wouldn't have been Jeremy Halavant, would he?"

Digweed smiled warmly at him.

"That's right. Jeremy, who had just recently had his half-built new house burned down, almost certainly at the instigation of the Guillemards, though no one could prove it. It cost him a considerable sum to put it right. How might he have felt if suddenly he found himself in temporary possession of what proved to be a very valuable painting belonging to the family who in his eyes owed him a considerable debt? He would have had the contacts to get a first-rate job done. And once back on Edwina's wall, if anyone ever did detect a difference, they would probably put it down to the cleaning and reframing which had taken place."

"But that would mean Job Halavant got taken in by his own grandfather's fake!" exclaimed Lillingstone.

"Not just Job," said Kee, looking significantly at Justin. "Justin too!"

"And not just me," said Justin, smiling fondly at Caddy, who shrugged and said, "There's no such thing as fakes, just good paintings and bad paintings."

Halavant began to laugh, Kee and Larry Lillingstone exchanged smiles, Digweed winked at Wield who looked away, Dalziel was looking as if someone had snatched an apple pie out of his mouth and given him a turnip instead. Only Franny Harding looked unhappier than the Fat Man.

"It's not funny," she said, half sobbing and leaning against Bendish, who patted her legs comfortingly. "It's all been for nothing and we're nowhere nearer saving the school."

Digweed coughed again. The group were fast learners. This time he got even quicker attention.

He held up a sheet of fax paper and said, "Things are not quite so black as they seem, perhaps. There could indeed be peace in our time."

"You've heard from your lawyer friend," said Kee.

"Indeed I have. Larry, that For Sale sign outside the vicarage. It may be that your masters are trying to sell what is not theirs."

"Not the old gift thing again, please, Edwin! A gift's a gift. You don't retain rights in it, especially not after two hundred years!"

"If you're a hardheaded Yorkshireman, you may do," said Digweed. "The gift was made in consideration of the annual remission of tithes. It was a quid pro quo. Since the Tithe Act of 1936 it seems the Church has had the quid without the village getting its quo. The deed is clear on this point, that possession is only vested in the vicar so long as the Church keeps its side of the bargain. It is learned counsel's opinion that the vicarage may well belong to the village, not the Church."

"But that's marvelous!" cried Fran. "It must be worth ... how much were they asking, Larry?"

Lillingstone was looking less than happy at the news. He said, "This will need some sorting out. . . ."

"It's all right, Larry," said Digweed. "I'm sure the Parish Council will sell it back to the Church at a very reasonable rate. Then they can turn the new bungalow into the first of this low-cost housing they're always preaching about. But I'm not done yet. I dug the school records out of the Council archives and sent them to my friend at the same time."

"Don't tell me we own the school too?" said Kee.

"If it ceases to be a school, we could do," said Digweed. "Stanley Harding saw to that. The land it was built on was part of the Green. The labor was the village's, the materials were paid for by local subscription, not least your dad's conscience money, Justin. And when the local authority took it over, Stanley Harding made damn sure, like the chap who drafted the deed of gift for the vicarage, that we didn't lose all rights in it."

"So if they closed it, the County Council wouldn't be able to sell the site and building off?" said Kee.

"Right. And that might just upset their calculations a little bit," said Digweed.

Fran Harding threw her arms around his neck and hugged him joyfully. Over her shoulder he caught Wield's eye and grinned rather sheepishly.

"Well, I'm glad that's all sorted," said Halavant. "You know, it must be about a century and a half since a Halavant attended a Reckoning. I think I might just look in and see what all the fuss is about."

"Oh, God, the Reckoning!" shrieked Fran. "Girlie will kill me. Harry, darling, you'll be okay? I have to go."

She rushed away around the side of the house toward the lawn. The others, too, reminded that they had civil and social responsibilities, began to follow.

"Sir," said Pascoe, "I think they're beginning to escape. What shall we do?"

"That'll likely be where the grub is, around there?"

"I expect so."

"Then what are we waiting for? Hot pursuit, lad. Hot pursuit!"

Two

I am afraid the young man has
some of your family madness.

And now the villagers began at last to sense that this year's Reckoning might hold some surprises, though none as yet could guess their full extent.

The first hint came when Girlie appeared and, instead of taking her customary place in the factor's chair, stood to one side. Behind her, looking very old, and assisted by Guy the Heir, came the Squire. Normally he didn't appear till the business was transacted and the feasting began. Now he allowed himself to be led to the table, seated himself in the only chair, and watched with gray indifference as Guy somewhat officiously laid the estate ledgers before him and opened them at the requisite page.

Then Fran Harding appeared, and the villagers realized that they had missed seeing her hurrying around at Girlie's beck and call.

Her cousin watched her breathless approach with a stony face.

"Nice of you to come," she said. "I don't know how we've managed without you, but we have."

"Oh, Girlie, I'm sorry . . . I can explain. . . ."

"What's to explain? You're a free agent. Obligations, responsibilities, desert, what the hell do things like that mean at Old Hall?"

There was a bitterness here which went beyond simple rebuke. Fran's attention had been so focused on her cousin that she hadn't noticed the Squire's presence till now.

"Girlie, what's happened? Why's Grunk collecting the rents?"

"He's entitled. They're his tenants, aren't they?"

The Squire had noticed Fran's arrival. He spoke briefly to Guy, who came toward them.

"My *favorite* cousins!" he said with gushing mockery. "Doesn't it give you a sense of the continuity of things, all the living Guillemards gathered here for this ancient ceremony? And I do mean all of them! I do so love history, the old traditions, that sort of thing. You, too, I bet, Girlie?"

"Within reason," she said with cold control.

"But reason has prevailed, hasn't it, my sweet? Good try, though. I'd say better luck next time, only I don't think there's going to be a next time. Fran, the Squire was a tad distressed to find himself deserted by his little accompanist on this important day——"

"Yes, I'm sorry, I'll go and tell——"

"No need. He's asked me to say that your services won't be required, as he has decided to dispense with the promised performance of his ghastly ballad. Good Lord! What's *he* doing here? And *him*? And *them*?"

His voice, rising in an accelerando of indignation, was clearly audible in the hush which the latest arrivals had caused.

First, and the object of greatest amazement, was Justin Halavant. That he should be here at all was astounding. That he should be here hand in hand with Caddy Scudamore was as far beyond explanation as it was precedent.

Alone, the limping figure of Harry Bendish might have raised a groundswell of speculation. In the wake of history-in-the-making he barely occasioned a ripple.

As for Kee, Larry, and the three policemen trailing along behind, they went almost unnoticed till the vicar detached himself from the group and approached Mrs. Pottinger with his message of hope. Soon the news was buzzing around the crowd. The vicarage belonged to the village . . . the school belonged to the village . . . the Morris and Hall belonged to the village . . . the greater part of Mid-Yorkshire belonged to the village! But not for this did the Enscombians, who were quite capable of juggling three or even more rumors in the air at once, cease to conjure up speculation about Justin and Caddy, while still analyzing the reasons for the unusual arrangements behind the big oak table.

Halavant, whose air of sangfroid concealed an uneasiness at the risk he ran of inspiring another Guillemard rebuke to match that which Jake had taken so badly all those years ago, advanced to the table, decided against offering his hand, but instead raised it and gave a cross between a friendly wave and a military salute to the Squire.

The old man gave him a puzzled frown and looked questioningly toward second slip. The village held its breath. The old man's gaze swung back, his hand rose to ear level, and the fingers twitched in a respondent wave.

The village breathed again, and voices rose up even more strongly as favorite theories were advanced and demolished. Then they were reduced to silence again as Guy the Heir banged his fist on the table and proclaimed that the Squire was now ready to collect his rents.

There weren't many of them and much of what there was was hardly worth collecting.

First to come forward were the pensioners to offer their pride-saving tokens. Next came a trio of smallholders who scratched a living out of poultry and rabbits and a few strips of vegetables. Then came the estate's cottagers, among them Elsie Toke, her myopic gaze still straining around in search of Jason. It was indeed rare that she was seen outside her home without her son, but her kindly friends and neighbors assured her the lad would be taking advantage of the occasion to pick up a few birds in the Squire's woods, and he'd be along just now as soon as the Feast began.

Finally it was the turn of the farmers. Only three remained of the dozen or more who had once owed allegiance to the Old Hall estate. Like the others before them they advanced in turn, declared the name of their property, paid their dues, watched while the payment was entered in the ledger, received formal thanks in their own name, then shook hands with the Squire in a gesture which owed more to feudal fealty than modern social convention.

George Creed was the last to come forward.

"Crag End," he announced loud and clear, and laid his rent on the table.

Guy Guillemard picked up the check and took his time examining it, underlining his offensive intention by holding it up to the light like a dubious banknote.

Neither Creed nor the Squire paid any attention to his pantomime but regarded each other steadily till at last Guy made the entry in his ledger.

"Thank you, George Creed," said the Squire.

"Thank you, Squire," said Creed, taking the proffered hand.

They shook. Creed took a little step back, but the Squire held on and used the leverage of the other's grip to draw himself upright. The watching villagers, already alerted to the possibility of something out of the ordinary by the Squire's active participation, abandoned hope of immediate encounter with Dora Creed's confections and with quite a different appetite concentrated their attention on her brother.

"George, will you come around this side of the table. Please," said the Squire.

Creed's eyes went from the Squire to Girlie. Then he nodded and went around the table, taking up a position between the woman and her grandfather.

"What's going off?" muttered Wield to Digweed while this was going on.

"I think," said Digweed, "that the Squire has at last discovered what most folk in the village have always known, that George Creed is his grandson."

"By God," said Wield. "Rider Haggard never wrote owt like this. Does this mean that Guy the Heir's going to get disinherited?"

Digweed shook his head.

"God, His angels, and everyone in Enscombe would certainly like to see it, but I fear that natural justice has never figured large in the calculations of the English gentry. Bastards and daughters rate only slightly higher than the horses in the stables when it comes to inheritance. No, I suspect the worst. The Squire looks far too unhappy to be about to do something as enjoyable as ditching the ghastly Guy!"

It was true. The old man's face was set in the grim mask of one about to set foot on the scaffold. Curiously it made him look younger. His back was straight, his eyes clear, and his voice strong as he started to speak.

"My friends, you are welcome as always to this our traditional Reckoning. Once it was purely the occasion of necessary business with some equally necessary hospitality thrown in. For many years the business has contracted and could be just as well carried on in other more casual ways, but the hospitality, the coming together of village and hall, has grown in importance. This is far from being the only day on which we meet and enjoy each other's company. But it is a good day and one I should be reluctant to see disappear."

There were several cries of "Hear! Hear!" and a scattering of
applause which he let die down before proceeding.

"Today, however, I do have some business to transact which can
only be dealt with on such an occasion, because I want all of you who
belong here in Enscombe to witness it. I have lately discovered what I
daresay many of you have long known, or at least suspected. That
George Creed here is my grandson."

He paused. The absence of *oohs* and *aahs* confirmed his guess at
general knowledge and he slowly nodded.

"I have always known him as a good tenant, a skilled farmer, and a
fine man, so the discovery causes me no pain save that of not having
had the pleasure of this knowledge long ago. It also means I have
another granddaughter, who happens to be the best baker in Yorkshire,
so there's another cause of joy."

He directed a smile of great charm toward Dora, who was looking
gobsmacked, then went on.

"Of course I have already been blessed by one granddaughter who
has been to me and to Old Hall a tower of strength, a helpmeet, a
friend. Without her . . . well, I am not sure where we would be today
without her."

Girlie had lit her pipe and was hiding her emotions behind a cloud
of smoke. George Creed reached out his hand and took hers, preparing
those who needed to be prepared for what was to come next.

"So when after telling me about George's relationship with me, she
went on to tell me about her relationship with George, I could only be
delighted for them both. For what she told me was that they are in love
and intend to marry."

More applause from the village, more gobsmackery from Dora. But
the smile which had touched the Squire's thin lips faded quickly to
prepare the watchers for bad news to come.

"But all this good news brought me sorrow, too, for naturally, once
I had digested it, my thoughts turned to the question of the inheritance
of the estate. I had wrestled with this problem before. My granddaughter has proved herself in every respect fit and worthy to run Old Hall.
She has known all her life that she could never inherit, but not for this
has she ever stinted her efforts on the family's behalf. And her great
desert some few years ago made me debate whether the time had not
come to cut through the old law of male primacy, bar the entail, and
make her my heir. You see how freely I speak to you."

This last was apparently addressed to the listening villagers, but to
Pascoe it seemed that for a moment the old man's steady gaze moved
away to that second slip with whom he seemed to be in such close
communion.

Now it jerked back and he went on, "But I felt that I, who was
Squire because my ancestors had stuck so rigidly to this tradition, did
not have any right to change it. By law, by custom, by right of birth, I
had an heir and I would be doing him great wrong to disinherit him on
a personal whim."

Guy tried to look serious but only succeeded in looking smug. A
couple of his colorful entourage clapped their hands but were quickly
shushed by the others, who were more sensitive to the mood of the
meeting.

"But now," resumed the Squire, "I find I have a direct male
descendant. What is more, a descendant who is soon to ally himself
even more closely with the family by marrying my beloved granddaughter. The struggle is renewed, and you may imagine how much
more fiercely it has raged this time even than last."

"Always a lot easier to leave unwanted daughters out on the hillside
to die," murmured Digweed.

Wield didn't respond. He was concentrating all his attention on the
drama going on behind the table.

"Yet basically I knew that nothing had changed. The laws of
legitimacy are as strong as, indeed are an integral part of, the laws of
male primogeniture. I am admitting you to the workings of my
thought today because I want you to understand the workings of my
heart also. Before you all I want to acknowledge, and to acknowledge
with pleasure and pride, this man George Creed as my grandson. But
equally, at the same time . . ."

He paused. Guy the Heir was regarding him with rapt expectation.
The villagers of Enscombe, too, were raptly expectant, but not, from
their faces, of ought for their comfort.

"Here it comes," hissed Digweed. "The face of tomorrow, God
help us every one."

The Squire was peering openly now at second slip as if hoping like
a monarch of old that even at this late stage a champion would ride
forth to defend his family's honor. But second slip had no help to
offer, and now the Squire shrugged and turned to Guy. At last he
showed every year of his age.

"But equally, at the same time," he repeated, "I have to acknowledge my great-nephew, Guy Guillemard—"

"Wait!"

And, as in all the best legends, at this very latest of last minutes, a
champion appeared.

It was Wield, moving steadily and purposefully forward. Digweed
took an anxious step after him, then stopped. Dalziel said to Pascoe,
"What's yon daft bugger up to?"

Girlie Guillemard stopped puffing at her pipe and wafted away the
concealing clouds so that she could more easily view the interrupter.

Wield advanced till he was standing directly opposite Guy the Heir.

He's going to issue a challenge! thought Digweed with mingled
anguish and delight.

"Guy Guillemard," intoned Wield in a voice which carried to the
furthermost corners of the garden, "I am arresting you for an offense
under the Protection of Birds Act 1954, Schedule One, Part One,
insomuch as it is alleged that on the banks of the River Een within the
Parish of Enscombe you did feloniously shoot and kill a protected
bird, to wit a kingfisher. You have the right to remain—"

But before Wield could complete the caution, the Squire had seized
Guy's arm and demanded in a voice strong with anger, "Is this true?
You shot the kingfisher?"

"So I shot a bird," said Guy, trying unsuccessfully to shake the
old man off. "You must have killed many a thousand in your time.
This stupid plod's jerking us about. What a man does on his own
land—"

"This is not your own land," said the Squire. "Have you no idea
what the kingfisher means to the Guillemards?"

Guy, suddenly aware that this might be more serious than the
humiliation of a public dressing-down, tried to compose his features to
conciliation.

"Look, if I did this, I'm sorry. But I'm not sure I did. Okay? I take
the occasional pot at a pigeon or a crow while we're working in the
woods, so do most of my team . . ."

He looked toward his team and a couple of heads finally nodded in
belated confirmation.

". . . and these aren't country boys, they wouldn't know the difference between a kingfisher and a capercaillie, so if one of them—"

"It was shot with a crossbow," said Wield. "The bolt was retrieved from the body, so there could be little doubt that the killer knew what he had done. The same bolt was later fired into the inn sign of the Morris Men's Rest. Assaulting this sign seems to be a hobby peculiar to the Guillemards, or do your team emulate you in this also?"

"How do you know it was the same bolt?" demanded Guy desperately.

"Forensic examination of blood traces," said Wield promptly. "DNA testing has linked the blood on the bolt to this precise bird."

Dalziel and Pascoe looked at each other incredulously, knowing this was pure invention. Guy, too, was trying to look incredulous but making a pretty poor fist of it.

The Squire said, "Guy, I have never been fond of you, but I always thought that at least you were a Guillemard. Now I hope that my poor dead brother, or his son, your father, was cuckolded, because it shames me to call you kin."

And now Guy finally abandoned hope.

"Well, I hope so too," he said, his good-looking face twisted in rage. "Because you don't think I ever got any pleasure out of having people know I was related to an antique loonie who spends his time composing doggerel that would disgrace a nursery rhyme, not to mention this pipe-smoking freak of a granddaughter. Helpmeet, you called her. What's that mean? That she rocks you to sleep with a hand job once a week . . . Jesus!"

The old man had released his arm and stepped back to give himself room for a one-hundred-and-eighty-degree swing of the right hand, which ended with a crack on Guy's face that sent the rooks squawking up out of the wilderness trees.

For a second Guy looked as if he might retaliate.

Then: "Fuck you," he said. "Fuck the lot of you."

And he strode away toward the house, and a few moments later they heard the roar of his Land Rover as he gunned it down the drive.

The Squire stood nursing his hand. Girlie and Fran rushed up to him.

"Grandfather, are you all right?" asked Girlie anxiously.

"I think I may have sprained my wrist," said the old man.

"Let me take a look," said Fran.

"In a moment," said the Squire. "Friends . . ."

As he raised his voice once more, the excited buzz of speculation faded away.

"Fuctata non perfecta," proclaimed the Squire. "The rents are paid."

"What's that mean?" demanded Dalziel.

"From the look of it," said Pascoe, "I think it means, 'Grub's up.' "

"About bloody time too!" said Dalziel. "Let's get stuck in while there's some left!"

Three

A Thing once set going in that way—one knows how it spreads!

Dalziel need not have worried, even though his assessing glance at the heroic deeds being performed all around convinced him he was in the company of peers. There was grub aplenty and of a quality he hadn't encountered since his childhood.

"If I weren't promised, I might marry that lass," he declared. "Where's she at?"

"I think she's being reconciled with her brother and to her new status," said Pascoe, looking to where George and Dora were huddled together in animated conversation. "Who are you promised to, sir?"

"Greasy Joan in the canteen who gives me extra chips."

"Is this a formal engagement?"

"Nay, I just told her if I ever did decide to get wed again, I'd give her first refusal," said Dalziel. "Pass me them cream horns, will you? Where's Wieldy?"

"Over there talking to Digweed."

"We'll need to watch him, Peter. He's been acting funny ever since he got back. What was all that crap about yon kingfisher, anyway?"

"What was all that about the kingfisher?" Digweed was saying.

"Guy shot it. It's an offense," said Wield stolidly.

"I see. So us burglars can be allowed to run free, but offenses against wildlife must be rigorously prosecuted.

Very green of you. So it was only incidentally that you did Enscombe in general and Old Hall in particular the signal service of disinheriting Guy."

"You think the Squire will disinherit him, then?" said Wield.

"I do love a man who knows how to change a subject," said Digweed.

"Are you really going to make Girlie and George your heirs?" asked Fran as she strapped the Squire's wrist.

"If I live long enough to see my lawyer," said the Squire. "What's that redheaded fellow hanging about for?"

Fran glanced to the doorway, where Harry Bendish was visible peering in.

"I think maybe he wants to ask if it'll be all right to marry me," said Fran.

"Good Lord. That's not what you want is it, my dear?"

"Very much," she said.

"Fellow's a striker, you know that?"

"No, he's not. That time you saw him on the wall, well, we'd been together in the garden, in the shed actually, and afterward he just sort of got carried away."

"Together? Doing what?"

Fran cast around for an idiom which might be familiar to the old man. All she could come up with was "spooning."

"Spooning?" he echoed, then threw back his head and laughed. "*Spooning* you call it? In my days we kept our clothes on to spoon, especially in midwinter! No, my dear, what I think you mean is at the very least canoodling, and possibly even coupling, eh?"

Fran flushed deep apricot and said, "I'm going to marry him, Grunk."

"Of course you are. You're like your gran, my sister Frances. Went off and married the vicar while I was chasing sheep around New Zealand. She'd gone by the time I came home. Never saw her again. Pity. She might have told me little Agnes was pregnant. I never knew that, you know. I thought I got sent away simply because she wasn't what they called suitable. A terrible man, my father. Most of them were, the Guillemards. Perhaps you think I'm a terrible man too?"

"No." She smiled. "I've never thought that."

"Good. I'll tell you something. First place Agnes and I ever *spooned* in, that was the garden shed too. What do you think of that?"

"I think it's great."

"You do? *Great,* eh? Well, I'll talk to young fellow-me-lad later. First things first. Soon as you bind me together, you slip off and get that big fiddle of yours."

"But I thought you weren't going to do the ballad today?" said Fran.

"Things have changed, haven't they?" he said. "Besides, there's probably plenty of folk out there thinking it's going to be all cakes and no ballad. Can't have them going home disappointed, can we?"

And he winked at her.

It took Fran a second or two to grasp his meaning. Even then she wasn't certain. She'd always been sensitive to the politely glazed boredom of most of his audiences, and it had been a constant worry that the Squire himself might one day detect and be hurt by it.

She said cautiously, "I'm sure most of them enjoy——"

"Oh, God. I hope not! After the years I've spent listening to them droning on at fêtes and shows and concerts and meetings, I hope I'm not wasting me old age entertaining them!"

She began to laugh, the Squire, too, and after a while, encouraged by their mirth, Harry Bendish came through the door, smiling shyly.

Kee Scudamore smiled shyly at Larry Lillingstone and said, "It's probably all for the best, Larry."

It was, she realized, at the very least an ambiguous statement. It could mean, it's all for the best that the object of an avowed celibate's desires should put herself out of reach by marriage. Or it could mean that in view of the kind of expectations Caddy would have of a husband, it was all for the best that someone else should be landed with her. What it really meant, of course, was that it was all for the best that her sister's availability had been so satisfactorily removed, thus clearing the decks for her own assault.

He said, "Never console a professional consoler, Kee. He's played that game too often not to know all its finesses."

Kee regarded him fondly, thinking how well despair became him. He was right, of course, he knew the cards of consolation as well as she did—the needs of the living, the healing powers of time. Eventually he would also recall that he knew these were not deuces and treys but mighty trumps. She wanted him body and soul. The one was still focused on Caddy, the other fixed on God. No problem, she thought. She was aware that the cure of unconquerable passions, and the transfer of unchanging attachments, must vary very much as to time in different people, but, late or soon, she had the patience to wait.

She said, "At least you can't think about leaving Enscombe until we get this business of the vicarage and the school sorted out."

He said, "Sometimes I get this odd feeling that I shall never leave Enscombe."

"That will be nice," she said lightly. "We would all love you to stay. That way, not only could you finish your history of the parish, you could write yourself into it."

"Talking of history, I think I see it coming," said Lillingstone.

And he pointed to the house from which approached, at a pace dictated by age, Fop's teeth, and an uncased cello, that (to Enscombian eyes) terrible trio of the Squire, Harry Bendish, and little Fran Harding.

As news of the sighting spread, most villagers accelerated their consumption to a rate which left even Andy Dalziel floundering.

"What's going off?" he demanded. "Has someone canceled tomorrow?"

"I think," said Pascoe with greater artistic sensitivity, "they may be trying to eat themselves insensible."

There were those whom the threat of balladry inspired to more direct forms of escape.

Digweed said, "I think the time has come to make an excuse and leave."

"What excuse is that?" asked Wield.

"I came out in such a hurry, I may have left the shop unlocked. With all these unsolved break-ins, a man can't be too careful."

"Aye, lot of desperate criminals in these parts," agreed Wield. "Talking of which, I don't see young Toke tucking in. Don't he come to these things?"

"Almost invariably. Perhaps the poor devil's got wind of this strange union between Caddy and Halavant."

"How'll he take it?"

"Badly, I should think. While Caddy was everyone's unattainable dream, he could be content. But now . . ."

"Might he do summat . . . daft?"

"Self-destruction, you mean?"

"I weren't thinking of self."

Digweed laughed and said, "Oh, dear. You're thinking like a policeman again."

"I am a policeman," said Wield heavily. "Nowt can change that."

The two men regarded each other cautiously, recognizing that almost imperceptibly their conversation was shifting onto another level. In the background the villagers chattered and chomped, distant birds sang, and Fran Harding's cello groaned in sweet agony as she lovingly tuned it.

"I'm a lawyer, a bookseller, a burglar," said Digweed. "These are labels, passport pictures to the world outside. They don't mean much in Enscombe. Here we tend to know the truth about each other."

"What the hell does that mean?" asked Wield, frowning.

"I suppose it means in a way that here everyone is *out*. We may laugh at, quarrel with, gossip about each other, but ultimately if everyone's business is everyone else's, then your own business is your own. A kind of emotional communism."

"You've lost me now," said Wield.

"I should hate to do that, Edgar."

"How the hell do you know my name?"

"It's like I say," said Digweed with a grin. "We know everything there is to know about our own."

"You're a right clever bugger, aren't you?" growled Wield.

"You'd be amazed. Listen, before I flee, something to occupy your mind while the Squire declaims. I mentioned before that I was thinking of putting in an offer for Corpse Cottage if your lot put it on the market. I suspect that could happen quite soon. You're not going to risk losing another young bobby to Enscombe, are you? Now, it will stretch my purse a bit. I'd be pleased if someone came in with me, spread the burden. You look the careful type, I daresay you've got a few bob stashed away, all those bribes! So how about it?"

The proposition took Wield's breath away. Finally he managed to say, "I'll think about it."

"Up to you. Purely commercial. If you want. Oh, God, I think he's going to start. See you later. I hope."

And Edwin Digweed slipped away from Old Hall and made his way back down the High Street toward his shop and his fate.

Others followed, or had preceded.

Thomas Wapshare left with a genial wave, claiming the imminence of a beer delivery. Dudley Wylmot left with an awkward bow, explaining to any who listened that he wouldn't offend for the world but the law required him to open the post office. Caddy Scudamore left without explanation, her mind full of the shapes and colors of the

Reckoning's excitements and her fingers aching to feel the heavy thickness of a brush. Justin Halavant, discovering his promised bride's absence, observed that to attend a Guillemard Reckoning might be history, but enduring a Guillemard Recital was mere masochism, so with a casual nod to the Squire and another to second slip, he hastened away.

And first of all to leave, convinced now that her son was not going to put in an appearance, and with foreboding increased once the amazing news of Caddy Scudamore's engagement had reached her, was the slight, pale figure of Elsie Toke.

But the vast majority of Enscombians, anchored by feudal loyalty, immobilized by self-indulgence, or intimidated by Girlie's fierce gaze, remained in their places and listened to the Squire's ballad, until the screaming began.

Four

It puts me in mind of the account of
St. Paul's shipwreck, when all are
said by different means to reach the
shore in safety.

Which one should it be?

The Good? The Bad? Or the Ugly?

He made his choice.

He raised his gun.

And he fired.

Wield felt the impact like a light punch on his chest. He looked down, saw the red stain blossoming, smelled the pungent raw vinegary odor of blood, and asked, more in bewilderment than bitterness, "Why me?"

Laundering might save his cotton shirt, but he knew from experience that there was no salvation possible for the Italian silk tie his sister had bought him for Christmas. His wardrobe was festooned with silk ties (his sister was an unimaginative present buyer), which spots of gravy, spatterings of soup, or even the fine spray from a rashly opened Guinness can had rendered unwearable. But blood was far worse than any of these. Blood was forever.

It occurred to him to wonder why the hell he was worrying about his laundry.

Dalziel and Pascoe had reacted according to their respective humors.

The Fat Man went hurtling forward with the speed which in his rugby days had amazed many a twinkle-toed stand-off. But fast as he was, youth and vengeful fury made Harry Bendish even faster. His injured leg forgotten, he leapt onto the table and launched himself in a bone-crunching tackle which caught the berserker in the midriff and swept him the full length of the polished surface till they shot off the end and crashed together onto the unyielding lawn.

Pascoe, meanwhile, put his arm around Wield and cried, "Oh, God, Wieldy, are you all right?"

It was not perhaps the question a man of education in such a circumstance would wish to have asked, but cliché comes in through the French window when deep emotion writes the script.

Wield, more practiced in control and more wedded to precision, examined and analyzed his feelings, and said with a mild surprise, "I'm a lot better than expected."

"But all this blood . . ."

"I don't know whose it is," said Wield. "But I'm pretty sure it's not mine."

And Dalziel, noting with admiration that Bendish not only tackled like a fullback but punched like a front-row forward, flourished the berserker's discarded weapon like a trophy and said, "It's one of them war-game guns that fires paintballs. Still, not to worry. It's the thought that counts. Tell you what, young Bendish. Pull that balaclava thing off and you'll get a lot better target to aim at!"

Harry paused in midpunch, nodded his acknowledgment of the superior wisdom of age and experience, and ripped aside the balaclava to reveal the slack, pallid face of Guy Guillemard.

The young redhead got in one more telling blow before Franny seized his arm and cried, "Enough!"

Bendish looked ready to disagree, but young love is a disciplinarian stronger even than old authority, and reluctantly he rose to his feet, then less reluctantly put his arms around the girl's yielding body and pulled her close for comfort.

Now the victims of the berserker's assault on his way through the village began to appear to express their outrage. Thomas Wapshare brought explanation as well as indignation.

"The bugger broke into the Morris," he said. "Drank a bottle of cognac, and he must have found a bucket of pig's blood, you know, what I use for the black puddings, and reckoned it'd be a lark to fill his ammo with that instead of paint. You should see the bloody mess he's made!"

Edwin Digweed, too, appeared. He and Wield took in each other's gory appearance and exchanged smiles.

"I thought I was dead," admitted Digweed.

"Me too," said Wield.

The bookseller touched his bloody front with his forefinger and held it up before his eyes.

"What I suggested before," he said, "—it occurs to me, a sensible chap like you might feel a very natural caution about letting yourself be picked up by a strange man. I assure you I, too, have been extraordinarily cautious since this new Black Death came among us. I have the certification to prove it."

"Me too," said Wield. "Don't worry. I was going to ask."

"You were? Does that mean you've decided yes?"

"From about five minutes ago," said Wield, looking ruefully at his bloody front. "Life's too long for silk ties, isn't it?"

Three of Guy's victims didn't return to the Hall.

Caddy Scudamore had looked over her shoulder at the blood trickling down her smock, then headed straight into her studio where Justin Halavant found her a few moments later, stripped to the waist, experimenting with this new material on a variety of surfaces. Smiling, he pushed a stool into a corner and sat down to watch her.

And Elsie Toke hardly paused in her stride as she headed past the pub and turned toward her cottage.

Here at her front gate she stopped and sighed with relief.

Her son was in the garden. He was wearing jeans and a white T-shirt and he was digging the ground under one of the windows.

"Hello, Ma," he said. "Thought we'd have some stock and petunias here. And some spuds and cabbage around the side. What's been happening to you?"

"Yon mad bugger, Guy Guillemard. Not to worry. It's the last time he'll be laking around here for a while. Fancy a cup of tea? I fetched you some cakes from the Hall."

"In a minute," he said. "Good Reckoning, was it?"

"Aye. Interesting. That Justin Halavant's going to wed young Caddy Scudamore, did you know?"

She watched him keenly.

"Aye, I knew," he said. "I thought mebbe some sweet peas over there. Warren were always fond of sweet peas."

"That'd be nice," she said. "I'll go and get out of these mucky things, then I'll make that tea."

Five

*There is very little story, and
what there is is told in a strange,
unconnected way.*

Evening was settling over the valley as the three detectives
drove out of Enscombe.

"And what the fuck am I going to tell Desperate Dan?"
asked Dalziel.

It was a rare, indeed almost a unique, dilemma. In the past
Dalziel had experienced very little difficulty in telling the
chief constable anything, from unpleasant truths such as that
his fly was open, to downright lies such as that his wish was
Dalziel's command.

"How about, all's well that ends well?" said Pascoe
brightly.

"Oh, aye? How about much ado about fucking nothing!"
retorted the Fat Man. "Two whole days, and what have we
got? Bodies in the morgue, none. Bodies in the cells, none.
Policemen resigned, one. Crimes committed, any number.
Citizens willing to bring charges, not a single one!"

"There is a positive side," said Pascoe. "Schools saved,
one. Marriages arranged, two, maybe three. Peace of mind
and ways of life preserved, a couple of hundred. And we can
still do Guy the ex-Heir for assault."

"What? When not a soul in the place except us is willing
to give evidence? Even Thomas bloody Wapshare says he's
not bothered by the breaking and entering. No, I may not
know much, lad, but I know better than to stand up in court
and complain about being showered with pig's blood. We'd
be a laughingstock!"

"The Post Office break-in's still an open case, though," said Pascoe. "We might still get someone for that."

He sensed rather than saw Wield stiffen. There was something there ... in fact there was a lot going on with the sergeant that he didn't quite understand. Ellie would fathom it, he comforted himself.

"I doubt it," said Dalziel disconsolately. "It'll probably turn out to be the Little People, or summat. Aye, that's it, it's bloody fairyland back there. I mean, look at yon spot, for God's sake!"

They were passing Scarletts, its exuberant shapes and colors gift-wrapped in the glow of the setting sun.

"What the hell's that got to do with Yorkshire?" demanded Dalziel. "It's like a tit show in a monastery!"

"Even monks need a night off," said Pascoe.

"Nay, lad, being an off-comer yourself, you'd not know what I mean. Wieldy, now, you understand. A tyke's a tyke even if it primps itself like a poodle. Wieldy, this Enscombe place, how'd it strike you?"

"Oh, I agree with you, sir," said Wield. "Definitely fairyland."

He glanced at Pascoe and winked, causing him almost to drive into the ditch as his mind clouded once more with vain speculation.

Dalziel didn't seem to notice.

"There you are," he said with satisfaction. "I'm glad at least one of you keeps his feet on the ground. A fairy tale, that's what I'll tell Dan! I'll begin, 'Once upon a time,' then lay out the facts. He can decide for himself how it works out, earn his overbloated salary for once. How does that sound to you, Wieldy?"

"Money for old rope," said Wield. " 'Cos if you start 'Once upon a time,' there's no bother at all deciding how it works out, is there?"

"Meaning what, clever clogs?"

"And they all lived happy ever after," said Wield. "The end."

FINIS